MW01102027

LIFECAST

LIFECAST

MARC OPSAL

GOLDSHIF

This is a work of fiction. Names, characters, places, and incidents are the products of the author's imagination or are used fictitiously. Any resemblance to actual events, locales, or persons, living or dead, is entirely coincidental.

Inquiries can be sent to:
heythere@goldshif.com

Publisher's Cataloging-in-Publication Data
Names: Opsal, Marc, author.
Title: Lifecast / Marc Opsal.
Description: Pasadena, CA : Marc Opsal, 2020. | Series: The Neurogem saga, bk. 1. | Summary: Noble Valet Bear must save his best friend from becoming The City's most famous person.
Identifiers: LCCN 2020915581 (print) | ISBN 978-1-7355495-1-4 (hardcover) | ISBN 978-1-7355495-0-7 (ebook)
Subjects: LCSH: Oligarchy—Fiction. | Dystopian fiction. | CYAC: Teenagers—Fiction. | Revolutions—Fiction. | Imaginary wars and battles. | Young adult fiction. | BISAC: YOUNG ADULT FICTION / Dystopian. | YOUNG ADULT FICTION / Science Fiction / General.
Classification: LCC PZ7.1.O67 Li 2020ber (print) | LCC PZ7.1.O67 (ebook) | DDC [Fic]—dc23.

ISBN 978-1-7355495-1-4

Printed in the United States of America
1 3 5 7 9 10 8 6 4 2
First Edition

LIFECAST website address: welcometolifecast.com

For Meryl—

my somewhere that's green.

LIFECAST

PROLOGUE

Welcome to LifeCast, by Neurogem.
You are: The Idol, Voxonica Aslanian.

You see the Idol, Vox, through her own eyes. She stands before a full-length mirror in a brilliant gold wedding dress. You can't influence Vox's actions or feel what she feels, but in this moment, you inhabit the Idol's life.

Stylists pull your lavender hair into place, add finishing touches to your makeup, and spout platitudes about what a perfect canvas you are. Whenever your champagne glass gets low, a composed blonde man in black formal attire refills it without a word.

Your dressing room door crashes open. A tall woman with broad shoulders enters. Her bright orange dress robes float as she speedwalks into the room. The woman shouts to herself in a furious, one-sided conversation.

"15 minutes until showtime!" the woman calls out. "Idol Aslanian, this came for you."

"Don't you know it's bad luck to open gifts before the ceremony?" you ask. "What kind of handler are you? Put it with the others!"

"Idol Aslanian, it is customary for the bride and groom to exchange small, meaningful trinkets before they meet down the aisle. Judging by the slate box and turquoise ribbon I assume this is from your fiancé."

"In that case, give it here! Stylists, scatter!"

The stylists scurry out of sight, while the handler breaks into another hurried conversation with someone unseen. You're left alone with the box.

"Valet!" you beckon, and the blonde man in black formal attire appears at your side. "Hold my glass."

"Yes, Idol Aslanian."

You pull the turquoise ribbon and let it float to the ground. With both thumbs you slide back the box's smooth stone top. A flash of bright white light envelops you.

"... and you, get a cool washcloth! She can't breathe, this dress is coming off!"

"We don't have time to redress her, Valet! Try another dose!"

"She isn't responding to the drugs!"

"You don't know what you're doing. Where's the medic?"

You hear a loud rip. Your eyes flutter open.

You're on the ground. Your gaze darts between all the faces staring down at you. You hear quick, panicked breaths. They're *your* quick, panicked breaths.

You examine the details of your dress as though you've never seen the garment before and look straight ahead. The mirror that previously reflected a confident girl at the center of everyone's attention is gone. She's been replaced by someone broken, crumpled to the ground, with a terrified expression.

"Idol Aslanian, are you all right?" the handler asks. "Can you go on?"

"Why am I wearing this?" you ask. "Where am I?"

"Idol Aslanian, this is no time for jokes!" the handler snaps.

You look around with more urgency than before, pop to your feet, and race out of the dressing room. Your long legs take you to the end of a hallway where you burst through a pair of huge double doors.

You find yourself in an open-air garden that overlooks several smaller stratoscrapers. A long white aisle extends before you. Rows of guests in chairs flank the aisle. All at once, the guests rise to look back at you. Their faces blur as tears well in your eyes.

You wipe away the tears and scan the guests' faces. They're all so beautiful, the most beautiful people you've ever seen.

No one moves to help you. A din of murmurs rises into the air. You fall to your knees.

"Why is this happening?" you shout. "Help me, please! Where are you?"

Sweat-drenched locks of lavender hair hang slack over your face. You brace yourself with open hands on the ground. Every blink drops more tears onto the aisle.

The shadow of someone approaches from behind. A large hand wraps around your shoulder. You brush it away and spring back up.

The guests' murmurs turn to screams as you climb onto the garden ledge. You stare down into the swirling layer of indigo mist far below. Dozens of camera drones hover in place around you.

Frantic pleas come from the guests. Once again, you scan their faces but don't linger on any one. You inhale a long, deep breath and release a shaky exhale.

"I'm sorry," you say. "There's nothing left of me to give."

The guests drop out of sight as you fall backward. A vast sky of bright stars opens before you until your body turns. You plummet straight down toward the mist.

Hysterical laughter overtakes you. Your arms flail. The only sound you hear is the air as it rushes past.

Light tendrils of mist kiss your still, outstretched hand. Frosted borders form at the edges of your vision.

LifeCast Terminated.

PART I

1

A single glass of Ol' Sassafras 205-year-old Appalachian bourbon balances on my sterling silver serving tray. I weave through throngs of distracted mourners and spin around self-absorbed socialites.

Reminders of the Fallen Idol hit me from all sides. Every wall displays a different highlight from her Idol reign. My eyes settle on one that triggers the audio.

"Bear, you're looking fit as usual!" Vox purrs. *"But no one can see those cute black curls against your dark complexion. Un-shade that fade with NuRoota's Chrome Slick Silver! Try it now for just 15 points! And if you love it, like I know you will, schedule a permanent coloration consultation at your nearest NuRoota Highland Spa! Come on, Bear; treat yourself!"*

Vox winks. She's been telling me to dye my hair silver since that ad launched.

I reach the East Study and locate Master Telladyne.

Bertram Telladyne, a stratoscraper of a man, is easy to spot. He's tall, even by Noble standards. His long black hair, peppered with champagne gold strands, bobs as he gestures.

I move to Master Telladyne's side and stare at the ground.

"What was in the box?" someone asks.

"At the bottom of the box," Master Telladyne replies. "Was a copy of the deed to my rival's last remaining diamond mine. At the top of the deed, my name was listed in bold as its new owner. The document was embedded with a retinal scanner. By simply looking at it, the poor fool was forced to acknowledge his witness of the transaction. And that, as they say, was that."

The small crowd breaks into applause. I've heard that anecdote hundreds of times. Master Telladyne loves to recount the tale of how he took complete control over The City's diamond trade. Diamonds aren't even his primary business—they're more of a hobby.

"What they say is true," someone says. "Never trust a gift from a Telladyne!"

I don't want to publicly interrupt Master Telladyne's adoration, so I send him a NeuroText.

"Master Telladyne, your drink has arrived."

He takes the glass and toasts the crowd.

"Will there be anything else, sir?"

"No, Valet. That will be all."

"Very well, sir."

I hear 3 beeps. It's a NeuroChat from Young Lady Kallista, Master Telladyne's daughter.

"Valet! Bring me and my friends... No, shut up! Stop that! Three bottles of champagne, Piper Leipzig Brut. You have five minutes."

"Yes, Young Lady Telladyne, right away."

That's odd, Kallista always drinks Svenson Ice Vodka on the rocks.

Of course, Kallista hasn't activated her NeuroTracker, so I have to tap into the Reinhold Palace security cameras to find her. She's with her twin brother, Kassian, and their horrible friend, Davis Vexhall.

I dart into the hallway. Everyone I pass holds a champagne flute. There's no way to know for sure, but I have a feeling it's the same champagne Kallista ordered.

As I approach the bar, the bartender sets out an ice bucket for me with a single bottle of Piper Leipzig Brut.

"I need three bottles."

"Sorry, that's the last one we have at this bar."

"How is that possible? This isn't even a rare vintage."

"There's a rumor going around that Piper Leipzig was secretly Vox's favorite drink. We got cleaned out."

I check the master inventory and locate more bottles at other bars. They'd take too long to get. I consider which is worse: being late or being wrong and decide to feign misunderstanding.

With 42 seconds left on my countdown clock, I gather the items and head for the West Garden. Once outside, I slow my pace to appear as though my task was effortless.

I see Kassian Telladyne first. He stands near, but almost apart from, his sister and Vexhall. He's tall with the same thin, but muscular frame and fair skin as his father. Waves of black hair fall over his large ears. His arms are folded, as usual.

Kallista and Davis Vexhall play-wrestle on the lawn. Kallista howls with delight as Vexhall tosses her through the air like a stuffed animal. With each throw, Vexhall's muscles bulge through his crisp, white, vintage naval jacket.

Vexhall freezes with Kallista suspended a few inches off the ground and drops her. The short, but hard impact looks painful. Vexhall grins as he extends his hand to her.

Kallista sees me once she's back on her feet. She's short, just over five feet tall, but her intense look lures people down to her level. A severe, angled black bob frames her bone white face of electric blue eyes and bright red lips.

"Young Lady Telladyne," I say. "Your order."

Kassian, Kallista, and Vexhall each take a glass. I move to pop the bottle's cork, but Vexhall stops me.

He takes the bottle and unsheathes a decorative sword from his side. With a single motion, Vexhall lops off the bottle top and fills each glass.

"It's delicious!" Kallista says. "No wonder people believed it was Vox's favorite!"

All three of them laugh. Kallista must have started that rumor before placing her order.

"Not bad," Kassian adds.

"It's fine, I suppose," Vexhall says. "I'd christen a ship with it, but I wouldn't drink it again."

"Well, I would love another glass, but it appears our Valet failed to fully deliver my order. Did I not request three bottles, Noble Valet Bear?"

"You did, Young Lady Telladyne. I apologize for my mistake. Please allow me to retrieve the remaining bottles."

Kallista throws back what's left of her champagne and steps closer.

"That's all right, Valet," Kallista says as she runs her hand down the lapel of my jacket. "There's no need to get more. We have other means by which to improve our mood."

Kallista flashes me a cold, emotionless smile. Her hand continues until her fingers rest around the top button of my jacket.

"Tell me, what's this gold chain here?"

"It is a pocket watch that Noble Valet Holt, under whom I apprenticed, gave me upon the completion of my training with the Yukita family."

"Beautiful, may I see it closer?"

"Of course, Young Lady Telladyne."

I detach the pocket watch chain and hand it to Kallista. She eyes the bobble with admiration, turns it over, and reads the inscription.

"Viventes serviamus, mori honeste," Kallista reads aloud. "'Live in service, die with honor.' Fascinating."

Kallista must have used a NApp to pronounce and translate the engraving, she doesn't speak Latin. No one does.

"It's the Noble Valet motto," I say.

"I see. This is such a lovely trinket. It would look fabulous with my outfit, don't you think?"

Kallista wears a black cape dress with a red, hand-painted silk lining. The watch would look fine with it, but that's beside the point.

"Young Lady Telladyne, it pleases me to know that you appreciate my watch's beauty, but it is simply too dear to me; I cannot part with it."

Kallista grips the watch tight.

"You know, Valet," Kallista says. "I really did want another glass of champagne. If you followed my original instructions, I would have it."

Kallista walks away with my watch and continues to examine it with obsessive focus. I follow.

"But you didn't follow my instructions, did you Valet?"

"Young Lady Telladyne, I apologize for my misunderstanding. Please, allow me make it up to you."

"Historically you've been so reliable. Why choose this of all nights, when we mourn the death of the Idol Vox, to flagrantly disobey me?"

Kallista keeps walking. She's headed to the garden's edge, which drops straight into the mist.

"Perhaps I was distracted by grief. Regardless, that is no excuse for my mistake."

"You're absolutely right, Valet," Kallista says and stops at the garden's stone border. "It is no excuse."

She climbs onto the low stone wall and sits down. Her legs dangle over the mist as she continues to look at the watch.

"I've wanted to be the Idol my whole life, but if I can't even get my own Valet to follow my orders, how can I expect the entire city to follow me?" Kallista asks. "Maybe I should just end it all, right here, like Vox did! She was supposed to show us how to live! Perhaps we should follow her example in death as well!"

Theatrics aside, Kallista's perched dangerously above the mist. If she slipped and fell, I'd be blamed for her death. It's too risky to forcibly pull her off the wall.

Kallista wants penance for my mistake with the champagne. The only way to get her down safely is to grovel.

"Young Lady Telladyne, I apologize for my incompetence. I will get you two, three, 100 bottles of champagne to make up for my negligence. Drop the watch, it means nothing compared to your life. Please, come down from there; I beg of you!"

"Is that so, Valet?" Kallista says and releases my watch.

I lunge forward. Before the watch falls out of sight, it stops. Kallista had the chain wrapped around her finger.

"You have a NeuroClock like everyone else, yet you check this thing constantly. Don't lie to me. Tell me what this watch means to you or I *will* drop it."

Vexhall snickers behind me. Kassian stands beside him but doesn't find the situation amusing. He shares the same worried expression that must be on my face.

"Very well, Young Lady Telladyne. That watch is probably my most cherished possession. It is a symbol of all of my hard work and how far I've come from my lowland birth. I am a peasant, a simple Valet, but that watch makes me feel significant—like my life actually matters for something in your family's gracious service."

Kallista looks out into the Highland while she swings my watch back and forth.

"Young Lady Telladyne, I implore you, please come down! You could fall straight to your death!"

"I'm fine, Valet, see," Kallista says and launches into casual upper body choreography. "I could stay up here all night!"

"I have a suggestion," Vexhall says.

He removes a narrow tube from his breast pocket. Several small, round, bright red capsules fill the tube. The capsules have no discernible markings, but given its recent popularity, there's only one thing they could be.

"Kallista, darling. Come down from there; it's time to be reborn!" Vexhall calls out.

Kallista looks straight to the vial in Vexhall's hand. She connects the chain of my watch to itself, drapes it over her head like a necklace, and climbs down.

Kallista approaches Vexhall with her palms out, ready to receive a capsule. Vexhall doles out three capsules and puts the vial back in his jacket.

"Young Master and Lady Telladyne," I say. "If that is ReBorn, I highly recommend that you do not dock it. ReBorn has been linked to numerous cases of blindness, hearing loss, temporary paralysis, nausea, loss of consciousness, and even death."

"We know the risks, Valet!" Kallista snaps.

"What of your father? What if he sees you dock a common street drug? At least dock something that Telladyne Pharmaceuticals produces!"

"It's competitive research, Valet," Kassian says. "Nothing more."

Vexhall produces three empty RXPens from his jacket. Kassian, Kallista, and Vexhall load their capsules into the pens. I have to think fast. The only thing worse than Kallista's untimely death is the untimely death of both Telladyne children from ReBorn overdoses.

Kallista stabs the pen toward her wrist.

"It could be counterfeit!" I shout.

Kallista stops with her pen hovered just centimeters above her dock.

"Counterfeit," Vexhall says. "Do you really think I would sling counterfeit ReBorn?"

"Not intentionally, sir, but reports have emerged from all over The City of fraudulent and impure ReBorn."

"Those reports are from the lowland. Of course they have dirty drugs. Besides, I've already docked seven of these capsules today and I'm fine!"

"Did you test them?" I ask.

"How dare you question me, servant! Your services are no longer needed. Leave us!"

"I apologize, Young Master Vexhall, but I do not take orders from you."

"You didn't test their purity, did you, Davis?" Kassian asks.

"Why would I? No one would dare sell me fake drugs!"

"Please, Young Master Vexhall, allow me to test your capsules with my RXSleeve. It will only take a moment."

Kassian unloads the capsule from his pen and gives it to me. Kallista lets out a huff, but follows Kassian's lead. I look to Vexhall. He doesn't move.

"Can't you just test theirs?"

"For the sake of due diligence, I should test them all. You will be able to see the results on my RXSleeve readout."

Vexhall rolls his eyes and hands me his capsule.

I drop the capsules into the medication testing compartment at the cuff of my RXSleeve. The results relay to my Neurogem before they appear in the sleeve's readout. The drugs are clean, so I prompt the readout to lie on my behalf.

"Paritan Phosphate!" Kassian shouts.

"I'm glad I tested these," I say. "If you continued to dock these capsules all three of you would be fully paralyzed by dawn and dead shortly after. Here, allow me to give each of you a pen of Veracort. It will break down the Paritan Phosphate in your system and let you pass it naturally."

"Impossible!" Vexhall shouts. "I've never purchased counterfeit drugs in my life! You're lying!"

"My RXSleeve does not lie, Young Master Vexhall. Please do not take this personally. Counterfeit ReBorn-related deaths have risen 347% in the last 12 hours. You are not the only one to be swindled by a lowland drug dealer, but you are one of the lucky few to survive."

"Swindled?" Vexhall replies. "By a LEF?"

There it is, Vexhall's favorite slur for people born below the mist. LEF, Lowland Educated Four, seems to work its way into every interaction I have with him.

Vexhall grabs my lapels and pulls me close. His light brown skin, with its subtle golden undertone, flushes red with rage. I'm so close I can hear Vexhall's teeth clench and grind.

"How dare you make such an absurd accusation!"

"Young Master Vexhall, even if I could alter the sleeve's readout what would I have to gain by doing so? My purpose is to serve the Telladyne family, which includes protecting their lives from the... mistakes of those around them."

"Mistakes?" Vexhall shouts. "I don't make mistakes!"

He pulls back to punch me, but Kassian grabs Vexhall's arm.

"Davis, that's enough! You're making a scene. My sister and I are headed inside for another drink. Do *not* follow us."

Vexhall snatches his arm from Kassian's grasp and stares me down.

"Before you go," I say. "Allow me to give you those Veracort pens."

I remove three empty RXPens from my jacket and stab them into the orange-black-yellow color-coded Veracort pin on my RXSleeve. Among the 128 drugs available in my sleeve, Veracort is one of the lesser used, which is why its pin is awkwardly located near my elbow.

Kassian and Kallista dock their pens. I extend the last pen to Vexhall. As expected, he knocks it to the ground.

"Get that away from me. It's probably full of poison! I can't believe you two trust him! This one's devious. They all are, but him more than the others. I'll have my eye on you, Valet," Vexhall says and stomps off.

Kassian and Kallista start to walk away, and I remember that Kallista still has my pocket watch around her neck.

"Young Lady Telladyne!" I call after. "My watch."

"What? Oh, right."

She pulls the watch chain over her head and tosses it away without a second thought. The watch flies in a high arc over the garden wall. Kallista flashes me a sarcastic smile.

Once the twins and Vexhall are gone, I run to the wall for one last glimpse of my mentor's thoughtful gift. I'm too late—it's long gone.

Perhaps if I reciprocated Kallista's romantic advances years ago, I'd still have my watch now. But that's absurd. She's practically my little sister, and in some ways, my daughter. Of course, she took my rebuff as a personal insult, and here we are.

Neurogem Tower stands in the distance, a striking glass spire wrapped in large silver neurons. The neurons illuminate to mimic the movement of information through the brain. Branch-like tendrils surround the landing where Vox was to be married and culminate to a sharp point above.

I suppose my watch, like Vox, froze solid when it hit the mist and shattered on the lowland street.

I take a deep breath and turn my back on the Highland view.

3 beeps. Aleks!

"Come find me when you have a chance. I have amazing news!"

I go inside to meet Aleks. She looks beautiful this evening in a long ice blue gown. Her platinum blonde hair lays in soft waves against her fair shoulders. Pale freckles travel across her cheeks and over the bridge of her nose. Most Noble girls would cover the freckles with makeup or have them removed, but Aleks likes them. So do I.

Davis Vexhall has her cornered beside a horrendous flower sculpture of Vox. He delivers every word through a toothy, forced smile.

"My father recently bought me a new boat for passing my corporate exams," Vexhall says. "It's the largest ship at the Lion's Chest Yacht Club, probably the largest in the entire bay. I'll have to take you out on the water some time."

"Oh, do you know how to sail?"

"Of course I know how to sail! Haven't you heard of the Vexhall Sailing Dynasty? We've won every major sailing competition since my grandfather took the cup at the very first-ever Windjam Regatta!"

Vexhall takes a beat to calm himself and resumes his advances with the same smarmy tone.

"Come out with me tomorrow. I'll show you the ropes, as it were. And maybe if you're good, I'll walk you through the ship's cabin. It's quite... comfortable."

"The only sailing event I've ever attended was the Neurogem Sea Dash last summer. It was a beautiful day, perfect for sailing I was told."

Vexhall's chest deflates.

"I didn't really follow the race, but I do remember one thing. There was a boat far ahead of the others that was tilted way over to one side. All they had to do was go around one more buoy and head back in to win. But right as it turned the whole boat flipped over! It was hilarious! I felt bad for laughing, but it serves them right for showing off. Did you see that race?"

"It's called 'tacking,' when a boat leans over like that," Davis replies. "And yes I saw that race. I was actually on that boat."

"Oh no! I'm so sorry, I didn't mean to laugh! It's just—"

"Tacking is a perfectly acceptable and often used tactic in yacht racing... it was lovely to see you again, Young Lady Yukita."

Vexhall departs with his eyes fixed on Aleks. His focus shifts to me for a brief moment before he turns away. Aleks and I try to stifle our laughter but fail.

"How may I help you, Young Lady Yukita?"

Aleks spins to face me and grips my arms in excitement.

"Ow!" she whispers, and shakes her hand. "I always forget about those sharp little pins on your sleeve."

She pulls my arms down so our faces line up.

"I heard the Monarchs are in the Northern Slopes for the rest of the week! Can you believe it? They actually left!"

"Really? Did their Valet go with them?"

"She did! It's hunting season. Are you free tonight?"

"Yeah. Meet me at the maintenance room when you're done here."

I try to suppress a broad smile and wind up with an awkward smirk. Aleks jumps up and down and shakes my arms, but I pull back. I can't risk word of my frivolity making its way back to Master

Telladyne. My face and body return to the same sturdy, neutral posture that all Noble Valets have mastered.

"Good evening, Young Lady Yukita. I look forward to serving you again soon," I say with a respectful nod.

Aleks is used to my sudden mood changes when we're around other Nobles. She dips into a low, formal curtsey.

3 Beeps. Master Telladyne.

"Valet, I am ready to leave. Bring the car around."

2

Inside the Reinhold Palace garage, I pass vehicles covered with explosion residue, bullet holes, and deep gashes. The faint smell of gunpowder wafts into my nostrils. This damage is fresh.

Every Noble has his or her own strategy for staying safe while traveling lowland highways. Some sacrifice speed for weaponry, while others forgo agility for heavy armor. Master Telladyne prefers to avoid conflict altogether, which is why his ride, the BT-27, is the only vehicle here without a scratch.

I step into the cockpit. Gauges and windshield displays spring to life with neon blue and champagne gold. I've logged so many drive hours in the BT-27 that it feels like an extension of my body.

I wait for Master Telladyne at the main palace entrance. As is tradition, I stand beside the BT-27's open rear door. The doors are automatic, and I already know his destination, so there's no practical reason for me to stand here. Noble Valet life is full of needless ceremony.

Master Telladyne says a few quick goodbyes at the palace entrance and locks into a split stare. He shouts at people in his virtual meeting and steps into the BT-27.

I'm 19 years old now and started working for the Telladynes at the age of 10. Even though I've spent almost half my life in his service, Master Telladyne rarely speaks anything aloud to me beyond, "That will be all, Valet."

We drive out of the Reinhold Palace grounds past Highland boutiques filled with rare treasures and hand-made items. The road ends at a lowland port.

The enormous, blast-proof port doors close behind us. Our slow descent begins. Bright white light illuminates the port car to make visual vehicle inspection easier.

I exit the BT-27 to manually test the tire pressure, confirm the external cameras' angles, and check the strut calibration.

An alarm sounds within the port car. 30 seconds until we reach the lowland.

I reenter the cockpit and affix my six-point harness. Master Telladyne is still immersed in his meeting.

The port car settles to a stop. Another alarm sounds, which is joined by flashing red lights and an audible countdown.

10.

I pull down on my black gloves and wrap my fingers tight around the steering wheel.

9.

I glance at the gauges. All of the BT-27's internal systems are fully operational.

8.

Black tire marks cover the port car floor. Some Valets let their nerves get the best of them.

7.

I understand their anxiety. Lowland port exits are the only places in The City where Noble vehicles dependably appear.

6.

If I were a radical and hated the Highland as much as they do, I'd gather a small arsenal and hold up outside the nearest port exit.

5.

Then again, Noble Guards in prismatic stealth armor guard every port exit. They'd apprehend me before my finger touched the trigger.

4.

But the Noble Guards, for all their strength and speed, can't stop everything.

3.

I release a slow, steady breath. There's no sense trying to understand the tactics of radicals.

2.

They're called radicals because they don't subscribe to traditional logic. They'd probably welcome Noble Guard capture if it meant one more dead Noble.

1.

I've seen some of the weakest Noble vehicles survive endless barrages of firepower and some of the strongest taken down by a single bullet. One lucky shot could end it all in an instant.

0.

Two sets of thick steel doors open before me. I stomp down on the pedal. The BT-27's tires spin before it launches into lowland traffic.

I lay a fresh pair of black skid marks in the port car. This happens every time. I try to stay calm and analytical but lose my cool at the last second.

I weave through countless LaborLiners. The blue and silver, retro-styled buses stop every few blocks and congest traffic like mad. Their enormous tires make it hard for them to accelerate quickly, which slows everyone down.

Those enormous tires have a purpose though—one I keenly appreciate right now. Harsh rumbles rise from the neglected lowland road, through the BT-27's hard racing tires and sporty suspension and vibrate into my arms. We're also assaulted from above, as rain from the lowland's constant storm pummels the windshield and glass roof.

Then there are the ads. Thousands of bright, gigantic ads play on the exterior of every building in view. Like the clips of Vox at the wake, if my eyes linger on any particular ad for a fraction of a second, its audio blasts in my ears.

Master Telladyne doesn't experience any of these distractions. For performance purposes, I need to feel every bump in the road, but Master Telladyne's compartment is equipped with advanced shock dampeners to ensure a smooth ride. Acoustic paneling blocks all exterior noise from Master Telladyne as well. For all he knows, we're still in the lowland port.

We reach the highway. Unlike the lowland surface streets, the highways are in pristine condition. Packed LaborLiners crowd all seven lanes, but I weave through them. Water flies off the windshield faster than it can collect.

Pa-khur!

I lose control of the BT-27 and veer toward a LaborLiner in the next lane. With a hard yank of the steering wheel, I avoid a full-on collision. Shrill damage alerts sound through the cockpit.

The rearview camera shows black smoke rise from the highway. A road mine. They're easy to hide but have unpredictable ignitions. Someone got lucky.

Two powercycles speed through the smoke. The riders raise their guns and open fire.

Ping-ping-ping!

They're far away, so only a few shots graze the BT-27. But that distance won't last long.

I engage the BT-27's prismatic stealth panels. The riders close in and fire more rounds.

Ping-ping! Ping-ping-ping-ping-ping-ping-ping!

A trail of direct hits runs down the BT-27. How can they see me so clearly? Some panels must have been damaged in the explosion.

I drop the stealth. No sense diverting power to a useless defense.

One rider holds back and fires at the rear wheel wells, while the other speeds ahead. The rider in front fires into the windshield. It's nearly impossible to see through all the tiny explosions.

My heart pounds against my rib cage. Beads of sweat form and tickle my brow, but I don't dare wipe them away.

The steering goes loose. A shredded black trail of rubber sprays behind us.

I grip the steering wheel hard and overcorrect at a rider. He drops back. My fierce momentum launches the BT-27 into a shipping truck.

The harsh screech of metal against metal pierces my ears. I turn the wheel but remain stuck to the truck. Somehow, we hooked together.

3 beeps.

"Valet! What's going on up there?"

"Just some road debris, Master Telladyne! Nothing to worry about."

The truck drags the BT-27 like a dead weight as we hurtle down the highway. Sparks fly while spider-web cracks spread over the roof and windows. With another hard tug, I break away and veer back into my lane.

Ping-ping-ping! Ping! Ping-ping-ping-ping-ping! Ping-ping!

I fight against the unpredictable steering to evade more direct hits. That truck collision made most of the bulletproof windows useless. If either rider gets a clear shot, Master Telladyne and I are dead.

I hear the BT-27's spoiler tumble onto the road. The rain stops, and my periphery turns white. We're inside an ad tunnel. Wherever I look, Vox appears.

"Bear, you haven't eaten anything since before the wakes, you must be starving! You should treat yourself to my favorite, a BurgerNite ChomperDeluxe..."

Ping-ping-ping-ping! Ping-ping-ping! Ping-ping-ping-ping-ping!

More shots connect. Where are the Noble Guard? There's no time to wait; I have to save myself.

I lock the front left wheel and spin the BT-27 180 degrees.

"... Premium wagyu beef," Vox continues. *"On a honey-infused black sesame bun with crisp iceberg lettuce, juicy heirloom tomatoes, artisan pickles, and bold garam masala aioli..."*

The smell of burnt rubber rises in my nostrils. I pop the BT-27 into reverse and drive backward down the highway while thin, pink slices of meat cascade down the tunnel walls.

I veer into another lane and lose one of the riders behind a LaborLiner. He'll be back any second.

Now!

I shift the BT-27 into drive, stomp down on the pedal, and rocket against oncoming traffic. The rider reappears right where I expected.

I engage the BT-27's emergency brake system, and stop dead in place. To my surprise, the rider accelerates. He lifts the front wheel of his powercycle and launches over the BT-27 like a ramp.

As if in slow motion, the rider aims his gun straight down at me. With the bulletproof glass roof compromised it won't deflect a single round. This is it.

Vox's face appears above the rider. She implores me one last time to try a ChomperDeluxe and gives her trademark wink.

Vox's wink.

People have fought over that wink—lived and died for that wink. Some would consider themselves lucky to see Vox one last time before they died. But I don't care about Vox. The last face I want to see before I die belongs to Aleks.

She's made me feel more whole and loved than any Idol who's ever lived—all the Idols combined for that matter. By some incredible stroke of luck, I stumbled into her life. Why haven't I told her that? I've wasted so much time!

I can't die like this. Not today!

As I open the door to dive out, a series of concussive blasts distracts the rider. He looks back, and lands behind us without firing a shot.

Chunks of cement and metal rain down from the tunnel ceiling. A single, bright red Noble Guard flies down through the new opening. He pursues the now-fleeing radical rider with a chain of bright white bullets that sends plumes of pulverized pavement into the air.

I turn the BT-27 around and follow the Noble Guard. Far ahead, I see the Guard's rounds clip the back of the rider's powercycle.

The cycle stalls, and the rider flees on foot. He barely gets three steps before the Noble Guard plucks him from the highway, stabs a sedative into his neck, and soars out of sight with the radical's now-limp body.

A second Noble Guard streaks across the sky. Vehicles up ahead crash into each other as the rider tries to divert attention away from himself. He has no idea how focused the Noble Guard can be.

A subtle smirk crawls across my face. The radicals came to kill a Noble, and by virtue of that mission, me as well. But their plan failed, and now they're the ones being hunted. I drive on the shoulder to get a better view.

The second Noble Guard's approach is different. As he closes in on his target, the guard raises his mechanical arm and fires once. The single, perfectly-aimed shot, connects with the front tire of a LaborLiner.

The tire bursts, which drops the LaborLiner hard onto the pavement right in front of the powercycle. The rider swerves and hits the highway barrier at full speed. His body catapults into the air. The Noble Guard catches the radical mid-flight and vanishes.

With my eyes back on the road, I take in the chase's wreckage-filled aftermath. Everywhere I look, vehicles lie crumpled into each other, some rendered motionless and smoking.

I approach the Noble Guard-hobbled LaborLiner, which sits amid a lake of shimmering broken glass. Some of the glass is tinged pink from the blood of people inside.

A muscular woman with a deep, bloody gash on her forehead stands atop the LaborLiner and pulls passengers up through the door. Everyone who emerges has a different injury; bleeding wounds, broken limbs, dislocated joints.

Dozens more bloodied and broken lowlanders huddle against the highway barrier. They weep to themselves, scream in agony, or sit frozen from shock. Camera drones fly over the scene with spotlights to capture every gory detail.

I pull over and slide back my door with a thought. Tears well in my eyes while my hands strangle the steering wheel. With the door open, lowland screams flood my ears. For some reason, I can't will my body out of the seat.

My skills and training could save lives out there, but I'm frozen. I clench my teeth, let out a primal scream, and beat the steering wheel until my palms ache.

3 beeps. Master Telladyne.

"Valet, why have we stopped?"

I take a deep breath to collect myself before I answer.

"A minor technical issue, Master Telladyne. We shall resume our travels straight away."

My door seals shut, the painful reality around me silences, and we resume our trip. Even though I fulfilled my primary objective, to keep Master Telladyne safe, something feels sunken inside me.

As we near our highway exit, Neurogem Tower comes into view. Down here it practically fades unnoticed into a landscape of similarly dilapidated buildings.

Most of the neuron details are broken off or rusted. A milky film coats the glass. Like all building sections in the lowland, scaffolding surrounds the tower to ensure that it's strong enough to support the Highland landscape above.

What am I doing? This isn't the time for contemplative observation. Even though we escaped with our lives, Master Telladyne's safety is still my top priority.

I dock a pen to stabilize my mood and increase my focus. We should be home soon.

3

I drop Master Telladyne off at the Manor main entrance. He's still NeuroSplit. For all I know, he's conducting two simultaneous virtual meetings, watching a Siloball match on NeuroCast, and running a NApp to move his feet up the stairs safely. It's no wonder he doesn't notice the BT-27's damage.

Once Master Telladyne is inside, I drive away to park and repair the BT-27.

A figure stands beside the garage. This must be my new Apprentice Valet. We've never met, but his facial scar is unmistakable. I pull up beside him and lower the window.

"You must be—"

"Carter," he says before I can finish. "CRTR, but it's not Critter, or Certer; it's Carter."

"Of course. Follow me inside."

I step out of the vehicle and stand beside Crtr for the first time. He's short and muscular. His hair is tamed into tied-back braids.

I prompt the garage to repair the BT-27. While the robotic repair arms get to work, we enter the maintenance room through a nondescript door.

"Room" is an understatement, it's more like a hanger. Metal catwalks crisscross through the cavernous space with all of Telladyne Manor's maintenance systems on the lowest floor.

As we descend a spiral staircase, I call up my task list in the upper right corner of my vision. Master Telladyne is due for his RejuviPod treatment in 24 minutes.

I audibly perform my regular system checks for Crtr's benefit until we reach the maintenance elevator that will take us inside Telladyne Manor.

"Service Elevator, Floor 3B, Northeast Chute," I command.

The elevator ascends and slides sideways.

Crtr observes the elevator's collection of wares with a scowl. His eyes fall upon dental procedure supplies, sporting equipment, a full wall of oil paints, and more. I can tell he has questions, but he doesn't say a word.

The elevator stops, and the doors open to a kitchen that's adjacent to the Telladyne Manor Sunset Lounge. We must prepare a light meal of fruit and tea before Master Telladyne's treatment.

Crtr collects fruit while I gather a formal tea set and put on the kettle. Like the formality of standing beside the passenger door, tea service must be done in the traditional, inefficient manner of boiling water by flame.

Crtr's already grabbed a knife and started chopping. He lops the tops off strawberries with reckless abandon, hacks the pineapple into chunks with the rind still attached, and throws it all together onto the plate.

"Valet Apprentice Crtr, stop! What are you doing?"

"Master Telladyne wants fruit, right? I'm chopping up some fruit."

"No, no, no. Consider presentation. Honor these ingredients with skillful preparation. Wasn't this covered during your introductory Noble Valet instruction?"

"I didn't have any introductory Noble Valet instruction, remember?"

That's right. Crtr was fast-tracked into the Noble Valet program. The Noble Valet Council must think highly of my skill.

"Right, of course," I say. "Let me show you."

I grab another pineapple. On my way back, I access the NApp Store, purchase a pineapple slicing NApp for five points, and gift it to Crtr with a flick.

"This time, use the NApp I just sent you. It will overlay slice lines onto the pineapple that you can follow to maximize the amount of edible fruit you retrieve."

Crtr lets out a sigh and hacks into the fruit again.

"Crtr, use smooth movements. You don't need to push down so hard. Let the blade cut for you—"

"This is ridiculous!"

"Excuse me?"

"This, all of this, it's ridiculous! You act like this pineapple is the most important thing in The City. It's just a pineapple!"

"I realize that it is just a pineapple, Valet Apprentice Crtr. But to you, in this moment, this pineapple *is* the most important thing in The City."

"More important than the lives of our brothers and sisters, the ones you left on the highway to suffer?"

Crtr holds the knife so tight in his fist that I briefly wonder if he's about to attack me. Frustrated tears turn his eyes glassy.

"Every chase ends the same way," he says. "The Noble escapes unharmed while every lowlander caught in the crossfire is ignored. How could you drive away? They needed your help!"

"It wasn't my place to help them."

"Have you been in the Highland so long you no longer see low-landers as living, breathing people?"

"Valet Apprentice Crtr, if Master Telladyne was captured or killed, the future of Telladyne Industries would be thrust into frenzied uncertainty. Hundreds of thousands of lowlanders would become Unassigned in the process.

"For this reason, my primary objective tonight was to keep Master Telladyne safe. I am proud to say that I succeeded. Right now, your primary objective is to prepare these strawberries and pineapple, and arrange them in an elegant display. We all have our roles to play, and we are fortunate to have them. Let me know when you're finished."

Crtr and I complete the remainder of our tasks in silence. When I return to Crtr, I find a plate of perfectly cut pineapple that encircles a pyramid of bright strawberry wedges. He must have downloaded a strawberry cutting NApp on his own.

I place the fruit and tea on the serving tray and bring it to the Sunset Lounge. The tray includes a supplementary RXPen, Master Telladyne's third and final wellness pen before his next pod treatment.

Crtr and I stand back while Master Telladyne eats the fruit as an afterthought. He's split for another meeting.

Even though we're in the Sunset Lounge, the sun is far out of sight. Dim, false candlelight chandeliers cast dramatic shadows around the room. I glance at Crtr to my right, and my eyes move to the scar on his face.

It's deep and runs clear from his hairline down to his chin. He got that scar because he values life in a way that most don't. It's no wonder Crtr was so upset about the chase.

Crtr never could have guessed he'd become a Noble Valet. Promotions from laborer to Valet are rare, but so are opportunities for true valor.

Crtr and I both came from corporate-sponsored birth pools. While I was selected for Noble Valet service, Crtr continued along the traditional occupational training path.

He was trained specifically in AeroPack-enhanced construction. Crtr and his team flew to the highest parts of new construction projects to guide beams, rivet scaffolding, and weld metal frameworks.

It was at one of these construction projects that Crtr first encountered his future master, Janson Carrington. The project was a new dual parabolic shuttle launch that would allow two jumpers to launch from the same location simultaneously—the first of its kind ever constructed. Carrington visited the site obsessively with his publicist in tow.

During a routine visit, Carrington wandered across a catwalk. Suddenly, a massive explosion erupted from the top of the launch.

The concussive blast disoriented everyone inside. Smoldering debris rained down as workers fled for cover and escape.

Seemingly out of nowhere, Crtr appeared. He grabbed Carrington and the publicist before a massive tank crashed through the catwalk. The Valet left behind plummeted into deadly darkness.

Carrington and the publicist clung tight to Crtr, which weighed him down. He needed to land soon, or he'd lose control of the AeroPack and they'd all crash.

Crtr flew to an opening in the launch's frame. As he moved toward the opening, a large piece of shrapnel fell from above. With limited maneuverability from the extra weight, Crtr couldn't avoid the sharp metal sheet.

Blood sprang from Crtr's face and ran down his neck, but he hardly grimaced. Shortly after he reached the landing, Crtr passed out. He awoke outside the launch.

A couple of RXPens of Lexiphene later, Crtr, Carrington, and the publicist watched the Noble Guard put out the critically damaged, flame-engulfed tower. Down a Valet, and never one to pass up a good publicity stunt, Carrington made Crtr his new Valet on the spot.

Of course, I saw this all happen live through the eyes of Carrington's publicist, as did most of the city. People even turned away from the Idol's LifeCast to watch.

Crtr's act of selfless heroism instantly became part of Carrington family lore. It's why Carrington demands Crtr wear his hair back, so his storied scar remains visible.

"That will be all, Valet," Master Telladyne says as he docks the wellness pen. "Prepare my RejuviPod."

"Yes, Master Telladyne."

I turn on my heel and motion for Crtr to follow.

"Service elevator, come to Floor 3B, Chute F."

We arrive at Master Telladyne's RejuviPod chamber. Dappled light from a large illuminated pool dances across the dark blue granite walls. As we walk along a narrow path to Master Telladyne's pod, Crtr marvels at the golden koi within the pool.

I touch an invisible panel on the wall, and a drawer extends. The drawer contains a blue stain sheet and matching pillow. Upon my approach, Master Telladyne's bespoke, champagne gold pod slides open. I dress the pod and stand back.

The wall behind the pod separates and Master Telladyne steps through. He wears dark blue pajamas that match the pod clothes I just placed.

"Sir, your RejuviPod is ready. May I assist you with anything else?"

"No, Valet, that will be all."

"Thank you, Master Telladyne."

Master Telladyne's pod closes with him inside and lowers into a lying position. On our way back to the service elevator, I send Crtr a list of simple tasks he can complete on his own.

The twins will bounce from wake-to-wake for the rest of the evening, and Master Telladyne won't have any work for me until his pod treatment ends.

For the next five hours I'm free.

4

Crtr drops me off at the maintenance room and rides the elevator back to Telladyne Manor.

"Bear!"

Aleks leaps off a catwalk into a cart of dirty laundry. She emerges with surprising grace, and runs to me.

"I saw the chase, are you all right?"

"I'm fine."

She lunges forward and hugs me. The feel of her body in my arms warms me all the way through.

"I was so worried about you," she whispers.

"Really, I'm OK. Let's go."

We ascend a staircase and bolt across several catwalks to my living quarters. Aleks pulls a black duffel bag from the cabinets above my workbench. She removes two boilersuits and throws one to me.

We change with our backs to each other. I feel a strong invisible force pull my eyes toward her body. It takes every ounce of discipline I have to resist.

"How was the rest of the wake?" I ask.

"Torture. I never have anything to say to those people, and Vexhall kept following me around. Whenever I caught him staring, he squinted and puckered up his face like he was at a photo shoot. Whatever, it's over now. I still can't believe we're finally going to see the Monarch archives!"

"I know, the Monarchs never leave! All it took was the Idol's death," I say, and realize my insensitivity. "Poor girl."

I hear the clang of equipment on the workbench, which means Aleks is finished changing. She lays out two pairs of grapplers and two safety line harnesses.

Her boilersuit zipper's undone. A thin strip of Aleks' fair skin peeks out from between the muted gray fabric and metal zipper teeth. She glances over her shoulder.

"Could you get that for me?"

I step closer and rest one hand on her hip, while I take the zipper in my fingers. She gathers her hair to one side, out of the zipper's path. As the gentle slope of her neck is revealed, the scent of her juniper shampoo fills my nose. It's the same shampoo she's used since we were kids.

I raise the zipper with a gradual pace—there's no reason to rush. My hands linger for a moment after I'm done. She looks back at me. My chest fills with warm soda bubbles. I feel the unseen force pull me toward her lips.

Aleks' eyes close in anticipation as our faces move closer. My fingers sink into her waist.

"Aleks, I…"

"What?"

Why is this so hard when my feelings were so clear on the highway? I've willfully sabotaged so many moments like this that my brain refuses to relent. I take a step back.

"I've never been to the Monarch Estate. Have you?"

We stand in awkward silence until Aleks pushes a pair of grapplers into my chest. I affix the grapplers to my arms.

"No, they don't throw parties or anything," Aleks says as she ties her hair back into a ponytail. "My father says Monarchs always come to you. Apparently, they don't like people in their home."

I grab the black duffel and head to the service line pick-up. We attach our harnesses and extend our grapplers. The small hooks at the ends of the katana-like grappler blades are meant for siloball cables but also work on service lines.

Access to the service line network requires a work permit. Workers use the lines to wash palace windows, patch cracked plaster, and perform other exterior maintenance tasks without disturbing any Nobles. Fortunately, I know someone who can forge permits.

Aleks jumps up to connect her grapplers to the line. I do the same. The service line pick-up's glass wall slides open.

Cold air rushes into the room. A visible shiver passes through Aleks' body. We slide forward on the gently sloped line.

Once we leave the room, the line bends down and our speed increases. With access to the greater service line network, we have a direct route to any palace in the Highland.

I've ridden the service lines hundreds of times but still feel a rush of adrenaline every time. The icy wind feels singularly refreshing and clean, almost purifying. The further we get from Telladyne Manor, the easier it is to breath.

After a few line transfers, the Monarch Estate comes into view.

Aleks drops onto a balcony without breaking stride. I catch the balcony with my legs and stumble to a stop beside her. After I finish loading our equipment back into the black duffel, we head for the door.

Before she touches the door handle, Aleks stops and looks me in the eyes. She taps her temple once. I do the same.

If we strolled inside the Monarch Estate with our gems enabled, the estate's security system would retrieve our unique NeuroSigs instantly. Tranquilizer darts would rain down upon us, and Noble Guards would arrive shortly after.

That temple tap tells me Aleks deactivated her gem. She's the only other person I've ever met who can do that. My temple tap confirms that mine's off, too.

Aleks pushes down on the door handles, and we walk inside.

We enter a study where leather-bound books line the walls. Aleks approaches a ruby-encrusted cocktail dress displayed inside a glass box.

"Phantasma Gerhardt wore this dress during her Idol Nomination Ceremony performance," Aleks says. "I remember wishing I could wear something so beautiful someday. Now I hope I never have to."

"Is that to say you do not aspire to be The City's next Idol, Young Lady Yukita?" I ask in an overly formal tone.

"How could anyone wish to be the Idol, especially after what happened to Vox? Her every move was broadcast to the entire city until the moment she died. I value my privacy far too much."

"But what about the fame, the points, the clothes, the immortality? None of that appeals to you?"

"Maybe the clothes. But I'd rather live a long life in obscurity than die young with notoriety. Come on, I saw the emergency access door on the way in."

We approach a tall bookshelf. The bookshelf looks different from the others, with a small gap around its edges. It's a manual access panel installed for emergencies in case of a power outage.

I pull one side of the shelf, while Aleks pushes the other. The panel rotates with a sharp break. Aleks stumbles through the new opening. I walk through to meet her in the service tunnel behind the bookshelf.

We travel down the tunnel to a service elevator shaft. I pry open the shaft doors with a crowbar from my black duffel, and we descend the shaft ladder several floors to the Monarch family archive. The archive, like those in every Noble home, spans an entire floor and is filled with heirlooms and keepsakes.

"Same bet as always?" Aleks asks.

"Of course. See you in the Reflection Lounge."

The archive overflows with antique furniture, artwork that once hung in now abandoned mansions, museum quality statues, shelves of photo albums and bobbles, outdated electronics equipment, and centuries-worth of other items.

I stop at a tiger oak vanity. The vanity's enormous mirror reflects back an image of what my life could have been. If Master Telladyne hadn't selected me to become his Valet, a boilersuit like this would have been my daily uniform.

I pull open one of the vanity's drawers. Inside, a strange golden rectangle sits on an orange pillow within a glass box. I open the box, and examine the rectangle. Holes line the rectangle's long edges. Two screws hold it all together. Though it's made of polished gold, this doesn't look like any piece of jewelry I've seen before. It's unusual and rare; Aleks will love it.

I look over to her. She kicks up her leg and pivots on one foot to ease between a pedestal topped with a bronze bust and an upright piano. Aleks' grace is what initially drew me to her so long ago.

I began my Noble Valet training at age seven, beneath Noble Valet Holt, at the Yukita Teitaku. One of my first independent tasks was gardening.

Through a tall rose bush, I saw Aleks dancing in a meadow. Whenever she lifted her leg or extended her arm, she was jerked into a more perfect position. I could tell she had a NeuroTrainer activated.

Most Noble children let their NeuroTrainers carry them through tasks like dancing, painting, or playing instruments, but Aleks fought against hers. She started over whenever the NeuroTrainer changed her position. I was intrigued.

I returned the next day. Aleks' movements were more fluid than before, but she couldn't escape the NeuroTrainer's awkward corrections. In a moment of unbridled frustration, she called out to me.

"Valet!"

How did she see me? Was I so obvious? Regardless, my curiosity was about to cost me my position. I set down my gardening equipment and met her in the meadow to accept my fate.

"How does this look?" She asked. "Be honest."

Aleks spun around and extended her leg back so it was in line with her forward extended arm. As she slowed, her torso twisted, her wrists locked, and her leg mechanically clicked into position two inches higher. The position in which she froze was textbook, but the last second correction ruined the movement's graceful effect.

"Young Lady Yukita, if you would like to study your movements, the dance studio on Level 4 is currently unoccupied."

"I just came from there. If I have to stare at myself any longer, I'll go crazy! Please, give me your honest opinion. Did that look good?"

"Young Lady Yukita, I must admit that I am no authority on dance. Yours is actually the first I've ever seen in person—"

"Stop calling me 'Young Lady,' my name is Aleks, just Aleks. I promise I won't be mad. Please, tell me what you thought."

"Well to be honest Young... Aleks, I don't know much about dance, but, and this does not mean that you aren't an excellent dancer... it seemed like everything was perfect until your NeuroTrainer kicked in."

"I knew it!" Aleks shouted. "I'm trying to learn the choreography for a school recital, but it's impossible with a NApp pushing and pulling at me!"

"Why don't you simply let your NeuroTrainer take over? It would seamlessly activate your muscle memory and move you through the choreography without issue."

"I don't want to move through the motions like everyone else, I want to actually *learn* the dance! What's the point of a recital if everyone's gem does everything? I wish they didn't make us download the NeuroTrainer."

"Why don't you just turn it off?"

"My NeuroTrainer? It won't release until the recital's over."

"Then turn off your gem."

Aleks burst into laughter so hard I thought she might fall over.

"A joke! From a Noble Valet! I didn't know you were allowed to be funny."

I remained stone-faced. After a few more chuckles, Aleks turned serious.

"Valet, no one can turn off their Neurogem, not even Nobles... Can you—"

"No, no, of course not... like you said, no one can turn off their Neurogem. Especially not a lowly Valet like me! I was just saying that if you could, then your NeuroTrainer wouldn't be a problem anymore. Please excuse me, Noble Valet Holt needs my help for dinner service. Good luck with your recital, Y... Lady... Aleks!"

I gave a quick bow and scampered back to the house.

From that point on, I stayed away from the West Garden. To reveal myself further would risk everything.

Given the size of the Yukita Teitaku, it was actually quite easy to avoid Aleks. After my Valet training I'd be placed permanently with the Telladynes, and would likely never speak to her again. The thought stabbed my heart, but I had no other option.

One afternoon, Noble Valet Holt ended our carpentry lesson early. He said we had to escort the Yukita family to Young Lady Aleksaria's school recital. A tinge of excitement surged through me. Even though I had successfully avoided Aleks, I longed to see her dance again.

My orders were to stay with the car during the performance, but I sneaked into the auditorium.

The stage curtains opened to reveal hundreds of boys and girls in sparkly purple body suits. Every child stared straight ahead while they sang and moved through precise choreography. They were all perfectly synchronized, except Aleks.

Aleks was at the back but stood out more than anyone. She didn't sing a note, but that didn't matter. Her transitions between positions were fluid and natural. Aleks brought life to the otherwise robotic performance.

The last move of the recital was a spin into an arabesque. Aleks' arm extended, her leg rose straight back, and she froze in place without any sudden shifts. At that moment I knew she'd figured it out.

By sheer force of will, Aleks learned how to turn off her Neurogem. Even more impressive was the fact that she did it in a matter of weeks, not months like me.

After the performance I wanted to tell Aleks how good she was, and reveal the truth I hid from her in the garden, but I didn't have a chance.

Master Yukita was furious. Aleks was admonished for embarrassing her entire family, and banished to her pod chamber.

Later that evening, I dropped onto the balcony outside Aleks' chamber. While her music blared, she practiced headstands at the center of the room.

I knocked. She saw me in the middle of a headstand, toppled over, and bounded to the doors.

"How did you get out there?" She asked.

"The service lines."

"Where have you been? You just disappeared, I thought you were mad at me."

"Mad? No, of course not. I was afraid."

Someone knocked on Aleks' chamber door.

"Young Lady Aleksaria, this is Noble Valet Holt. Please open this door."

"One second!" Aleks shouted. "Quick, get into the pod."

I climbed into her bright pink RejuviPod. The pod smelled like Aleks' juniper shampoo. I focused hard on the scent to remain as quiet and still as possible.

Holt entered and sat down with Aleks beside the pod.

"Aleks, why weren't you singing with the other children this evening?" Holt asked. "Your father is quite cross and would like an explanation."

"I didn't feel like it. That song is boring!"

"Boring or not, it is your school's anthem. Do you not like your school?"

"No, I like my school fine. I just don't like singing."

"But you have such a lovely voice!"

"It's embarrassing."

"You know, if you ever want to be the Idol one day you will have to dance *and* sing."

"I know. I'm sorry I didn't sing tonight. I promise I will next time."

"Excellent, see that you do. And I'll tell you a secret. I love to sing. If you ever wish to practice, call on me and I will happily sing with you. Now come along, it's time to brush your teeth before your pod treatment."

I left that night without saying goodbye but returned the next night and almost every night after.

At parties, Aleks and I turned off our gems to sneak away and explore Noble family archives together, which we agreed were the most interesting part of any Noble palace. But waiting for parties got tiresome. We started using the service line network to traverse the Highland at will. The possibilities were endless.

"Bah!"

An angry, bright red mask pops into view. I stumble backward, trip over something, and catch myself on the same bronze bust Aleks maneuvered around before.

She laughs, with the red mask in her hands.

I walk forward to look closer at the mask, and my leg catches on something. A little hidden door juts out from the base of the bronze bust pedestal. Cold gas pours from the door.

We crouch down to find several large metal disks inside. I remove one of the chilled metal disks. They're containers. I open one and remove a spooled wheel of long plastic tape. The tape must extend for hundreds of feet.

"Someone went to a lot of trouble to keep these cool and hidden," Aleks says.

"Yeah, I wonder what they are."

"Look at the little notches on the sides. This tape must feed into something. Maybe it's some kind of information format. Here."

Aleks takes an end of the spool and hands me the rest. We walk backward to unravel the tape.

I hold the tape up to the moonlit archive windows and see a vague form in it. This gives me an idea. I dig into the duffel for a flashlight to confirm my suspicion.

"It's a string of images! Shine your flashlight up through it!"

Each image is slightly different than the last. I walk back toward Aleks with my eyes and flashlight fixed on the tape. As I walk, I see two men throw a white ball back and forth. They use padded gloves to catch the ball. I'm oddly mesmerized by the crude motion created by the strung-together images.

"This must be some primitiv—" I start to say when Aleks and I bump into each other.

"Did you see the two men throwing the ball?" Aleks asks.

"I did! How many more of these are there?"

We go back to the pedestal and find three more canisters. Aleks and I have discovered countless strange and valuable artifacts, but nothing this intriguing.

After I stuff the canisters into the duffel, we move to a tufted leather sofa in the Reflection Lounge.

Aleks reaches into her backpack and removes a flat, square box. The box has a brushed copper finish with a dark blue ribbon tied around it. She unties the ribbon and opens the box.

Nine perfect, handmade Schollner du Sant chocolates sit inside the box. Each chocolate is a distinct work of art.

We always choose our favorites first. Mine's a chocolate dome coated with liquefied cinnamon, dusted with cherry powder, perched on a thin honeycomb wafer. Aleks takes the Cone de Saveur. On the outside, it looks like a simple chocolate cone, but inside it's layered with strawberry jam, mint foam, stem ginger, and clotted cream.

With a bite, Aleks tells me to go first. I lick the melted chocolate from my fingertips, wipe them on my pants, and show her my find.

She's never seen anything like the small, golden rectangle. We think it could be some kind of cooking device used to seal dough, or maybe an ornamental attachment for multiple necklaces. Finally, Aleks takes the rectangle and blows into it. The resulting high-pitch note startles both of us.

"It's an instrument!" Aleks says. "How strange."

We pass the instrument back and forth to try and string together some kind of melody. Each little hole screams its own note. This thing must take incredible precision to play.

"What'd you find?" I ask.

Aleks presents a heavy marble box. A small stand comes out from the top where a long handle rests. The handle has large, knob-like bulbs with tiny holes in them on each end. A gold dial with numbers 0 - 9 covers the box's face.

"Those bulbs kind of look like showerheads," I say. "But there's no water hookup. Maybe it's some kind of massage device?"

"And you use the number to select the strength?" Aleks suggests.

"Could be."

"Let's see if it works."

Aleks jams one of the knobs into my ribs, and makes a whirring sound. It tickles, and I squirm away. She comes at me again and presses the knobs to my chest.

Every time I move, twist, or push away the device, Aleks finds a new way to pester me with it. I can hardly catch my breath from laughter.

The massager meets my neck. Aleks looks down into my eyes. The weight of her body on top of mine feels natural. My hands move to her waist. Hers was the last face I wanted to see before I died.

Our faces near each other, and for the first time, our lips touch. The familiar soda bubbles that course through my limbs whenever we make contact explode through my bloodstream.

The sweet surrender of this moment feels like the culmination of our entire, beautiful shared history. Her Noble status and my Noble Valet duty mean nothing. All that matters is her and me.

Each kiss pulls me further from reality, until I'm catapulted back by something in the back of my mind. Master Telladyne's treatment will end in a couple hours. I pull away.

"What's wrong?" Aleks asks.

"There's just never enough time. If we want to learn more about those reels, we should go soon."

Aleks lets out a sigh, and crawls off of me.

"You're more responsible than me."

She rests her head on my chest while my fingers move through her silken hair. There's truly nowhere in The City I'd rather be. I want to live in this moment forever, sheltered by the warmth of Aleks' body against mine, fed by the electricity that surges between us whenever our skin touches.

"Yours was the stranger find," Aleks says. "You win."

My victory means the last chocolate in the box is mine, but we always share it. I take a bite of the crushed nut and nougat-filled chocolate and pass it to Aleks. While she chews, I braid the side of her hair. She looks out at the enormous Reflection Lounge windows.

"That jumper looks like it's about to collide with that red satellite," she says.

I turn my head to see two exhaust trails burst into existence behind a parabolic jumper.

"That's a Saben Industries navigation satellite," I reply. "It's in intermediate circular orbit about 1,400 miles above sea level."

"How do you know that?"

"They made us learn all about the different satellites during parabolic shuttle pilot training. See that solid orange one that looks still?"

"Mm-hmm."

"That's the Neurogem transmission satellite in geosynchronous orbit. That purple flashing one is Patel Robotics. And you probably know that light blue one."

"No, whose is that?"

"Yukita Transit. It relays positioning information for all your LaborLiners, MagLev trains, and ferries."

"I didn't even know we had a satellite. Daddy doesn't exactly see me as the heir apparent."

"What does he expect you to do when he retires?"

"I don't think he's given it much thought."

"I'm sure that's not true."

Nobles always have plans for their children whether they've conveyed those plans or not. I don't know what Takeshi Yukita has in mind for Aleks, but I know his plans don't involve his daughter falling in love with a lowlander like me. If he found out about Aleks and me, he'd do everything in his nearly limitless power to keep us apart.

5

We take a worker lift down to the lowland. Thin metal grates surround us. This thing's no frills, purely utilitarian.

After we left the Monarch grounds, Aleks and I reactivated our gems. This let us identify the objects we found. Aleks' marble box was a crude analog communication device called a telephone. It was heavy, so she left it behind.

We confirmed that my discovery was a small wind instrument called a harmonica. It fit easily inside my pocket, so I kept it.

We also identified the spools of tape. They're celluloid film reels that must be ancient.

To play the reels, we need something called a reel-to-reel projector. Neither of us has ever seen such a device in person, and we can't simply order one on the NeuroNet. Luckily, we know someone in the lowland who might be able to help us view the reels.

Aleks is enamored by the harmonica. As we approach the mist, her notes get shaky from shivers. I pull her close and wrap my arms around her. We look out beyond the lift in silence.

The opulent Highland architecture appears weightless on a bed of indigo clouds. White wisps of fog float in light streams that give the sturdy buildings a sense of movement.

Thick, thermal panel walls surround the lift as we travel through the mist. For the moment, we're truly alone again. The heat generated from our bodies combats the cold.

Aleks turns to face me. She raises her arms to wrap them around my neck, and coaxes me down for a kiss. I live for these stolen moments but wish we could own just one of them.

We clear the mist and the thermal panels. Torrents of lowland rain spray into the lift. Bright, colorful ads invade our vision from every angle. The bombardment of water and ads shocks us out of our embrace.

Aleks grabs hold of the metal grates and looks out with wonder. Even after all her trips down here, she still finds the lowland novel.

The lift stops in a fenced-in supply yard, and we depart. Two bright red Noble Guards appear. They aren't usually stationed at maintenance lifts.

The wakes.

They're doing random travel clearance checks tonight. I should have known.

The Noble Guard technically work for the Highland, but only answer to their commander. Anyone, even Nobles, who test their strict security measures are subject to persecution. It's best to avoid them whenever possible.

"Please present travel documentation," one of the Guards says in the same deep, authoritative, robotic voice that all Noble Guards use.

Aleks' face flushes with frustration. She's a Noble, and I'm a Noble servant, which means we're both cleared to travel anywhere in The City. Even so, to verify our travel clearance, the Noble Guard require access to our Neurogem central logs.

"Please present travel documentation," the guard repeats.

In addition to travel documentation, central logs house a complete list of Neurogem activity. With that kind of access, the Noble Guard can view NeuroNet searches, purchases, conversations, and much more. The request is invasive and unnecessary, but there's no way around it.

"Here's our clearance!" Aleks snaps, and holds up her dock.

Aleks has always resented the Noble Guard. She's witnessed their disregard for collateral damage and general thuggishness her entire life. Most Nobles turn a blind eye to the Noble Guard's tactics, but Aleks refuses to accept their authority. It's one of my favorite things about her.

"This is Styrolex!" Aleks shouts. "What lowlander could possibly afford a Styrolex RXDock mod? We're obviously from the Highland! What more do you mindless, destruction-bots need?"

Per ounce, Styrolex is the most valuable synthetic substance in existence. Styrolex mods aren't just stylish, with swirls of tangerine-red; they also absorb the chill from RXPen docking. Everyone in the Highland has them, even Valets.

"Thank you for your cooperation, Noble Valet Bear," says the second guard.

"Bear! What are you doing?"

"Aleks, just give them access," I say. "Master Telladyne's treatment will be over soon."

"No! I'm not letting some faceless sociopath into my central log. Take this as my clearance and get out of our way!" Aleks pushes her dock into the Noble Guard's facemask.

The guard grabs Aleks' wrist so fast I don't even see him move.

"Get your hands off her!" I shout.

Before I can step forward, the second guard hoists me off the ground and pins me against the lift. I kick and struggle, but it's useless.

"Please present your travel documentation," the first guard says again.

"No! What are you going to do, arrest me? Take me back to your Noble Guard clubhouse and make me hang out with all the other lost boys?"

The guard squeezes his hand around Aleks' wrist, and she lets out a tortured scream.

"Thank you for your cooperation, Highland resident, Aleksaria Yukita."

The guard releases Aleks' wrist. Three pieces of Styrolex fall along with a stream of bright red blood. Aleks crumples to the ground. I'm released and run to her side.

I tear the sleeve off my boilersuit and wrap it tight around her wrist.

The Noble Guards have retaken their posts nearby with stoic disregard for the pain they just inflicted. My teeth clench and my hands shake. I want nothing more than to fill them with sedatives, throw them into the lift, ride it above the mist, and kick them out.

My shaking hand forms into a fist. Aleks gently grasps my arm.

"Bear, don't. Just get me to Zola. She'll take care of me."

We leave the supply yard. I lead Aleks through the relentless river of oblivious pedestrians. Navigation NApps move their feet and help them avoid collisions with other walkers while they're split.

I pull Aleks into a nearby building, and we cross a dilapidated lobby to an elevator bank.

"Where are we?" Aleks asks.

"The hospital, this is the main entrance. You can't climb the fire escape with your wrist like that."

We reach floor 18, the Breaker Ward.

The elevator doors open to neat rows of metal beds. The ward is generally silent, except for monitors that beep, compressed air devices that hiss, and the soft shuffles of patients who move like ghosts through the solemn floor.

Pach, the man we're here to see, spots us and smiles. He's one of the floor's few conscious inhabitants.

Pach sits hunched over and gaunt from a lifetime of hard labor. Fine wrinkles draw an intricate topographical map across his dry brown skin. His enormous, deep-set eyes float around the room with a lazy lilt.

"Aleks... Bear... it's good to see... you," Pach struggles. "To what... do we owe... the pleasure of... this... visit?"

Most of the Breakers are here because they attempted to overclock their Neurogems, expand the number of splits they could perform, or run complex algorithms that were only possible by hacking the Neurogem's fail-safes. The consequences of this kind of tinkering are typically disastrous, but Pach managed to avoid the same catatonic fate as his fellow ward-inhabitants.

He didn't come out unscathed though. Pach's nervous system was fried, which resulted in significant speech and motion delays. Luckily, his mind remained unaffected. Despite his sloth-like movements, Pach can carry on a fast-paced NeuroText conversation on any topic. Even so, he chooses to speak aloud whenever possible.

"Pach, where's Zola? Aleks is injured!"

"I see that. Let me take... a look."

Aleks unravels the bloody cloth from her wrist. Pach's eyes widen. He eases himself off his bed.

"Sit... down."

Pach shuffles toward a large metal cabinet. His half-time pace tests my patience. I follow him to the cabinets and pull at random drawers. Before I find a single useful item, Pach has gathered everything he needs and is on his way back to Aleks.

"Give me... your wrist."

Pach leans over the wound and blows on it. Aleks winces.

"Good," Pach says. "Nerves are still... alive. Easy to... graft a new... dock."

Pach shakily lifts a bottle of rubbing alcohol to Aleks' arm. He tips the bottle and accidentally pours half of it onto the wound.

"Here," I say. "Let me finish up."

I dress Aleks' wound with a simple bandage.

"What brings... you... here this eve... ning?" Pach asks.

"This," I reply.

Aleks pulls a reel from the black duffel.

"We need something to play it."

"Loomi... she can help."

"Who's Loomi?" Aleks asks.

"An old... friend. Best tech I... know."

Pach pushes the reel under his pillow. I hold onto the others. If the reel I gave him gets lost or confiscated, I'll still have the rest of them.

"Who's that over there?" I hear from across the room. "Is that Aleks and Bear?"

We look over to find Zola, matron of the Breaker Ward. She's a slight woman whose limbs are so thin they practically float as she walks. She tames her wild, frizzy hair with a long green scarf that falls over her pointed shoulders.

"What are you two doing down here with us lowlanders?" Zola asks. "Don't you have enough trouble up there?"

Zola catches sight of Aleks' bandage.

"My sweet girl, what happened?"

"A pair of Noble Guards met us at the lift," I say. "Aleks didn't want to give up her travel clearance, so they crushed her dock."

"What possessed you to stand up to a Noble Guard over something as silly as that?"

"I don't want them poking around my central log. No one should have to accept such a violation!"

"Everyone... has secrets," Pach says. "I under... stand."

"This isn't about secrets," Aleks replies. "It's just none of their business what I do!"

"Privacy, such a Noble concept," Zola says. "Now what are we going to do about your wrist? If you can slum it for a spell, I can give you one of our docks."

"That would be great. Thanks, Zola."

"In all the excitement I forgot to give you two hugs!" Zola shouts. "It's good to see you, sweets. Come here."

Zola wraps her fragile arms around Aleks.

"And you, Bear. My pride. How is the Highland treating you?"

"Good. Same, but good."

"That's all you ever have to say, 'same, good, fine.' You're hopeless."

Zola reaches around me. Even though I stand almost two feet above her, I feel enveloped by her embrace, just like when I was a kid.

"All right you two, come with me."

Zola leads us to an elevator that we take down several floors.

The elevator doors open to a dark, cavernous room that plunges deep into blackness. Enormous glass cubes suspended from thick cables glow bright blue and purple. Composed nurses in white lab coats cross over catwalks that extend above and below us.

Zola walks ahead while Aleks hangs back in awe. It occurs to me that she's never seen a place like this in person before.

"Welcome to the Birth Pools," I say.

One of the enormous glass cubes high above our heads pulses red. Nurses all around sprint toward the cube. Zola grabs a nurse who runs past us.

"Level 1 temperature spike!" The nurse shouts. "Third one this week! If we lose another stack, UteroCube will pull our license!"

We travel down another fifteen floors to the bottom of the Birth Pools. Glowing cubic stacks of UteroCubes stand in-wait before us. Aleks approaches a stack and touches the cube of a baby boy.

The boy's eyes are closed, but he kicks with life within a cloudy solution. An umbilical cord at the top of the UteroCube anchors the boy face-up.

"I can't believe you were born here like this," Aleks says.

Like that, but not exactly. My UteroCube malfunctioned and was destroyed after I was born. They wanted to destroy me too, but Zola stopped them. From that point on, she took a special interest in me.

A large robotic arm lowers onto the stack and lifts off the top layer of 25 cubes.

"Where are they going?" Aleks asks.

"Let me show you."

We walk into a bright white hallway. Zola stands at a large window that overlooks a room full of waist-high pedestals.

A woman in a pale green dress joins us in the hallway. She looks like Zola but younger and plump.

"Caretaker Mint!" Zola calls to the woman.

"Zola! It's been too long! How can I help you?"

"This one decided to play chicken with a Noble Guard and got her dock broken."

Aleks smiles and waives at Mint.

"Can you spare a dock?" Zola asks.

"Oh yeah, no problem," Mint says. "Wait, is this Bear?"

"Yes! I forgot you haven't met him!"

I extend my hand to Mint, but she lunges forward with a powerful hug that nearly knocks me over.

"It's so good to meet you, Bear! I've heard so much about you! How is the Highland? Those Nobles aren't giving you too hard a time, are they?"

"No, no. It's fine."

"Fine? You live in the Highland and that's all you have to say about it?"

"It's... beautiful. The architecture, the people, everything is very nice."

"Well, that's a little better. I'm glad you get a chance to visit Zola now and again."

I hear a loud whir from the pedestal room and look back. A robotic arm, like the one Aleks and I saw, lowers into the room with a stack layer. The arm separates the layer into 25 individual UteroCubes and sets each one on its own pedestal.

As the arm ascends out of the room, it takes the sides and top of each cube with it. Fluid from the cubes rushes onto the floor. Shrill cries ring out from the newborn babies.

Multiple doors inside the room slide open. Nurses in pale green dresses and facemasks file into the room and take their positions beside the babies.

The nurses move with practiced precision. They suction the babies' noses and mouths to clear their airways, remove and discard the umbilical cords with a few quick slices, and swaddle the babies in black blankets. Each infant's left arm is kept out.

With their tasks complete, the nurses disappear back through the doors.

"Looks like I'm up!" Mint says.

We follow Mint into the nursery. While most of the babies scream, some sleep peacefully. Regardless of the automated nature of their birth, they already have unique personalities.

Mint pulls over a cart that contains a small refrigeration unit, a bright silver gun device, and a box of pre-filled Opiex RXPens.

"There's another fridge over there with some docks and an extra gun. We don't have any Styrolex down here, but these work just the same. Help yourself."

"I don't need Styrolex," Aleks says.

"That's big of you, m'lady. Most Nobles would throw a fit if they had to put Austenite in their body."

"How'd you know I'm a Noble?" Aleks asks.

"Honey, it's obvious to anyone in the birth pools that your coloration is custom. No Noble would select a pricy HeritageLine for their order, the licensing fees would be outrageous."

We follow Zola past a row of new babies. I can't help but feel sympathy for these little creatures. They've just entered the world and their cries are already being ignored.

A single blood-curdling scream rises above all the others. I turn to see what happened, but it's already silenced. I watch Mint wheel her cart to another baby. She removes an RXDock from the refrigeration unit on her cart, loads it into her silver gun, presses the gun to the baby's left wrist, and fires.

The baby reacts with a horrific scream of his own. Mint docks a pen into the new dock, which stifles the scream. She continues down the line.

Zola opens the fridge Mint mentioned, removes a basic dock, and loads it into a gun.

"This will hurt, but just for a second," Zola says.

She presses the gun to Aleks' wrist and fires.

"Youch! You weren't kidding. That really stings!"

"Remember that the next time you want to test a Noble Guard," Zola says. "You're lucky they only broke your dock."

"I will. Thank you, Zola."

"You're welcome. This should hold you over until you can get a new Styrolex dock in the Highland. They can probably put your old one back together, if you still have the pieces."

"I do, but this is fine. Here, buy some new equipment for the Breaker Ward or something."

Zola raises an eyebrow to the shards of Styrolex Aleks offers.

"I'll take these, but only because you two kept me from my work. I'll need to make it up to my patients."

The timer connected to Master Telladyne's RejuviPod gives me a 60-minute warning.

"Thanks, Zola," I say. "We really appreciate it. I need to get back to Telladyne Manor."

"A Noble Valet's work is never done! I'm so proud of you Bear. We all are."

We both hug Zola and return to the Highland.

6

Aleks and I stand on her pod chamber balcony with just a sliver of air between us. My arms are wrapped around her. She looks up at me with large eyes that sparkle in the moonlight.

"You've always pulled away whenever we were about to kiss," Aleks says. "What changed?"

How do I even answer that question? Tonight, I nearly died and my thoughts immediately turned to how much I would miss Aleks. Just a few hours later, I saw Aleks bleed at the hands of the Noble Guard and never felt such rage. Aleks has my heart entirely. It would be insane to deny that for a second longer.

"Aleks, I never wanted to pull away, but fear compelled me. Fear that we'd be torn apart. Fear that you'd suffer social banishment for being with a lowlander. Fear that us being from two different worlds would be an impossible obstacle to overcome. But tonight, I realized I can't live without you. I can't keep fighting how I feel. I want you, whatever that means."

"You're so good at masking your emotions. There were so many times I was convinced you loved me and others where I was certain you thought of me only as a friend. It drove me crazy! But now we're here, we're finally here, together and honest.

Now that I know we want the same things, I know we can make this... us work."

We kiss once again before Aleks walks inside. I travel back across the maintenance lines in a haze of elation and adrenaline. I know that Aleks and I will figure out a way to have a real relationship despite our positions. We just need time.

Back at Telladyne Manor, I stack the reels inside my armoire.

3 beeps. It's Holt.

"Noble Valet Bear, I trust that you are available. Please allow me entry. We must talk."

Holt never visits. What could he possibly want? Did he see Aleks and me kiss?

Another 3 beeps.

"Noble Valet Bear, please let me inside at once."

"Of course, Noble Valet Holt. I shall be there right away."

I meet Holt at the maintenance room's main entrance. I've seen him at numerous Highland events since I left his apprenticeship but haven't spoken to him in such close quarters in years. He looks exactly like he did the day we met.

Holt is tall and slender with combed back grey hair and a thin mustache that curls at the ends. His look is dated, but Holt started as a Noble Valet in another era.

"Noble Valet Bear, I attempted to NeuroChat ahead but received no answer. You must have been busy."

"Yes, extremely. The Telladynes can be quite demanding."

"Nobles are never demanding, Noble Valet Bear. They are simply burdened with the responsibility of maintaining our society. We can hardly fault them for that."

"You are right, of course. How may I be of service, Noble Valet Holt?"

"I understand that Master Telladyne is nearly finished with his RejuviPod treatment, so I shall be brief."

"How do you know—"

"Never mind that. I am here because I witnessed your chase earlier this evening."

If Holt knew about Aleks and me, he would have led with that. For some reason he wants to discuss what happened on the highway.

"I am not proud of my performance," I say. "Unfortunately, the radicals managed to detonate a road mine that crippled our vehicle early on, which complicated matters."

"The ever-increasing desperation of these radicals has escalated their aggression. In my day, they simply built crude roadblocks or lobbed a few grenades and fled. So much has changed in such a short amount of time."

"Then we will change with them! Faster vehicles, better security measures, less unnecessary trips to the lowland."

"Yes, my boy, those suggestions are all well and good, but there comes a time when we must take up arms to defend our Masters and ourselves. This brings me to the purpose of my visit. I have brought you something."

Holt moves a finely crafted, dark wood box from his side and presents it to me.

"What's this?"

He opens the box to reveal a pair of antique pistols. A quick NeuroNet scan identifies them as 8-inch long, 18th century, flint-lock dueling pistols. The handles are made of ivory, and have doves in-flight engraved into them.

"These were gifted to me by Master Yukita on the anniversary of my 25th year of service. They once belonged to the Marquis de Lafayette. Of course, they have since been modified with fully automatic firing capabilities, a magazine compartment that holds 55 rounds of ammunition, and advanced accuracy modifications."

"Holt, I—"

"The radicals will never stop!" Holt interrupts. "Their irrational hatred of the Highland knows no limits! They will throw people, and bullets, and fire at us infinitum. It is a sad symptom of the times in which we live. The Yukita family has assured their safety by investing in the most modern weaponry available. I no longer have use for these. Please, accept this gift in good faith."

"I appreciate your concern, but you know how I feel about guns. I cannot take these."

"Nonsense! If you had these weapons today you could have easily dispatched those radicals! You're young now and think you're invincible, but you can't stop bullets. One shot to the head or the heart, and you're done! Do you understand? Dead. There's no coming back from that!"

"You've seen the destruction and bloodshed left by trigger-happy Noble Guards!" I shout back. "I refuse to share a single quality with those brainless monsters!"

Holt straightens up and recomposes himself.

"I did not come here to argue. I came to help you. Now listen very carefully. You need to take every advantage that you can. The radicals are not going to play fair. Given the chance, they will slice your throat without a second thought. If something happened to you I couldn't... I would have failed you. And for that matter, failed the Noble Valet Council, the Telladyne family, the Yukita family, and Young Lady Aleksaria. Please, Bear. Please, accept this gift."

I've never seen Holt so sincere about anything. He cares for me as much as anyone in The City, in some ways more. Holt taught me how to survive in this world of privilege and ceremony. I owe him my life, many times over.

I close the beautiful wood box and take it.

"Thank you, Noble Valet Holt."

"Of course, Noble Valet Bear. May they serve you well."

3 beeps. It's a visual message from the Idol Selection Committee. I accept the message. The Idol Selection Committee's insignia overtakes my view, five hands raised in a conical shape toward a glowing ball of light.

"Attention: Please stand by for an important message from the Idol Selection Committee in 5, 4, 3..."

Holt and I receive the message, along with everyone else in The City. The countdown ends and Dahlia Delachort appears.

She wears a heavy dress covered in prisms that shimmer in shades of purple, blue, green, and white. Delachort's voluminous blonde hair falls over her broad shoulder pads. Her makeup is severe, as always, with sparkling metallic eye shadow, sharp contour lines, and lipstick that makes her lips appear three times larger than their actual size.

It's hard to imagine that all the sparkles and paint are an applied persona. Beneath Delachort's elaborate façade stands a tall, slender Noble man with an impossibly small waist named Dylion.

"Good evening, Dahlings!" Delachort says in her familiar drawl. *"It's me, Dahlia Delachort here to tease with your new Idol Nominees!"*

Whenever Dahlia Delachort's face appears, I can't look away. She's drama personified, and impossibly engaging. It's no wonder why she hosts practically every Highland event and news story in The City.

"I am beyond ecstatic to announce that the nominees for this cycle's Idol have been selected! These nominees were chosen for their staggering intelligence, striking beauty, exceptional fitness, intrinsic kindness, and natural charisma.

"Of course, we were all saddened by the loss of our previous Idol, Voxonica Aslanian, but we are confident that your selection this cycle will bring us ever closer to the ideal we all strive for. To become the Idol is to embody the potential of our society. Now, without further adieu, I present your Idol nominees!"

That was even faster than usual. I didn't expect the nominees to be announced for another day, at least. Master Telladyne is still in his RejuviPod. He'll be furious that he missed the live announcement, but there's no way I could revive him in time.

The shot pulls back. Delachort motions to her right, and a full body hologram of the first nominee appears.

"Vitinia Flynn!"

I only know two things about Vitinia Flynn. Her family controls the ElectroField system that powers the entire city, and she's the most celebrated singer alive. That combination of resources and talent could make her the one to watch.

"Prianka Patel!"

Oh great, Kallista's going to love that. Kallista and Prianka are best friends. She'll act excited to Prianka's face, but Kallista's jealousy will consume her. I can only imagine the scathing rumor campaign that will unravel Prianka's campaign.

"Kallista Telladyne!"

Or even worse, they're both nominated. They'll act civil in each other's company, but it's only a matter of time until the war begins.

"Marena Vexhall!"

Everyone knows Marena Vexhall. She's been nominated for the Idol two cycles in a row; now three.

"And last but not least, Aleksaria Yukita!"

Wait, what?

"Congratulations to all of our nominees! Tune in for the Idol Nominee Ceremony in one week for an evening of spectacular entertainment and the chance to get to know this cycle's nominees better. Remember, your selection of the Idol puts the evolution of our entire species squarely in your hands. Congratulations again to all of the nominees and best of luck in your decision, dahlings!"

The transmission ends. I stand stunned and speechless. How is this possible? Kallista speaks gossip fluently, is obsessed with her appearance, and has 100 times more NeuroFeed followers than Aleks. With so many eligible Noble girls, how could they choose her?

"My boy, it appears we have cause for celebration!" Holt exclaims. "I must go! There are so many preparations to make! Good evening, Noble Valet Bear and congratulations to you! Congratulations to us both!"

Holt disappears. Eventually, my feet carry me to my armoire, where I set down the box Holt gave me. Now that Aleks is an Idol Nominee, I won't be allowed within 100 feet of her. And if she wins… no, I can't think like that.

3 beeps. Kallista.

"Valet! Meet us in my textiles archive! I know the perfect outfit for my first appearance as an Idol Nominee! It has midnight blue feathers and ties all up

the back... whatever, you'll see the sketches when you get here. And bring a few bottles of ice vodka, you know the one I like. What, Jiffers? Oh, OK. And bring gin for Jiffers; he only drinks gin. Actually, just bring the whole bar cart, but don't forget the ice vodka. You have 9 minutes."

PART II

7

"Valet, bring me beluga caviar with water crackers and a glass of champagne. You have 4 minutes."

"Yes, sir, Young Master Kassian."

"Valet, we are practically the same age, 'Master Kassian' will suffice. Make that 3 minutes."

"Yes, sir."

After I retrieve his order, I meet Kassian on the wide shared balcony of the Telladyne's luxury box at Vanderbilt Coliseum. The balcony connects every box to make networking easier, not that Kassian cares about that.

He stands by himself, as is usual when Kallista isn't around. She's the social butterfly. Without Kallista, Kassian isn't much fun to be near. He's been in an even fowler mood than usual since the Idol Nomination announcement. For possibly the first time ever, I can empathize with Kassian.

Aleks hasn't responded to any of my NeuroChat or Text requests for the past week. She's been busy with all the same Idol Nomination pre-performance arrangements as Kallista.

It's strange not to hear Aleks' voice or know how she's feeling. Right before our first kiss, she told me she never wanted to be the Idol. This all must be so overwhelming for her.

"Your requested items, sir."

Kassian's hand trembles as he brings the champagne flute to his lips. He dabs his forehead with his pocket square.

Kassian's movements are typically so sure. I check his vitals. His resting heart rate is up 12%. This, along with the shaking and perspiration are all symptoms of acute anxiety.

"Sir, you seem agitated. May I offer you a pen of Clopenezal?"

"No, I'm just hungry."

Kassian dollops a bit of caviar onto a cracker.

I can't move unless Kassian releases me or another family member request pulls me away. Despite my advanced training in a variety of skills from etiquette to combat, Kassian has decided to utilize me as a side table.

I look out to the seven tall silos within the Coliseum. They're the same silos I'll climb tonight during the mandatory Idol Nominee tribute match. Vibrant montages of previous Idol Nomination Ceremonies play across each silo.

"What do you suppose they're doing right now?" Kassian asks.

"The Idol Nominees, sir? Unfortunately, I have no idea."

"I wish this damn event would start already. The screams of all these lowlanders hurt my ears, and the lights are so bright."

"Sir, your Neurogem can dull external sounds, and I would be happy to provide you with an Iris-darkening agent to limit your light sensitivity."

"I am perfectly aware of my options, Valet. If I require such items I will let you know. In the meantime, please keep your mouth shut."

As if to answer Kassian's request, the music fades, and the lights dim to black. Random flashes provide enough light to see the silos lower, while a huge platform rises. The silo tops and stage meet to create a massive elevated stage.

The ceremony is starting. Part of me is excited, the same part of me that's watched these ceremonies since I was a kid. But this one feels so different from the others. No one I ever cared about has been a nominee.

My first instinct has always been to cheer for Aleks, to support her in every performance from my place in the audience. But tonight I want her to fail. I want her to fail so hard that the lowland forgets she ever existed.

Warm orange light illuminates a level of drummers that wraps around the Coliseum below the luxury boxes. The drummers strike huge drums in perfect synchronization. Nobles pour out to the balcony.

Dahlia Delachort rises from the middle of the stage. She wears a voluminous orange Victorian-style dress with an impossibly cinched waist, tortured cleavage, and enormous panniers. Delachort's blond hair is pulled up into a cartoonishly large bouffant.

The drums come to an abrupt stop.

"Thousands were considered, but in the end, just five were selected," Delachort proclaims. "For generations, we have looked to the Idol for guidance. She is our mirror, our voice, and our emissary to the future. Through her, we not only see who we are, but who we can become. Tonight, we take one more step toward perfection! Ladies and gentlemen, welcome to the 47th Idol Nomination Ceremony!"

Gold fireworks explode from the Coliseum roofline while cheers rise from the general admission seats below. The balcony Nobles join in with demure applause.

"I'm finished," Kassian says. "Take this away."

"Yes, sir."

Kassian's dismissal unleashes a flood of guest requests into my task queue. I'm so busy gathering and delivering items for guests that I can't see what's happening onstage.

A massive ball of light forms in the sky that shatters into five pieces. One of the pieces takes an unnatural flight path back toward the Coliseum.

As the stray shard gets closer, I see it's a giant mechanical bird. The bird's gleaming metallic purple feathers and long tail pull back as it dive-bombs.

A Peahawk. They're absolutely stunning birds with the fierce temperament of a predator. I've only seen them on the Patel grounds, this must be part of Prianka's performance.

"Valet, drink!" A Noble man shouts, and I hand him his beer stein.

Several concussive blasts ring out. The Noble startles as he grabs for the stein and drops it. Rather than blame me, he looks straight ahead. I follow his gaze.

Columns of mist-high purple flame burn all over the Coliseum. Loud Peahawk caws ring out. I'd love to tune into a NeuroCast of the proceedings, but all four of my splits are in use to orchestrate service, and I don't have time to spectate at the rail.

After Prianka's performance ends, the air grows hot and arid. Requests for refreshing cocktails, like Mojitos, come through.

Bone-rattling roars mix with the sound of machines being brutally torn asunder. Red fireworks, sparks, and smoke fill the air. While I hold out a box of VaporLite Classics to a party of Nobles, we're enveloped by thick, bright red fog.

I can't see anything an inch from my face.

There it goes. The fog lifts, as if sucked up by a giant vacuum in the sky.

Velvet vocal notes weave through the air like a silk tapestry. Vitinia Flynn's performance has begun. Her curio-jazz arrangement is a far departure from Prianka's bouncy, sitar-heavy track, but it's just as compelling.

3 Beeps. It's Mariposa Monarch, Kallista's Idol Nomination handler.

I've never actually seen her in person, but Mariposa's pompous, nasal voice is familiar to me now.

"Valet, Idol Nominee Telladyne's performance will follow Idol Nominee Flynn's. Please distribute the appropriate noise makers and supplements in preparation."

"Yes, Lady Mariposa."

Crtr and I pass out slender, champagne gold horns and predosed pens of Hilodopa to everyone outside the Telladyne box.

Sweat beads on my forehead. The air flipped from bone dry to humid. Leafy tendrils crawl over the Coliseum walls and balcony banister. Several mighty trees grow into existence that form a leafy canopy overhead.

A simple, ominous drum beat starts. Something's coming; something big.

"How's this possible?" Crtr asks.

"What?"

"All of it! The giant mechanized animals, the trees that grow before our eyes... It's like magic."

"It's not magic, Crtr. It's science, used for theatre. Don't worry about how it's all done. Just enjoy the show."

Long vines drop through the forest canopy. I practically jump out of my shoes when an enormous mechanical beast leaps over the Telladyne luxury box to catch one of the vines.

Leaves and branches fall as the hulking beast swings from vine to vine. Its mighty exhales send warm fronts through the Coliseum. Long, champagne gold strands cover its body like jacket fringe.

The beast swings back toward the Telladyne box, and I see its face for the first time. With a full view of its furrowed brow, small black eyes, and muscular limbs, the animal's natural dominance feels thrust upon me. My Neurogem identifies it as a golden-back gorilla.

As it powers toward our box, the gorilla opens her wide mouth and lets out a hot, deafening roar. The roar pushes everyone in the box back a few steps.

I continue with my tasks as electric guitars, horns, and synthesizers join the drum beat. The Hilodopa's kicked in. Everyone around me sways and flails awkwardly, like it's the first time they've ever danced.

Someone at the rail orders a drink. I fight my way through and see the stage.

Ashen gray statues of the peahawk, golden-back gorilla, and a Bengal tiger strike dramatic poses on-stage. 12 women in golden safari outfits perform a synchronized dance with champagne gold rifles that match their gold, diamond-strung outfits.

Kallista dances provocatively at center stage with her own champagne gold rifle. Instead of a safari outfit she wears a perfectly tailored, dark blue, men's suit with no under shirt that drips with long diamond necklaces.

With vacant eyes, Kallista spits lyrics she obviously doesn't understand. She's always wanted to be The Idol but refused to ever take a single dance or singing lesson. Why bother when you can simply activate a NeuroTrainer?

More requests pull me away. Everyone on Hilodopa keeps double-ordering, changing their request, or cancelling after I've already gotten their drinks.

Thankfully, Hilodopa has a short effect. They'll be zombies during the next performance, but that's fine with Master Telladyne and Mariposa Monarch. The less interested his contingent of supporters looks, the better.

Kallista's performance ends.

Several waterfalls burst from the roofline and the canopy of trees falls into raindrops. Laser-sharp images of rolling tides and crashing waves undulate across every surface.

An enormous ivory and yellow gold orca whale leaps straight into the air.

The whale gains altitude fast. Body parts slough off the whale as it climbs. Something bright white glows inside it. Patches of synthetic flesh and pieces of graphene boning fall away, and the light's shape clarifies. It's a person, the next Idol Nominee, Marena Vexhall.

"Valet! Drink!" A Noble woman snaps.

"I apologize, ma'am."

I hand off the drink and look back. Marena, free of her whale costume, dives head-first toward the stage. She hardly seems concerned about impact. As a hologram, Marena isn't burdened by the same laws of physics as the rest of us.

A drumbeat starts that's joined by tambourines, horns, maracas, xylophones, and other instruments. Each new instrument layers seamlessly into the song and brings everyone to their feet. I catch a glimpse of the stage and see multiple copies of Marena all over the Coliseum with different instruments.

As expected, everyone outside the Telladyne box has crashed. They can hardly muster a foot tap. Regardless, their lethargic requests continue throughout Marena's performance.

"Your VaporLite, sir," I say, and my breath hangs in the air.

A chill passes through me. Are those snowflakes? I look up and confirm a light dusting of snow coming from the mist.

This must be Aleks' performance. I'd love to see it, but unless someone at the rail orders something, I'll miss every note.

A flurry of requests for scarves and heavy coats enter my queue. I move to retrieve the coats and hear a loud howl echo through the Coliseum.

My attention snaps to the howl's source; an enormous, silver, mechanical wolf on the roofline. The wolf lets out more howls toward the mist, as if to invoke an invisible full moon. That's Aleks. She's the last nominee to perform. At least I got to see her once.

Smack!

A fist connects hard with the side of my face. I stumble back into a high table. Glasses shatter all around me. I look up to find Davis Vexhall stomping toward me.

"I tested the rest of my capsules, Valet!" He says. "They were clean. I knew you were lying, you filthy LEF."

Master Telladyne approaches with a confident, unhurried swagger.

"Young Master Davis, so good of you to visit our box!"

"I'm not here for a social visit, Telladyne. I'm here to put your Valet in his place."

"My dear Davis," Master Telladyne says with a chuckle. "What could my simple Valet possibly have done to warrant such theatrics?

Come, I recently acquired a box of Cohiba Habana VaporLites. Let's have a smoke while you tell me all about your new yacht."

Master Telladyne drapes his long arm over Vexhall's shoulders and leads him away.

"Valet," Master Telladyne calls back to me. "Clean up this mess."

He flashes me a slight smile. I can't imagine why Master Telladyne would extend such an appreciative gesture.

I rise to my feet and see a swarm of camera drones around me. The whole torrid scene where Davis Vexhall attacked an innocent Valet was caught on dozens of NeuroCast channels. No wonder Master Telladyne was pleased. Vexhall's outburst will reflect poorly on his Idol Nominee sister.

Vexhall actually did me a favor, too. Master Telladyne gave me a specific task, which means I can ignore the general task queue for now and use a free split to watch the rest of Aleks' performance.

I access a NeuroCast that shows the Coliseum awash in light blue. The camera looks down on Aleks from above. She lies on the wolf's back, wrapped in a long wolf-pelt robe. Aleks moves her arms with fluid elegance to soft flute notes and string instrument melodies.

Even with the blue light, I can tell her previously white-blonde hair has been dyed into shades of icy blue. She wears a long side braid, identical to the one I gave her in the Monarch archives.

Aleks dismounts the wolf with a spin and leaps across the stage. At the crest of each leap, she seems frozen in mid-air for a moment until she floats back to the ground.

Years as a member of the Highland Dance Company have molded Aleks into a truly exquisite dancer. She moves with such perfect synchronization to the music that she appears to control it.

It's a beautiful display of grace and control, but I can tell the lowland crowd is bored. Even the Nobles seem unappreciative of the technically masterful performance. No one here cares about subtle nuance. They're here to be beaten over the head by over-the-top spectacle.

The music fades into barely audible notes. Aleks flutters her wrists into her chest and lowers her head. A few confused claps ring out. No one knows how to react. The Coliseum feels uncomfortably still. Was this Aleks' plan, to bore everyone and lose their interest?

I can hardly mask my smile while I sweep. She did it. Aleks found a way to take herself out of the running. The hope that Aleks and I could actually be together was shredded a week ago, but now it's returned even stronger than before.

A single powerful reverb note barrels through the silence. And another. And more until they form a steady rhythm. Horns, keyboards, and a symphony of other instruments join in. Powerful vibrations penetrate the Coliseum walls and travel through my body. I drop my broom, and run to the ice-cold banister.

The music crescendos with a glass-shattering bass drop. All the snow onstage explodes upward and swirls around the Coliseum. A team of dancers bursts up from trapdoors around Aleks. They're all members of the Highland Dance Company in wolf pelt capes and hoods.

Aleks spins and whips off her long wolf pelt robe to reveal a fitted wolf pelt crop top, skin-tight silver micro-shorts, and silver ankle boots. As her long robe flies through the air, the entire company breaks into aggressive choreography that brings everyone to their feet.

The audience dances like it's the end of the world; like this is the last time anyone's going to see dancing, and it has to mean something. The beginning was just a vamp, a fake-out. Aleks wasn't throwing the performance, she was lowering our guard so she could hit us with a surprise left hook.

What is she doing? The crowd's loving every second of this. It's probably the best performance she's ever done! Does she actually want to be the Idol now?

With the last note and last step, Aleks plants her feet in front of a nearby camera drone. She stares down every NeuroCast viewer with confidence that makes me feel unworthy of her attention.

Aleks breaks the intensity with a relieved, exhausted smile. My chest relaxes. I didn't even realize it was clenched. She and the dancers wave as they lower into the stage to the sound of thunderous applause.

A few boxes down, Nobles shake Takeshi Yukita's hand, pat his back, and whisper things to him that elicit deep, satisfied laughs. Their celebration sickens me.

I move through the luxury box to a maintenance room, and drop the bag of broken glass shards down an incinerator chute. The bag falls out of sight with a satisfying crunch as it reaches the first level of disposal blades.

3 Beeps. Mariposa.

"Valet, drop what you're doing and meet Idol Nominee Telladyne and me at your assigned locker room. It's time to suit up for tonight's siloball match."

8

I hang up my Noble Valet uniform in the room's sole locker and step into a brand new, dark blue siloball suit. As the weightless, water-resistant fabric slides over my body, a rush of anxious energy surges through me. I'm unsure if it's excitement to play again or fear I refuse to accept.

I slip on magnetic gloves, climbing boots, and a grappler to each arm. The gloves and boots are new too, but the grapplers are the same I've used for years. New ones are lighter and faster, but these grapplers have taken me all over the Highland; they're reliable and familiar.

On my way out into the hall, I catch sight of myself in the mirror. The siloball suit is covered in diamond-shaped champagne gold stitching. For a second, I almost forgot the Telladyne's practically own me.

"What took you so long?" Kallista asks.

She wears a perfectly tailored, golden-back gorilla fur coat.

"I apologize for the delay."

"We have sixteen minutes until the match begins," Mariposa says. "Come with me."

Mariposa's severe look matches the tone I've come to know. She's tall and strong-looking in a flowy orange blouse and white palazzo pants. Her slicked-back hair explodes into a meticulously messy ponytail.

We follow Mariposa to a green room that's nestled in the Coliseum stands behind a massive one-way window. All of the Idol Nominees, their handlers, and the players who will compete in their honor are here except Aleks and her camp.

"Valet, get me a Svenson ice vodka martini."

"Idol Nominee Telladyne," Mariposa interjects. "I recommend a glass of champagne rather than a martini."

"But I always drink Svenson ice vodka."

"That may be true, but as an Idol Nominee your promotion is a valuable commodity. Until we secure a sponsorship contract with Svenson ice vodka, you should stick to ubiquitous beverage choices. Valet, fetch a glass of champagne for Idol Nominee Telladyne."

"Put the bottle on ice, too, to keep the label covered," Kallista adds.

"Very good, Idol Nominee. You are a natural. But please, exercise moderation. You still must escort your player to the siloball pool."

"Hey hey, hello!" A familiar voice rings out.

Prianka Patel waves to Kallista from across the room. Both girls raise their arms high and run toward each other with quick baby steps. I go to the bar for Kallista's champagne.

Crtr stands behind the bar. He must have been assigned to tend bar in the green room. I order the champagne.

"Who's that Valet over there?" Crtr asks. "He's been glaring at you ever since you walked in."

I turn to see Pinz Baylor. He's hardly changed since the last time we met four years ago. His empty, black eyes match the greasy black hair that he combs back with a tight side part. Pinz flashes me a broad smile that reveals two missing front teeth.

"He isn't a Valet," I reply. "That's just a costume. Pinz Baylor is a mercenary. Nobles hire him to compete in dangerous competitions, like the siloball match tonight, on their behalf. He's actually Noble-born, from a family that manufacturers medical devices but chose not to join the family business."

"Why not?"

"He'd rather inflict pain than ease it."

"Can you beat him?"

"I have before, but that was years ago. I'm the one who knocked out his front teeth."

"Well, good luck. Please excuse me."

Crtr moves to serve someone else at the bar. I pop the champagne bottle cork and pour Kallista's glass.

"Noble Valet Bear, how fortunate to run into you."

Marena Vexhall stands beside me in a white gown with pointed shoulders and a neckline that plunges to her waist. She raises a glass of water to her lips.

"Fortunate?" I ask. "How so?"

"I have some information that may help you and Idol Nominee Telladyne."

"Why would you want to help your competitor?"

"Because Kallista must become the next Idol. She's the only choice."

I don't care who wins so long as Aleks loses. If Marena can actually help Kallista win, I'm all ears, but this could be some kind of sabotage tactic. She is a Vexhall after all.

"With all due respect, Idol Nominee Vexhall, why should I trust you? This is your third attempt at becoming the Idol, and you're telling me that Young Lady Kallista should win? That doesn't make sense. I'd be a fool to think this isn't some sort of trap."

"Aleks said you were clever. You're right. You have no reason to trust me. But I can tell you this: Aleks doesn't deserve to be the Idol. None of us do; not even Kallista."

"What do you mean?"

"No time to explain. Just listen. My player, Pinz Baylor, has a weakness that you may be able to exploit in the match tonight. He recently underwent extensive left knee joint reconstruction. The new joint is so technologically complex that it requires passive Neurogem operation to function."

"I can't take control of his knee without access codes."

"I know and, unfortunately, I don't have those. But I can tell you that it's a Baylor Paradigm 750, by Baylor Medical. Perhaps you can retrieve the codes before the match begins. I have to go. Remember, it's his left knee. Baylor Paradigm 750."

Marena leaves her glass on the bar and walks away. After a few steps, the holographic glass dissolves out of existence.

I return to Kallista and NeuroText her upon my arrival.

"Regardless," Kallista says, as she takes her glass. "You're so lucky you got a peahawk. I got stuck with that oafish, smelly-looking golden-back gorilla."

"Abs! Daddy supplied all the mechs for tonight's ceremony on the condition that I got first billing and could pick my entrance animal. The Monarchs couldn't refuse."

Niko, the Patel family Noble Valet approaches. His sandy blonde locks fall over his bare, sun-toasted shoulders. As usual, he isn't wearing a shirt. Niko likes to keep his lowland-born, Highland-sculpted physique on display at all times. He dips into a low bow to present Prianka's drink.

She takes the drink and gives Niko a thorough look. I can tell by her leer that Prianka never misses an opportunity to appreciate Niko's body.

I hear an obvious throat clear behind me and turn to find Noble Valet Holt. He wears an ice blue, snowflake-covered siloball uniform.

"Noble Valet Bear," Holt says. "I apologize for the interruption, but have you seen Idol Nominee Yukita recently?"

"Not since her performance, why?"

"I'm afraid that she's gone missing."

"What do you mean, missing? For how long?"

"No one's seen her since the end of her performance. She just vanished."

"Have you told Master Yukita?"

"Not yet. Could you please NeuroChat Idol Nominee Yukita? She may be more eager to accept your request than mine."

I nod and send the request.

3 beeps.

3 more beeps.

3 more beeps still.

No answer.

The green room door slides open, and Aleks strides through. She's dressed in a pristine yellow and black siloball suit, and all the necessary equipment to play. I lose my breath at the sight of her after so long apart.

"Noble Valet Holt," Aleks says as she marches forward. "I will be competing for myself this evening. You are relieved."

"Idol Nominee Yukita, I am afraid that is impossible. I have explicit instructions from your father to play in your honor during tonight's match."

"Idol Nominee Yukita, what is the meaning of this?" I ask.

"Valet, as an Idol Nominee and the daughter of the Noble family that employs you, I order you to lay down your grapplers and return to the Yukita luxury box."

Aleks stares at Holt but sends me a NeuroText.

"I can't let Holt get slaughtered out there."

"No, it's too dangerous! Just let him compete."

"Do you really think Holt has a better chance of surviving than me? It's not as if I'm untrained. It's the only way to save Holt. We can also work together to win the match for Kallista."

"All right, fine. But promise me you won't get caught up in any battles with Pinz. Run, zip away, jump into the water if you have to. Just stay away from him!"

"Not that I need your permission, but OK, I promise. Now we have to convince Holt to stand down."

"I have an idea."

"Holt, listen," I say. "Idol Nominee Yukita is right. You should not compete tonight."

"That is not for you to say. Do you forget that I am the one who trained you?"

"I know you trained me, and you did an excellent job, but siloball has changed since you were last in the pool. There's no such thing as sportsmanship anymore. It's become pure blood sport. You saw what Pinz did to me after our match. They're all like that now because that's the mentality you need to win."

"I still have some tricks up my sleeve, Noble Valet Bear. You would be wise to respect experience over age."

"And you would be wise to know your limitations. There's no way you can keep up with the other players. Holt, if you play tonight you will *die*."

"Siloball is about more than mere speed."

"You're too old and slow, Holt! I know it's hard to hear, but please listen to what I'm saying."

"I understand that the prospect of competing against your former Mentor Valet is intimidating, but if you keep your wits about you, you may have a chance at besting me yet!"

"Holt, I'm not afraid of you, I'm afraid *for* you! You've left me no choice."

I call Crtr over with a NeuroText and he appears at my side.

"Crtr, give me two pens of Diazapax."

"Noble Valet Bear, what are you doing?" Holt asks.

Crtr hands me the pens.

"Here," I hold out one of the pens to Holt. "Take this. On the count of three I'm going to drive my pen into your dock."

"You're going to what?"

"If you're fast enough to stop me, then you're fast enough to play."

"This is preposterous, I'm not going to—"

"1, 2, 3!"

I lunge at Holt and twist his arm into a painful hold that forces him to drop his pen. I catch Holt's pen, spin around, and dock it into his wrist.

Holt's eyes flutter. His body goes limp, and I lay him on the ground.

Slow, loud claps from across the room catch my attention. Pinz stares straight at me. I just gave away my one tactical advantage.

Going into tonight's match, no one had seen me play in years, which means my combat skills were a wild card. But thanks to Holt, Pinz just got a sneak peek.

"Idol Nominee Yukita, where have you been?" Someone shouts.

A tall man with broad shoulders and a narrow waist approaches. As he walks, his long straight silver hair shimmers with orange undertones. The black suit he wears looks constructed from a single sheet of folded and creased fabric. He smells of fresh-ground coffee.

"I've been looking everywhere for you! And what are you wearing? And why is your player on the floor?"

This must be Aleks' handler. I slip both Diazapax pens into my sleeve.

"Change of plans, Balliat," Aleks says. "I'm playing in Holt's stead."

"Idol Yukita, this is unaccept—"

The green room lights dim, and a holographic projection of Dahlia Delachort appears at the center of the room.

"Good evening, dahlings, and thank you for volunteering for tonight's Idol Nominee tribute match! You've probably seen Siloball played on NeuroCast, in-person, or even played in an actual match before, but in case you're unfamiliar, here's a quick refresher on the rules."

A three-dimensional schematic of the siloball pool appears in front of Delachort. The game's seven silos rise from the pool. I've always imaged their configuration as the five-side of a dice, with extra pips to the right and left.

"The action of Siloball takes place across silos like these. The center silo is exactly where you'd expect it to be, in the center of the pool. This is where you will start the match. When the match begins, select a cable, and use your grapplers to zip to any of the four corner silos.

"When you reach one of the four corner silos, climb to whichever cable you like and zip to your corner silo's corresponding outer silo. The outer silos are located furthest from the center silo at opposite ends of the siloball pool. One glows bright orange while the other glows bright blue. You can't miss 'em.'

"There is a small tube at the top of each outer silo. If you're the lucky first player to reach an outer silo, you'll find a bright yellow siloball atop the tube. Take possession of the siloball, and book it back to the center silo. But be careful! Your opponents will do anything to steal your siloball!

"When you return to the center silo, you'll find a point tube at the center of the platform. If you managed to stave off your opponents, or capture a siloball from one of them, deposit, or 'cash' your siloball into the point tube. It's that simple!

"Now keep in mind that while you were headed to your chosen outer silo, some of your opponents pursued the opposite outer silo. If you meet an opponent at the point tube who also has possession of a siloball, get ready for a fight!

"The first player to cash their siloball during each round earns 10 points. The second player gets 5 points. Once both balls are cashed or taken out of play by hitting the water below, two more siloballs will appear at the outer silos, and a new round of play will begin.

"But don't go thinking you can just wait around on an outer silo for a new ball to appear. Any player on an outer silo or the center silo platform without possession of a siloball will be power-washed into the pool after ten seconds. The only exception to this is if a player with possession is on the platform with you. Any player who hits the siloball pool is disqualified, so try not to get swept away.

"Now let's talk about your... equipment. Unless you wandered into this match from the wilderness, you'll recognize those metal things on your arms as 'grapplers.' Your grapplers will let you zip across cables and climb up and down silo rungs while keeping your hands free. With enough skill, you can use your grapplers to pluck a siloball right from an opponent's hand or defend against oncoming threats.

"Grapplers make for powerful weapons by themselves, but if you ever need an extra power boost, you can knock your grappler blades together. This will illuminate and electrify your grapplers with ElectroField energy. This extra charge can equalize even the most one-sided grappler battles.

"Now pay attention. This part's important! Never let your grapplers remain electrified if you fall off a silo! If you think a swim's in your future, knock your grapplers together to power them down. Hitting the water with electrified grapplers will fatally electrocute you. In other words, you'll be dead, dahling.

"Finally, there are no rules of conduct in siloball, so play well and stay vigilant. The first player to reach 50 points wins. Good luck!"

The projection of Delachort disappears, and the green room's massive glass wall slides open. Screams, cheers, and chants fill the room. I split to hear the Siloball announcers, Chip and Bulloxy. They're good for information about unseen surprises or dangers.

"Ladies and gentleman, the glass has risen! It's going to be an all-out slugfest in the pool tonight, and I for one can't wait to get started!"

Neckties and nipples, me neither, Bully! This is the Idol Nominees' last chance to make an impression before the 12-hour LifeCast event!"

After tonight's ceremony, every nominee will host their own LifeCast for 12 hours to prove that they're the most compelling choice. Aleks must be dreading it. But 12 hours is nothing compared to a lifetime of constant scrutiny.

The gigantic window that overlooks the Coliseum rises to let in the deafening roar of the crowd. Deep purple paints the silos in the pool, which have risen once more from the stage. Poppy sitar music from Prianka's performance plays.

Prianka's handler gestures toward the silos. Niko ties his long hair into a ponytail, and he and Prianka step out onto the ramp. All the silos erupt with purple flames while Niko flexes his muscles.

"Wickets and waistbands, what an entrance! Bulloxy, did you turn the heat up in here or is it just Idol Nominee Patel's player, Niko?"

"I didn't change the thermostat, Chip, but when Niko hits the cables it's going to get hot in the pool for his competitors. Don't let the ponytail and baby face fool you, at 6' 7" tall, and 284 pounds with just 3% body fat, Niko is a serious threat."

Vitinia Flynn and her player step onto the ramp next. Their body types couldn't be more different. Vitinia stands elegantly in an emerald bodycon dress that hugs her curves, while her player is short, muscular, and poised for battle. The only thing they have in common is their bright orange hair.

Green lights fade up while Vitinia's player knocks her grapplers together so they glow neon green. She launches into an elaborate acrobatic routine that demonstrates her speed and skill.

"Jumping and jacks, Noble Valet Jita has made her debut! Tiny, but deadly!"

"She's only 5' 5" tall and a 120 pounds, but she can easily break the bones of men five times her size. Noble Valet Jita once fought off six radicals with her bare hands when they infiltrated a Flynn factory. Those fighting skills will certainly come in handy tonight."

"I can't wait to see her in action! The suspense is killing me!"

I present my arm to Kallista and we approach the ramp. On my way, I send a NeuroText to Crtr.

"Crtr, how much do you know about Siloball?"

"I've seen every Siloball match ever NeuroCast, it'd be easier to tell you what I don't know."

"Perfect. Get back to the luxury box and find a good vantage point at the rail. We need eyes above the pool during the match."

As my foot hits the ramp, a remixed version of Kallista's performance song plays. Champagne gold leaves fall over the Coliseum.

"Tonight," I shout, and hear my voice carry through the Coliseum. "I compete in honor of Idol Nominee Kallista Telladyne!"

"Windmills and wingdings, would you look at that! Noble Valet Bear back in the siloball pool and ready for action! Our viewers may be surprised to know that Bear has only played in one other siloball match ever!"

"And what a match it was, Chip! Until now only a select few Nobles had access to that match's NeuroCast, but for a limited time you can watch it for just 150 points! That match ended Bear's siloball career before it began, and tonight he'll face the man who ended it, Pinz Baylor."

Shivers run through my spine as we approach the center silo. There's no turning back now. To win, I'll have to find strength in my emotions. I just hope Aleks isn't too close when I finally unleash the vicious cocktail of fury, fear, and rage within me.

"Crutches and candlesticks, who could forget that ruthless assault? Bear's one tough lowlander, that's for sure. If Pinz did that to me, I'd never look at another siloball pool again!"

"Chip, if Pinz Baylor breathed in your direction, you wouldn't look at anything ever again. At 6' 5", and 250 pounds, Bear's gained some weight since his last match, while Pinz has gained muscle and experience. These two have history, and they're the ones to watch tonight."

I feel propelled forward by the incredible roar of the crowd. A refreshing, cool breeze of ionized air flows through the mesh of my siloball suit. I look out at the network of black cables that awaits my grapplers. They're so thin, frictionless, and fast.

All the things I love about siloball flood my mind with crystal clarity. For a moment I feel 15-years-old again, at the start of my first-ever siloball match. Unfortunately, my fond recollection is overtaken by the memory of what Pinz did to me at the end of that match.

Tied at 40-40, Pinz and I grappler battled at the top of the center silo. His size and my speed locked us in an aggressive stalemate of slashes, kicks, and dodges. We'd already dispatched the other three players and were down to 1-on-1 siloball rules with only one ball in play.

With possession of the ball, and only enough strength for one last power move, I blind-elbowed Pinz in the face. Blood sprang from his mouth. The momentary distraction let me spin around Pinz and cash the ball to win.

I collapsed to the ground in exhaustion. The clear blue Highland sky never looked more beautiful. I had just won my first siloball match. Even better, it was an exhibition match for Master Yukita's birthday, and Aleks saw every step of my victory.

But Pinz didn't zip away to lick his wounds. He never left the platform.

Pinz appeared above me with a gruesome, bloody smile of newly missing teeth. He lifted my body into the air, broke my back across his knee, and threw me off the silo.

Fortunately, my extended grappler caught a silo rung on the way down. I only know what happened because I demanded Aleks show me a visual slice of it. In the slice, my body hung limp from the side of the silo, a sweat-drenched sack of bones.

I spent the next several weeks in a recovery pod while my spinal tissue and bone regenerated. Aleks visited me whenever she could. She told me about her day at school, read me books from the Yukita library, and rarely left my side. Over time, my hatred for Pinz dissolved and was replaced by my love for Aleks.

Kallista and I find our marks on the Center Silo, P for Player and a gold star for the Idol Nominee. Neither Niko nor Jita look at me. They stand at attention like soldiers prepared for battle.

Kallista motions for me to lean down so she can tell me something.

"Win tonight or I'll make sure daddy kicks you back down to the lowland."

"Of course, Idol Nominee Telladyne. I shall try my best."

"You'll have to do better than that," she says, and kisses me on the cheek.

Eerie synthesized music fills the air. At the top of the ramp, Pinz's silhouette appears against bright white light.

"Tonight!" Pinz shouts. "I will win this match in honor of Idol Nominee, Marena Vexhall!"

Pinz raises his arms and drops them back down to trigger a torrent of water that fires up from the pool. As the water rains down, he and Marena descend the ramp.

"Swells and seagulls, we're all soaked!"

"If there's one man who can personify the power of a high seas storm and the rage of a tsunami, it's Pinz Baylor. At 7' 2" and 345 pounds, there's a reason they call him The Bone Crusher!"

I can feel Pinz stare at me as he approaches the center silo. Despite his intensity, I know he won't do anything before the match starts. Pinz is getting paid a small fortune to win for the Vexhall family. He wouldn't risk embarrassing his benefactor for a cheap shot at me.

Pinz and Marena take their marks. They're the first ones to face the orange outer silo.

Soft blue light fills the Coliseum. A thin layer of ice crawls over the silos, ramp, and walls. Aleks appears at the top of the ramp. She stands arched in a balletic backbend.

More lights reveal the bright gold dress Aleks wears. She dances to formal music that sounds like a bridal march.

"Sirens and steeples, I don't see a player! Is the Idol Nominee Aleksaria Yukita playing in tonight's match? And what is she wearing? Is that the fallen Idol Vox's wedding dress?"

"Tonight," Aleks shouts. "I play in honor of myself!"

Aleks runs and slides down the ice-covered ramp on her knees. As she slides, the thin layers of ice all around explode into frozen dust.

"Igloos and icicles! Is this intro a reference to the fallen Idol Vox?"

"Whatever it is, she's lost some of the crowd, Chip. I see a lot of angry faces out there who find this homage downright distasteful. Whatever your opinion, there's no denying the Idol Nominee Yukita knows how to make a memorable entrance! She's almost in place. Let's go back to the center silo for the start of tonight's Idol Nomination Ceremony Siloball Match."

Aleks walks to her mark and stands tall in her yellow and black siloball suit. The V-Pro wedding dress disappeared during the ice explosion.

The center silo rises, and the Idol Nominees' marked platforms lower into the silo. Giant silver tens appear all over the Coliseum. Everyone inside shouts the numbers aloud.

10.

"Real subtle, Aleks. I can't believe you wore her dress."

9.

"I wish! Manchetti never released a V-Pro of the actual dress, so I had to find a convincing knock-off. Hopefully I offended enough people to lower my LifeCast views."

8.

"Crtr, you in position?"

7.

"Yeah, I can see the whole pool from here.

6.

"Aleks, I'll follow you to the orange outer silo. Pinz is hyper aggressive. He'll probably jump on your cable and try to take you out early.

5.

"He's heavy, so he'll gain on you fast. Just stay out of his way."

4.

"Crtr, contact my friend Pach. Tell him I need access codes for a Baylor Paradigm 750 knee joint replacement."

3.

"Why, do you need those?"

2.

"Don't worry about it, just send me the codes when you have them."

1.

"Good luck, Aleks."

"You, too, Bear."

Go!

9

"And here we go! Jita and Niko split toward the blue outer silo, while Bear goes for the orange! He's bringing the fight to Pinz early! Pinz has leapt onto the same cable as Idol Nominee Yukita!"

I grab the free orange corner silo cable. Pinz gains on Aleks as I expected. Even though he's out of striking range, he swipes the air. He'll be close enough to hit her any second.

"Aleks, drop!"

"No, I can make it!"

"You promised not to engage Pinz, drop!"

Aleks whips off her cable and falls to another one. She's further from the siloball but safe. Pinz's intimidation tactic worked; there's one less obstacle between him and the first ten points.I reach the corner silo and overtake Pinz on my climb to the next cable. Aleks would have smoked him up the silo, but I couldn't risk her getting hurt by a lucky blow.

I zip to the orange silo, reach the platform, and sprint for the siloball. As I lay my hand on the ball, a bright white streak slices toward me. I somersault backward to dodge.

Pinz follows-up with more powerful slashes that I deflect. He envelops me like the shadow of a planet and forces me to the platform edge. I can't get around him.

Suddenly, a foot comes out of nowhere that connects with Pinz's head.

Pinz slashes the air behind him, but it's too late. Aleks leaps off the platform to catch a cable away. I flee with the siloball.

"Water in 10, 9, 8... and Pinz wastes no time pursuing Bear and the siloball! That last minute assist from Idol Nominee Yukita may have kept Bear in the game! What was she thinking?"

I reach the corner silo without interference from Pinz. Aleks is already on her way back to the center silo. She'll get there well before me.

3 Beeps. Crtr.

"Aleks, you're in position to intercept Niko before he cashes his ball! That'll leave Bear open for the first ten points."

Aleks hits the platform and sprints ahead. Niko barely takes three steps before Aleks checks him hard with all her momentum. He tumbles off the platform. With no competition, I easily cash my ball.

Images of Kallista celebrating on the luxury box balcony play across the Coliseum interior. Every point I collect is another promotion opportunity for her. If I win, she'll star in a lengthy trophy ceremony with everyone in The City's eyes on her.

"That's 10 points for Idol Nominee Kallista Telladyne!"

"Theme tunes and thimbles, Valet Bear has the Idol Nominee Yukita to thank for that round! She's full of surprises!"

With my siloball cashed and no one else on the platform with a siloball, the water penalty countdown starts.

3 Beeps. Crtr.

"Niko still has possession. Drop onto the rungs and wait for him."

We do as Crtr says, which ends the water penalty countdown. Niko has to come through here for his five points, and when he does, we'll be ready for him.

"Niko's retreated to a corner silo to control the game's pace. I see Yukita, Bear, and Pinz, but where's—Jita! There she is with a surprise assault on an unsuspecting Niko!"

"Poplars and potstickers, those punches are ferocious! Niko's lost! Two head blows, three kidney jabs. Oh no she just slammed his beautiful face into a rung!"

"Niko's swinging blind! Jita's all over him! He can't— A savage uppercut! Jita... she has it! She took the ball right from Niko's glove!"

Jita zips for the center silo, but instead of going straight for the point tube, she drops onto the silo rungs. Aleks and I climb sideways to engage her.

"Gophers and golf balls, there she goes!"

Jita pops onto the platform. Aleks and I follow. Pinz appears as well. But we're all too slow. Jita cashes her ball for five points.

Two new siloballs emerge on the orange and blue outer silos.

Aleks and I take different lines toward the blue outer silo. Niko's already almost there. He camped out on a corner silo in anticipation of the next round. He'll have possession any second.

"Aleks, if we each wait on our corner silos, one of us can cut Niko off before he gets to the center!"

"No! There's a better way!" Crtr adds.

"What do you mean?"

"Take the fight to him!"

"How? He could go either way.

"Trust me. Both of you, zip to the blue outer silo!"

Niko leaps onto a cable away from the blue silo as we zip toward it. His cable travels directly beneath Aleks.

"Aleks, drop onto Niko's cable! That'll put you on his heels! Bear, once you hit the blue silo, jump onto the same cable as Aleks and Niko!"

Aleks drops and lands a few feet behind Niko. He feels her arrival, releases a grappler, and slashes at her. Aleks parries his attacks with her own free grappler.

I hit the blue silo and follow after Aleks.

Once I reach the corner silo, I scramble up. Niko and Aleks are locked in a silo-side grappler battle above my head. I try to ascend unnoticed.

"Hammers and hemlines, here comes Bear to break up the fight between Yukita and Niko!"

Thanks, Chip.

I reach up and catch the top of Niko's boot with my grappler hook. Without a second thought, Niko raises his powerful leg, along with me, and kicks down hard. My grappler unhooks, and he flees up the silo.

We climb after Niko, but somehow lose him. Where'd he go?

Just as I think this, Niko leaps over our heads from atop the corner silo. He soars in a free fall toward the center silo, catches a cable, and zips off. Aleks and I share a brief glance of disbelief before we give chase.

Niko hits the center silo platform in a full sprint. Aleks and I land shortly after. I'm almost in striking distance when Niko whips around and catches me in the cheekbone with his grappler blade.

Dull pain spreads across my face. My right eye clenches, but I can still see Niko. The momentary distraction worked. Aleks crashes into Niko and pushes off him.

She has the ball!

Niko electrifies his grapplers and engages Aleks. She does the same. When Niko attacks, Aleks throws the ball to me, and I cash it.

"Kudos and kaleidoscopes, that's another 10 points for Idol Nominee Telladyne, for a total of 20! Yukita and Bear are definitely working together! I can't believe it!"

"Neither can Niko. He's desperate for points and on his way to join the fight between Jita and Pinz at the edge of the center silo!"

Jita has possession, but struggles to hold off Pinz, who pushes her to the platform edge. Looks like he has a favorite move. Niko jumps into the fray. All three players launch into a three-way grappler battle for the only ball left in play.

Pinz and Niko tower over Jita. She knows what could happen and powers down her grapplers. Her ball is as good as lost. I run to the nearest corner silo with Aleks, but Crtr stops us.

"Attack Jita!"

"No way! I'm not getting caught in a five-way grappler battle for five points!"

"If Jita's threatened by two more players, she'll throw the ball to save herself! I'm sure of it!"

Aleks and I electrify our grapplers and run to the three-way battle. As Crtr predicted, Jita launches her ball at the point tube to divert attention. Niko splits off like a dog chasing a bone, but Pinz stays on Jita.

Aleks reaches the ball first and bats it to me. I cash it with a dive for another 5 points.

"Make that 25 points for Idol Nominee Telladyne, or should I say Team Yukita-Telladyne? They've all but kept their opponents off the board, and are already halfway to victory!"

The water penalty countdown begins. This time Aleks and I head for the orange silo. I get there first and grab the ball. On my way back to the corner silo, Niko appears.

I don't have a second to defend myself before Niko connects an electrified grappler slash to my chest. My torso feels cleaved open.

I land on top of him and manage a desperate head-butt. Blood gushes from Niko's brow. While he's disoriented, I scurry up the silo.

Pain surges through my chest with every rung I pull, but I can't slow down. I'm not just playing for points anymore; I'm playing for my life.

I leap for the center silo cable, hear Niko behind me, and twist in mid-air. Niko slides after me with an onslaught of slashes.

My unsure feet hit the platform. I stumble, and Niko charges to keep me off balance. Searing hot electric slashes hit my legs and ribs.

Niko hits me in the collarbone, and I fumble the siloball. We both dive for it, but I manage to swat the ball away toward Aleks. Thankfully, Niko chases after it.

Aleks crouches to catch the ball. Niko runs at her with his grappler raised. He drops his grappler at Aleks' head. With just inches between her skull and the blade, Aleks deflects the attack.

Niko follows up with a series of complicated maneuvers that Aleks dodges and parries with ease. Aleks' brother, Takeo Yukita, is one of The City's greatest-ever siloball players, and she was his sparring partner for most of their childhood.

Feeling comes back to my limbs, and I rise. Once Aleks gets the ball back to m—

Ah!

A sharp slash hits my shoulder, and my arm goes limp.

Jita. She comes at me with a flurry of bright green slashes. Her hits are weak, but with just one arm it's impossible to block them all. She lands blows to my hips, arms, and legs. My nerve endings scream with each hit.

Now I know how Niko felt when Jita attacked him. She's relentless. If Jita can knock me out, my points will go away and the match will essentially reset.

Some feeling returns to my arm. I can block her attacks, but am sluggish from the twin assaults of Niko and Jita.

"Here comes Pinz Baylor, totally unchallenged on his way to the center silo! Can anyone stop him?"

"Absinthe and apple seeds! Pinz is almost to the point tube and all of his opponents are caught in grappler battles!"

I need those ten points, but Aleks can't pass me the ball with Jita all over me like this. Without my full strength, I have to fight smart.

Jita relies on fast combos. She especially likes to left lunge, right slash, then leg sweep. I need to make her speed into a weakness.

From the corner of my eye, I see Aleks clap her grapplers together. With fluid motion, she wraps Niko in ribbons of blinding ice blue light.

Jita lunges. When she sweeps at my legs, I stomp down hard on her blade. With my free foot, I kick her hard in the head. Jita stumbles back onto the ground.

"Aleks, I'm open!"

Aleks unleashes her full assault on Niko. With staggering grace, she paints burning lines across Niko's face, chest, and arms. He collapses, and Aleks passes me the ball.

I pump my arms and sprint hard for the tube. Pinz charges like a bull with singular focus; I can practically see smoke come out of his nostrils.

"Crtr, I need those Baylor Paradigm codes!"

"I don't have 'em yet!"

Pinz electrifies his grapplers. He had a head start, but I'm faster, so we reach the tube at the same time. Pinz launches himself high into the air with a gigantic slash meant to scare me. Just as Pinz hooks his arm over his head to cash his ball, I lob mine at the top of the point tube.

He can't stop. Pinz drives his ball down onto mine and slams both balls into the tube.

"Haystacks and hollyhocks, what just happened? Bear's ball went in first, but Pinz hit it in! Who gets the points?"

"What a play, Chip! Technically the player who touches the ball last gets the points, so that's another ten points for Bear for a total of 35! Thanks to his showboating, Pinz collects just five. He can't be happy about that!"

With both balls cashed, the water penalty countdown begins. I look back to see if anyone's following Aleks and me off the platform.

Jita's almost fully recovered. She's powered down her grapplers but is taking a moment to regain her bearings. Niko still lies unconscious with fully electrified bright purple grapplers at his sides. If the water penalty triggers while Niko's grapplers are activated he'll be killed. Aleks would blame herself. I can't let him die.

"Go ahead, I'm right behind you!"

"What are you doing?"

"Just go!"

I run to Niko. Pinz barrels past me without a glance and plows into Jita before she fully returns to her feet. Her body flies off the silo like a ragdoll.

"And that's it, tonight's match is over for Idol Nominee Vitinia Flynn and her player, Jita. Is Bear trying to finish off Niko the same way? If so he better hurry, he's only got 7 seconds before that water penalty shoots him into the drink!"

No time to rouse Niko back to consciousness. I knock his grapplers together to power them down.

As I run to the nearest cable, I feel the ground shift under my feet. Millions of tiny holes appear on the platform. A sharp hydraulic noise cuts through the air. The point tube grows fifteen feet tall, and is covered in more tiny holes.

"Here we go, Bulloxy. It doesn't look good for Niko and Bear in 3... 2... here come the water works!"

Too far from any cable, I jump off the silo and grab a rung.

Torrents of water rush over me. Even though I'm not directly in its path, the air itself pulls me down. I grit my teeth, shut my eyes, and hold tight to the rung with both arms. Pain from my grappler injuries surges through every cell of my body.

I can't let go. No pain is worse than Aleks becoming the Idol.

"Ooh, make that a double, Chip! So much for Noble Valet Niko! If Bear can stay out of the water, we're looking at a three-player match. If not, it's just Yukita and Pinz in a one-on-one!"

The water stops. I'm drenched, but still in the game. The slow climb back up reveals the true toll on my body. Any more beatings and my muscles will shut down in protest. I throw an arm onto the platform and pull myself over.

Pinz has Aleks beaten back to the platform edge!

Their grapplers are electrified, and they both have possession. I run to help Aleks.

Pinz seems resistant to Aleks' blows. She jabs and weaves to hold her position, but she can't regain any ground.

I pass the point tube. Hold on, Aleks!

3 beeps. Crtr.

"Aleks, Bear's at the point tube. Can you get him the ball?"

Aleks crouches down and sweeps at Pinz's legs. The slight diversion lets Aleks pass me her siloball. We lock eyes for a moment.

Pinz's weight shifts.

"Aleks!"

Pinz delivers a savage backhand slash to Aleks' face. She flies backward off the silo with her grapplers still electrified!

"Aleks! Aleks, can you hear me!"

She's out. Even if I jump off the silo to disqualify myself, she'd still hit the water first and be electrocuted to death.

Pinz dashes after Aleks' ball, but he's too far away. I scoop up the ball and cash it for 10 points.

Pinz and I sprint toward each other. If he knocks me into the water, I'll be out and points won't matter. I need his siloball to win.

"Crtr! The codes!"

"I don't have them! You have to end the match before Aleks hits the water!"

"I know!"

With just a few feet between us, I pull one of the Diazapax pens from my sleeve. While Pinz focuses on the pen, I drop into a slide and use all my remaining strength to slice through his cybernetic knee.

I feel Pinz's knee shatter to pieces inside his body. As he crumples to the ground, I grab his siloball, spring up, and cash it for another 5 points. That's 50.

Champagne gold and dark blue fireworks burst above the Coliseum while I run and dive off the silo. Aleks' body floats face down in the water.

She never should have played. I was afraid to lose Aleks to the Idol, and now I might have lost her for good. Please be alive, Aleks. Please.

I hit the water, emerge beside her and turn Aleks face-up. A long, cauterized, gash runs across her face. I hardly remember the swim to the beach, but we get there.

No pulse. She isn't breathing. I start chest compressions. Nothing. I tilt her head back, seal my lips around her mouth and breath long, deep breaths into Aleks' lungs. Her chest rises, but her eyes stay closed. More compressions.

"Aleks, wake up! Stay with me!"

I breathe into her mouth again. She's still out. No pulse. I start another round of compressions.

"Aleks, come back! The City needs you! I need you!"

As I move to put my mouth over hers again, Aleks hacks up the water in her lungs. Her eyes flutter open.

She's confused, and exhausted from what her body's just gone through. Her gaze settles on my face, and she flashes me a soft smile.

"Hey, Bear," she says through soft coughs. "I missed you."

She reaches up and wipes the bottom of my eye with her thumb. A stream of pooled tears releases down my cheek.

Her polished silver eyes reflect my deepest truths. Aleks is my life—the bright spot in my world of servitude and violence. I have no true family and own no property, but for a moment I understood what it means to lose everything all at once.

"I missed you, too."

Aleks winces as bright light shines into her face. I look up to find dozens of camera drones assembled above us.

Mobs of lowlanders close in on us from both sides. Every Idol Nomination Ceremony ends with fans rushing the siloball pool beach. I never gave much thought to the tradition, but in this moment I'm absolutely terrified.

"Can you run?"

"Yeah."

I lift Aleks to her feet. The nearest exit has already been overtaken by fans.

We charge into the adoring fray with our heads down. Fingers grasp at our clothes, open palms smack our bodies, and fingernails drag across our exposed skin. They push and pull at us like a vicious ebbing tide.

Aleks' arm slips from my grasp.

"Bear!"

A crazed man has both his hands wrapped tight around Aleks' wrist. Someone else has a fistful of her hair. I fight my way to her, wrestle Aleks away, and continue to fight through the gauntlet of rabid lowlanders.

"Holt! I'm with Idol Nominee Yukita. She needs my protection to escape unharmed! I will escort her to the Yukita Teitaku as soon as possible."

"Message received. I will alert your house."

We reach an exit tunnel. Two Noble Guards prevent any fans from following us down the long, dark corridor. We continue to run until the tunnel goes quiet. Aleks leans against a wall and slides to a seat.

"Is that what it means to be the Idol?" Aleks asks. "If you weren't there, they would have torn me apart. I'd rather die than live like that."

Aleks runs her hands through her ice blue hair and exhales a stuttered breath. I lower beside her. She crumbles into me but stares straight ahead.

For the last seven days, Aleks' every move has been surveilled. Idol Nominees are expected to behave a certain way in public, maintain composure under any circumstances, and accept invasive analysis in stride. Her LifeCast hasn't even started yet.

She must feel so trapped; trapped and helpless. I recognize the feeling from my childhood in the lowland.

"Give me your hand," I say.

"I can't go back to the Highland, not yet."

"I know. Turn off your NeuroTracker and come with me."

10

We exit the Coliseum through a service door. Lowland rain re-saturates our hair and cascades down our water repellent siloball suits. Right now, Aleks and I are two of the most recognizable people in The City. We'll need disguises to get away from here unnoticed.

We approach a group of Unassigned. Their heavy, hooded overcoats are perfect for concealing our identities. Unassigned never stay any place for long, so we'll have to act fast.

The group greedily devours pieces of rotisserie chicken. A man with bright orange hair and beard strips huge bites of flesh off two drumsticks in his enormous, pillowy hand. Something tells me he's their leader.

"We need your coats. Yours and..." I scan the group for someone about Aleks' size. "Yours. I'll give you 1000 points for them. That'll get you a roof over your heads and food for a few weeks."

The orange-haired man doesn't look up and ignores the Unassigned who nudge him.

"We need to go! This offer's good for another five seconds. 5, 4, 3, 2—"

"What makes you think we want a roof over our heads?" The orange-haired man says. "Can't you see? This is paradise."

The Unassigned laugh with mouths full of chicken.

"Look, we don't have much time. I'm offering you a better deal than you'll ever get."

"Have you seen the mist on an unusually warm night?" The orange-haired man asks. "When it gets really hot out the mist swirls with all kinds of blues, indigos, and violets. It's really quite a sight, one I can't imagine living without. We'll need enough for a nice place, one with a view. 2500 points, each."

"That's outrageous! 750 points each."

"Bear, we have to get out of here!"

The orange-haired man locks eyes with me and stands. He's bigger than I initially thought, a few inches taller than me but padded thick all around.

"4000 for both."

"Fine, deal! Now hand 'em over, we don't have all night!"

"Dalo!" the orange-haired man says. "Give your coat to this nice lady with the cut-up face."

A thin Unassigned, tosses his coat to Aleks, and the orange-haired man gives me his. It's far heavier than I expected. There's something inside the coat's lining. I shake it out, and countless vials of bright red ReBorn capsules fall to the ground.

"You don't want the ReBorn?" The orange-haired man asks.

"No, of course not! Is that why you wanted so much for these coats?"

"Does it matter?"

"No. What's your name?"

"Rork. It's a pleasure doing business with you, Noble Valet Bear."

We shake hands, and I transfer 4,000 points to Rork's NeuroBank.

Aleks and I put on our expensive new coats. The coats reek of sweat and machine grease. We flip up the hoods and start through the lowland crowd.

We run over several blocks until we reach an alleyway. The alley contains a dumpster that overflows with construction debris.

"What is all this stuff?" Aleks asks.

"Scrap from the plant next door. They're constantly refurbishing their lines. It's a good thing too, we need it to get where we're going. Help me move this."

Aleks and I lift a heavy metal pipe into place, along with more of the alley trash, to build a small platform. From the platform, we jump up to a rusted fire escape.

The city noise dissipates with each new landing we reach, and the air grows colder. Aleks seems unfazed by our ascent, despite the fact that we're 22 stories up, and only secured to the building by a decayed metal lattice.

When we reach the top, Aleks looks back down at the alley.

"We're so high."

"Yeah, high enough to get a little privacy. Come on, we're almost there."

"Where?"

"I guess you could call it my vacation home."

We continue along the roof ledge to a slab of pebbled concrete. I push the large slab aside to reveal a small, dark archway.

"After you," I say.

Aleks crawls through, and I follow. We stand back up inside a modest space with three walls, and a ceiling to keep out the rain. Aleks runs her hands across stacked burlap sacks that line the walls.

"The bags are salvaged from lowland res-hall dumpsters," I say. "The food courts use tons of rice and beans. I actually filled them with other burlap sacks. They block the wind well enough."

Aleks' eyes hover to the ceiling. She walks beneath a skylight and watches the rain patter over her head.

"Those are hard to get. Most windows I find are broken. If I ever find one in good shape I haul it up here and fix it to the ceiling. It's taken me almost ten years just to find these six windows."

"You've been working on this since you were nine?"

"Yeah. I found this place before my Valet apprenticeship started. Over the years I've added little bits here and there. The scraps in the alley below were perfect for constructing the frame. The rugs are actually discarded from renovations at Telladyne Manor."

While I talk, Aleks looks to the room's open wall. She darts toward the view. The side of the building drops straight down to the street far below, but Aleks doesn't seem to care. I run after her, grab her arm, and pull her back.

"Be careful!" I shout.

"Bear, I didn't climb all this way just to jump."

Aleks looks up at me with a smirk. Her rain-soaked, ice blue braid sticks to the side of her face. I brush away the braid, and my hand lingers.

Every beat of my heart pounds like a bass drum against my rib cage. Aleks moves her fingertips down my arm. The familiar unseen force draws our faces closer.

"Bear," Aleks whispers.

"Yes, Aleks?"

"My face stings like mad. Do you have any medical supplies up here?"

Of course, the gash that Pinz gave her. It cauterized on contact, but must still be brutally painful. Fortunately, I have exactly what Aleks needs in a small trunk.

I retrieve a basic first aid kit. Aleks stares out at a recap of the Idol Nomination Ceremony that plays against the side of Neurogem Tower. The recap shows a clip of Vitinia Flynn singing atop a sleeping copper tiger.

Aleks lets me dress the wound with a DermaBandage. As I place the bandage, I wonder when we'll kiss again. Now doesn't feel like the right time—the memory of how her face got slashed feels too fresh.

I stretch out onto my stomach to face the view. Aleks lies down beside me. The open wall looks over the busiest intersection in The City, Neurogem Square.

Throngs of lowlanders in purple, green, light blue, dark blue, and white V-Pros walk in all directions. The V-Pros show their support for different Idol Nominees.

"I've wanted to show you this place for the longest but never had the chance."

"It's spectacular."

"You still haven't seen the best part. Turn off your gem."

I can tell Aleks has done as I asked when her face drops in awe. I turn mine off too.

All the ads and infotainment news coverage blink out of existence. Wet, grey, scaffolding-covered buildings fill our view. Only the sound of rainfall and the dissonant noise from distant factory machinery is audible.

The V-Pro outfits and hairstyles below disappear to reveal the lowlanders' true appearance. Everyone wears the same dark grey boilersuit, skin tight so it doesn't distort their V-Pro images. The unpleasant smell of garbage creeps in, which isn't helped by the trash I used for insulation.

"It's all so... drab," Aleks says. "The clothes, the lifeless way everyone moves, the total lack of color. It's beyond drab. It's tragic."

"This is the lowland behind the veil. Can you blame them for buying V-Pros and everything else that's shouted at them from ads? Without all the distractions there's just this—a sickly silence that would force them to hear their own thoughts."

Tears pool in Aleks' eyes.

"No one sees this," I continue. "Not lowlanders. Not even Nobles. This is the truth hidden in plain sight. I know it's shocking, but we're lucky to see it."

"I don't feel lucky. All I feel is sadness for all those people down there."

"I'm sorry, I didn't mean to—"

"No, it's fine. I'm glad you showed me. I just... it's too much to take in right now. I have to turn my gem back on."

Aleks leans back on her hands and pushes herself further from the edge. I move beside her. The sudden rush of color and noise can be shocking, so I close my eyes to turn my gem back on.

"Bear, look!"

Coverage from the evening's siloball match plays on Neurogem Tower, specifically the battle between Aleks and Pinz.

"Maybe we shouldn't watch this," I say.

"No, I need to see what happened."

It's bad enough that Aleks had to experience the battle first hand, let alone be forced to relive it in Hexographic Ultimate Definition fifty stories tall.

Pinz slashes Aleks' face and sends her over the edge. She winces in real life when the blow connects.

The next clip shows me shattering Pinz's knee. Aleks' jaw drops. We watch as I cash the ball and dive after her. I didn't know until now that Aleks' grapplers powered down mere inches above the water.

The coverage cuts to me dragging Aleks' still body onto the shore. There's no audio, but my panic and desperation are obvious. Aleks spits up the water in her lungs, and I hold her. We appear frozen, painted by flashes of firework light.

I wouldn't blame Aleks if she got up and stormed away. I wouldn't even blame her if she never spoke to me again. We were supposed to look out for each other during the match, and she was nearly killed.

The view cuts to Kallista accepting her trophy for winning the siloball match, with Master Telladyne, Kassian, and Mariposa Monarch by her side. I look over to find Aleks staring into my face with glassy eyes.

"I should have known better," I say. "It was too dangerous."

"No, that's—"

"If I let Holt play you would have been safe."

"And he would have died. You saved both our lives tonight. You saved me."

Aleks rests her palm on my cheek and releases a shaky exhale. The scent of her juniper shampoo draws me in. We lean in closer until our lips touch.

A concussive blast explodes the roof. Shrapnel rains down while a thick cloud of dust envelops us.

At the open wall, a single Noble Guard hovers in mid-air, flanked by several camera drones. His arm cannons are lowered; he didn't cause the explosion. I look back.

With lightning-fast speed, another Noble Guard tosses me across the room. Aleks screams and kicks as the other guard grabs her. I pounce to my feet, but the guard flies off with her before I take a single step.

I run to the ledge. Aleks shouts my name, and I shout hers back. All I can do is watch as she vanishes into the distance.

I don't care that the roof of my hideaway and all my years of work were just destroyed in a flash. All I care about is Aleks. Where are they taking her? And what will they do once she's there?

Noble Guards work for the Highland, so that's my first stop. I'll start at the Yukita Teitaku. They won't just let me in, I'll have to break in unseen.

Am I really going to interrogate Takeshi Yukita and his family? If it comes to that. I wish Aleks was here to help me strategize; she's always been a better planner than me.

3 Beeps. Marena Vexhall. What could she want?

"I know where they took her."

"You know where Aleks is? Tell me!"

"Meet me at the following coordinates."

"Is she OK? If she's in danger tell me now!"

"She's safe, for the time being. Please, meet me and I will explain everything."

11

A central lake anchors the Vexhall compound of limestone palaces. The lake acts as a not-so-subtle reminder of the Vexhall's control over The City's water supply—a vast hydrological empire that exploits every human's need for a resource that makes up over 70% of the planet and 60% our own bodies.

I approach the huge yellow gold gate of a high stone wall. The gate opens, and I continue down a wide path lined by waterfalls. All I can hear is the loud crash of water.

The path ends at a gigantic, ballroom-like foyer. Chandeliers made of thin streams of water float overhead. Beyond the chandeliers, the foyer continues up at least 15 stories to a spotless glass ceiling.

"Marena!" I shout. "I'm here! Tell me where Aleks is!"

"It's OK, Bear. She's safe."

Marena's voice carries through the room like a light breeze.

A microdrone flies into sight. Marena materializes around the drone. She's dressed down in loose brown leather pants and a simple V-neck t-shirt.

"Where is she?"

"At home. The Noble Guard were dispatched to ensure her safety. They wouldn't dare harm her."

"What do you mean, 'dispatched?' I didn't call them, and I know Aleks didn't."

"She did call them, just not intentionally. If an Idol Nominee's heart rate increases above normal parameters or her cortisol levels spike to a level that suggests potential danger, the Nominee's NeuroTracker activates automatically, and the Noble Guard are deployed to extract her. You must have gotten her really worked up."

"Aleks would never agree to such an invasive security measure."

"Oh, she did, she just didn't realize it. It's buried deep in the 110,000-page Idol Nominee agreement. I'm probably the only person who's ever read the whole thing."

"Why isn't she answering my NeuroChats?"

"They most likely threw her into a RejuviPod. You're what, a 44 long?"

"You mean my jacket size? What does that have to do with anything?"

Marena walks over to a smooth white wall. The wall splits to reveal a rack of white AeroPacks.

"The third one from the right should fit you. Go ahead. Try it on."

"Why?"

"I know how to keep Aleks from becoming the Idol. Meet me on the top floor, and I'll explain everything."

Marena disappears and her microdrone flies away. I should have been back at Telladyne Manor hours ago, but for Aleks' sake, I need to hear Marena out.

I strap on the AeroPack. My Valet training taught me how to pilot all kinds of vehicles, including AeroPacks, but this one's unusually light and thin. Of course, the Vexhalls have the best of everything. Why should their guest AeroPacks be any different?

I sync my gem to the AeroPack and kick off the ground. Each floor passes so fast I lose count.

What's tha— my reflection! I jerk sideways.

I hit a grass landing and tumble over the soft ground. Marena laughs as I brush blades of grass from my jacket.

She's changed her outfit again. Now Marena wears a long white robe with gold sandals. Her make-up is more subdued than before with only a bit of blush and nude lipstick.

I'm surrounded by bright green grass, rose bushes, and sculpted shrubbery. Overhead, the nearly-invisible glass ceiling reveals a sky of ever-brightening daylight.

It all seems so natural, but there's a silent eeriness to the landscape. Outside this building birds squawked and the wind brushed past my ears, but not here. This is a facsimile of life, a strange disconnected production that misses the finest details.

"Sorry, I should have told you about those AeroPacks. They're meant for high performance racing. Some flyers find them a bit... sensitive."

"What is this place?"

"This is my home, my real home. Come."

I move to take off the AeroPack, but Marena stops me.

"Keep that on, you'll need it again."

I follow Marena to an archway of flowers within a wall of dark green hedges. A stone marker among the flowers reads,

"Born from tides that have no end,
Oceans and rivers with futures to tend,
Righteous swells and ebbs that stir,
Now rest with you because we were."

Through the archway, a series of white marble boxes surrounded by headstones dot the landscape. We pass one of the boxes and I see that the headstones are etched with four-letter names. These are the graves of dead Nobles and their servants.

We stop at the edge of another artificial lake. This one is far smaller than the one outside but still quite large. The water stands perfectly still like a smooth sheet of navy blue glass. A tall, yellow gold step pyramid sits at the center of the lake.

Marena dematerializes, and her microdrone floats to the pyramid. This must be why she told me to keep the AeroPack.

I fly over the lake to meet Marena and follow her inside the pyramid.

We walk through a long corridor that acts as a shrine to Marena. Oil paintings of her at various ages are interspersed with clips from her numerous NeuroCast episodes that range in topic from hang gliding to carpentry.

The ground rises as we make a sharp left turn. More Marena-based content bombards me. She walks among the portraits and clips with aloof indifference.

The corridor narrows and shrinks with each turn. We must be climbing to the pyramid's top.

"So," Marena says. "What do you think?"

"I don't think any Noble has ever cared to learn so much about so many different things," I reply. "You've lived an incredibly rich life."

"Life... that's one way to describe it. I suppose I have to fill eternity somehow."

I follow Marena around another corner, and we stop at a heavy-looking golden door covered with gears, levers, and cranks.

"Go ahead," Marena says. "Touch it."

I press my palm against a flat section of the door, and it explodes with activity. The gears turn, the levers rise and fall, and the cranks spin.

Suddenly, the entire chaotic process stops, and the door splits down the middle. We step over the threshold into a small, frosted glass booth.

There's hardly enough room for both of us inside the booth. Sure, Marena's a hologram and I could step right through her, but there must be some kind of hologram etiquette about that.

The gold door closes behind us, which makes the space feel even smaller.

"You're about to step inside a respiration chamber," Marena says. "The room itself will breathe for you, so you'll want to disable your automatic breathing reflex."

"You want me to what?"

"Do you actually believe I would go through all of this just to kill you now? You have to trust me. It's the only way to save Aleks."

I take a deep breath, and nod. It's true, if Marena wanted me dead, she could have made that happen easily.

Marena counts down from three. At one, I turn off my breathing reflex with a Neurogem command, and the frosted glass walls lower. To my amazement, my lungs inflate and deflate on their own.

The taste of saltwater and feel of thick humidity hit me. A pathway stretches out before us, but the air is too dense to see where the path leads.

Violently boiling water surrounds the pathway. Glass walls that match the angular step pyramid's exterior reach overhead. If the glass was ever transparent, it's been long-covered by an opaque film of condensation residue.

As I walk down the path, the outline of what looks like a reclined, stark white RejuviPod comes into view.

I move closer. The pod doesn't have a face. Through the hazy atmosphere, I make out the shape of a small person. She's rail thin, with long blonde hair that lies in frizzy, voluminous curls.

Fluorescent, multi-colored tubes run all over her body. My face contorts with heartbreak when I realize what I'm seeing. It's Marena, the real Marena.

Her eyes are closed but active beneath the lids. Holographic Marena's limbs are strong and healthy, but her actual body looks too weak to scratch her own nose. I've never seen someone in the Highland look so vulnerable.

My feet unconsciously carry me to Marena's side. Unsure if my intention is to comfort her or myself, I move to lay my hand on her arm.

"Stop! Don't touch her!"

Marena's projection appears across from me and I leap back. She's changed her look again, this time to match the simple appearance of her actual self. There's no make-up on her face and she wears the same basic, form-fitting, sleeveless navy blue boilersuit as her physical counterpart.

"I wish you could touch her, I mean me, but you can't. There are sensors everywhere. If you laid a single finger on my body, you'd be shot full of Diazapax and taken by the Noble Guard."

"Are there any other hidden dangers I should know about before we continue?"

"Sorry, I'm not used to visitors."

"What about your family, don't they come around?"

"Not for a long time. My pod used to be in the main palace, but when I turned 17 for the fifth time, I got my holographic projection, and my father moved my body here. I begged to stay in the palace, but he ignored me."

"What do you mean, 'when you turned 17 for the fifth time?'"

"My doctors bio-locked me at the age of 17. It supposedly improves my ability to regenerate tissue and fight infection. The lock was supposed to be temporary, until they found a cure, but I'm still waiting."

"A cure for what? Are you dying?"

"We're all dying. I just live a bit closer to death than most people."

"What happened?"

"It was quite sudden actually. I had just turned seven and was running around the grounds. Suddenly my ankles went numb and I collapsed.

"After days of testing, my doctors determined that I had some kind of undiscovered neurological disease that affects the basal pons of my brain. The disease spread fast. Within a few weeks almost my entire body was frozen. Miraculously I maintained the use of my eyes, which are now my only connection to the physical world."

Marena's eyes flutter open. She blinks a few times and looks right at me.

I stare back at her for a moment and take in the significance of what she just shared. The thought of being trapped in one's own body is utterly horrific. My eyelid twitches, and my throat clenches a bit, but I stifle my emotions.

"How can this be?" I ask. "Any Highland hospital can regrow an entire circulatory system in a matter of days. Curing this can't be more difficult than that."

"I've endured hundreds of operations and treatments to replace or repair different areas of my brain. The best pathologists in The City have all come up short. Eventually my father simply gave up and decided it would be easier to lock me away out of sight."

"How long has it been since anyone visited you, other than me?"

"I could give you a number, but time has become meaningless to me. Some days feel like minutes, and some minutes feel like days. Without age, I have no marker by which to personalize the passage of time. I'm fortunate, however, to have full control of my mind. It's how I've kept from going crazy all these years.

"Lowlanders and Nobles alike constantly tell me how much they appreciate my NeuroCast channel for showing them untold wonders. But my channel isn't for them. It's for me. I crave new experiences because it's the closest I can come to living a real life. Everyone knows you learn more when you teach, which is why my NeuroCast channel has an educational bent."

"So why wouldn't you want to become the Idol? It's the most unique human experience you could possibly have."

"I thought the same thing, but I soon realized that to become the Idol is to lose yourself. It is all-encompassing, all-consuming, and never-ending. Fortunately, I've managed to avoid being selected."

"If that's how you feel, why keep running?"

"My Idol nomination is a fantastic promotional tool for The Vexhall Group."

"Can't you refuse?"

"If only it were that simple. While I can travel beyond the wildest imaginations of most people, I'm still burdened by my physical existence. My father controls the machines that keep me alive, and while calling this 'alive' feels like a cruel joke, it's better than the alternative."

"He wouldn't... how could he possibly?"

"He's all but abandoned me here already. It wouldn't be much of a stretch for him to simply turn off the lights and walk away, so to speak. But that's not why you're here. I'll be fine. It's Aleks I'm worried about."

"Why? What's Aleks to you?"

"It's not what Aleks is to me, it's what she is to The City. During the Idol Nomination rehearsals, we got to know each other. Aleks is different from most Noble girls. Somehow, she's developed a sense of empathy for the lowland. Do you know how rare that is among Nobles? With her Highland resources and genuine concern for the world below the mist Aleks could accomplish great things."

"But wouldn't that mean..." I say with careful words. "If Aleks became the Idol she would be in a perfect position to do some good. Wouldn't she?"

"Bear, I've known 12 Idol nominees since my first nomination. For the most part they're vapid, spoiled brats like Kallista Telladyne, but a few have been good like Aleks. Vox was good once, until she changed. And how much better did anyone's life really get after she became the Idol?"

"How did Vox change?"

"It started after she was selected. Vox adopted new habits and mannerisms that I initially chalked up to nerves, or stress, but those little quirks built until she was practically unrecognizable."

"What kinds of quirks?"

"The first thing I noticed was her impatient dancing. She did it whenever she had to wait more than a few minutes for anything."

"So, what? Lots of people do that."

"Vox didn't. If a wait was too long, she'd confront someone about it, not dance. She also used to squint when she spoke in a way that indicated meaning and thought behind her words. After she became the Idol, Vox adopted a sing-songy lilt, and her eyes were always wide open and vacant. But that's nothing. The strangest change was her sudden interest in men."

"What do you mean?"

"Vox and I hung out together all the time in bars and clubs all over the Highland. Even when the most attractive, eligible Noble bachelors approached us, Vox dismissed them out of hand, usually with a barb about their pick-up lines or their overcompensation. She told me the only time she ever kissed a man was when she was drunk, and it absolutely repulsed her. Fast forward to a month after she became the Idol when Vox was attached at the lips to whichever male musician, athlete, or socialite was popular at the time."

"You're sure she wasn't attracted to men? Not at all?"

"Not. at. all. Bear, if there's one person in the entire city who's sure of who Vox really was, it's me."

"Does that mean you two were together?"

Marena's hologram freezes for a moment and resumes with a sigh.

"We were as close as two people could be when one of them is made of light. I would have done anything for her, just like you would for Aleks."

"I won't let that happen to Aleks. She doesn't even want to be the Idol!"

"Neither did Vox. The best way to save Aleks is to make sure someone else wins. At this point, Kallista is the most viable nominee."

"How am I supposed to help Kallista become the Idol?"

"The LifeCast. Kallista should play to her strengths, whatever those are, so she seems natural. Statistically, LifeCasts that involve the lowland in some chartable fashion do well, as long as they don't come off as condescending. On the other hand, make sure Aleks' LifeCast is absolutely, mind-numbingly boring. The City has a short attention span. Understand?"

"I do. What are you doing for your LifeCast?"

"Not sure yet. I have to skirt the line between tedium and intrigue. If I finish in last place my father might not be able to convince The Vexhall Group board to sponsor my fourth Idol nomination."

"I thought you didn't want to be a nominee?"

"I don't, but I fear that my participation is the only thing keeping me alive at this point. Don't worry about me. Just make sure Kallista's LifeCast outshines everyone else's and that Aleks' fades out of sight."

Marena looks at me with eyes that sparkle with life within her motionless body. Everyone who's supposed to care about Marena has given up on her.

Sure, Marena's showered in praise for her NeuroCast channel, but what good does that do her? At the end of the day, she's still trapped in this lonely, cramped tomb. Who knows how long it's been since she felt the touch of another human?

I look around the room to inspect the security measures. With the performance AeroPack I wear and my grapplers, I might stand a fighting chance against the tomb's defenses. There are panels along the ceiling for dart guns. Openings in the walls are probably there to pump in fog or other substances to disorient anyone trying to escape. I could overlay a clear route to the door with my gem—

"Bear, what are you doing?"

"Just taking in this structure," I lie. "It really is incredible."

"I appreciate your intention, but it's not worth the risk. You wouldn't last five seconds against the tomb's security. And for what? A comforting gesture that I couldn't even feel? My disease renders my body's nerve endings useless. You could stab me in the leg and I wouldn't even flinch."

"It's not about the feeling," I say. "When I lived in the lowland orphanage, my caretaker Zola kissed my forehead every night. She went out of her way to do so. It was a small gesture, but it made me feel safe like someone actually cared what happened to me."

"I think I'm starting to understand where Aleks gets it."

"What?"

"Her empathy for the lowland. Remember, Kallista must become the Idol."

"I will. Thank you for your help, Marena. Aleks and I are lucky to have met you."

"I'm the lucky one, Bear. You've given me hope that there are still kind hearts left in the Highland."

Marena waves her hand, and I hear the glass booth at the tomb's exit lower.

12

I check my NeuroChat and NeuroText messages from the service lines back to Telladyne Manor. There aren't any angry messages from Master Telladyne. Crtr must have things under control in my absence.

Weighty, metallic clangs greet me at the service line dock. I follow the sound and find Crtr waist-deep in the back of a washing unit. He could use my help, but I need a moment to collect myself first.

I NeuroChat Aleks to see if she's been released from her RejuviPod yet.

"You've reached the NeuroChat channel of Aleksaria Yukita. I'm not available right now, but please leave a message and I'll get you back!"

"Aleks, chat me back as soon as you get this. It's important."

I need to tell Aleks what Marena said about her LifeCast. She's surely under Noble Guard watch, so I couldn't stop by the Yukita Teitaku on my way back here.

The dissonant pounding of Crtr's repairs follows me up to my loft space. I leave a scattered trail of clothes on my way to the shower.

Hot, soapy jets hit my aching body. I rest my head against the shower stall's cool tile and take a deep breath. The cauterized gash on my torso stings as water runs over it. My muscles are exhausted to the point of uselessness. I'm long overdue for a pod treatment, but there's no time for that.

The rinse cycle completes, and the shower stall blasts me dry. I step out and approach my armoire. It feels comforting to change back into my Valet uniform. With my crisp white oxford shirt in place, I slip on my WristVac, and put on my black jacket. Finally, I attach my RXSleeve.

Highland hair and skincare products of the finest quality lie in neat rows on my standing vanity. I put in a bit of product to give my hair body. Next, I oil my skin and apply a light coat of cacao foundation to my face.

I draw two thin champagne gold lines around my eyes with confident strokes. The lip-gloss I use only has a slight tint—just enough to give my lips a bit of contrast. Some Valets indulge in more elaborate makeup rituals, but Holt taught me the subtle art of facial minimalism.

I prep a pen to counteract my drowsiness. It's basically a Hot Shot but modified to mitigate shakiness and excessive sweating. There's no substitute for a few hours in a RejuviPod, but this will have to do.

An immediate jolt of energy surges through me after I dock the pen. The drugs course through my veins like battery acid that turns to ice water. My vision wavers for a moment, and I clutch the vanity to stabilize myself.

I might as well eat something while I have the chance. I choke down a ProTerra energy bar. It tastes like mint-flavored tar but is packed with enough vitamins, protein, and carbohydrates to stand in for a full meal.

The heavy clangs continue. Crtr, he's still at it! He needs my help!

I run down the catwalk and launch myself down the stairs three at a time. My heart flutters so fast that my body feels obliged to stay in constant motion. This initial surge of frenetic energy should pass soon.

"Crtr, get out of there!" I shout.

"Noble Valet Bear! It's all right, I'm almost finished! Here, hold this!"

Crtr reaches back to hand me a metal arm that controls the door's locking mechanism. He has no clue what he's doing.

"Crtr, get out of there now! You're making the problem worse!"

I see Crtr's legs jostle back and forth. He doesn't respond.

"Crtr, did you hear me? Come out of there. That's an order!"

"I'm trying... I... I think I'm stuck! Can you give me a pull?"

I grab Crtr's feet and yank him out of the machine. A flood of tiny, white, absorbent beads cascade out with Crtr's body. He topples into me, and we fall to the floor. Crtr laughs, and despite everything on my mind, I do, too. Even after Crtr goes quiet, I stay doubled-over in hysterics.

I finally catch my breath and rise to the machine. If Crtr thinks I've completely lost my mind he doesn't show it. Masking one's true feelings is a fundamental Noble Valet skill he appears to have mastered.

I show Crtr how to diagnose and repair the machine.

"This happens all the time with water-free washing units," I say. "It's an easy fix once you've done it a few times. The next tasks in our queue are a color change for Young Lady Kallista's toe nails and the preparation of refreshments for her guests."

"I've already prepared the refreshments," Crtr says. "A variety of hand-made sushi. I used a NApp so it's perfect."

"Where is it?"

"Outside Young Lady Kallista's pod chamber."

"How long has it been there?"

"22 minutes. Don't worry. They're in a chilled, odor-proof compartment."

"Crtr, you can't just leave food!" I reply, but calm myself and resume. "Valet Apprentice Crtr, I appreciate your proactivity, but it is best to deliver refreshments just before the arrival of guests so they are fresher."

"I guess I could make more—"

"It's fine. Just keep what I said in mind for next time. Please head to the service elevator and prepare a cart for Kallista's color change. I will be there shortly."

Crtr leaves with a bow. My hands move in a blur to complete the repair, and it only takes a moment to WristVac up the white beads.

I meet Crtr at the service elevator, and we careen toward Kallista's wing.

"Kallista is extremely particular about her nails," I say. "So, I'll handle the color change. While I do that, you tidy up her room."

"How? I don't know where anything goes."

I retrieve a blueprint of Kallista's pod chamber suite and send it to Crtr.

"Keep this open while you work. Whenever you look at a particular item, its most common locations will glow along with location likelihood percentages. If you look at a fur cape, for example, multiple closets will light up, and the one with the highest percentage is where it's most often stored. Make sense?"

"Yes sir, Mentor Valet Bear."

"NeuroText any questions you have. If Kallista thinks you're distracting me from her nails she'll throw a Highland-grade fit."

"15 seconds to destination: Master Suite - Kallista Telladyne Wing," the service elevator announces.

The elevator slows, and I reach for a support strap. Crtr wanders a few steps away, likely absorbed by the blueprint I sent. When the elevator stops, Crtr gets launched into a wall of sporting equipment.

I run to help him. Crtr's crouched beneath a pile of tennis rackets, skis, grapplers, ping-pong paddles, and balls. He stands up and aggressively brushes himself off.

"You all right?"

"I'm so tired of making mistakes! Now we have to clean all this up, which puts us even more behind!"

I haven't been available to Crtr like Holt was to me. His frustration stems from my failure as a teacher. Before I ever met Crtr, Holt gave me a piece of advice about training a Valet Apprentice.

"There will be times when you're too tired to care," Holt said. "But for the sake of our city, you must be patient. Every mistake is a chance to improve."

If not for Holt's dedication to my training, I would have been cast out of the Highland and unassigned long ago. The least I can do is attempt the same level of commitment to Crtr.

"Check this out," I say.

I lift the right leg of my trousers to reveal a long scar across my knee.

"I got this from doing almost the exact same thing you just did. Instead of grabbing one of the bright orange support straps, I grabbed the strap of one of Kallista's handbags. I flew straight into a rack of gardening tools. A hand rake, with tangs four inches long and razor sharp, dragged across my knee."

"Why didn't you DermaBandage it? You wouldn't even have a scar."

"There wasn't time. I was behind schedule and needed to get a bird in the oven. Don't be too hard on yourself. That's what I'm here for."

It only takes a few minutes to re-organize the equipment. I push the service cart toward the elevator doors. Before they open, I hear 3 beeps.

"Valet! Where are you? My handler and her crew will be here in 25 minutes, and I'm still wearing toenail polish from this morning!"

"I apologize for the delay, Young Lady Telladyne. We will be there shortly."

"What do you mean, 'we?' Don't tell me that simpleton with the braids is still following you around. Whatev, I don't care. Just be here in two minutes or both of you will be out of a job!"

Kallista and Mariposa are meeting to finalize Kallista's upcoming LifeCast. This is my last chance to influence it.

Aleks will meet with her handler soon, too, which means she'll be out of her RejuviPod. The information Marena gave me is too sensitive to leave on a NeuroChat message. When I'm finished with Kallista, I'll go to the Yukita Teitaku in person.

The service elevator doors open to a wide hallway with dark blue marble floors. Strings of illuminated diamonds hang from the walls and ceiling like glittering cobwebs.

Loud bop-woo-pop floods into the hallway as the doors to Kallista's pod chamber suite open. Numerous NeuroCasts play on the walls. Clothes and jewelry lie scattered across the floor. The glimmer of a single diamond earring catches my eye. It's probably five carats, small enough to be swept up by the automatic vacuuming system.

Kallista bursts into view mid-conversation.

"Last time he gave me a pen, I wound up naked in the fountain of some Southland Noble. I had to wait in the bushes while my Valet came with a hideous outfit he picked out... Jiffers didn't know either, said he woke up at a baby farm. He almost ordered a kid! Can you believe?"

As she passes, Kallista docks a pen and throws it behind her. Crtr catches the pen without taking a step. Kallista realizes we're here and turns to us.

"Set up my color change over there. What are you here for?"

"I'm here to tidy up, Young Lady Tella—" Crtr says.

"Fin-fin, just do it!"

I push the service cart to the sofa Kallista indicated. A floor-to-ceiling NeuroCast of "Sirens of Nouveau Monaco" plays across a dark blue velvet curtain. The curtain covers a glass wall with a stellar view of the Highland, but Kallista never opens it.

A round, mirrored table sits in front of the sofa. I root through the table's hidden drawers and replace the more powerful drugs with innocuous counterfeits or lower doses. Left to her own devices, Kallista would be dead by now.

Kallista flops onto the sofa and presses her sneaker into my face. She continues her NeuroChat without acknowledging me. I remove her shoe, and she drops her foot into the still-filling footbath.

"Ow!" Kallista shouts and kicks me in the shoulder with her wet foot.

"I apologize, Young Lady Telladyne. Is the water too hot?"

"No, too cold!"

"I apologize once again, Young Lady Telladyne. Please allow me to remove your current nail polish while the bath warms to your preferred 103.6 degrees Fahrenheit."

Kallista rolls her eyes. I hold her tiny foot in my hand and wipe away the ombre coral polish on her nails. When I'm finished, I present a palette of nail polish options to her.

"Give me the China Seafoam with a gold base."

"Very good. Would you like a particular design as well?"

"I *would*, but there's no time for that now because you disappeared after the siloball match! Where were you?"

Either she didn't see the footage of Aleks being snatched away from me in the lowland or she wants me to bring it up so she can scream at me. While I consider my answer, I rub pale purple granules of salt over Kallista's leg and foot with smooth, circular motions. She's preferred the same lavender lime menthol exfoliate scrub since the age of 12.

"Valet, do we need to get your hearing checked? I asked you a question!"

"I apologize, Young Lady Telladyne. There was a fatal emergency that required me to escort the Idol Nominee Aleksaria Yukita from the premises."

"You do realize you work for me and not her, right? I saw you two on the beach. Would you rather work for the Yukita family? Is that what you want?"

"Of course not Young Lady Telladyne. I do not wish to work for anyone other than the Telladyne family. Our interaction was purely transactional. I negotiated Idol Nominee Yukita's cooperation to win the siloball match for you."

"And what did she get in return?"

"Her Valet temporarily forgot his place. She needed me to remind him on her behalf."

"Ha! I didn't think Yukita had it in her. I've never liked her more... I've never liked her at all actually. She spent every ceremony rehearsal sulking and crying to her Valet. It was so annoying. I suppose some people simply can't handle the pressure of Idol nomination."

Aleks must have been desperate to abdicate her nomination. Her parents surely ignored her pleas, so she confided in Holt.

3 Beeps. Crtr.

"Where's this notebook go?"

"Use the map I sent you."

"I did, but it's split 50-50 between a shelf beside Kallista's drafting table and a stand next to her pod-side chair."

"What's it look like?"

Crtr sends me the image of a large, black, leather-bound notebook. He thumbs through the pages, which are covered in sketches of various outfits on models of Kallista. Unlike most Nobles, Kallista designs all of her own clothes.

"You'll find lots of those. Put them on the shelf with any others like it. If there's no ID tag on the spine, add one."

"She didn't tell you what she's doing for her LifeCast, did she?" Kallista asks.

"Who?"

"Yukita! Who do you think I'm talking about?"

"No, she did not reveal any details about her LifeCast. Speaking of which, how are your LifeCast plans coming along? Surely your handler has something in mind at this point."

"Everything Mariposa suggests has been done before. There isn't an original synapse in her tiny brain. I can't fight off muggers like Vox, and I'm not about to fly across The City in a hot air balloon like Ambrosia."

"What about Kassian, he must have some thoughts on the matter."

"He locked himself in his wing the second we returned from the ceremony. He won't even answer my NeuroChats. Said he's got something big in store that will 'ensure a favorable outcome in the Idol race.' Tell me, Valet. What do your people like? At this point I'm willing to take suggestions from anyone."

This is my chance. Marena said the most successful LifeCasts play to the nominee's strengths and involve the lowland in a charitable fashion... fashion! That's a start.

"You do have a talent for clothing design," I say.

"I can't sit and design clothes for 12 hours. That sounds profoundly boring to watch."

"Well, you could—"

"Wait, shut up, Valet! I could do a fashion show! I could get all of the hottest models in the Highland to walk for me. It would be epic! Those lowland dummies couldn't peel themselves away from all that beauty!"

I start on the seafoam top coat and consider Kallista's LifeCast idea.

A fashion show might get a few views, but no one would stay tuned for 12 hours. Her LifeCast needs a narrative, something that draws viewers in and keeps them.

I might have something, but I need to make Kallista think it's her idea.

"Young Lady Telladyne, lowlanders like stories more than anything, stories with characters that they can see transform over time. Your fashion show idea is brilliant, but the lowlanders won't understand its visual story. All they know is ugliness, perhaps you can show them how to transform their ugliness into beauty?"

"You mean like a makeover?"

"A marvelous suggestion! The closest things lowlanders have to your beautiful designs are knock-off NApps. They would tune-in in droves to see how actual outfits look on people like themselves."

"How many lowlanders would I have to makeover?"

"Ten is a nice round number. Perhaps they could be selected from your top ten potential sponsor companies. You could do short profiles on them, design entire new wardrobes for them, get their hair and makeup done. All of it! The lowlanders would love it, and they would love you for doing it."

"Hmm... you over there! What do you think of this idea?" Kallista shouts. "It's for my LifeCast! I take a bunch of tragic lowlanders, put new stunning outfits on them, and give them full makeovers so they're less ugly. Would you watch that?"

"Just say 'yes,' Crtr. Say 'yes' emphatically."

"Yes, Young Lady Telladyne," Crtr agrees. "That sounds great! I can't think of a single lowlander who wouldn't want to watch that!"

"Thanks."

"Then it's settled!" Kallista says. "Are my toes done yet?"

"They are, Young Lady Kallista. What do you think?"

"I think they'd look better with a design. Now get out. Mariposa will be here any second."

I pack up the cart and meet Crtr at the door. He turns to bid Kallista good-bye, but she leaves our sight without a word.

"Do you really think people in the lowland will watch Kallista's LifeCast?" I ask Crtr on our way back to the elevator.

"Yeah. People love a good makeover show, especially if it's about lowlanders for once. Can Kallista really fake interest in the lowland for 12 hours straight?"

"I hope so."

We meet Master Telladyne at his closet, where he stands naked before a bank of mirrors. Master Telladyne has used countless fitness training NApps to sculpt his body into a study in long, lean, muscular strength. Regular small surgical procedures mean there isn't a single wrinkle or sag on his skin.

While Master Telladyne continues his meeting, I explain Highland men's fashion rules to Crtr via NeuroChat. During the lesson, we select a solid dark blue, two-button suit with diamond thread stitching; diamond cufflinks with a large T emblazoned on them; and a pair of dark blue loafers with diamond tassels.

I send NeuroTexts to Master Telladyne so he raises his legs, holds out his arms, and lowers them back down as needed. With

Crtr's help, it only takes a moment to dress Master Telladyne. We finish with a spritz of cologne that Master Telladyne walks through on his way to his styling chair.

I wrap a cape around Master Telladyne's neck and trim his hair with a straight razor and comb. Every flick of my wrist sends another tuft of hair to the floor.

3 Beeps. Crtr.

"Why don't you use scissors?"

"My Mentor Valet, Holt, taught me this technique. If you use only a straight razor and comb, you don't have to fumble with a bunch of different instruments."

After the trim, I shape Master Telladyne's eyebrows, give him a shave, blow-dry and style his hair, and apply his makeup. With his morning beauty regimen complete, Master Telladyne wanders off into the manor without a word.

Crtr and I return to the maintenance room where we're met by a microdrone. The drone hovers in mid-air with a small pink envelope clutched in its tiny claws. The envelope reads "Bear" in crooked, black script.

Whoever wrote this didn't trust the envelope's contents to the NeuroNet. Few people in The City can write by hand, but these letters are especially crooked. The author was afraid to look at the paper while he or she wrote.

Before I open the envelope, I turn off my gem, so there's no visual record of the note's text.

Friend saw reels. Wants to meet. IDOL.
Bring A friend. 12pm. Destroy note.
40.7500718999999
-73.9922025999998

It's about the reels. Must be from Pach. 12pm? That's in 22 minutes!

With everything that's happened I forgot all about the reels Aleks and I found. "Bring a friend," with a capital A; he's talking about Aleks. I try her again, but there's still no response. Even if I could reach her, she couldn't get out of working on her LifeCast with Balliat.

Pach had to write "Idol." I probably would have ignored the note if not for that one word. He knows I'll do anything to keep Aleks from becoming the next Idol. I search the note's coordinates.

Great, they fall right in the middle of an enormous clave. I've been all over The City, but have avoided claves at all costs. No curiosity warrants that kind of risk.

"What's it say?" Crtr asks.

I was so deep in thought I forgot Crtr was beside me.

"Nothing. Don't worry about it. I have to go."

"You're leaving again? Where? Can I come?"

"No, stay here and..."

Pach did say that it's dangerous and to bring a friend. Crtr hasn't had any formal Noble Valet combat training, but I know he's strong.

"All right, you can come, but you have to follow my orders explicitly. Understand?"

"Yes, understand-ed."

"I'm serious. This place is deadly. If you forget where you are or lose focus for even a second, we could both be killed."

"I promise to follow your orders, Mentor Valet Bear."

"Good. And starting now, drop the 'Mentor Valet.' When we aren't around Nobles, call me 'Bear.'"

13

I change into my boilersuit and the coat I bought from Rork. Crtr changes into Aleks' boilersuit. It busts at the seams and hangs long over his hands and feet. He looks so ridiculous we can't help but laugh.

I request a stand-in Valet under the guise that Crtr and I need to run an errand for Master Telladyne. Someone should arrive soon to manage the house in my absence.

The BT-27's doors slide back as we approach. Crtr's excitement is palpable. He flops into the luxurious back seat, while I take my position up front.

As we pull out of the garage, I see Mariposa Monarch and her team emerge from a luxury cruiser at the Telladyne Manor main entrance. I hope she listens to Kallista's LifeCast idea and that Kallista hasn't already forgotten what we discussed.

I try Aleks again. No answer.

We pull into the lowland port. I exit the vehicle to perform my standard maintenance checks. Crtr gets out and follows me around the BT-27.

"You haven't told me where we're going yet," Crtr says. "What makes it so dangerous?"

"We're going to a clave."

"Seriously? You realize we'll be driving into the middle of an Unassigned turf war, right?"

"I do, but I have my reasons. Still want to come?"

"They must be good reasons. I'm in."

We get back into the BT-27. The lowland port doors open and we reach the highway in seconds.

"It's so light!" Crtr shouts over NeuroChat. *"I feel like we're flying!"*

He slaps the wall between us and begs me to go faster. I've always wondered how fast the BT-27 can go, but if I punch the accelerator we might blow past our exit, and there's no time to turn around.

"There you go, now we're moving!"

I speed up, but not for Crtr. All traffic accelerates on clave borders. No one wants to risk getting hit by stray fire.

A brilliant orange blast in the distance grabs Crtr and my attention. The explosion blossoms across the horizon and illuminates the pitch-black clave. A massive central palace stands surrounded by small, boxy buildings. Empty, ashen roads stretch throughout the compound. I blink, and the area is once again cloaked in darkness.

Dozens of construction signs come into view as we approach our exit. The signs say the exit is closed and redirect us to distant detours. There's no way improvements are being made to a random clave exit. The signs are meant to keep people out.

I speed ahead. We quickly approach wooden barricades, spike strips, and bright orange signs, but I'm not worried. The BT-27 can withstand point blank gunfire, and the tires are puncture proof.

"Crtr, brace for impact!"

I expect to hear splintered wood, twisted metal, and deep scrapes along the BT-27's body, but don't. We pass straight through without a scratch. The signs were holograms. There must be regular traffic on this exit.

I turn off the BT-27's bright headlamps and activate the prismatic exterior tiles.

Collapsed brick buildings, charred LaborLiner frames, and lakes of broken glass crowd our view. The road has degraded into gravel that crackles beneath our tires. Even though the clave appears desolate, there's a subtle motion to everything.

Silhouettes run through shadows, empty windowpanes flicker, and rusted doors open and shut on their own. The BT-27 runs in near-total silence, and with the camouflage tiles it's invisible to anyone who might glance our way. Even so, I feel a strong suspicion that we're being watched.

I look in the rearview camera. Three powercycles approach from behind. They don't have weapons raised, but I duck into a nearby alley to be safe. The powercycles drive right past.

"This place is super creepy."

Crtr was all laughs on the way here, but he left that on the highway. There's a quiet unpredictability about this place that demands vigilance.

We're still about a quarter-mile from Pach's coordinates, so I pull back onto the road. Up ahead, a lowland trash hauler dumps its payload at the side of the road. Among the trash, there are entire powercycle frames, shoulder-mountable rockets, and scores of other weapons. Why would The City dump such an arsenal in a clave of all places?

Between the powercycles and truckload of weapons, the roads don't feel safe anymore. I park between two crumbling buildings.

"What are you doing?"

"We'll go the rest of the way on foot. Keep an eye out for anything strange."

We creep through the darkness. I move with my hands against a brick wall to feel for incoming movement.

"Do you at least have a knife or something?" Crtr asks.

"Why would I need a knife?"

"For protection. You saw that explosion from the highway."

"What's a knife going to do against a bomb?"

I peer around a corner and see the same derelict palace we saw from the highway. Once mighty columns lay crumbled over a wide staircase, fire damage creeps up the exterior walls, and the domed roof has collapsed.

"Bear!" Crtr sends, and pulls my arm.

"What?"

To my left, a small girl glares at us. Her irises glow like two backlit sapphire rings. She wears a heavy leather apron and welding goggles on her forehead. Her pale, soot-covered face is framed by a bushel of long, stringy hair with bolts, nuts, and screws tied into the strands.

The girl's relatively small stature and round cheeks make her seem harmless; but perhaps that's her greatest weapon.

"You're Bear, right?" She asks.

"Yeah, and this is Crtr. Who are you?"

"Loomi, that's L, double-O, M, I. Take these."

Loomi pulls a pair of sticks from her apron, lights the ends, and throws them to us.

"Cool scar," she says to Crtr. "We've had eyes on you since the exit. The only reason you're still breathing is cuz you're with me. I know you Noble Valets think you're pretty deadly, but if you try anything clever your story'll be over before it started. Got it?"

"We wouldn't—"

"Got it?"

"Got it," we say in unison.

"Follow me, and stay close."

Loomi takes us toward the palace, around a courtyard of dead grass with two powercycles lain in the middle. I have no doubt those bait powercycles are surrounded by landmines.

Even with our torches, Crtr and I trip over mounds of rubble inside the palace. Loomi moves like a cat through the dark.

"Are we almost there?" I ask.

Loomi doesn't answer. We slide along a wall past a gigantic hole in the floor. Past the hole, Loomi flings open a pair of rusted double doors. Tile backsplashes, steel tables, hooks in the ceiling; this must have been a commercial kitchen.

Loomi walks to a bright red porcelain cake tray that looks totally out of place.

"What's under there?" I ask.

"Your tickets to the True Born Collective, where all of your questions about that reel will be answered."

Loomi opens the cake tray to reveal two RXPens.

"What are they?" Crtr asks.

"A little of this, a little of that. Don't worry. It won't kill you."

"Are you joking?" I respond. "We've followed you this far, but I draw the line at blindly docking some mystery drug!"

"Do whatever you want, but I can't take you any further unless you dock these pens. The choice is yours. Return to your lives of mindless servitude or come with me and learn the truth about the Idol. I'll leave you to it."

Loomi strides out the double doors.

Crtr looks to me for guidance. I came to find out what was on those reels and can't go back to the Highland before I do.

I pick up a pen and Crtr does the same.

"You don't have to do this. I won't think any less of you for going back."

"How could I leave now? I have to see the True Born Collective, whatever that is."

We dock our pens. I feel the drugs spread quick through my blood stream. My pulse and breath slow. The corners of my mouth creep into a smile.

Every muscle in my body relaxes as the weight of all life's concerns float away. Aleks's Idol Nomination, her LifeCast, Kallista's LifeCast, the clave, and the drugs we just docked, none of it bothers me. A few carefree chuckles escape my mouth.

I lean back on a cool metal tabletop. Crtr stands with a slack jaw and blank stare. He sees something, I don't know if it's a projection, a hallucination, or what, but he's captivated.

My palms slide back until I lie flat on the table with my arms outstretched. My eyelids flutter. Everything in the dark room is easier to see, as if someone's turned up the lights. I hear a trickle of water through a crack in the wall, the crumble of plaster, the rattle of broken tile on the floor, and the clang of old metal pans that sway into each other.

My eyes close. The room's ambient soundtrack picks up more elements: Shattered glass in the distance, an animal that scurries through the wall, wind that howls through broken window panes overhead. It all sounds new and exciting. I want to hear everything.

A dirty, yet sweet smell floats past. I can't place it. Mildew? The scent of sawdust follows shortly after and is joined by something else... charcoal. Oddly, I want to shovel all those smells into my mouth, feel them between my teeth, and bite down.

My eyes pop back open. Orange patches of rust on the stove, intricate spider webs spun across the ceiling, and colonies of black mold blossom before me like exotic flowers. They all pulse in time with my heartbeat.

My muscles, skin, and bones feel warm and relaxed. I move my hand before my face. Each movement of my fingers sends a rush of excitement through me. This is my hand, and I have another. My body is mine. It's under my control. I slide from the table onto the floor.

I hear 3 beeps. Where's that coming from?

I move to my hands and knees. The same 3 beeps sound, but this time a short message appears in my field of vision: "Noble Valet Council for Noble Valet Bear." I look at the message for a long time, come to my senses, and accept the inbound NeuroProjection Call.

A massive, black marble room overtakes my vision. On elevated platforms before me, 12 Noble Valet Council members stand behind individual pulpits. Each council member wears a unique mask to hide his or her identity.

Single spotlights illuminate each council member. A council member in a blue kabuki mask with angry eyes speaks first.

"Noble Valet Bear, thank you for joining us. We have called this hearing to address complaints that you have been unavailable to your assigned Noble family as of late."

Another council member, in a dark wood carved mask painted with white dots and accent lines, chimes in.

"We all understand that the demands on a Noble Valet whose master is an Idol Nominee are great. But this is no excuse to ignore your responsibilities..."

As the wooden mask drones on, the projection fades and I catch a glimpse of Crtr in the hall. He runs past the kitchen door in an awkward, uncontrolled sprint. I crawl forward to see him better.

"Tell us," says a polished silver mask with bulbous features. *"Where were you following the siloball match this evening?"*

I stare at the silver-masked council member. The eyes of his mask burn in a kaleidoscope of reds, oranges, and yellows.

"Fa-fa-fa-follow... ing... the... syyyy-loooow... ba-aaall... ball match... ball match!" I stammer out.

The syllables feels unfamiliar, but satisfying to say. Each word is easier to say than the last. It's as if I'm re-discovering how to speak.

"Yes, where did you go following the siloball match?" The silver mask repeats with obvious frustration.

"I was making sure Aleks... the Idol Nom-i-nee Aleks-aria Yu-ki-ta... was safe. She was in danger..."

"We understand that Idol Nominee Yukita was in danger, Noble Valet Bear," interjects a long purple mask with orange fringe around its edges. *"Our primary concern is the amount of time that you were gone and the resulting necessary evacuation by the Noble Guard."*

Crtr trips to the floor. He stands up and runs back down the hall at full speed. His boilersuit is unzipped and pulled down to his waist. One of his braids hangs unraveled. As Crtr careens toward me, I notice that his auburn eyes glow bright the same way Loomi's did.

"Crtr, your eyes! They're glowing!"

Did I say that to Crtr or the council? I never should have accepted a NeuroProjection Call from the Noble Valet Council, but if I hadn't answered they would have judged me guilty by default.

"Noble Valet Bear!" shouts a bright pink mask with upside-down V-shaped eyes that glow purple. *"What does your Valet Apprentice*

have to do with this hearing? You clearly do not understand the gravity of your situation! We are here to determine your commitment to your work as a Noble Valet, and frankly, you are not doing a very good job of convincing us of that commitment!"

I pull myself up the kitchen doorway to a standing position. Once I'm upright, I lean against the wall and refocus on the trial. The trial. If they understood a fraction of what I was dealing with they wouldn't just find me innocent, they'd probably give me a promotion. None of them have ever cared about anyone the way I care about Aleks.

"Noble Valet Bear," says a grey bearded mask with ringlets of more grey hair down its sides. *"We are willing to concede that your instincts were correct in protecting the Idol Nominee, Aleksaria Yukita. We primarily take umbrage with your general lack of availability to your assigned family, the Telladynes."*

"Oh, come on," I spit back. *"I don't take any more break time than the allotted ten hours per week. Kallista's just mad I wasn't there to paint her toenails this morning."*

"Noble Valet Bear, you will watch your tone and maintain formality when speaking with the Noble Valet Council!" shouts a dark red mask with thick black eyebrows and golden horns. *"Greater Noble Valets than you have been Unassigned for less than your transgressions!"*

"Enough!" shouts a teal mask with delicate swirls of silver lines. *"Noble Valet Bear, we simply wish to know where you spend your time away from the Telladyne family. It is extremely rare for Valets to take the entirety of their break time, especially when they have a Noble Valet Apprentice under their tutelage."*

"Why do you care about my break time? That's none of your business! Wait a second. Is this about what happened in the green room? Look, Holt, that was for your own good, you have to understand that—"

I instantly regret the words that got away from me. Even though the identities of the council members are often obvious from their self-styled masks, it's considered highly disrespectful to address them by name.

"No this is not about what happened between you and Noble Valet Holt in the green room!" The teal mask shouts. *"The Noble Valet Council works at the pleasure of the Highland. It is standard procedure to present a full audit of a Noble Valet's free time to a Noble family when their Valet's dedication is called into question!"*

"My free time?"

"What about your free time?" Crtr asks.

"Sorry, that was meant for someone else. I'm on trial right now, can you believe it?"

"What for?"

"Doesn't matter."

"Noble Valet Bear, you have served the Highland well in your previous nine years of service," The teal mask says. *"You have never been brought up on any kind of charges to date. We are willing to put this entire nasty business behind us if you simply submit records of your free time to the council."*

"Why would I record my free time? That's my time, it isn't meant for anyone else."

"Noble Valet Bear," adds the pink mask with the upside-down V eyes. *"We should not have to tell you that your Neurogem records all of your actions and archives them each day. Simply access the recordings from your time off and send them to us. It should not take more than a few seconds."*

"But I don't save those recordings. I delete them when I get back to work."

"You what?" The teal mask shouts.

All of the council members turn and grumble to each other.

"Come here," Crtr says. "I found some pigeons! They're amazing!"

I follow Crtr on shaky steps to a large broken window. The window overlooks a bombed-out courtyard. It looks like the kind of place where people used to eat lunch and take VaporLite breaks.

"Shoot, they're gone," Crtr says. "But they were just here. See? Still warm!"

Crtr sticks his finger in a fresh dollop of white pigeon poop. We both laugh at the gross, unnecessary verification.

We hear a few synthesizer notes emanate from the kitchen. The notes are followed by more instruments and melodic hums. We head back to hear the music better.

"Are you still on trial?" Crtr asks.

"Oh, right, I forgot."

"Noble Valet Bear, this hearing is over!" Shouts a zebra-striped mask with a black mane and bright blue eyes that overflow with smoke. *"Your insincerity and lack of remorse for your actions, along with your general uncooperativeness should make our decision an easy one. We shall be in touch with our verdict shortly. Do you have else anything to say on your own behalf?"*

We reenter the kitchen. The entrancing music envelops us. Soft vocals seamlessly combine with complex, experimental electronic arrangements. I've never heard anything so beautiful.

Crtr and I lie down on the ground to watch colorful shapes streak across the ceiling in time with the music. The luminescent visuals trigger new scents that fill my nostrils. Dark yellow swirls smell of pine, green and white checkerboard patterns emit the scent of fresh-baked cookies, and purple raindrops reek of roofing tar.

"Noble Valet Bear! Have you anything to add before we adjourn?" The zebra mask shouts.

I take a deep breath.

"Please, go easy on me," I say. "I am small. Everything seems so new, and I'm still trying to figure out how this all works... I've made mistakes, and I know that I will make more. But please be patient... I have so much... potential..."

The music swells. New combinations of visuals and aromas merge with the general warmth that courses through my body. From the moment I docked that pen, I've felt like nothing can hurt me. The anxieties and concerns that dictate so much of my life dematerialized and left me to exist as my truest self.

My eyelids flutter and feel heavy. I look over to Crtr. He's passed out. Each blink lingers a bit longer until my eyes stay closed.

14

Drills, hammers, and metal-cutting blades fill my ears. The ground vibrates beneath me. My head feels like a washing unit full of rocks. I press my palms against the cool dirt floor and rise to my feet.

With a few blinks my vision comes back into focus. Huddled workers, fixated on long workbenches, surround me. They wear tattered clothes and have the strong scent of Unassigned. Their eyes all glow like Loomi's did.

A surge of pain rockets up my neck and into my head. I drop back to the ground.

"Bear!" I hear over the room's cacophonous din. "Bear!"

Crtr! I try to access my NeuroTracker, but it's unavailable. Nothing's available for that matter; NeuroText, NeuroClock, even NeuroWeather they're all gone. Wherever we are, Neurogems don't work here. How is that possible?

I find my way to Crtr. He sways back and forth in an unsteady fighting stance.

"Crtr!" I shout.

He spins to face me. His still-glowing eyes are wide and shaky with intense panic.

"What's happening?" he asks. "My gem isn't working!"

"Neither is mine..." A wave of pain envelops the side of my head. I lose my balance for a second but remain upright. "We need to stay calm and assess our surroundings. Panic only leads to mistakes."

I set my hands on an empty section of workbench nearby. No one looks up. They couldn't care less about me.

I climb onto the table for a better view. The workbenches continue indefinitely within the colossal expanse. Scavenged antique chandeliers and street lamps paint the massive space in dim orange and yellow light.

Something flickers in my periphery. Two powercycles approach through the mass of Unassigned. I recognize one of the riders as Loomi. She rides beside a tall woman with long dreadlocks and dark skin.

I startle when a sharp glass explosion bursts. The Unassigned below me laugh and clap each other on the back. An empty UteroCube between them lies shattered on the table. All the other tables have UteroCubes on them too.

I climb down.

"You find anything?" Crtr asks. "How do we get our gems back online?"

Crtr's never been without NeuroNet access before. He must be terrified. To make matters worse, he's probably in the same pain as me, and he can't look in any direction without seeing unpredictable Unassigned.

"Crtr, relax. Our gems don't work here, but you'll live. Understand? You're going to be fine—"

Another wave of searing pain moves through my left ear and spreads across my skull. I clutch my head and fall to my knees. The powercycles stop before us, and the riders dismount.

Loomi's companion stands about a foot taller than her and has the fit, defined musculature of a Noble. The woman's skin is a darker shade of brown than mine but with pale beige patches all over her arms, neck, and face. I've never seen a skin treatment like this, but I'm sure the Highland would love it.

I start to speak, but Crtr lunges forward and cuts me off.

"Where are we? Why don't our gems work?"

"We're too far underground," Loomi says. "All the dirt and concrete overhead blocks the NeuroNet signal. Come with us."

Loomi pats the seat of her powercycle, and Crtr mounts it without question. His desperation to regain NeuroNet access has made him eager to comply. I'm not at all desperate—just furious at the lack of explanations we've received.

"You coming?" Loomi asks.

"No," I say from my kneeling position on the ground.

"Excuse me?"

"We proved our trust in you by docking those pens, but now our gems don't work, and we still haven't heard anything new about the reel! What's on it? Where are we? Who's this? All you've given me is questions! I'm not taking another step until I get some answers."

Loomi charges at me.

"You're lucky we've taken you this far! You want to stay here, fine! Good luck finding your way out. You'll need it! Especially once people start recognizing you."

"Loomi, that's enough!" The muscular woman snaps. "Bear is right, we have insisted upon a disproportionate amount of blind faith. Allow me to introduce myself. My name is Locke."

"That's Locke with an E," Loomi interjects.

"You could say that Loomi and I are the custodians of this place. We don't really believe in complex hierarchies or chains of command, but we are, more or less, responsible for ensuring that the vision of our collective remains clear. What else would you like to know?"

"How about telling us what was in those pens," Crtr says. "My head's killing me."

"Oh, Loomi, you didn't give them the recovery pens?"

"Must have slipped my mind."

"Here," Locke reaches into a leather satchel at her side and removes two pens. "Dock these, you'll feel better soon."

We dock the pens. My vision sharpens and the violent riot inside my brain ceases.

"Just tell us what's on the reel and show us the way out," I say.

"A fair request. Come, let us take you to our lab. All your remaining questions will be answered there."

I sit on the cycle behind Locke. It whirs to life and we ride past more busy workbenches.

"Where are we?" I shout to Locke.

"How rude of me!" Locke shouts back. "Welcome to the True Born Collective! A sanctuary for those who understand that science is the only true path toward revolution!"

"As opposed to what?" I ask.

"Violence! The Highland throws away more weapons every day than we could produce in a year! Even with the excess artillery they offload in claves, we could never mount a true uprising against them."

"I saw one of those dumps! Why would they risk arming people who hate them?"

"The Nobles don't see it as a risk! They see it as population control! Those dumps fuel clave civil wars all over The City! Fortunately, we've been able to use their discarded weaponry for a higher purpose!"

"How so?"

"Powercycles! We use them as a sort of entrance exam. Anyone who can reactivate and take control of a decommissioned powercycle proves their mechanical aptitude. Releasing the reactivated cycle to us proves their vision."

My coat gets yanked from behind, and I fall backward off the powercycle. As I catch my breath, I see someone with mounds of familiar bright orange hair. He stomps over to Locke, who must have stopped when she felt me leave my seat.

"You can't bring Nobles down here! What are you thinking?" Rork shouts.

"He isn't a Noble," Locke replies. "He merely works for them."

"Even worse, he's their servant! He can't be trusted!"

"You didn't mind me so much when I bought your coat for a thousand times its value," I say.

"It's one thing to overcharge you for a coat and another to endanger me and my family by bringing you to our home!"

"Rork, I wouldn't bring him here if it wasn't safe for all of us. Come along, Bear."

Locke reactivates her powercycle and stares Rork down. I climb back on. Rork doesn't follow, but as we speed away, I hear murmurs and feel hundreds of eyes on me.

We enter a long, dark tunnel and re-emerge in another massive space. Locke and Loomi park their powercycles and we proceed on foot.

Huge silver tanks stand throughout the room. A network of hoses carries red liquid to various locations. There are conveyer belts everywhere. We pass a large machine that drops round, bright red capsules into clear tubes. I know those capsules.

"To answer your question, Crtr," Locke says. "This is what was in those pens. ReBorn, The True Born Collective's greatest export. We also mixed in a bit of Luminex so you could see better down here."

They don't just use ReBorn as a sedative to transport people, the True Born Collective manufactures it. There must be thousands of workers making this stuff around the clock. Not to mention scores of True Borns, like Rork, who sell it in the lowland.

"How do you mask ReBorn's chemical make-up?" I ask. "I've never been able to get an accurate analysis with my RXSleeve."

"We mix thousands of chemical red herrings into the solution to obscure its active ingredients."

"So Telladyne Industries can't create a knock-off?" I ask.

"That, and to hide ReBorn's true effects," Locke says with a smirk.

"Locke!" Loomi snaps. "What are you doing?"

"Relax. ReBorn's already swept The City. Even if I told him what ReBorn actually does there's nothing he could do to stop it."

"If there's no stopping your ReBorn plan, tell me what it does. I need to know what to expect."

"Don't worry, you'll find out soon enough," Locke says.

We follow Locke and Loomi up a rusted escalator. At the top of the escalator, a large archway opens to a narrow, but extremely deep lab.

The lab's split down the middle. On one side, caged animals sit beside beakers, burners, centrifuges, and other scientific equipment. The other side is filled with hand tools and stray electronics.

"Is that an actual rabbit?" Crtr asks.

"It is! How do you know rabbits?" Locke asks.

"I studied all kinds of animals from some old veterinary training mods I found. Rabbits were one of my favorites, but I've never seen one in person, not even in the High..." Crtr remembers where we are and stops himself.

"Come then, let's take a closer look. Loomi, go ahead and get started. We'll be over in a moment. I call him Rosco..." Locke says as she leads Crtr off to the cages.

I follow Loomi to a cramped edge of the lab where instruments and broken machines hang from the ceiling and walls. Loomi digs through a low cabinet. My Noble Valet training already has me re-organizing the lab in my head. I could have it working at optimal efficiency in a few days.

"So, Locke does the chemistry and you handle the tech, is that right?"

"More or less. There's some overlap with stuff like gem science, which is why we share a lab."

"Gem science? I thought you didn't get the NeuroNet down here."

"We use external gems on a closed network. Here, hold this," Loomi says, and hands me a clumsy contraption with two metal arms, a glass lens, and an ancient-looking motor that's jerry-rigged with a power coil.

"External gems have been out of production for generations. Do you make them here?"

"No, we harvest them from paupers' graves all over The City."

"You take them off dead bodies?"

"Yeah, it only takes about 30 seconds to wipe and reset a corpse gem, then they're good as new. That's actually where we get most of our clothes too. Here we go, look familiar?"

Loomi pulls out the reel I gave to Pach.

"Locke, Crtr, get over here!" Loomi shouts.

Crtr and Locke join us. Loomi loads the reel into her makeshift player and flips it on. Scratchy footage of a happy group of people waving and smiling appears on the wall.

Wherever the video was shot is lush green, with tall trees, and wood cabins. The video cuts to some kind of competition where a line of people step into sacks and bounce in a race toward the camera. As the winner comes close, I read the words "Monarch Family Reunion '75," on the man's shirt.

15

The video continues with scenes of people throwing a brown, oblong ball, lighting crude fireworks, and running on a sandy beachfront. I can't imagine any Noble family engaging in such relaxed, joyous activity together, let alone the Monarchs.

The video goes black. All I hear is the repetitive snap of film as it flicks over itself on the projector's receiver spool.

"Did people really used to do stuff like that?" Crtr asks.

"Apparently," Locke says. "It's amazing how differently people thought about family in those days. If that was my family, I'd hold onto those memories for as long as I could."

"Maybe you would," I say. "But Nobles aren't exactly sentimental. Why would the Monarchs go to such lengths to preserve that film?"

"My thoughts exactly," Loomi says. "I watched that reel over and over again, backward and forwards, in half-time and double-time, and didn't find a thing. Then I put the film under a micron microscope, and that's when I found it."

"What?" Crtr and I say in unison.

"1s and 0s, hundreds of billions, no, hundreds of trillions of them, in a specific order. It was binary! When I translated it into modern NApp code, I found this."

A beam of light fires from the ceiling that projects a new, crisper video on the wall. The video begins with a black screen and white letters that read, "Part 3: Rebuilding the Self."

I hear applause, and the screen fades to the empty stage of a large auditorium. A tall, thin man, with dark gray hair and severe, angular features walks out. He wears a long black lab coat, with an orange necktie. The name, "Dr. Vanguard Monarch" appears at the bottom of the screen. The applause peters out.

"Now comes the fun part!" Dr. Monarch says with a huge smile of electric white teeth. "This is where we can begin introducing new preferences to the subject. With newly-available Neurogem technology we can track whether or not the subject has a positive or negative reaction to a particular product. But that's just the beginning. Surely you remember this from the start of our experiment."

The video cuts to a bright room with tiled walls and no windows. A buxom girl with thick eyebrows and voluminous waves of black hair sits at a sterile metal table. I recognize her immediately; she's the first-ever Idol, Maya Sandivall.

She leans back in her chair with casual indifference. Dr. Monarch, in dark sunglasses, sits across from her at the same table. A small paper cup and glass bottle sit between them.

"Is that the drink I'm supposed to try for you?"

"It is. Let me know what you think."

Maya takes a sip and immediately spits out the milky yellow liquid.

"That's disgusting, what is it?"

"Pomelo Fizz. BevCo plans to release it later this month."

"Who would ever drink that? It tastes like grapefruit-flavored vomit... with bubbles!"

"Would you like another sip? Maybe it will grow on you."

"No, get that away from me! It's vile!"

"You're sure you don't want to try another sip, just a little one?"

"No! How dare you waste my valuable time like this!" Maya shouts, and kicks away her chair as she stands.

"I'm afraid you cannot leave," Dr. Monarch says.

"I can do whatever I want!"

Maya stomps toward the door, but two black-clad men in reflective facemasks stop her. She struggles and screams obscenities as the men force her back into the room. Maya stomps on one of the men's feet, and runs for the door. Before she makes it, the door slams shut.

"What is this? I am the Idol! I could have you all disappeared with a snap of my fingers! Let me out immediately!"

The black-clad men close back in on Maya. She punches one of them straight in the facemask, but the punch only hurts her hand. Maya is planted back into her seat across from Dr. Monarch.

She wriggles beneath the men's hands. Eventually, she breaks free and leaps over the table at Dr. Monarch.

The video freezes with Maya in mid-air. She has the rabid look of a crazed animal. Her eyes bulge, her hands are ready to claw, and her teeth are poised to tear Dr. Monarch's throat from his neck. The video cuts back to the auditorium where Dr. Monarch and the entire audience roar with laughter.

"Now let's get back to the experiment at hand," Dr. Monarch says.

The video returns to Maya, but she's in a different room. No, it's the same room, but instead of blinding white light, it's filled with a warm orange glow. Maya sits at the metal table. She looks different now, like a tattered, faded copy of herself.

Her silk dress is soaked through and clings to her emaciated body. Maya's thick waves of hair lie flat against her sunken cheeks. She hardly looks capable of lifting her head.

Dr. Monarch sits across from Maya. He looks exactly the same as he did in the last clip.

"How are you feeling, Idol?"

"OK," Maya says with a wet sniffle.

"Good. Are you thirsty?"

"Yes."

"Excellent, I have something for you. Here."

Dr. Monarch pours liquid from an unmarked bottle into a paper cup and slides it forward. Maya lifts the cup with a shaky hand and drinks from it. Her face twinges, but she says nothing.

"What do you think, Idol?" Dr. Monarch asks.

Maya stares down at the cup.

"Idol, what do you think of the drink you just enjoyed?"

"It's... I don't know."

"That little tang you tasted, that's tartness, refreshing tartness. Try it again."

Maya takes another sip. This time her face reacts positively.

"I like it," Maya says. "It's... refreshing. What is it?"

"That is Pomelo Fizz. Most people call it Pomm Fizz. You told me once that it's your favorite drink in the whole City. Go ahead, have more. I'll leave the bottle."

Maya swallows the rest of her cup, grabs the bottle, and finishes it off with a chain of gulps. A tiny burp escapes her lips. She covers her mouth in embarrassment but relaxes when Dr. Monarch chuckles.

"Very good, Idol."

The video cuts to Dr. Monarch onstage.

"Thanks to new Neurogem technology, I was able to track the subject's level of enjoyment in real-time as she tasted the Pomm Fizz. Our data indicated definitively that her initial reaction to the drink was negative. However, our training methods kept her from expressing that opinion and left her open to accepting a new one.

"At this stage, the subject has come to rely on me, her trusted confidant, to guide her decisions. What is truly amazing is that through subtle suggestion, and Neurogem assistance, her dopamine levels rose with each successive sip of Pomm Fizz. By the end of this experiment, further data indicated that Pomm Fizz truly became the subject's favorite drink!"

The auditorium explodes with a standing ovation, and the video fades to black.

"What happens next?" I ask.

"That's the end of the reel," Loomi says. "Do you have more reels?"

"Yes, three others. How long will it take you to decode them?"

"Not long, maybe a few hours."

"I always wondered why every Idol liked Pomm Fizz so much," Crtr says.

"They're monsters, inhuman monsters." I say. "Sure, the Idols are usually vapid Nobles, but they're still people! The Monarchs hallow out their personalities and stuff them with sound bites and slogans to shill products! How can they do that?"

"The Monarch family must make a fortune off the sponsorship of Pomelo Fizz alone," Locke responds. "Imagine how many points they earn from all the products they promote through the Idols."

"But why forcibly change their minds?" Crtr asks. "Can't they just tell her what to say and do? Can't the Idol just fake it?"

"No one works harder, or is more convincing, than a true believer," I say. "Wouldn't you agree, Locke?"

Locke responds with a glib smirk. She knows the True Born Collective's greatest resource is their belief in revolution; it's the reason why so many Unassigned pack ReBorn and research UteroCube sabotage for hours on end.

Several projections spring to life around us. The projections show Rork on a powercycle with more riders behind him. He's in the ReBorn manufacturing facility outside. Rork didn't let us go after all. He just needed time to assemble a mob.

"Loomi, take Bear and Crtr through the bug-out tunnel. Go!"

We chase Loomi through the lab where we exit through a wall of file cabinets. Two dormant powercycles wait for us within a dark, damp tunnel. Loomi pulls something from her hair and tinkers with one of the cycles.

"There's an abandoned mailbox in the courtyard of a lowland res-hall called Delightful Towers on 23rd and 6th. Drop the other reels there and I'll decode them."

The powercycle whirs to life.

"Don't stop, or it'll power down."

"Crtr, you drive," I say.

I know Crtr will test the powercycle's speed limits in a way that I won't, and his AeroPack experience means his reflexes are sharp.

"Follow the lights in this pattern: Orange, Green, Blue, Yellow, and repeat," Loomi says. "You won't be able to see far down the tunnels. Drive straight at each light when you see it."

"OGBY, got it," Crtr says. "What if I follow the wrong color?"

"Don't. You could starve before you find your way out of the tunnels. After the colored lights, you'll see the surface exit. You can't miss it."

We hear shouting from the lab, with occasional reactions from the mob.

"Is Locke OK?" Crtr asks.

"She's fine, but Rork should have pushed past her already... you have to go. Now!"

Crtr twists the powercycle's handle and we rocket down the dark tunnel. I hear the hum of other powercycles behind us. Rork was stalling while his gang circled around the lab.

Indiscriminate gunfire erupts behind us. Bullets ricochet around the tunnel, but the riders are too far to shoot clean. Even so, one lucky shot could kill either one of us.

I look back. All I see are quick flashes through the darkness.

Crtr accelerates into the first orange light. We drown on stale air from the long-disused tunnels. Crtr turns toward a white light up ahead, but quickly realizes his mistake and stays on course. This gives me an idea.

I remove my coat.

A stray shot grazes my ear. It stings like mad, but I ignore the pain.

The green light appears. Crtr attacks it. I hold out my coat and whip it over the light as we pass.

Crtr follows the rest of the colored lights. I no longer hear the riders behind us, which means my plan must have worked. The ground pitches to a steep incline, and we see the exit ahead.

I see the indigo mist first, followed soon after by ads painted on stratoscrapers. Our gems have reactivated.

We emerge from the tunnel ramp, and our momentum catapults us through the air. I don't realize where we've come out until we land on an elevated MagLev train track. Crtr keeps a steady line as we sail over the narrow platform with sheer drops on both sides.

I look back to see if a train is coming. There isn't one, but that could change in an instant.

The sheer drop off to our right turns into a rider platform. Thousands of lowlanders wait for the train with split stares. They don't even notice us.

Crtr steers up a maintenance ramp, pulls the brakes, and we skid to a stop. Smoke from the burnt powercycle wheels dissipates as we leap off the bike. Before I can think of our next move, ads on the platform pillars catch my attention.

"Tune in to Aleksaria Yukita's LifeCast, and you could win!"

The pillars play scenes of Aleks' Idol Nominee Ceremony performance, intercut with past dance performances and shots of her posed inside various Yukita Transit vehicles.

"A mansion in the Highland, unlimited transportation on all Yukita Transit lines, and 10,000 points a day for life! Tune in to Aleksaria Yukita's LifeCast tomorrow at 10am for your chance to live like a Noble!"

I NeuroChat Aleks, but get her away message again. Why won't she answer?

I can't wait to tell her what Marena said, there's too much at stake. My words have to be discreet, but meaningful.

"Aleks, It's Bear. Just wanted to say good luck during your LifeCast. Try not to be too boring!*"*

I hope she hears my emphasis on "too boring." It's the best I can do. With Aleks' LifeCast on the horizon, I won't be allowed within 1,000 feet of her.

"What should we do with the powercycle?"

I hear Crtr's question, but the pain in my ear distracts me. I reach up and feel blood on my fingertips. Two inches over and I'd be dead, shot straight through the skull.

"Leave it," I say. "If I never see another powercycle again it'll be too soon."

Crtr and I walk to the nearest lowland port and return to Telladyne Manor. The trip takes forever on foot, but it's our only option. As we cross the catwalk to my living quarters, I give Crtr instructions.

"The rest of the reels are stacked in my armoire next to a black duffel. Drop them where Loomi said. I need to see what's on those as soon as possib—"

"There he is, the man of the hour!" Kassian shouts from a chair beside my pod.

He leans back with his legs crossed. Kassian wears a plush, dark blue robe. His long, black hair is wet and combed back like he just got out of a shower.

"Master Kassian," I say. "What an unexpected surprise. How may I help you?"

"Noble Valet Bear, what are you wearing?"

"A lowland boilersuit, sir. We had to run an errand for your father and needed to blend in."

"Yes, yes, I'm sure, no matter! I'm here to thank you for the excellent job you did during the Idol Nomination Siloball Match! Your performance was truly remarkable."

"Thank you, sir. I was just doing my job."

"And a fine job you did! Granted, Kallista was rather upset that you couldn't join us on the podium to receive her trophy, but I understand that you were indisposed."

"I apologize sir, I would have loved to be there."

"I'm sure. And this must be your Valet-in-Training, Crtr, right?" Kassian asks. "Pay attention to what Bear says, he's very good at what he does."

"Yes sir," Crtr replies.

"Master Kassian, of course, you are welcome here any time and certainly do not need an excuse, but may I help you with something in particular?"

"There's no need for such formality, Valet! Call me Kassian. I've actually come to deliver a gift on behalf my family. Here."

Kassian hands me a small, dark blue box that he coaxes me to open with his eyes. I lift the box top to find an exact replica of my pocket watch, the one Kallista tossed into the mist.

"It is beautiful," I say. "Truly a remarkable recreation. How did you replicate my watch with such fine detail?"

"Oh, it wasn't terribly difficult," Kassian replies. "The hardest part was waiting for the damn thing to print! So many tiny parts."

"Thank you again, Mast... Kassian. It is lovely."

"It is my pleasure. In addition to the watch, my family has hired a stand-in Valet to handle the rest of your duties between now and the LifeCast tomorrow morning. Please, use this time to relax and regroup. You deserve it. Now I must run, have an excellent evening gentlemen."

"And you, Kassian," I say.

"You too, Kass!" Crtr adds.

Kassian stifles his obvious irritation at Crtr's informality and saunters away. Once he's out of sight, I examine the watch in greater detail.

Crtr moves to collect the reels from my armoire.

"That was nice of him," Crtr says. "I didn't think Kassian was capable of generosity like that."

"He isn't," I say. "Haven't you heard the saying, 'Never trust a gift from a Telladyne?' Kassian's up to something. This watch is set to 10am, when the LifeCasts start. That can't be a coincidence. And the inscription..."

"Optimum auxilium in morte, dat honore in vitam," Crtr reads aloud. "The Noble Valet motto."

"Not exactly. He switched the words for Life and Death, so it roughly translates to 'Superior service in death, gives honor to life.'"

"What are you going to do?"

"Nothing. Kassian understands I've been with the Telladynes long enough to know their gifts are laced with treachery. If I don't engage with the watch, it can't hurt me.

"After you drop off the reels, check back in with the Carringtons. They'll likely need assistance during the LifeCasts. Speaking of which, make sure everyone you know watches Kallista's."

"Will do," Crtr responds. "See you after the LifeCasts."

"Until then."

Crtr starts to leave, but I call back to him.

"Thanks for coming with me tonight, by the way. It was good to have you there."

"No problem. That was way more fun than scrubbing floors."

I set the watch Kassian gave me on my workbench and undress for a long-overdue RejuviPod treatment. Stand-in Valets aren't always reliable, so I set the pod to wake me a few hours before the LifeCasts begin.

The pod door closes over me. Warm pink vapor fills the pod and relaxes every cell in my body. As the pod leans back into horizontal position, my arms, legs, and head sink into plush cushions that make me feel weightless.

Through the pod's round face window, I see the maintenance room lights lower to deep purple and blue tones. My eyelids flutter, my mind slows, and with a few deep breaths, I slip into a calm, peaceful...

16

It's so cold. Everything's wet. If my treatment's over the pod face should be open. Something's wrong.

I pry the pod face open. My muscles feel so weak. I squeeze through the opening and flop onto the ground. Why are the lights so bright?

The lights won't follow my commands to dim.

A thick film covers my body. Sweat. Cold sweat. I need clothes.

I wobble to standing. My armoire floats in space, like everything else around me. I take a step, stumble, and smack onto the floor.

Could this be a side effect of the True Born drugs? I NeuroChat Crtr, but the chat fails for some reason.

This combination of symptoms is unlike any drug side effect I know.

I crawl to the armoire and fling open the door. My jacket and RXSleeve hang out of reach. I lunge up to grab them both, and crash back down.

The jacket doesn't relieve my shivers, and the pens I dock are useless.

Poison. It's the only explanation. But when? How?

I squint to examine the room. This all started with the pod treatment.

Kassian!

Never trust a gift from a Telladyne. The gift wasn't the watch, it was the time off. He knew I needed a pod treatment. I played right into his hand.

Knowing Kassian, he put some clever little clue about what's happening to me inside the watch. I crawl to the workbench.

Invisible hands clench my lungs. I gasp for air. A pen of Albutol releases the hands. At least I can treat one of my symptoms.

The workbench feels impossibly high. It takes all my strength to pull myself up. I grab the watch. It reads 10:25am. If that's true, the LifeCasts have already started.

The watch blurs and shifts. I drop back to the floor.

Optimum auxilium in morte, dat honore in vitam... Superior service in death, gives honor to life. Service in death. It wasn't a mistake. Kassian switched the words on purpose. He's trying to kill me! But why?

My bones feel like glass; my skin like paper. Deep scratches run down my throat. The taste of blood sits on my tongue.

I can't reach anyone for help. I can barely move. Inducing vomiting won't do anything, the poison's already run through me.

My NeuroClock confirms the time. The LifeCasts have begun. If nothing else, they'll take my mind off the fact that I'm dying a slow painful death alone.

I check Kallista's first. She talks into a mirror to address her audience. A line of haggard lowlanders stands behind her. One of the girls is so young, she can't be older than 11.

"Now that we've found 10 of The City's most tragic, painfully grotesque lowlanders, we're ready to start their journey from garbage to glam!" Kallista says. *"Over the next 12 hours, you'll watch me transform these half-cocked zeroes into high-class heroes! With a little Highland magic, some of them might even pass for Nobles! Stay tuned as we 'Refresh the Lowland!'"*

"Refresh the Lowland," that must be the title of her LifeCast. Kallista needs all my view points, but I need to see what the other nominees are doing.

Prianka stands at a machine press in a factory. Instead of a practical boilersuit, she wears a purple gown with feathery cuffs. The cuffs are already matted down with thick black sludge.

A chain of violent coughs pulls me from the LifeCasts. Icy shivers run through me. My lungs freeze. I dock another Albutol pen.

Vitinia Flynn sings to a room full of Nobles. Her voice carries through my ears, as if I'm singing. When the song ends, the audience jumps to their feet with ecstatic ovation. Their sudden movement turns my stomach. I cough, gag, and produce a mucousy solid.

Marena walks through a Highland shop. She casually picks up rare jewelry and trinkets, looks at them, then sets them back down without a word. In her NeuroCast she'd describe everything she touched, but she's trying to be uninteresting.

I don't want to give her any view points, but I have to check on Aleks.

She's running through a dark space. The space looks familiar. I hear footsteps clang on a metal catwalk. They sound so close, even for a LifeCast. Aleks runs into somewhere impossibly bright.

She walks further into the space. I see myself through Aleks' eyes. Is this some kind of hallucination? I lie huddled in my jacket on the ground. My hair and skin shimmer with sweat.

"Bear!"

I force my eyes open. She's really here.

Coughs erupt from my chest. I can't catch my breath. My eyes unfocus.

I awake to a cool damp towel on my forehead. The lights are lower. It's easier to look around now. There's a blanket over me, but I still feel frozen to the core.

Aleks sits above me. My head lies in her lap. She flashes me a smile and strokes my cheek. Despite everything, the sight of her face soothes me.

"Aleks..." I say in a strained whisper.

"Here," she says, and pours water into my mouth.

I swallow with awkward gulps. The drink stings on the way down.

"Did you get my mess...age?" I ask.

"I did."

"Then why... are you here?"

"Because of Kassian, actually."

"What?"

"He dropped off a 'good luck' basket to my house. Said he came himself because you were on death's door. I dropped the basket and came straight here."

I would have done the same thing if our positions were reversed, but Aleks can't be here. She needs to go home, be boring, and lose LifeCast views. I motion for more water and Aleks complies.

"Go away."

"No, you need help."

"Not from you. You know why. Please go."

This is all too interesting for her viewers. I hoist myself up and move away from Aleks. A desperate wheeze escapes my throat, and I dock another pen.

"I can't," Aleks says.

"You can and you should."

"No, I actually can't. There's an army of Noble Guards outside locking this place down under quarantine. They said if I go in, I can't come back out."

"Quarantine?"

A red tinge falls over the room. Something's covered all the windows. Aleks runs to get a better look.

I turn on the Highland News and see an aerial shot of the Telladyne garage complex. It's covered in a massive red tarp. A graphic at the bottom reads, "Virus in the Highland."

"You're watching live breaking coverage of an unknown disease discovered here at Telladyne Manor," Dahlia Delachort narrates. *"All we know now is that the Idol Nominee Aleksaria Yukita has been quarantined inside the Telladyne maintenance room along with the Telladyne family's Valet, who has contracted the disease."*

Kassian didn't poison me. He infected me. But with what? There are vaccines for everything, no one's been sick for generations.

"Come on," Aleks says. "Lie back down, you need to relax."

I do as Aleks says, and she pulls the blanket up to my chin.

"How'd you get the lights down?" I ask.

"I found the manual switchboard."

Kassian set the stage with studio lighting. He knew Aleks would run to me.

Ding!

"What's that?"

Aleks doesn't answer, but she returns with a bowl of hot miso soup.

"You need to eat to keep your strength up. Here."

The room feels untethered from gravity. My muscles are sore for no apparent reason. I take the bowl from Aleks, but shake so hard that I almost spill it. She takes the bowl back and prepares a spoonful for me.

"Careful, it's hot."

She feeds me like a helpless child. No one's cared for me like this since I was actually a child with Zola. It's a comfort I'd long forgotten until now.

The soup's warmth travels through my body. For a second, I forgot that Aleks' LifeCast is live. This is the most stable I've felt since I escaped my pod, but she can't be here. My health isn't worth her life.

"Aleks," I say. "You have to... stay away from me. Go read some technical manuals about... garden irrigation systems or something."

"Bear, eat."

Several sets of loud footsteps clang across a nearby catwalk. A team of hazmat suits appears. The suits read "TDCA."

Aleks rises to her feet. Two suits come straight for us while the others scatter throughout my loft.

"Idol Nominee Yukita," One of the suits says. "Please come with us for examination."

"I'm not leaving him."

"We need samples from both of you in order to better assess the situation," the other suit says.

"Go with them," I whisper.

"No, you need me."

"I don't want you to get this. If they can help you, let them."

Aleks nods and turns to a suit.

"You have five minutes," she says, and walks away.

Aleks stares down the suits with conspicuous distrust. They take her temperature with a digital thermometer, listen to her heart with a stethoscope, and perform a variety of other tests with archaic-looking tools. Whatever's happening to me is so unusual that they don't even trust Neurogem readings.

Two more suits descend on me to perform all the same tests but with less care. They poke, prod, and stab me with different implements. After the tests are done, one of the suits connects a blood-draw adaptor to my dock and starts filling vials.

While countless glass tubes fill with my blood, I watch the other suits trample through my loft. They seem to stuff items into giant red plastic bags at random.

"Is this the last thing you wore before your initial symptoms came on?" One of the suits asks, as she holds up my boilersuit.

I nod. She wads up the suit and stuffs it into a bag.

My eyes weaken and my vision goes hazy. A burning rash tickles my ankles then rages up my legs like an inferno. I rub and scratch my skin, which makes the burn worse. I start to convulse. The tube connected to my dock snaps loose and blood splatters across my blankets.

My eyes flutter open. The suits are gone. Chills course through my body. This vacillation between ice and fire is dizzying. It's impossible to focus on anything other than how miserable I feel. Thankfully, Aleks is back.

She wipes my nose. The cloth is covered in blood. Aleks has a concern in her eyes I've never seen before.

I want to tell her everything that's happened since she was taken by the Noble Guard—about Marena's tomb, the True Born Collective, and the reels. But I can't say anything without telling the entire city. NeuroChat fails to Aleks, just like it did with Crtr.

"Wait here, I made you something."

Wait here? Where am I going?

Aleks walks over to my small stove. The windows are still covered in red. I check the news to see if there are any new developments.

"The Telladyne Disease Control Agency has isolated the disease, which they are calling 'Valet Hemorrhagic Fever,' or 'VHF.'" Delachort says to the camera.

She's on the Telladyne grounds now with the red-tarped garage complex in the background. Delachort matches the magic hour sunset in a hooded, burnt sienna sequined jumpsuit. A bright gold microphone completes the outfit.

"While reports of unexpected fever surge throughout the lowland, the TDCA continues to come up empty-handed regarding a treatment or vaccine for VHF. Panicked viewers have flocked to the LifeCast of Idol Nominee, Aleksaria Yukita to see how this devastating disease progresses..."

Oh no. That will drive even more people to Aleks' LifeCast. I better give some view points to Kallista. It's not much, but maybe I can offset a few of Aleks' points.

Kallista sits beside one of her lowland contestants. The contestant's hair is shock white, and his skin is thick and weathered. He's obviously experienced a lifetime of exposure to harsh chemicals at his job. Dotted ink lines cover his face.

The famous Highland surgeon, Serge Washington, also sits beside the contestant. He has long black hair that's combed straight back, unnaturally golden skin, and mathematically-symmetrical features. Serge fondles the contestant's face.

"Not to worry, we can easily sculpt them," Washington says. *"After that, we insert implants here and here, suck out the excess fat, and voila! New cheekbones to make his eyes pop!"*

"Speaking of his eyes, what do you think of spearmint green?" Kallista asks. *"I think it would really add some drama to the hickory skin treatment we discussed."*

"An excellent suggestion, I couldn't agree more! Iris swaps are lava right now. Once we're done, he'll have more NeuroFeed followers than me!"

Kallista and Washington laugh while the contestant stares straight ahead. He seems indifferent to the extreme proposals, which means he's probably drugged.

Kallista looks into a wall mirror to address her viewers.

"Now that we have Roth's facial reconstruction plan finalized, let's check on the others!"

Kallista walks to a bright white surgical parlor. She looks down on several simultaneous surgeries being performed on "Refresh the Lowland" contestants.

"They're all coming along marvelously!" Kallista says. *"I can't wait to see the results! I'm especially excited about Niya. Where is she?"*

Kallista looks at each table until her gaze settles on the youngest girl from the line-up. A bushel of dark red hair falls in large curls around Niya's face. Two dark eyebrows lie above her closed eyes like sleeping caterpillars.

A surgeon cuts into the girl's lips with tiny movements that are obscured by his arms. What are they doing to her?

This is my fault. I should have known Kallista's desperation to become the Idol would take her LifeCast to inhuman extremes.

The lowlanders unlucky enough to be selected by Kallista will wake up with new faces and bodies that look and feel foreign. And for what? So a spoiled Noble girl can have a chance at even more undeserved wealth and fame?

Aleks returns with a clear drink. The warm liquid tastes horribly salty, and sickeningly sweet at the same time. I start to gag, but choke it down.

"W-what is... this?" I ask.

"An electrolyte drink I found on the NeuroNet. It's supposed to keep you hydrated and raise your blood sugar. Is it OK?"

The liquid hits my stomach like a bomb. I gag, roll over, and projectile vomit a mixture of bile and blood. It's been days since I've had a decent meal. Each round of vomiting sends knives through my abdomen.

People aren't used to seeing sickness like this. They won't be able to look away. Aleks is racking up LifeCast views and I'm powerless to stop it.

When I finish, Aleks puts my head back in her lap. The blood flow from my nose feels constant.

While my limbs lay like heavy stones, my heart moves like a hummingbird's. Every breath is a battle, but at least I can breathe, for now. My symptoms get worse every minute. After everything I've survived, this might be it. I need to say goodbye, while I still can.

"Aleks," I whisper, and take several sharp breathes in. "The day we met... in the garden was... the best day of... my life."

"Bear—"

"You gave me hope... showed me that the world w-wasn't such a c-cold place after all. You are my... confi-dant, my p-p-partner, and the love..."

I turn to cough. Blood sprays onto the floor, but I continue.

"My fondest memories are... of watching the stars... with you."

Fluid floods my lungs. My skin turns to absolute frost as my organs throb.

The chill ignites, and the burning rash returns stronger than before. My vision goes black, but I'm still conscious. I seize as Aleks shouts my name over, and over, and over again.

I awake with a strained wheeze. My eyes open to a different room. I'm on a plush blue sofa. Straight ahead, large crescent windows look out onto the mist. The full moon hangs distant in the sky.

"Bear!" Aleks shouts with tears streaked down her face. "Bear, you're alive! You're alive!"

She buries her face in my chest and hugs my aching torso.

I try to ask how we got to the Telladyne family archives, but the words don't come. My lungs and throat have given up. Aleks seems to read my mind.

"I used a motorized flatbed thing in the maintenance room to move you," she explains through a veil of tears. "The service elevator took us straight here."

Aleks nestles beside me, and places my arm around her shoulders. My fingers fumble in a poor impersonation of how I used to stroke her hair.

Aleks pulls herself up and looks into my eyes.

"Sharing so many strange and beautiful things with you has been amazing, but it's nothing compared to the world you've shown me beyond the Highland. Even without our trips, the joy I feel when we're together outweighs all the points and luxury of Noble life. You are my person, Bear. And I am yours. Forever."

I stare at Aleks from behind wet eyes. She just said all the things I could ever wish to hear. I hope she knows I feel the same.

Loving Aleks has given my life meaning. I don't want to die, but if I'm about to, I'm glad it's her face I'll see last.

My chest rises with a stuttered breath. I can feel my whimpering organs strain with their last pathetic efforts.

Before I go, I split to give a few more view points to Kallista.

All 10 contestants of "Refresh the Lowland" strut down a catwalk. Their new faces are covered with extreme make-up, and their new bodies are adorned with Kallista-designed outfits.

Niya, the youngest contestant comes out. Kallista's kept Niya's curly hair, but made her eyes more cat-like, bleached her skin bone white, given her a tiny up-turned nose, and blown her lips up into a cartoonish heart shape. Niya started as a fresh-faced young girl, now she looks like an aged Noble woman trying desperately to look young again.

This is the climax of Kallista's LifeCast. Hers, and all the other LifeCasts, will end in about 15 minutes.

I switch to the Highland news.

"Confirmed cases of VHF currently total 157,446, but reports continue to come in from every corner of The City. There is still no official word from the TDCA regarding a treatment for VHF, but we received a statement from Kassian Telladyne just moments ago.

"In the statement, Telladyne said: 'With each passing second, we understand more about Valet Hemorrhagic Fever, and Telladyne Industries will not rest until this horrific disease is eradicated. Our primary goal at Telladyne Industries is to keep The City healthy. It always has been, and it always will be.

"Until further notice, please stay where you are. Any travel between locations risks spreading VHF..."

Aleks takes my hand in hers. My eyelids flutter again. I've lived as good a life as I could, and am lucky to die beside the person I love. I try to smile one more time for Aleks.

Her lip quivers as she suppresses sobs. She's trying to stay strong for me. My eyelids grow heavy.

Maybe there's something after all of this; a higher plain where our collective consciousness exists and Aleks and I will see each other again. I hope so... I'm not ready to leave her... I'm not ready.

17

"Valet, wake up! Valet!"

Someone shouts and shakes my shoulders. Fingers pry open my eyelids.

Kassian?

I feel the sofa on the back of my head. Aleks is still beside me. I can't have been out long.

"We found a cure!" Kassian shouts. "Here!"

He docks a pen into my wrist.

"Idol Nominee Yukita, you must dock this pen as well. It contains both a cure and a vaccine. Do it now!"

Aleks takes a champagne gold pen from Kassian and does as he says.

"That was a close one," Kassian says. "But as always, the TDCA came through. We've already administered cures to all of the lowland cases. A vaccine, called Valaviran, will be available in every Telladyne mobile pharmacy across The City within 10 hours. I implore everyone in the Highland and the lowland to take it."

This information isn't meant for Aleks or me. It's for everyone watching Aleks' LifeCast. I check the time; there's still 1 minute left. Kassian continues.

"And as a special thank you for your patience during this trying time, each pen of Valaviran comes with a free sample of Telladyne Industries' new anti-fatigue and sensory enhancement supplement, MaxDrive! Telladyne Industries: Wellness for Life."

The chill in my body vanishes and air pulls into my lungs easier, but I still feel incredibly weak. I check the time again. The LifeCasts are over.

It's all so clear to me now. Kassian nearly killed me and put everyone in The City at risk to sell vaccines and distribute samples of whatever MaxDrive is.

"How... could you do this?" I ask.

"Relax, Valet, you'll need your strength for what lies ahead. Now if you'll excuse me, I have a city-wide distribution effort to lead."

"You're a monster, Kassian," Aleks says. "How can you be so selfish and cruel?"

"I'm not selfish, or cruel; quite the opposite actually. I simply take calculated risks to ensure the betterment of our fine city as a whole. Some day you'll understand, Young Lady Yuki... or should I say, *Idol* Yukita. Good evening."

"What?" Aleks asks. "They haven't announced the Idol winner yet, have they?"

"I don't think so—"

3 beeps. It's a visual message from the Idol Selection Committee.

Dahlia Delachort appears on the same balcony where she introduced the Idol Nominees.

'Wow, what an incredible series of LifeCasts from this year's Idol Nominees! Some of us gave a stirring performance met by standing ovations. Others got to explore the Highlands cutest boutiques. We even learned how difficult it is for a Noble to step into a lowlander's shoes. And speaking of shoes, 'Refresh the Highland' changed the shoes and so much more of 10 dowdy lowlanders who were transformed into dazzling swans before our eyes!'

And through all of this, we watched as the Idol Nominee Aleksaria Yukita uncovered a deadly new disease that threatened The City. We were glued to the nominee's LifeCast as she rushed to her beloved's side, showed us the horrific symptoms of the unknown disease up-close, and nurtured us all back to health. And what better way to end her LifeCast than with a cure discovered in the last dramatic minutes! Needless to say, with a record-breaking 92% view rate, I am pleased to announce your newest Idol, Aleksaria Yukita!"

Light blue and silver confetti bursts around Delechort. Shots of celebrations in Neurogem Square, Yukita manufacturing facilities, and the Yukita Teitaku flash before my eyes. Delachort returns.

"Congratulations once again to Aleksaria Yukita on becoming The City's 47th Idol! Don't miss the Idol Coronation in two weeks. The red carpet starts at 6pm City Standard Time. See you there!"

Delachort waves good-bye, and the camera swings around to reveal a party in full swing on-set. The entire city will celebrate their new Idol tonight—the Nobles for the profits they'll see from a fresh face to promote their products, and the lowlanders for a new lifestyle emissary to guide them.

No, no, no, this can't be! Aleks isn't supposed to be the Idol! She never even wanted it, that must count for something. What am I thinking? The Highland doesn't care about what Aleks wants, they never did.

Camera drones have already assembled at the archive windows, but we're too far into the dark room for them to see us. Aleks stares blank into the distance.

"Aleks?" I whisper. "Aleks..."

"They need me back home..." she says. "To join the festivities. As soon as I leave here it begins, everything changes... Maybe I can stay here, in the Telladyne archives. Eventually they'll forget about me, and find a new Idol, right?"

My muscles ache as I push up into a sitting position.

"Listen, Aleks, I didn't get to tell you this before everything started. Those reels we found, they showed the Monarchs doing mind control experiments on the first Idol."

"What? It was just people throwing a ball back and forth."

"There was hidden information inside the film reel. We stumbled onto something big, something no one outside the Monarch family was ever supposed to see. Whatever you do, don't trust the

Monarchs. Don't dock anything they give you, don't drink anything they pour for you, and stay vigilant. Promise me."

"I promise, but it doesn't matter. I'm going to stay here, right? I'll throw some curtains over those windows and partition out rooms with bookshelves. It'll be lovely once we're finished."

I grip Aleks shoulders and prepare to drive my warning home but stop myself. She heard me perfectly well. My features soften, and I gently rub her arms with easy strokes. She needs a little fantasy before everything becomes painfully real, we both do.

"And I'll bring you three meals a day," I say. "And fabulous clothes to wear. We can clear away some of this furniture and make a space for you to dance over there. We'll have to do something about the lighting, but that's easily fixed..."

I hear footsteps.

Holt emerges from the shadows. He's come to bring Aleks home. Holt was the one who first introduced me to Aleks, and now he's the one who will take her away from me.

"Idol-elect Yukita, your presence is requested at the Yukita Teitaku."

"Oh, hello Noble Valet Holt!" Aleks says. "That won't be necessary. I've decided to stay here indefinitely. Could you please inform my family and the Idol Selection Committee? They should be able to find a replacement easily enough."

"I am afraid that is not possible, Idol-elect Yukita. Your father has authorized," Holt sighs. "The use of sedation to retrieve you if necessary."

"There's no way I'm... letting you knock her out and... take her away!" I say through hoarse coughs.

Holt looks back into the darkness with tired eyes. Heavy, metallic footsteps approach. A Noble Guard marches into view and stands at attention beside Holt.

"I take no pleasure in this," Holt says. "Idol-elect Yukita, please collect your things and meet me at the service elevator. I need to speak with Noble Valet Bear for a moment."

I squeeze Aleks so tight I'm afraid she might suffocate. Warm tears pool at my chest as Aleks softly weeps into me.

I spread my fingers to feel as much of her back as possible. I don't want to let go, but I also don't want our memory of this moment to be marred by the Noble Guard tearing us apart.

"Aleks, it's time," I whisper. "We will see each other again. Soon. I'm your person, and you're mine. Always remember that."

Aleks releases her grip. I wipe a few wet streaks from her cheeks and kiss her forehead. My lips linger as I take in the scent of her juniper shampoo. I don't know when I'll smell it again.

We rise from the sofa. Our eyes remain locked as her fingers travel down my arm to the end of my hand. It feels like she's floating away, and I have no choice but to release her into the void. I hold onto her fingertips for a moment before I let go.

After Aleks disappears into the darkness, Holt steps forward. He lets out another deep sigh.

"Noble Valet Bear, I have some unfortunate news."

"How could you possibly make this any worse?"

"The Noble Valet Council has reviewed your case. I am sorry to say that they have ruled against you. Your title as Noble Valet is hereby stripped, effective immediately. You have one hour to vacate the Highland. Noble Guards are standing by to escort you from the premises."

"How could you let this happen?"

"I am so sorry, Bear. Of the 12 valets I have mentored, none have shown more natural aptitude and potential than you. This is not just a grave personal loss for me, but for the Highland at large. It breaks my heart to deliver this news."

"What about Aleks? You've seen what happens to the Idols! Forget about me; focus on her! More than anything, you need to keep Aleks safe!"

"I will do everything in my power to ensure the Idol-elect Yukita's safety."

There was a time when I thought Holt might be different, but he's just another mindless Highland servant. My only hope now is that some part of him remembers Aleks as a little girl, the one he would have done anything to protect. Even so, he's old, and he's not me.

"Everything in your power?" I say. "If that's the best you can do, then Aleks is already lost."

PART III

18

The next in an endless stream of micro circuit boards slides in front of me. A green "14" counts down in the upper right corner of my vision.

I pick up the board with a pair of tweezers. Magnification goggles allow me to see the board in exquisite detail. It looks like a miniature version of The City with complex networks of conduits that deliver information all across the board. There's probably some kind of significance to the similarity...

The countdown clock turns an angry red and beeps louder as it hits ten. I'm already behind schedule.

I perform five quick solders on the board, flip it over, make three more solders, and set it down with two seconds left. That was close. Another board slides into view.

No one's told me what the boards are for, but I don't really care. This job requires no critical thinking or artistry whatsoever. I'm only here because it's cheaper to replace a human worker than it is to repair a machine. Thanks, UteroCube.

A high-pitched chime rings out, and the gold Success Point counter in the lower left of my vision increases from 10 to 11.

My SPs are low because I paid 200 for the privilege of switching my original shift and working a double. That way I'll be off before the Idol Coronation starts tonight, and I'll get to watch it alone.

This is the least alone I've ever been. There are hundreds of us side-by-side on the assembly line. We're all focused with unblinking diligence on our own repetitive tasks.

Everyone here, except me, is newly out of basic job training. They just started making points of their own, which have all gone straight to outrageous V-Pro hairstyles, clothes, and NApps.

When I was their age, I was above the mist learning the difference between Rhone and Loire Valley wines. Yet here I am. Holt couldn't save my job as a Noble Valet, but he pulled some strings to get me this position.

I had no choice but to take the job. Like everyone else in The City, I need points to live, and I need to live if I ever hope to see Aleks again.

A genderless robotic voice, that I've come to despise, sounds through the room.

"Attention: Current shift ends in 5, 4, 3, 2, 1. Your shift has ended. Please complete your work, and evacuate the assembly line."

My replacement on the line steps into position across from me. I lower my facemask and remove my goggles. Everyone on my side of the assembly line lets out a collective exhale.

Trumpets blare, fireworks explode, and glitter rains from the sky. It's all virtual but still abrupt. Aleks spins into view before me.

"Congratulations, you are now a Level 5 Assembler! Very impressive. You've unlocked an assembly time modifier that lets you earn more Success Points for high assembly combos! Check out the NeuroNet for more information about your promotion! Here are 10 bonus Success Points! Keep up the good work, Bear! The City needs you!"

Aleks blows me a kiss and vanishes. I must have assembled enough boards during my double shift to reach the next job level.

Hopefully the time modifier will help me get SPs faster so I can take more time off. I need all the free time I can get to strategize a way back into the Highland.

Lowland rain pummels my body as I leave the factory. A swarm of workers rush past me on their way out. I look like a weathered gray stone in the middle of a rainbow-colored river of vibrant V-Pros. No V-Pro can help me see Aleks again, so what's the point?

I head to the Breaker Ward. Pach wants to show me something before the Idol Coronation.

Pach sits cross-legged on his bed. His mouth forms into a broken smile as I approach.

"Bear!" A synthesized voice says from a speaker on Pach's bedside. "So glad you made it!"

"What's that thing?"

"New voice box. Our mutual friend made it for me. It translates NeuroText dialogue into audible speech. Quicker than waiting for me to get the words out."

"What about practicing speaking?" I ask.

"My abilities plateaued, pointless to continue. How's work going?"

"Meaningless, unstimulating. The usual. What did you want to show me?"

"Take a seat."

I sit at the end of Pach's bed. There's a black and white checkerboard between us with rows of soldier figurines on each side. The game looks familiar, I've probably seen it in an archive before.

He says the game's called "Chess," and explains the rules. It seems pretty straightforward—defend your king while trying to capture your opponent's. Pach gives me the first move.

I examine the board and try to remember what each piece does. After I move a knight, Pach edges his pawn forward.

"If you truly hate your job," Pach's speaker says. "You could always join the revolution underground. I'm sure with your knowledge of the Highland they would welcome you with open arms."

"That'd be moving in the wrong direction," I say. "I need to get above the mist to save Aleks, not further below The City. Besides, your band of revolutionaries is hardly more than a minor nuisance to the Highland. Locke alluded to some master plan with ReBorn, but from what I can tell it just makes people giggly from hallucinations."

"That's the advantage of an arrogant adversary, they're easily caught by surprise. The Highland will never see ReBorn's true effect coming."

"What's it supposed to do?" I ask.

Pach looks down at the board and back to me.

"It's your move."

"Aleks is in the Highland," I say, and move a pawn. "If she's in danger you have to tell me."

"From what I saw in her LifeCast, I'm certain Aleks won't be affected by ReBorn."

"What does that mean? Just tell me what it does! Locke said herself that ReBorn can't be stopped at this point."

"I'll tell you what," Pach says, as he moves his bishop forward. "If you win this game, without using your gem, I'll tell you everything I know about ReBorn."

"And if you win?"

"You promise to never ask me about it again. I've already said too much. Deal?"

"Deal," I say, and consider the board with newfound interest.

We go back and forth at a steady clip. Pach and I take each other's pieces as we both advance across the board. He leaves his queen unguarded at the board's center, and I snatch it with my bishop. I have his king surrounded. The game should be mine in a couple moves. Pach moves his knight.

"Checkmate."

"How did you?"

I study the board. He's trapped my king. I lost.

"The game was over as soon as you took my queen. You were so focused on her that you lost sight of your own position. It's a classic trap, maybe one you can learn from."

"Are you saying I should forget about Aleks?"

"I'm saying you need to remain open to the bigger picture. You say joining the collective would send you in the wrong direction, but how do you expect to get into the Highland by yourself?"

"I don't know yet, but I'll figure something out."

"OK, and then what? You'll just zip in through Aleks' window, sweep her up, and run away with her before anyone notices?"

"No, of course not, I... I just need time."

"You've already had two weeks. How's your plan coming?"

"I liked it better when it took you ten minutes to say a sentence."

"If you can't answer that question, then tell me what level Assembler you are."

"I just hit level five."

"Exactly. You're in the system now, a full-fledged lowlander. You can't do this on your own. If you really want to save Aleks, you need to join forces with people who have the same goal as you."

"The True Borns don't care about Aleks. All they want is to tear down the Highland."

"Don't you think freeing the Idol would facilitate that?"

"I—"

"Bear!" Zola shouts from across the ward.

Zola couldn't have come at a better time. I never realized Pach was so radicalized by the True Born Collective.

"Aw, Bear, you look terrible," Zola says. "I could swim in those black pools beneath your eyes, and your shoulders are slumped down to your knees! Why don't you log some hours in the ward pod?"

"Thanks, but I can't. The Idol Coronation starts in 20."

"But you just got here, why don't you watch it with us?"

"Sorry, I have other plans. It was good to see you both. Congrats on the new voice, Pach. I'll drop by again soon."

"Make sure you do, sweets."

I kick through scraps of charred rug, shattered glass, and chunks of rock where my lowland hideaway used to stand. Miraculously, a single overhang remains. Long cracks span the skylight, but it still keeps the rain off my head.

I sit down amid scattered used Hot Shot pens. They make it easier to extend my time between pod treatments. I managed to avoid pod treatments for 7 days, but Zola caught me talking to myself and insisted I use the ward pod.

I open the bright purple wrapper of a BurgerNite ChomperDeluxe that I picked up on the way here. As always, it looks exactly like the ads, down to the last sesame seed.

I sink my teeth into the ChomperDeluxe. It's good, but in the same way all lowland food is good. I can practically feel the pleasure centers in my brain light up from the salt, fat, and sugar. A savory wax coats my tongue that somehow makes me crave each coming bite.

Coverage of the Idol Coronation plays across every building in Neurogem Square. Aleks hasn't been introduced yet. They're saving her for last. Holograms of past Idols perform before the Coronation's main event. It's the one time deemed acceptable for The City to remember past Idols.

I watch the famously rotund fallen Idol, Paris Serpentine, dance alongside two other fallen Idols: Michiko Thomas and Oksana Reyn. The three Idols are depicted in their prime. None of them looked like this when they died. Everyone chooses to ignore the Idols' gruesome deaths, but it's all I can think about.

Paris was incinerated in a fiery highway crash while she fled from an army of camera drones and NeuroCasters. Michiko Thomas was smothered to death when she fell off the stage during a concert and the audience rushed her. Oksana Reyn was vaporized by a crazed fan who exploded himself, along with 36 innocent bystanders, during a routine factory visit.

I walk to the ledge. Rain drenches my face and boilersuit. I take another bite of my now-soggy burger. An icy breeze moves through me.

The square's been blocked off to traffic and filled with dirt. The dirt, meant to limit injuries during the raucous celebration below, has turned to mud. Thousands of lowlanders dance and slide through the mud as they partake in free pens and drinks that flow from numerous kiosks.

Most of the revelers have pulled down their boilersuits, or stripped naked and projected iridescent V-Pro skin paint onto their bodies. Some have joined forces to capture and defend particular kiosks. A few bodies lie motionless on the ground; their muddy skin washed clean by the rain.

I've spent too much time in the Highland to enjoy the crowded, mud-caked festivities below. Until now, I've spent almost every Idol Coronation working in the Coliseum luxury boxes, but I don't belong there either. My status as a sort of hybrid in The City used to make me feel free. Now I just feel untethered.

I take another bite of the ChomperDeluxe.

It's only a matter of time until I get fired from my assembly job. Then what? I join the True Borns? I can't spend the rest of my life pretending to share their ideals. Besides, it would just be another low-level assembly job, except I won't get paid.

That leaves the Highland. Of course, I should just become a Noble and return to the Highland! Pach was right, there's no way back there. Even with my gem off, the Noble Guard would recognize and disappear me before I took a single breath of Highland air. Disappear me...

I take another bite.

Nowhere feels like home because Aleks was my home, and she's lost to me. Every time I tried to help her, I just made things worse.

I helped her lose the siloball match, and she nearly died. I helped her escape the Coliseum, and she was captured by the Noble Guard. Worst of all, her affection for me was used against her. If I hadn't been around, Kassian couldn't have infected me, and drawn Aleks into an impossibly gripping LifeCast that made her the Idol.

It's good that I can't help Aleks now, I'd probably get her killed, or worse.

I take the last bite of my ChomperDeluxe and drop the wrapper.

If my body splattered in the middle of Neurogem Square, especially tonight, no one would notice. I'm already dead to Aleks anyway. At least this way, she'd be safe from my attempts to help her.

I take a deep breath. A shiver runs through my body. The tips of my toes move past the ledge. My heart races while my body begs me to step back.

This is the only option left. Despite all our shared history, it's better for Aleks that I go.

The sole of my shoe slides forward. One more inch, not even that, and I'll be off. A building in view switches from Coronation coverage to Aleks' face.

"Bear, do you ever have days where everything seems to go wrong?"

The ad cuts to Aleks as she slips on her way out of the shower, spills coffee on her dress, and gets lost during a dance performance.

"I know I do. With each new disaster, my mood worsens, my senses feel more dulled, and I don't have the strength to be my best self! That's when I reach for Telladyne Industries' latest breakthrough, MaxDrive."

Holt hands Aleks an ice blue pen. She docks the pen and smiles. More scenes play that show Aleks masterfully lead a dance troupe, operate an antique espresso machine, and high-dive into a pristine pool.

"So Bear, don't wait! Dock a pen of MaxDrive today and feel the difference! During tonight's Coronation you can try MaxDrive for free at any Telladyne pharmacy kiosk. Feel alive, with MaxDrive!"

That's it, the last thing I'll ever hear from Aleks is an ad for Telladyne Industries' latest drug. My gem detected low serotonin levels and the NeuroNet served up a corrective measure. The real Aleks would never try to shill pens to me if I was depressed. She'd empathize with me, listen to how I felt, and find a way to make me laugh.

I turn off my gem. If I'm about to die, all I want to hear are my own thoughts.

The city quiets. Trash fumes and factory exhaust fill my nose. A powerful gust of wind blows rain into my face. The drops taste like burnt rubber. No one should have to live like this.

Somewhere in The City, somewhere that looks beautiful and smells nice, Aleks is warming up for her performance. If nothing else, her short life will be filled with a level of luxury that most people only see in their wildest fantasies.

I lean forward.

Aleks never needed the opulence of an Idol life, all we ever needed was each other. Each other... all we ever needed was each other... I need her... and she needs me.

She needs me!

I leap back from the edge and crawl backward. What was I thinking? The lowland has my mind in knots. I lost myself among the rain, the darkness, and the incessant ads. The only way to save Aleks is to rise above it all.

I lie flat and let the rain fall over me. My back aches from hunching over the assembly line, my muscles are weak, and my tendons are tight. I'm broken but still able to work, just what the Nobles want.

Enough waiting. My plan to save Aleks has to start now.

I turn my gem back on.

3 beeps. It's a visual message from Holt.

An ice blue envelope appears. The envelope opens, and a sheet of silver paper rises from it. The top of the sheet is embossed with the Idol Selection Committee seal, which is followed by swirling calligraphy:

The Idol Selection Committee
requests the honor of your presence
to witness the coronation of
Aleksaria E. Yukita
as The City's forty-seventh Idol
on Friday, the eighth of July
at 8 o' clock City Standard Time

How is this possible? I've been trying to reach Holt for weeks, and now he sends me a Coronation invitation out of the blue? Something must be happening with Aleks—something Holt needs to tell me in person.

No time to for questions. I need to get to Vanderbilt Coliseum.

19

I push through the congested lowland sidewalk. As usual, no one reacts to my hurried shoves. They're all split to watch the Coronation.

The ground turns from asphalt to slippery mud. Crazed revelers, like the ones in Neurogem Square, surround the Coliseum.

A wall of mud-covered lowlanders slides toward me. I try to leap over but get clipped and fall hard to the ground. As I climb to my feet, a man closes his hands around my head, scream-laughs in my face, and sprints away.

I see the Coliseum energy field up ahead. There's a distinct invisible line where the mud and merriment end, and the pristine Coliseum grounds begin. Bright red Noble Guards stand posted every 100 feet along the field.

I dodge more lowlanders on my way to the energy field. RXPens crunch beneath my feet. They're all full-size, light blue pens with gold lettering: MaxDrive.

My invitation lets me step through the energy field. Before I reach the other side, someone grabs my arm.

I try to shake off the wide-eyed man, but he won't budge. Despite his spindly frame and mud-covered grip, he's locked on tight.

In a flash, the spindly man falls to the ground. He grips his shoulder in agony. A thick rubber bullet rolls through the mud beside him. I look down the field, and see a Noble Guard move back into position.

Once I pass entirely through the field, a bright silver V-Pro suit appears over my mud-covered boilersuit. New, manicured nails cover my actual dirty, gnarled ones. The patchy beard on my face is probably filled in, too, but I can't see it.

I run inside Vanderbilt Coliseum. Light snowfall clings to my body. Each breath hangs in the air for a moment. Oddly, I don't feel cold at all.

Aerial dancers in precision AeroPacks fly over the stage while the fallen Idols Maya Sandivall and Frederica Solis perform a remixed medley of their greatest hits. The audience dances and screams along.

More ice blue pens litter the ground. Instead of drink fountains, uniformed servers distribute teal drinks that overflow with vapor.

I could use a drink, but I'm not here to celebrate. Holt sent me that invitation for a reason. I NeuroChat him, but as usual, my request fails. He's probably in the luxury boxes. How am I supposed to get all the way up there?

The Coliseum lights flick out. A giant sphere of ice blue lasers appears onstage. Faint chimes and rhythmic drums carry through the air. The sphere illuminates to reveal nimble silhouettes inside.

The sphere starts to spin, and the air around me shifts to match the sphere's rotation. Pens and stray articles of clothing soar in laps around the Coliseum.

Heavy snow obscures the sphere. The drums pound louder, louder, louder still until they merge into a single heavy note. People scream. Glasses crash to the ground. The Coliseum feels like it might shake apart.

Silence.

The music and wind stop. Everything falls back to the ground.

Aleks crouches at center stage. Her eyebrows are thicker, her cheekbones are more defined, and her skin has a subtle sparkle.

Cheers erupt from the crowd. Aleks remains so still that snowflakes collect on her head, shoulders, and arms.

The music returns. Aleks and her dancers launch into a complicated routine of crisp isolations and acrobatic moves. The routine fuses Capoeira dance fighting with classic B-boy style. No Highland choreographer could conceive of such a dance. This is all Aleks.

Everyone in the Coliseum is enthralled. If I'm going to sneak up to the luxury boxes, now's the time. I wrestle my gaze from the stage and head for the Coliseum's outer wall.

The most direct and least guarded route from here to the luxury boxes are the garbage chutes. They carry trash straight down through the Coliseum walls into a huge basement incinerator.

I reach my entry point, a small square panel.

Before I open the panel, I access a schematic of Vanderbilt Coliseum, and NeuroText Pach.

"Bear! Have you given any more thought to what we discussed?"

"No. Can you forge a maintenance permit for panel 86B in Vanderbilt Coliseum?"

"Vanderbilt Coliseum! How'd you get in there?"

"Don't worry about it. Can you forge and file the request?"

"Done. I underestimated you, my boy. I apologize. Be careful."

I kick the panel, and it buckles and tumbles down the chute. Orange light from the incinerator flickers within the opening.

No Noble Guards, Pach's maintenance permit worked. I contort my body into the chute. Hot air blasts up at me. I wedge myself into the chute and inch upward with tiny steps.

The sour, foul smell of burnt garbage wafts up the chute. Neurogems automatically filter out most offensive odors, but this is a new level of stink.

Spinning disposal blades high above my head grow louder with every step. I didn't even consider the blades before climbing into the chute. That's the kind of detail Aleks always remembered when we planned our hunting trips.

Something hits the blades. Oh no.

I clench my lips shut, close my eyes tight, and push hard against the chute walls. A torrent of wet sludge rains down on me. The smell is unbearable. It's mostly food, but the toxic smoothie also contains bits of RXPens, and VaporLite butts.

After the slurry passes, I continue up, and slip.

I slam my feet and back so hard against the chute walls that they bow. How far did I fall? Not far, only a few inches.

Another mistake like that could drop me straight into the incinerator. I need to stay focused, keep a clear head.

I close in on the first layer of disposal blades. The blades spin like a cruel torture device. Without any tools, I have to improvise. Luckily, the blade gears are exposed for easy maintenance.

I reach through my silver V-Pro suit, tear off my boilersuit sleeve, and feed it through the exposed gears. The blade mechanism jams. Even though the blades are stopped, they still block my path.

I wedge myself tighter into the chute and kick up at the blades again and again. The metal frame dislodges. I pry the frame aside and continue my ascent.

My muscles ache, and my spine feels like it might burst out of my back. I can't even see the top. Giving up isn't an option. There's too much at stake.

After I dispatch the second layer of blades, another load of trash falls. Thick sauces, strips of meat, and nests of unidentifiable refuse cover my body. A vomitus cocktail of slime oozes down my face. I take a few quick breaths, regain my composure, and push upward.

I reach the third, and final level of disposal blades. With no more sleeves left, I tear off my boilersuit pant leg, jam the blades, and push through.

A bright light comes into view overhead. I have to be careful. That light means there's a Noble Valet up there who just opened the chute. If I'm discovered, the Noble Guard will rip me out of here like an Adam's Apple from a throat.

I brace for impact. A heavy bag of trash drops onto my stomach like a wrecking ball. I rotate my body to drop the bag, and wait for the light above to go out. When it does, I continue my climb.

I crack the trash chute hatch to confirm no one's around and slide out. The room is freezing. It doesn't help that beneath my V-Pro suit, I'm practically naked.

The trash room sits off a main hallway that connects all the luxury boxes. Nobles never use the hallway, but that doesn't mean I can casually stroll through looking for Holt. I try to NeuroChat him again, no luck. Crtr and Marena don't answer either.

I call up the Vanderbilt Coliseum schematic. The Carrington box isn't far from here. I'll knock on the kitchen door. If Crtr answers, I'll lead him back to the trash room to regroup. If another Valet answers, I'll have to incapacitate him.

I pop my head out into the hallway. With the area clear, I run for the Carrington box.

A door up ahead crashes open. Niko and Prianka Patel burst into the hallway. They're joined at the lips as they paw at each other's bodies. Niko spins Prianka and pushes her against the wall with a passionate kiss.

I retreat with light, swift steps. Niko moves down to Prianka's neck. She lets out a moan and opens her eyes. Her lustful, distant gaze tracks straight to me, and she screams.

"Lady Patel, what is—" Niko starts to ask before he sees me.

I sprint back to the trash room.

"What are you waiting for!" Prianka snaps. "Catch him!"

Niko chases after me. He's fast, but I have a head start. If I can get back into the trash chute, I might have a chance of escape.

A bright red figure materializes before me. I collide at full speed with the Noble Guard's solid armor.

The guard grabs hold of me in a flash. He lifts me into the air by my arm like a doll. I kick and struggle, but can't shake his tight grasp.

A sharp sting drives into my neck. My vision blurs and my eyelids grow heavy. I fight to stay conscious with several blinks, but my limbs go numb, and the hallway goes dark.

20

I awake in a dim cell, closed in by cinderblocks and metal bars. The Coronation V-Pro is gone. My torn-apart, trash-soaked boilersuit is fully visible.

A low whir fills the room. This place is hot like the trash chute.

I try to access a Coronation NeuroCast, but I'm locked out. The Noble Guard must have blocked me.

My neck stings at the injection site. The spot is swollen and sensitive to the touch. I notice a small mirror above the cell's sink.

The angry lump on my neck is merely one aspect of my haggard appearance. I've surpassed the general worn out look of most lowlanders and reached a new pinnacle of pathetic-ness. Aleks probably wouldn't even recognize me.

Zola wasn't kidding about the circles under my eyes. They look like two ladles of crude oil. Remnants of trash chute sludge shimmer in my unkempt beard and hair.

I hear the loud click of stiletto heels. Each step comes quick after the next. She must be short. Short, stiletto heels and eager to see me at my lowest point. Of course.

The stiletto steps stop in front of my cell.

"Kallista," I say. "How nice of you to visit."

She stares at me with smug, narrow eyes and a smirk. Kallista's fair white face with broad gold eye shadow and bright red lipstick pops against the drab surroundings.

"Bear, Bear, Bear," she says with a scolding click of her tongue. "I knew you were in love with the Idol but never thought you'd be foolish enough to show your face here."

"Someone has to help her."

"Help her? She's the Idol, everyone wants to help her!"

"Aleks never wanted to be the Idol. She just wants to live her life."

"She *is* living her life; she's living the best life imaginable! No one chooses to enter this world, but we *can* choose to make the most of our circumstances. Like you."

"What do you mean, like me?"

"Right, I forgot you're a lowlander. Let me simplify... You were born in a batch with hundreds of other Telladyne employees, right? Yet somehow you managed to slither your way into my family. Why my father picked you I'll never know, but he did, and you enjoyed a life that all those other four simpletons below the mist could only dream of."

"I was lucky. What's your point?"

"Lucky or not, you were given a chance to live beyond your station, and you took it!"

"Of course I did. No sane person would choose the promise of misery in the lowland over even the most uncertain future in the Highland."

"Exactly. You didn't know what to expect, but you knew it was better. Your problem is you got too comfortable and started to think you were one of us. Now look at you. Two weeks in the lowland and your true form is revealed, a sad, desperate lowlander, covered in trash and barely able to stand."

Kallista looks me up and down with a sneer and continues.

"Who wouldn't forget their old life in exchange for a better one? That's what Yukita did. You were a pastime, Bear, a novelty that made her feel rebellious. But now her life as the

Idol is so much grander than a few memories of flirting with some LEF."

I stare at Kallista as I grip the cell bars so tight my knuckles turn white. She smiles back, pleased to have gotten under my skin.

"Oh, don't get upset, little four," Kallista says. "Here, I brought you something."

Kallista reaches into her diamond clutch, and tosses a pocket drone into the air. The drone projects a live feed of the Coronation proceedings on the wall beside her.

Snow falls on the Coliseum while floating blue lotus flowers add a reverent glow to the scene. The crowd is silent. Trumpets blare to mark the beginning of the Idol Coronation oath ceremony.

A jewel-tone blue carpeted ramp extends down to the elevated stage. Aleks appears at the top. She wears a fitted silver robe that moves in soft waves as she walks. Aleks' parents, her three brothers, and Holt follow.

"Her flat chest and straight hips don't do that piece justice," Kallista snaps. "She doesn't even know how to work the robe's weight. I can't believe she's the Idol. That robe is sleek though. Don't you agree, Valet?"

"I'm not a Valet anymore," I remind Kallista. "And that robe doesn't do *her* justice. She's the most beautiful person in the entire city."

"Clearly your time in the lowland has affected your taste."

Aleks reaches the stage. Her family stops at the edge while she continues to meet Dahlia Delachort, Balliat Monarch, and a hologram of Vox.

"Idol-elect, Aleksaria Elizabeth Yukita, thank you for joining us here today," Delachort says through the Coliseum speakers. "Are you prepared to make your coronation oath and officially become The City's Idol?"

"I am," Aleks responds.

"Aleksaria Elizabeth Yukita, will you promise and swear to act as a paragon of virtue for all citizens of The City? To guide them in their daily lives and act as a model for their decisions?"

"I will."

"Will you, to the utmost of your power, maintain the laws of The City and preserve the system of commerce that drives our economy and supports the lives of our city's inhabitants?"

"I will."

"Will you promise to maintain the highest standards when it comes to the products that you endorse and the companies with which you work? To lead The City by example and never stray from the taste and style that allowed your election?"

"All this I promise to do."

Balliat presents an ice blue silk pillow lined with silver rope. A silver ring with a single, large sapphire sits atop the pillow.

"This ring symbolizes the unbroken bond between the Idol and The City," Delachort says.

Delachort slips the ring onto Aleks' left index finger.

"Ladies and Gentlemen of The City, I present to you, your 47th Idol, Aleksaria Elizabeth Yukita!"

Blue and silver fireworks explode above the Coliseum, while confetti canons fire mirrored flakes into the air. Energetic music sends the crowd into frenzied celebration. Vox vanishes to symbolically make room for the new Idol.

Aleks bursts into tears.

"You see that, Valet? Yukita just fulfilled the dream of every Noble girl in The City. She's done with you. She was done with you a long time ago. It was stupid to think otherwise."

I glare back at Kallista. She mocks me further with a series of faux-sympathetic faces and laughs a terrible, rehearsed laugh.

"I suppose you've seen enough. It's time for you to go."

Heavy metallic footsteps echo through the corridor. Two Noble Guards come into view and move toward my cell.

"Oh, wait!" Kallista shouts. "I want him to see this last part, too."

The guards stop in place. I look back to the projection.

Delachort rejoins Aleks. I forgot all about what happens next, the first act of every new Idol.

"Idol Yukita, before we sign-off, you must make your Proclamation of Desire! Tell us, what do you want, more than anything in the entire City. Just say the words, and it's yours!"

Aleks stands silent. She scans the Coliseum as if she's looking for the answer in the stands. The first Idol, Maya Sandivall, requested Pomelo Fizz. Vox asked for Naturalese Hair Color. This is Aleks' moment to declare her allegiance to her flagship sponsor, but something's wrong.

"Idol Yukita! Tell us what you want?" Delachort repeats. "Anything in The City— anything at all!"

"Say it!" Kallista shouts. "MaxDrive! You want MaxDrive! How is this difficult?"

"I want..." Aleks starts.

"Just say it!" Kallista shouts again. "What are you waiting for?"

"Perhaps a pen of something to engage your senses and brighten your mood?" Delachort coaxes.

"I want..." Aleks repeats. "I want a Valet!"

Delachort laughs at the request.

"A Valet?" Delachort replies. "You are the Idol, you can have ten Valets!"

"No, I want *my* Valet... I want, Bear!"

"What?" Kallista shouts. "Yukita is so annoying! Whatever. Even the Idol can't have everything. Guards, remove this trespasser at once!"

The guards throw open my cell door and grab me by the shoulders.

"Take him away, and make sure no one ever sees his face again!"

"Negative," one of the guards replies. "Cannot fulfill orders."

"Then where are you taking him?" Kallista asks.

"Classified, you are not authorized to receive that information."

The guards lead me out of the cell. I'm pinned under their impossibly strong hands. There's no use struggling to escape.

"Wait. You aren't taking him to the Idol, are you?"

"Classified, you are not—"

"No! Unacceptable! This lowlander trespassed on Noble property! He must be punished! He wouldn't even be here if I hadn't ordered him back! Tell the Idol I had him first! *I* say what happens to him, not her! Do you hear me?"

Kallista leaps onto one of the guards' back.

"He has to be punished for his crime! Disregard the Idol's order and take him away this instant!"

The Noble Guard throws Kallista to the ground with a sharp twist, and we continue down the corridor.

Are they really taking me to Aleks? I try to suppress my excitement for fear of being crushed completely.

We enter a freight elevator. The guards stare straight ahead with stoic purpose as we pass each floor.

The air cools. I look down to discover a new V-Pro outfit over my body. It's a Noble Valet uniform.

The elevator stops, and the doors open.

"Proceed forward to the gold star," one of the guards says. "Remain still until the lift has come to a complete stop."

The guards release their grasp on me. I walk, as instructed, to the gold star, which is stuck to the center of a circular platform.

The aperture of a circular hatch above my head opens. Confetti rains down through the opening as the roar of thousands of Coronation attendees floods the chute. The platform rises.

My head pops up from the stage, and the celebration hits me like a tsunami.

I can hardly see through the storm of confetti. Eventually, I find Aleks. Every muscle in my body wants to run to her, scoop her into my arms, and hold her so tight that we can never be torn apart again. But I can't.

Aleks defied Balliat and her sponsors when she said my name. If I'm going to stick around, I need to act like I'm on board with the Monarch agenda.

Delachort introduces me as I step forward. Aleks holds back, too, but cracks a wide smile. The magnetic force between us has grown impossibly strong during our time apart.

All I want is to touch her face, kiss her lips, and weep tears of relief, but now isn't the time. I lower into a deep, formal bow. Aleks responds with a curtsy.

"And there you have it, folks!" Delachort shouts. "The Coronation of your new Idol, Aleksaria Yukita has come to a close! Stay tuned for the Idol Tour immediately following this NeuroCast. Good night from Vanderbilt Coliseum!"

The Idol Tour: Five days of sponsored ad placement, with a LifeCast Dinner interlude. After that, the Idol's full-time LifeCast starts. That means I have just five days to save Aleks— whatever that means.

More fireworks erupt over the Coliseum while clips of the evening's Coronation play on every surface. The clips will play until Aleks reaches her first tour stop.

"That's a wrap kids," Delachort says. "Forgive me for saying so, Idol Yukita, but you really stepped in it now. I hope he's worth it."

Delachort walks off-stage.

Aleks and I wrap our arms around each other. I bury my face in her ice blue, juniper-scented hair and try to feel her in my arms with every cell of my body. We're together again, after what felt like an eternity apart. Nothing has ever felt this good.

Aleks pulls back and laughs.

"You smell awful," she says. "What happened to you?"

"The lowland. I was afraid you forgot about me."

"Forgot about you? Bear, you were all I could think about."

I stare into Aleks' wet eyes. The ecstatic celebration around us fades to muffled static. Right now, in this moment, there's just her and me.

I brush Aleks' hair aside. Our faces move closer. Her soft breath grazes my lips.

"Idol Yukita!"

Aleks' body jerks back. Balliat has her by the arm. He glares at her with impatient rage.

"We need go, *now*."

"No, you need to let go of her, *now*," I say, and eye Balliat with a furious, unwavering stare.

He releases Aleks' arm but continues.

"The Telladynes are incensed! Your last-minute script change has made our first tour stop more vital than ever. We have a jumper waiting... I suppose you will be joining us."

"Of course, I am the Idol Valet. I go where the Idol goes."

"Then hop-to, Valet. We don't have a second to lose."

21

The Noble Valet Council informs me of my official reinstatement en route to the jumper. I should be excited, but the bitter taste of my sudden dismissal still lingers. Despite being one of their best Valets, the council discarded me like an easily replaced machine part.

My feelings about re-entering Noble Valet service aside, I know it's the best way to protect Aleks. I'll have constant access to her and no one will think twice about us being alone together.

Aleks insisted on sitting up front with me on our way to the jumper, but we don't have a chance to talk. Every few seconds, she gets another urgent NeuroChat request.

She answers each request with over-the-top enthusiasm and sickening-sweet platitudes. Aleks' sponsors all want an explanation for her improvisation at the Coronation and assurances that she's still committed to them.

Between requests, Aleks tells me her plan was always to name me as her most desired thing. The invitation from Holt was also her doing. Unfortunately, she couldn't fill me in on her plan without raising suspicion.

Inside the jumper launch, I park the limousine at the end of a long, jewel-tone blue carpet. Aleks reaches across the seat and puts her hand on mine. With a simple, earnest smile, I'm convinced that all she wants is to be with me.

I walk around the car to open Aleks' door. She takes my arm, and we move toward her new, custom jumper. With its sharp lines and stark, aerodynamic design, the reflective silver jumper looks like a deadly sharp arrowhead.

A door slams behind me. Balliat. He looks furious, but his expression softens when two more limousines pull up.

The jumper's interior is more opulent than any I've seen before. Each swivel chair looks keenly designed for maximum comfort and style. Every fixture from the arm rests to the accents around the windows shines with luminous chrome that matches Aleks' eyes. A wash of dramatic blue light gives the entire cabin a cool, sensual feel.

"I don't want to, but I should sit back here for take-off," Aleks says. "Balliat's been trying to reach me since we left the Coliseum."

"Sit here," I say. "If we can't be together at least we'll be close. If you need anything, I'll be just on the other side of these doors."

The scent of freshly pulled espresso shots enters the cabin.

"Valet, don't you have pre-flight arrangements to make?" Balliat says from the jumper doorway.

"At least change into your uniform," Balliat continues. "It's bad enough that you stood beside the Idol in a V-Pro, but the stench of whatever you're wearing beneath is horrendous."

"As you wish, Master Balliat. Idol Yukita, may I get you anything before we depart?"

"No, Valet, I'm fine. Thank you."

"I'll have a—" Balliat starts.

"Very well, Idol Yukita. Please contact me if you desire anything at all."

Balliat doesn't even acknowledge that I cut him off. He sits beside Aleks and leans over to tell her about potential new sponsors as I walk away.

The cockpit door hisses closed behind me. Like the jumper cabin, the cockpit is appointed with polished panels and switches.

I put on the fresh Noble Valet uniform left for me. It doesn't take long thanks to years of muscle memory.

"How was your sabbatical in the lowland?" I hear a voice ask behind me.

I look back to see Marena Vexhall materialize into view.

"Lovely, thanks. The constant rain, lack of decent food, and endless work hours really calmed my nerves. How can I help you, Marena?"

"I came to see how Aleks is doing. Have you noticed anything different about her?"

"No, and I don't plan to. We're out of here the first chance we get."

"How do you propose to do that?"

"Not sure yet, but we'll think of something."

"I see. Well, in the meantime stay close and let me know if you see any changes in her personality."

"Will do."

Marena fades away.

I return to the cabin. The other losing Idol Nominees and their Monarch handlers have boarded. They sip drinks, puff on VaporLites, and cackle with boisterous laughter. The only Idol Nominee who's missing is Vitinia Flynn; she's on her own tour.

"Idol Yukita, you must pay attention!" Balliat snaps. "This information is vital to the success of your Idol reign, especially in these first few days."

"I'm trying. There's just so much to keep straight."

"Don't worry, Idol Yukita, with my help this will all feel like second nature soon enough."

"May I get you anything, Idol Yukita?" I ask.

"Looking good, Valet! Doesn't he look fit, Balliat?"

"His appearance is acceptable. Valet, bring us a bottle of Pom Fizz and two glasses."

"Pom Fizz? No thanks. That stuff's disgusting. I wouldn't mind a glass of water though, with bubbles. If it's not too much trouble."

"No trouble at all, Idol Yukita. I shall return shortly."

I walk through the cabin toward the jumper galley. Kallista and Prianka sit together up ahead. They're rapt in flirtatious conversation with Niko and Prianka's handler. I sneak past unnoticed.

In the galley, I'm surprised to find Crtr behind the bar. He pours the contents of a cocktail shaker into two chilled martini glasses and carves two perfect lemon peel twists. When he looks up, Crtr's mouth forms into a wide smile.

"Bear!"

"Crtr! What are you doing here?"

He comes at me with an extended hand, but I give him a hug instead. Once he realizes my affection isn't some kind of test, Crtr embraces me fully with a few back pats.

"I work for the Telladyne's now!"

"You do? How?"

"When you were... uh, excused from your post, the Noble Valet Council analyzed how much time I'd spent at Telladyne Manor versus Carrington Palace and thought I could better serve the Telladyne family."

"But Carrington chose you specifically because of the accident."

"I thought the same thing, but he gave me up, no problem. Said my story already ran its course."

"Whatever the reason, it's good to see you here. I hope the Telladynes haven't been too hard on you."

"It's nothing I'm not used to, which I suppose was the Noble Valet Council's reasoning."

"This is your first time in a jumper, right?"

"Yeah."

"Meet me in the cockpit when you're free. I'll show you how to get this thing in the air."

"Great, I'll see you up there! Now please excuse me, I have to get these drinks to Kallista, or she'll, well, you know."

Crtr speeds off down the cabin. I collect Aleks' drink and return to her seat. She stares out her window while Balliat talks at her.

"As I was saying, our first tour stop is to Telladyne Industries Factory #168. It is imperative that you stay on message during this tour stop. After your little stunt at the Coronation, Telladyne Industries threatened to revoke their sponsorship."

"So, what? Don't I have loads of other sponsors?"

"Yes, but Telladyne Industries is your *flagship* sponsor. They provide the base upon which your entire lifestyle campaign is constructed."

I set down Aleks' drink, and she looks back to me.

"Valet, we're scheduled to launch in ten minutes," Balliat says. "Don't you have somewhere to be?"

"As a matter of fact, I do. Idol Yukita, I will see you again shortly."

I return to the cockpit, hang up my jacket, and release the jumper brakes. The cockpit door opens, and Crtr bounds in as I reverse the jumper into launch position.

He sits in a chair beside me, and I explain what I've done already. The jumper shakes as metal clamps close around the body.

"Ladies and gentlemen," I say over the jumper intercom, "that gentle shake you felt means that the launch clamps have engaged. If you haven't already, now is the time to buckle yourselves in as we prepare for take off."

"You see that light there?" I ask Crtr. "Once it turns green, everyone's harnesses are fastened. You have to make sure it turns green before you're in launch position or you could send a Noble tumbling 50 feet straight down through the cabin."

"Can we tell who's buckled in and who isn't?"

We both chuckle. When the harness light turns green, I reach between our seats and ease back a lever to tilt the jumper into vertical launch position.

"Ladies and gentlemen, we are prepared for launch," I say over the intercom. "Please note during our flight you will temporarily lose NeuroNet access. I recommend that you take this time to enjoy the majestic view of our beautiful planet. If you would like a sedative for the flight, feel free to dock the Diazapax pen located in your seat's armrest. We should reach the Everglades in approximately 57 minutes. Thank you, and enjoy the flight."

"No one ever takes in the view," I say. "The notion of being without NeuroNet access, even for a few minutes, drives them all to the Diazapax."

"If someone offered me some Diazapax when we first got to the collective, I would've offered up my wrist before they finished talking."

"The collective... That feels so long ago. You haven't told anyone about it, right?"

"No. Who would I even tell? The only person I've had a real conversation with since you left was Aleks."

"You spoke with Aleks?"

"Yeah, she sent me NeuroChats every day to see if I'd been able to reach you. We were afraid you got disappeared."

Crtr is a true friend. I don't have the words to express my appreciation for his concern, so I flash him a quick smile and refocus on the jumper controls.

"All that's left is the countdown button which will engage the launch chute. Would you like to do the honors?"

I motion to a bright blue button in the center of the jumper dashboard. Crtr rubs his palms together and depresses the button with slow drama. We're about to move faster than any vehicle in The City. He's going to love this.

The launch chute springs to life with spooling mechanisms, surging power, blue-lit rings, and massive metal arms that click into place. A countdown sounds in the cockpit.

10.

Crtr cranes his neck forward to watch the chute's busy technology.

9.

I double-check my harness.

8.

A dash-mounted screen reveals that almost everyone in the cabin has already docked a Diazapax pen.

7.

Aleks stares straight ahead with a calm expression.

6.

Balliat's already passed out.

5.

If Balliat was unconscious between Aleks and me, we'd take turns drawing on his face with lipstick.

4.

The chute hatch far above opens.

3.

Crtr grips the arms of his chair and beams with the biggest smile I've ever seen.

2.

My heart jumps. I've piloted hundreds of flights, but something about this launch makes me anxious.

1.

There are people on this flight whom I care about more than anything, and I'm responsible for their safety.

0.

The jumper kicks forward like a bullet. I'm thrown back into my seat. The chute walls scream past in a neon blue blur.

The chute arms that pull us crash to a stop and propel us upward. We soar high into the clear morning sky on momentum alone.

Crtr laughs like a maniac. The altitude panel ticks up in increments of a thousand feet. I push the thruster throttle in my chair's armrest.

The jumper shoots up with even greater force. After we break through the atmosphere, the jumper evens out. The G-force pressure on our bodies turns to weightlessness.

I take a deep breath and look at Crtr. He points to the buckle of his chest harness. I nod. Crtr releases his harness and floats up from his seat into a slow motion, backward roll.

"We'll re-enter soon. Head back to the galley and prepare for landing."

"Sure thing. Thanks for the flying lesson!"

Crtr flies out of the cockpit.

I confirm the jumper's trajectory and prepare for re-entry. It's so calm up here without any ads or artificial light. I gaze out the cockpit window at the limitless, star-filled expanse before me. Without The City's light pollution, every star is visible—trillions upon trillions of them. The view feels wasted without Aleks here.

I push out of my seat to the cockpit door. Before I touch the door, it slides open. Aleks floats in front of me.

We stare at each other. Chills run through my limbs as my heart races. For a moment, my breath stops. My arms vibrate, unsure whether to stay still or reach out and grab her.

"Aleks, there's so much to say. I don't know where to—"

She pushes off the doorframe into me. Our lips collide, and we careen into the cockpit. Aleks tears off my RXSleeve while I rip off her coat. The sleeve pins hit a wall, depress, and send dozens of capsules flying. A galaxy of accessories surrounds us.

I pull her closer. Her skin feels cool against mine. Surges of pure adrenaline course through my veins with every kiss. Our furious rhythm matches the years of suppressed desire between us.

I grab a handle on the ceiling to steady our course. We float in a gentle spin. There isn't a single drug in my RXSleeve that could match this sensation. I want to spend forever like this.

Ding!

Ding!

"What's that?" Aleks whispers.

Ding!

"Onboard alarm... means we have... 60 seconds... until... descent. We should... should..."

"Don't worry," Aleks says. "We'll continue this later."

It's torture, but I have to pull away. If I don't, we'll overshoot our mark.

I pull Aleks in for one last kiss. We loosen our grasp, and I stare into her silver eyes. The City sees her as The Idol, but they don't know her heart like I do. They don't know about her generous spirit, her sense of humor, the way she navigates the Highland with unmatched intellect. I know the real her, and she is spectacular.

"Buckle in."

Aleks lowers into the co-pilot seat. I begin re-entry preparations and address the cabin.

"Ladies and gentlemen, we are about to begin our descent into the Everglades parabolic shuttle port. Please fasten your harnesses and prepare for re-entry. We will touch down shortly."

I flip more switches and engage the jumper's secondary thrusters, which push us back down into the Earth's atmosphere.

Waves of bright orange air, heated by the friction of our descent, travel over the windows. After we break through the atmosphere, I glide the jumper down to the runway, deploy the aft parachutes, and we roll to a stop.

Aleks and I leap from our seats and put ourselves back together.

"What now?" she asks.

"We figure a way out of this. Until then, we can't let Balliat, or anyone else, separate us."

"That won't be easy..."

"The only thing that's ever come easy to me is loving you," I say. "It may not happen tomorrow, or the next day, but we will be free."

I flip a switch that releases a light mist of salt gas into the cabin. The gas revives everyone from their Diazapax-induced comas. It's not harmful to anyone who's awake, but it smells awful. Sorry, Crtr.

"I should get back to my seat."

"You're always getting pulled away from me," I say.

"And someday I won't be, but until then..."

Aleks gives me one last kiss and steps back into the cabin. The door hisses closed between us.

22

Aleks sits in back of the limousine with Balliat to keep up appearances. Ever since we left the jumper, I've craved Aleks like never before. The sound of her soft breath as I kissed her neck rushes to memory. I can still feel the tremble of her body as my fingers ran across her skin.

I shake my head and refocus. There's no excuse for distraction as we travel through this unfamiliar region.

Up north, stratoscrapers are bound together by a mess of intricate steel scaffolding. Down here, in the Everglades, standalone modular factories dot the landscape. They rarely reach the mist and are separated by large swathes of marshland.

The Telladyne factory comes into view. Beyond the grey horizon and black forest of thin, bare trees, a colorful ad plays across the factory's exterior.

In the ad, Aleks rehearses choreography in an empty studio, laughs and talks while her hair and make-up are done, poses for a photo shoot, attends a siloball match, and meets friends at a cocktail party. With each event, the ad's color fades and the sound lowers.

By the time Aleks leaves the cocktail party and slumps into the back of a limousine, the ad is silent and in black and white. She removes a MaxDrive pen from her bag. Aleks docks the pen, and the ad's color and sound return, more vibrant than ever.

Aleks finally looks straight into the camera with a satisfied smile. The words "MaxDrive, by Telladyne Industries" appear. She exits the limousine, walks into a dance studio, and the ad's loop resumes.

We stop in front of the factory. Thousands of Telladyne employees wait to see the Idol in person, along with an armada of camera drones.

I step out of the car onto a gated-off, jewel-tone blue carpet. My skin feels sticky with humidity while the smell of rotten wood and mildew fills my nostrils.

I open Aleks' door and all the cameras flash. Balliat emerges first, followed by Aleks. A shockwave of emotion explodes around us. Some fans scream with clenched eyes, while others burst into tears at the mere sight of the Idol.

3 Beeps. Aleks.

"This is insane!"

"I know, right? They don't even know you."

"No, look around. All the men here look just like you!"

Everyone around has the same dark brown skin and blue eyes as me. The men are all tall, with broad shoulders, ideal for hoisting heavy bags of ingredients into high vats. All the women are short, with long fingers good for packaging and testing.

If not for my selection as the Telladyne's Valet, I would have lived and died beside these people. I'm one of them but luckier for whatever reason. My guilt makes it hard to look into their eyes.

Aleks shakes hands and smiles on her way down the carpet. I stay close. Chants of "I-dol Yu-Ki, I-dol Yu-Ki" mix with one-off exclamations like, "We love you, Idol!"

A man climbs over the gates. As I throw him back into the crowd, I see a woman with both her hands clasped around Aleks' hand. I move to separate her but stop when she speaks.

"Why's your dock like mine?" The woman asks.

"I had a run-in with the Noble Guard a while back!" Aleks replies. "The only replacement handy was this one!"

"The Noble Guards don't respect no one!" Another fan shouts. "They busted my lip open and broke my eye socket just last night!"

"Show me," Aleks replies.

The man turns off his V-Pro to reveal a swollen-shut black eye surrounded by an enormous purple bruise that covers his cheek. Clumsy stiches close up the man's bulbous, torn lip. Aleks gasps.

"What happened?"

"Reds crashed into my apartment looking for stolen pens."

"And they did that to you?"

"Sure did! I grabbed a chair, told 'em to get out. Gave me a nice smack for my trouble."

"They came to my place, too!" Someone else shouts.

3 Beeps. Balliat.

"Valet, we don't have time for this, move the Idol along."

"I can't control what she does. You want me to pick her up and carry her into the factory?"

"If you have to."

"Noble Valets are never to lay hands on their masters against their will except in emergency situations."

"This is an emergency!"

"For whom? She's in no danger, and I don't take orders from you!"

"Grabbed me by the neck," Another man shouts. "Threw me across the room like a trash bag! Spent every last point I had getting my collar bone reset!"

He drops his V-Pro and pulls down his boilersuit to reveal a mangled scar that travels down his neck and over his shoulder.

"They didn't find a single pen!" He continues. "Don't know if they ever found 'em!"

"They did!" A woman shouts. "Skag took the pens, a whole case of Breathex! They were for some Unassigned kid he took in!"

"What happened to Skag?" Aleks asks.

"Disappeared. The kid, too."

"That's... unconscionable! The Noble Guard can't storm into your homes and treat you like this!"

"Now, now, Idol Yukita," Balliat interrupts. "You shouldn't speak ill of the Noble Guard. Remember, they keep our city safe, they keep *you* safe."

"Keep me safe! They crushed my dock without a second thought! The Noble Guard are bullies! Bullies with too much power! How many of you have been hurt by the Noble Guard?"

No one raises their hand or calls out in response. Instead, one-by-one, workers throughout the crowd drop their V-Pros to reveal a dense landscape of broken bodies. There are countless bruises, open wounds, mangled scars, and patched eyes.

This is the true reality of life below the mist. Neither the lowland nor the Highland news chronicles this kind of abuse. Why would they? Monarch Media controls all news coverage, and they have nothing to gain by revealing how Nobles use excessive force to maintain control.

"You don't deserve this!" Aleks shouts. "No one in the lowland or even the Highland deserves this kind of treatment! We are brothers and sisters. All of us. All of us!"

The crowd breaks into screams, cheers, applause, and whistles. The "I-dol Yu-Ki" chants start back up, but are joined by new chants.

"No more guard! No more guard!"

"All of us! All of us!"

Balliat grabs Aleks' arm.

"Come along, Idol Yukita," he says through grit teeth. "We're already behind schedule and need to get inside."

I can tell Aleks wants to argue with Balliat but knows she's already pushed him too far. Her face softens, and she lets him rush her toward the factory. I keep step beside them while the crowd continues to chant.

Kassian meets us at the factory entrance. He extends his hand to Aleks with a broad smile that reveals his indifference to the crowd's fervor.

"Idol Yukita, it is lovely to see you again," Kassian says. "Thank you for visiting our factory today."

Aleks stares at Kassian's hand until he lowers it.

"Let's get this over with, Kassian."

We step inside, and the factory's massive metal blast doors close behind us.

"This will be a quick photo op," Balliat says. "Please try to forget the unpleasantness outside, Idol Yukita. You don't want it to affect your appearance. Remember, Telladyne Industries is your flagship sponsor! Where would you like us, Master Telladyne?"

"The packaging belt will give us some nice, active shots. Please follow me."

Scores of workers inside the factory are busy with all manner of tasks. There's a frenetic energy in the air as forklifts move across the floor, bags of seeds pour into metal vats, and pre-loaded pens are boxed. The workers' eyes, visible above their crisp white face-masks, look worn and bloodshot.

"Here we are, one of our hyper-efficient, state-of-the-art packaging lines," Kassian says. "We've kept a space open for you right here, Idol Yukita. Don't worry, we don't have the line at full speed."

Kassian shows Aleks where to stand and demonstrates how to package MaxDrive pens that come down the line. She takes over when the short training ends. Camera drones cover every second.

The workers beside Aleks wear full makeup and their eyes sparkle with life. They're merely set dressing in this curated scene.

"What was that out there, Valet?" Balliat asks, with his eyes on Aleks. "You do realize that it is your job to protect the Idol, don't you?"

"I did my job; no harm came to her."

"No *physical* harm... The Idol cannot simply denounce the Noble Guard. There are consequences."

"If you didn't want people asking about her dock, you should have replaced it with Styrolex."

"Our analysis indicated that lowlanders find her metal dock relatable. I told her to avoid questions about it, to keep an air of mystery, but as usual she failed to listen... That's excellent, Idol Yukita!" Balliat shouts to Aleks. "Hold the pens up near your face so we can get clean shots of the Idol with MaxDrive!'

"No matter, she will eventually acquiesce, they always do... Idol Yukita, kiss one of the pens! There you go! I wonder who the lucky lowlander to get that pen will be?"

Aleks kisses a distinct silver lip print onto one of the pens.

"And that's a wrap, Idol Yukita!" Balliat shouts.

"That's it?" Aleks asks. "It was so short."

"A testament to how much the camera loves you!"

Sirens sound throughout the factory and yellow lights flicker overhead. I hear the same robotic voice from the factory where I worked.

"Attention: Please evacuate the facility at once. This is not a drill. Abandon your posts and exit the facility immediately. Attention: Please evacuate the facility at once..."

"What's happening?" Aleks asks.

"Don't worry, Idol Yukita," Kassian says. "This is not a drill, but I assure you that everything is under control."

"Indeed, come with us, Idol Yukita," Balliat says and leads Aleks further into the factory.

"The doors are that way!" I shout.

"You don't expect the Idol to wait outside with all those fours, do you?" Balliat replies.

Aleks, Balliat, Kassian, and I snake our way through the factory as workers pass in the opposite direction. We emerge outside at the factory's rear. An enormous white hovercraft bobs in a river that runs behind the factory.

"What is this?" Aleks asks. "Where are you taking me?"

"Idol Yukita, relax, you are in excellent hands," Balliat replies. "I have a delicious surprise in store for you at the Splendido Resort and Spa."

There's motion from the hovercraft. A figure steps out of the navigation room. He wears pristine dress whites with a matching captain's hat and decorative sword.

"Davis Vexhall!" Aleks shouts. "I'm not going anywhere with..."

Something in the sky catches Aleks' attention. I follow her gaze.

A team of bright yellow, dual-propeller Hewgo Corporation helicopters closes in on the factory. There aren't any building materials in sight; this is a decon team. They're here to tear down and relocate the factory.

"I'm afraid you have no choice," Balliat continues. "Your limousine has already been moved to our next stop. This location is no longer safe for you, Idol Yukita. We must go."

Streams of decon agents in AeroPacks drop from the approaching helicopters. The decon agents secure themselves to the factory and get to work. Within seconds, the factory roof is detached and removed. More decon agents pour into the factory from above.

The alarm sounds again, followed by the same robotic voice.

"Attention: Telladyne Everglades Factory #168 is slated for relocation effective immediately. For your safety, please maintain a distance of 1,000 feet from the deconstruction zone. Thank you. Attention: Telladyne Everglades Factory..."

Furious roars, punctuated by the shatter of glass bottles, erupt from the other side of the factory. The newly-evacuated workers are being forced to watch their jobs dismantled before their eyes. They won't stand idly by while this happens.

"Why would you move the factory now when she's still on the premises?" I ask.

"Time is points, Valet. Even without the Idol's Coronation promotion MaxDrive has proven wildly successful! To meet demand, and lower shipping costs, we must move the factory north."

"What about all the workers you just made Unassigned? They don't care about your profit margins! Once they destroy everything at the factory entrance they'll come around back!"

"Don't worry, Valet." Balliat answers. "We've enlisted the Noble Guard to contain the emotional fours until our departure."

"You mean the same Noble Guard Aleks just denounced?"

A Molotov candle flies through the air and shatters mere feet from Aleks. Waves of enraged workers run around the factory. I grab Aleks' arm and run for the hovercraft.

The craft eases away from the dock before we reach it. What's he doing? Vexhall's fleeing to save himself. What chivalry.

Aleks and I leap aboard. Balliat jumps on after us. The hovercraft picks up speed. Kassian's still on the shore. He can't catch up. His flat-soled dress loafers are terrible for running, especially on wet grass. The mob will overtake him soon.

A loud, excitable part of me wants to see Kassian die. He used Aleks and me for his own gain and was rewarded for his treachery.

No. I want him to suffer, but in a way that matters. Death would be too quick.

"We have to help him!" I shout. "Look for something to throw, a life preserver, rope, buoy, anything!"

We scour the deck but find nothing. Balliat disappeared, not that he'd be any help. More Molotov candles burst around Kassian as he chases us.

For some reason the hovercraft slows. I pull Kassian aboard. Once his feet hit the deck, the hovercraft kicks hard and speeds away. The workers lob more bottles and trash after us, but we're long gone.

"Thank you, Valet," Kassian says. "I don't think those savages would have listened to reason."

"Thank Vexhall, he's the one who slowed down for you."

"I will have to do that."

Kassian straightens his jacket and walks off.

The Hewgo decon agents have already stripped the factory to its frame. Teams of agents fly enormous machine parts to the other side of the river. They stack the parts in neat, organized piles.

A menacing chain of Noble Guards creates a perimeter around the raw materials.

I see a chill pass through Aleks, and drape my jacket over her shoulders.

"What will happen to all of them?" she asks. "They're all Unassigned now?"

"Every single one of them. It's too expensive to move them with the factory, so the Telladynes will re-staff with a new workforce fresh out of training. Surely your father has modular factories. He hasn't told you about any of this?"

"My brothers are meant to take over the business. I, it turns out, was born to be the Idol."

Aleks' face drops. She stares down into the black water. I rest my hand on the small of her back. Her muscles feel tense enough to snap.

"How can they perform atrocities like this right in front of me and expect me to turn around and shill their products with chirpy enthusiasm? I'm complicit in all of this."

"There's nothing you could have done. Kassian probably gave the relocation order hours ago and planned the factory move even longer before that."

"Those people opened up to me. They dropped their V-Pros to show me their true selves, and I betrayed them. I didn't give the order, but I played my part for Kassian, Balliat, the Hewgos, and every other Noble who will profit off what happened today."

Her stare turns to a determined squint.

"Points," Aleks mutters. "What even is a point?"

"How do you mean?"

"Points! It's all for points! They drive people like Kassian to do things like this! Why? Points aren't even real things. You can't touch them, or see them, but the Highland's obsessed with them! How can something so intangible have so much value?"

"I don't—"

Aleks pushes off the railing. She shoots up a spiral staircase and flings open the navigation room door. Davis Vexhall stands alone with his back to the door. Puffs of white vapor float above his head.

Soft lounge music wafts through the toasty warm room. Dark polished wood covers every surface. An unbroken wall of windows provides a 180-degree view of the marshland.

Aleks marches straight to Vexhall.

"Where's Kassian?" She shouts.

"Oh, hello Idol Yukita. He could be anywhere. It's a big ship. Can I help you with something?"

"How do you justify treating lowlanders like this? What makes you any better than them?"

"I don't know what you're talking about."

"You know exactly what I'm talking about, Vexhall. The factory relocations—"

"That was a Telladyne factory, my dear Idol," Vexhall says with his eyes fixed on the water ahead. "I had nothing to do with it."

"But you've done it before. All of you have! And for what, a few points?"

"Surely you realize that the Yukita family has relocated plenty of factories. Why don't you ask your father these questions?"

"He isn't here. You are. Now tell me, how can you value points over so many human lives?"

Vexhall glances over with a smirk.

"I like your jacket, Idol Yukita. If I'm not mistaken that belongs to your Valet, correct?"

"What? Yes, he let me borrow it. Here!"

Aleks throws my jacket to me.

"Idol Yukita, why don't you dock a pen of something and enjoy the rest of the ride. You seem... agitated," Vexhall says.

"How can you be so dismissive? All those people, thousands of them, just lost their jobs! They won't be able to buy food or pay their rent—"

"Do you want to go back?" Vexhall snaps. "I'm sure those rabid LEFs would find your theories about points and the value of human life fascinating."

"I—" Aleks starts.

"I was asked to give you a ride, and that is exactly what I'm doing, but I did *not* volunteer to explain how the world works to a naive girl who clearly cares more about a bunch of fours than she does her own people!"

"This is pointless. I should have known better than to try and have an actual conversation with you, Davis."

"Well at least we can agree on that," Vexhall replies. "Your regrettable little outburst aside, I still expect you to make good on our agreement."

Aleks scowls at Vexhall and walks out.

23

Aleks stands at the hovercraft bow with her hands clenched around the rail. She doesn't even look up as we enter a lowland port and travel above the mist.

The lowland port opens to a grassy knoll where scores of eager Nobles stand. They cheer at the sight of Aleks, but she doesn't respond.

The hovercraft glides to a stop, amid the crowd, before an ice blue-lit hotel. Heavy footsteps shake the deck boards beneath my feet.

"Idol Yukita," Davis Vexhall says. "It's time. Shall we go?"

Aleks turns around. Vexhall stands with a toothy smile and his hand outstretched. After a few seconds of silence, Vexhall's smile wavers.

"Idol Yukita take my hand. We had a deal, remember?"

"What's he talking about?" I ask.

"I asked Davis to slow down so Kassian could catch up to the hovercraft. In return, he insisted that I let him escort me off the hovercraft when we arrived."

Aleks lets out a sigh, shakes her head, and plasters on a smile of her own. She takes Vexhall's hand, and they walk down the hovercraft ramp together.

Camera drones surround Aleks and Vexhall. Every news outlet and gossip NeuroCaster needs coverage of the Idol's latest arrival.

Balliat appears at Aleks' side the second her foot touches the grass. How dare he bound up as if he's innocent. I'd love nothing more than to smash a camera drone over his head.

I step off the ramp and expect to feel the spongy give of grass but instead, feel the crack of an RXPen. It's a MaxDrive pen. They're scattered all over the lawn.

"Master Vexhall," Balliat says. "Thank you so much for saving our Idol from that horrific riot at the Telladyne factory! We are all in your debt!"

"It was my pleasure," Vexhall replies. "I'm just relieved she's safe."

Vexhall kisses Aleks on the side of her head like she's a powerless child.

"Indeed, aren't we all?" Balliat says. "Now, Idol Yukita, allow me to be the first to welcome you to the Splendido Resort and Spa! With 184 luxury suites, 34 meeting and conference rooms, a full-service spa that's open around the clock, two 18-hole golf courses, and its own private white sand beach, the Splendido Hotel is the perfect spot for a weekend getaway, corporate retreat, or extended vacation. The Splendido Resort and Spa: The Art of Luxury, Refined. Are you excited for your stay Idol Yukita?"

Aleks stares at the ground.

"Idol Yukita, the Splendido Resort and Spa! Can you believe it?" Balliat insists. "Aren't you excited to be here?"

"What? Oh, yes. I'm very excited to be staying here."

Balliat coaxes Aleks with his eyes, as though she's missing something.

"At the Splendido Resort and Spa," Aleks finishes.

"Excellent! Come, let's see the magnificent interior!"

We approach the hotel entrance. On our way, someone grabs my arm. It's Niko.

"Noble Valet Bear, I apologize for my intrusion, but I was not sure when I would have the opportunity to speak to you again."

"Noble Valet Niko, can I help you with something?"

"Can you help me with something? Ha-ha-ha! You've already done more than enough!"

"Is this some kind of joke? If so, I'm not in the mood."

"Oh, Idol Valet Bear you are hilarious! The siloball match, don't you remember? You powered down my grapplers and saved my life! Now I am in your debt, a debt that I will happily repay!"

Niko leans in to whisper.

"I apologize for not coming to your aid during the Idol Coronation. Young Lady Patel had already called the Noble Guard. There was nothing I could do."

"Niko!" Prianka snaps from the crowd. "Bring these bags to my room at once!"

"Yes, Young Lady Patel, right away!" Niko says and turns back to me. "Idol Valet Bear, I swear my fealty to you here and now. If you ever need anything, anything at all, do not hesitate to ask. I am at your service."

"That won't be necessary, Niko. You would have done the same for me."

"Oh no, I most certainly would have let you die. You are truly among the most noble of Valets."

Niko scurries away to Prianka. When I saved Niko during the siloball match I didn't expect him to feel indebted to me. Regardless, it never hurts to have a favor from another Valet.

I catch up with Aleks at the hotel entrance. A short, stalky man with slicked back hair and puffy side burns greets us.

"Idol Yukita, hello!" the stalky man says. "Welcome to the Splendido Resort and Spa. I am Alfred DiMelino, the owner of this establishment. Please come in. We have so much to see!"

DiMelino claps his hands together and ushers us through the hotel. He talks at length about the Splendido's bejeweled chandeliers; one-of-a-kind, hand-carved marble fountains and every other extravagance we pass. Between listing ostentatious hotel features, DiMelino runs through the hotel's amenities such as instant room service; a 24-hour gaming parlor that plays every mechfight, siloball match, and e-quine race; and air that's purified with 106 levels of filtration.

DiMelino finally escorts us to a set of thick, gilded doors.

"The suite behind me," DiMelino begins, "hosts unparalleled views of our grounds; a private Olympic size, salt-water pool; museum-quality works of art; and six RejuviPod chambers like you've never seen before. But why tell you when you can see for yourself? Idol Yukita, I present to you the Idol Suite!"

The doors open. Everyone who walks inside, myself included, is awestruck by the suite's opulence.

Beautiful and ancient oil paintings hang side-by-side with mere slivers of wall between them. Vivid frescos that depict epic scenes of romance and battle sprawl across the high ceilings. Every rail and fixture gleams with polished gold that reflects off the bright marble mosaic tile floor.

Aleks moves straight for the nearest wall of windows where she watches the sun sink beneath the mist. When I arrive beside her, Aleks lets out a long exhale and looks into my eyes.

3 beeps.

"Aleks, I'm standing a foot away from you. We don't need to NeuroText."

"I'm afraid to speak. Someone's probably listening to us right now. My every movement and word are captured. It's maddening. How can anyone live like this?"

"I don't know, I think some people crave that kind of attention, like a drug."

"Well, there was obviously some kind of mistake because I'm not one of those people. I can't simply resign. Trying would probably make me more famous. The first Idol to ever try to step down! How could she do it? What was she thinking? And what was she wearing? This can't be how I spend the rest of my life."

"It won't be. We just have to bide our time until we can think of a plan to get you out of this."

"We don't have time to bide! Once my tour's over, my LifeCast will begin, and I'll be bound even tighter. I'm already maxed out on splits from interviews,

schedule updates, NApp pitches, and everything else. If anything drops, I pay for it tenfold with meetings about what happened and why. Bear, I'm sorry, but if there's a way out of this, you're going to have to think of it."

"Idol Yukita, there you are!" Balliat bellows. "Please join us in the formal dining room for the delicious surprise I told you about!"

Aleks pushes off the window to join Balliat.

This is Aleks as the Idol. She's thoughtful and defiant, which is what I love about her and precisely why she can't survive like this.

The suite's formal dining room hosts a massive, round table that seats 30. Only one place is set with crystal glasses, fine platinum cutlery, and an ice blue napkin folded into a howling wolf.

A chef with bright orange hair bursts into the room. He wears a black chef's coat with award patches all over the sleeves. The chef greets Aleks with an aggressive handshake.

"It is an absolute pleasure to meet you, Idol Yukita! I am Chef Casper Fiori. You may know me from my restaurants in the Highland."

"Yes, I believe I've eaten at one or two before. It's nice to meet you, Chef Fiori."

"Good to hear! I hope you enjoyed your dining experiences!"

"I'm sorry, I don't remember," Aleks says. "I eat at so many restaurants... but that's probably, good, right? I mean, your restaurants weren't memorably terrible."

Chef Fiori looks stunned. He's used to people fawning over his cuisine.

Balliat pounces to salvage the awkward moment. He moves Aleks and Chef Fiori together and places Fiori's arm around her shoulders. A publicist in a gold robe dances around the room while his FilterFlash glasses pop from various angles. When he's finished, the publicist resumes his neutral position at the edge of the room.

"Idol Yukita, thank you for inviting me to your suite this evening," Chef Fiori says. "I have curated a culinary expedition especially for you. I hope you're hungry."

Aleks grabs Chef Fiori's shoulders and looks him dead in the face.

"I'm starving."

"Fabulous! Please, have a seat. My Valet will bring out your first course straight away! Hopefully you will find this meal more memorable."

Aleks sits down while Chef Fiori looms behind her. A Valet, accompanied by several camera drones, enters the room. He hoists a bright silver-domed serving tray with his bird-like arm. His long blonde ponytail falls in curls down his back. He's clearly had his skin bleached to a near-glowing white. I hate when Nobles make extreme changes to their Valet's appearance.

"Idol Yukita, this evening's 12-course tasting menu will take you on a journey through the ancient world from the comfort of your chair! The first item on our menu is one that honors the great frozen north..."

Chef Fiori goes on with his description for what feels like hours. When he finally finishes, the thin Valet lifts the silver dome with a flourish. Aleks stares down at a bowl covered in dark red spines that contains a teaspoon of bright green liquid topped with gray flakes.

"I present to you, your first course, celery root and cuttlefish puree with Norwegian sea salt in an arctic sea urchin bowl. Enjoy."

Aleks can hardly mask her disappointment. It'll take the entire evening to get through all 12 bite-size courses of this meal.

She tastes the soup. Chef Fiori stares in anticipation.

"Very good, Chef Fiori, thank you. Is there more?"

"Oh yes, Idol Yukita! Our next course is on its way now! You know, I've catered events for Nobles all across the Highland, but lowlanders can enjoy my cuisine as well," Chef Fiori replies. "I'm excited to announce that Fiori's Fire Grill has just opened our 5,000th location in the lowland residence hall, Scenic Vista. The fare isn't quite as painstakingly crafted as this, but a piece of my heart goes into every dish we serve at Fiori's Fire Grill."

3 Beeps.

"Bear, I need some of that instant room service we heard about on the tour."

"What would you like?"

"I don't care, anything, everything. I just need some real food. Now!"

"Of course. What will you tell Balliat?"

"Don't know, I'll think of something."

"Idol Yukita, is everything all right?" Fiori asks.

Aleks' silence during our NeuroText exchange must have made Fiori insecure.

"Chef Fiori, I have no doubt that the food you've prepared this evening is among the finest in The City. The cuttlefish and rhubarb, or whatever it was, soup was delicious, but I must bid you good evening. You know, the life of the Idol, always on the go! It was lovely to meet you; I wish the 5,000th Fiori Fire Grill location, and all of your endeavors, great success."

Aleks squeezes Chef Fiori's arm and leaves the room. I follow behind. As the door closes Chef Fiori expresses his displeasure to Balliat in hushed, but angry tones.

"Hopefully that'll be enough," I tell Aleks. "Fiori's livid, but you left him with some good sound bites and footage."

"The soup really was tasty, I just needed about 200 times more. Did you order my food?"

"I did. It's waiting in the Master RejuviPod Chamber."

"Idol Yukita!" Balliat shouts. "Idol Yukita, stop right there!"

Balliat stomps toward us with his eyes ablaze.

"Idol Yukita, *the* Chef Fiori has personally created a tasting menu just for you. You can't walk out on him! This is insanity! Get back in there at once!"

"Balliat, I need a pod treatment and realistic quantities of food. Tell him there's some kind of emergency or something. I'll make it up to him later in the tour. I just need to do what's best for me right now."

"What's best for *you*?" Balliat asks. "Are you joking? There is no *you* anymore! You're the Idol! Whatever's best for you is what's best for your sponsors! Do you have any idea how much work goes into orchestrating promotional deals with people like Chef Fiori?'

"If you're tired, I'll give you another Hot Shot. If you're hungry, I'll give you a pen of Syminex to suppress your appetite. I don't care what it takes, but you *are* going back in there and you're going to eat every last bite of whatever Fiori puts in front of your entitled little face!"

Balliat's impassioned commands push him forward. I keep him at bay with a stiff arm.

"She's not going back in there," I say.

"Shut up, Valet, this doesn't concern you."

"How dare you speak to the Idol Valet like that!" Aleks snaps. "Apologize immediately!"

"The last thing I'm going to do is apologize to your pet four."

"How dare you! I've had enough of this. Good night!"

Aleks continues toward the Master RejuviPod Chamber. I follow with my eyes locked on Balliat. He won't try to fight past me to get to Aleks. Balliat's power comes from his words. Even so, I wouldn't dare turn my back to him.

"Idol Yukita, if you do not start listening to my advice and following instructions, I will be forced to take extreme measures to ensure your compliance!"

Aleks and I stop.

"What do you mean, 'extreme measures'?" I ask.

"Every Idol has a short adjustment period, but yours seems endless. Follow my instructions, and we might be able to salvage your Idol reign."

"What happens if my Idol reign can't be salvaged? Will you let me go and find a new Idol?"

"Let you go? Do you honestly think you could simply return to your old life after being the Idol? If you don't start cooperating, yours will be the shortest Idol reign in history, and we all know that Idols don't simply retire."

"Is that a threat?" I ask.

"No, merely a statement of fact. I worked so hard to make you the Idol, Aleksaria. I would make your Idol reign last forever if I could! But it's not up to me. It's up to the fine people of The City. With their support your every whim will be met, your every desire fulfilled with a snap of your fingers! Let me be your guide. I can make them love you unconditionally. But for that to happen you need to do as I say."

Memories of the reel flash through my head. I see Maya Sandivall, soaking wet and shaken to her core. I see Dr. Monarch, Balliat's ancestor, twisting her mind to his will. The thought of that happening to Aleks makes my whole body burn with unassailable fury.

"I'm going to ask one more time. What did you mean by 'extreme measures'?"

"You couldn't possibly understand, Valet. Not everything can be punched into submission. Now Idol Yukita, what shall it be? A moment of rest or a lifetime of luxury?"

"I choose rest. Good night, Balliat."

Aleks and I walk into the Master RejuviPod Chamber and slam the door in Balliat's face. He doesn't shout or bang his fists on the door, but he does send a chain of NeuroChat requests to me. I can tell by her face that Aleks is under the same request assault.

"You have to block him!"

"I don't know. That seems pretty drastic."

"It's the only way he'll stop!"

"All right, done."

There's no way for Balliat to reach us now. I didn't expect Aleks' departure to be such a big deal, but Balliat was clearly at his wit's end. If he's capable of the same brainwashing horrors as his ancestor, I'll have to keep constant watch over Aleks.

Aleks stares upward. Schools of fish, long white sharks, silver stingrays, and a host of other sea creatures swim across the vast aquarium ceiling. Dappled blue light paints the room.

"Maybe I should have gone back to the dining room," Aleks says.

"No, you need to eat. Here."

I slide back the mobile buffet table covers. Lobster tails stuffed with buttered breadcrumbs, beer battered onion rings, Cajun seasoned waffle-cut french fries, fried jalapenos with cream cheese filling, Buffalo chicken wings, and a smorgasbord of other delicious snack foods lay on the buffet. Aleks lunges at the table like a ravenous beast and tears into everything she sees.

"What do you think he meant by 'extreme measures'?" Aleks asks with a mouth full of food.

"I don't know, but now that we're alone, I need to tell you something. Balliat and the Monarchs... the reason I told you not to trust them, is because I saw what they've done to past Idols."

"What?"

"Remember the reels we found in the Monarch archives? They weren't just family videos."

I tell Aleks about visiting Marena's tomb, the True Born Collective, and most importantly, what was on the reel. When I finish, her mouth hangs slack in shock. I prepare her RejuviPod while she processes everything.

"You think they've brainwashed all the Idols," she asks. "Even the ones like Kallista who just want to be famous?"

"Probably. It didn't seem too difficult and why risk an Idol ever going off script?"

"But Balliat's never tried to lock me away in any kind of room."

"I saw footage from the *first* Idol. Who knows what kinds of indoctrination techniques they've developed since then?"

I double and triple check the solution in Aleks' pod. No one's tampered with it.

"You need to come up with a plan during my treatment, at least the start of one. Balliat hasn't done anything suspicious yet, but I can tell..."

"Aleks?" I look back to see her push away from the table.

Aleks eyes the chicken wing in her hand as if she's never seen one before and drops it to the floor.

"Are you all right?"

As I move to her, she bites into a fried jalapeno. Her face contorts into a wince, and she spits it out.

"What is... how could you serve the Idol such garbage?"

She's referring to herself as the Idol now? Aleks must really be losing it.

"Garbage? Aleks, these are all foods you've described as your favorite. I didn't know what you wanted, so I just got you everything I know you like!"

"Right, yes... I'm just... tired. So tired."

"Of course. Your pod is ready. You'll feel better when your treatment's complete."

I take Aleks' hand. She stumbles with her first step. Aleks is normally so graceful that I'm barely prepared to catch her. Her walk steadies after a few steps.

When we reach the pod, Aleks stops, looks down at herself, and giggles.

"What's funny?" I ask.

"Nothing... Thank you for your assistance, Valet. You are dismissed."

I'm dismissed? First, she referred to herself as the Idol and now she's talking to me like I'm any other Valet.

I pull a wellness report that shows me Aleks' fatigue levels are off the chart. She's actually delirious with exhaustion.

I help her into the pod. She closes her eyes as the twin pod doors close. I've seen her tired after countless performances but never so absolutely spent. Being the Idol is Aleks' most grueling performance to date.

I'm pretty beat myself, but I can't rest now. Aleks expects me to have the pieces of a plan by the time her pod treatment's over; I don't intend to fail her.

The pod fills with pink vapor and reclines into position. I grab an onion ring and move a lounge chair beside the pod.

There's no need to stay in uniform now, so I remove my RXSleeve, WristVac, and jacket, and loosen my collar. Last, I dock a pen of FocusAll and some other stimulants to help me strategize.

I flip the empty pen through my fingers and stare up into the aquarium.

The City won't let Aleks escape, especially once her LifeCast starts after the tour. It has to happen before, when we can still be somewhat secretive.

We'd need a distraction, a grand diversion to pull everyone's attention away from the Idol. I can't imagine such an event. It would have to be a monumental surprise that catches the entire city off-guard.

ReBorn!

The way Locke and Pach talk, ReBorn's true effect could be the diversion we need. But I still don't know what it actually does.

Something catches my eye in the tank above. Marena.

She somersaults and spins through the water as if she's weightless in air. I send her a NeuroChat request.

"Marena, I'm right below you."

"Oh, hello Bear! I was just enjoying a quick dip. I saw the aquarium and couldn't resist."

"How'd you get in there?"

"Water-adapted microdrone. Is Aleks in that pod?"

"Yeah."

"And naturally you're standing guard. Mind if I join you?"

"No, not at all. Actually, maybe you can help me with something."

I crack open the veranda door and Marena's drone flies inside. She rematerializes beside Aleks' pod.

Marena appears soaking wet. She bundles her hair together and rings it out onto the floor. Realistic projected water splatters against the tiles. Marena's sheer, white silk jumpsuit clings to her body and reveals lacy, dark blue undergarments.

"Marena, what is all this? You weren't actually in the water."

"I like to maintain realism whenever possible."

Marena shakes like a dog. Her hair snaps back into its familiar golden curls, and her jumpsuit becomes opaque. She flops onto my chair and crosses her legs over the armrest.

"Please, Bear. Sit."

Marena gestures to another chair, which I pull up.

"What can I help you with?" Marena asks.

"ReBorn, what do you know about it?"

"ReBorn... I've been dying to try it since capsules were found in Vox's estate. Sadly, it isn't available to me. The tubes that keep me alive can dose me with any current or discontinued Telladyne pharmaceutical, but I don't have access to street drugs. I have, however, researched it extensively."

"Have you uncovered any unusual side effects—maybe something that could be weaponized?"

"ReBorn does appear to affect women differently than men."

"How so?"

"Women experience significant libido spikes during ReBorn trips. Davis used it to sleep with half of the Highland's female population. It's revolting but hardly lethal. If you're looking for sinister side effects, I recommend shifting your focus to the Idol's flagship product."

"MaxDrive?"

"Yes. On the surface, it's simply a knock-off of ReBorn with focus and energy supplements added, but I discovered something else. After samples of MaxDrive were packaged with Valaviran, Davis got right to abusing it. The more MaxDrive he took, the more pliable he became."

"Pliable? How do you mean?"

"One day, after Davis docked 10 sample pens in a row, I jokingly told him to take a swim. Without a beat, he leapt into the pool, fully-clothed, and started doing laps. He swam 14 before I got worried and told him to stop. For all I know, he would have kept going until he drowned."

"So MaxDrive makes people illogically submissive. How?"

"That I don't know," Marena says. "But a drug that eliminates critical thinking is the perfect tool for anyone with a large workforce they want to easily control."

With enough MaxDrive, any Noble could build an army of perfect employees willing to work themselves to death.

I have to go," Marena says. "Our conversation has given me a great idea for a NeuroCast about Environmental Dependency Syndrome."

"Let me know if you learn anything new about ReBorn."

"Sure thing. See you around, Bear."

Marena winks with a finger gun and fades away.

After I let Marena's drone out, I walk back to Aleks' pod. Her face looks so peaceful behind the veil of pink vapor inside. I'm sure Balliat would love to get some MaxDrive into her; she'd be so much easier to control.

I remove all the MaxDrive capsules in my sleeve and replace them with a harmless energy supplement. If we wind up in a situation where Aleks has to request MaxDrive to keep up appearances, she'll be safe.

Aleks' vitals look good. I sit back down by her side.

Hundreds of escape plans come to mind, but none of them seem viable. Nonetheless, I can't stop thinking. Sometimes good plans start out terrible. Aleks taught me that.

24

Aleks' RejuviPod emits a soft melody and rises to standing position. Pink vapor cascades onto the floor as the pod doors slide open.

So many ideas sped through my mind over the past hours, but I still don't have a fully realized escape plan. It's so much harder to strategize without Aleks' help. Hopefully she can make sense of my flood of disparate ideas.

"Good morning," I say. "How was your treatment?"

Aleks looks me up and down.

"Where's my handler?"

"I'm sure Balliat will knock any second."

"Knock? An Idol's handler should never have to knock."

The room's door unlocks with a loud click. Mariposa Monarch strides into the room, followed by a swarm of hair and make-up artists, wardrobe stylists, publicists, and other members of Aleks' Idol team.

Mariposa approaches with hard, quick steps. Every muscle in my body instinctually tenses at the sight of her.

"Idol Valet Bear," Mariposa snaps. "What are you wearing?"

"My Idol Valet uniform, as always, Lady Monarch. Where is Balliat?"

"Not that it's any concern of yours, but my brother is momentarily indisposed. I will be acting as the Idol's handler in his absence. When did you last change your clothes?"

"Not since the jumper flight, I'm afraid."

"So, while the Idol received her treatment, you just sat around in yesterday's uniform? What could possibly—"

A bellhop wheels a room service cart between Mariposa and me.

"Ah yes, here we are. Valet, the Idol will take her breakfast on the veranda. After you've set her place, change into a fresh uniform."

"The Idol can speak for herself," I say. "Idol Yukita, where would you like to eat your breakfast?"

"Outside," Aleks replies through a split stare. "On the veranda."

"Well then, what are you waiting for?" Mariposa snaps. "You heard the Idol, go!"

Stylists usher Aleks into a nearby make-up chair and get to work. I don't want to leave, but I can't ignore her order either. It'll only take a second to set a place outside, then I can run back here and try to figure out what's going on.

Groomed shrubs, vibrant flower bushes, tall hedges, and multiple fountains fill the magnificent veranda. Early morning sun paints the sky in shades of pink and orange that cast dramatic shadows throughout the grounds.

In the distance, a diamond chandelier reflects sunlight patterns inside a small gazebo. The gazebo, while beautiful, is too distant for a quick breakfast. I set up Aleks' meal at a shaded banquet table nearby.

I push back the cart's silver top to find a half grapefruit, a small bowl of unseasoned rice, a doppio macchiato, and an ice bucket with a bottle of champagne. Aleks would never order this. She hates grapefruit and prefers tea to coffee. Is she trying to abide by some new Idol diet Balliat has prescribed?

As I prepare Aleks' place, I notice three objects in the sky. I recognize that color. It's the Noble Guard. The middle one has uncommon gold accents on his suit.

The guards land on the veranda. After what Aleks said about the Noble Guard they could be here for vengeance.

I drop the bowl of rice and run to evacuate her. Before I reach the door, it swings back at me. Aleks strides through with a wide smile and outstretched arms. For some reason she's got soot all over her face, fresh cuts and abrasions pepper her body, and she wears a tattered silver gown.

"Is that my dear Unkie Jervis in there?" Aleks asks.

Unkie Jervis? The gilded Noble Guard removes his helmet. He has a strong jaw, chiseled features, and scars all over his face.

"Little Aleksaria Yukita," Jervis says. "Look at you, all grown up and now the Idol! The City sees you as its beacon of virtue, but I will always remember you as the little girl who put on shows during her daddy's parties at the Teitaku."

The two laugh and share a warm hug. What is this? Aleks despises the Noble Guard more than anyone and now she's waxing nostalgic with their leader?

Mariposa looks at me then to the shattered bowl of rice.

3 Beeps.

"First your clothes, now this! You're a disaster, Valet! Clean that up before the Idol sees. And change your uniform immediately!"

"Noble Jervis," Mariposa says. "Thank you for coming on such short notice! I realize that you are extremely busy."

I move to the shattered bowl and out of earshot of the conversation between Aleks, Mariposa, and Jervis. As I crush the ceramic bowl into pieces and WristVac it up, a loud burst startles me to attention. I look up to see a rocket fire straight into the distant gazebo.

The rocket explodes the gazebo to splinters in a perfect, fiery sphere. I roll to protect Aleks, but she doesn't need protection. She and Mariposa applaud with approval.

"Contained detonation rockets," Jervis says. "They were designed after the Second Lowland Revolution. Our goal was to neutralize threats while reducing collateral damage to Noble property."

The Aleks I know would never co-sign senseless destruction like this. Why play nice with the Noble Guard now? Balliat must have threatened her somehow, that's the only explanation.

After the guards finish wreaking havoc on the veranda with more weaponry demonstrations, Aleks and the Noble Guards commence a photo shoot in the wreckage. That explains why Aleks came out such a mess, this was all premeditated. I duck away quickly to change my Valet uniform.

Back on the veranda, I see Aleks hug Jervis and bow to the other two guards. Once the guards fly out of sight, Aleks turns to me.

"Valet, fetch me a glass of champagne."

She walks back inside with Mariposa and the rest of her team. I run to retrieve the glass and catch up with her.

"That should smooth things over with the Noble Guard nicely," Mariposa says. "After today's tour stop at Turner Leather we will head straight to the LifeCast Dinner."

"I still haven't selected my gown," Aleks says.

"We have procured a selection of exquisite options from which to choose, Idol Yukita. Right this way."

"It has to be perfect. This will be The City's first taste of what to expect from my full-time LifeCast when the tour ends. We have to please my sponsors and make a splash. Valet!" Aleks shouts. "My champagne!"

"Here you are, Idol Yukita."

Aleks snatches the glass without breaking stride and stops before a rack of flower-covered gowns. A stylist pulls outfit after outfit from the rack. Aleks dismisses each gown with a wave of her hand.

"None of these are suitable for the Idol," Aleks says. "They're all so... pedestrian. Pull that, that, and that one. I will decide on the ship."

Aleks holds out her champagne flute and shakes it. I've been so focused on her sudden change in personality that I didn't think to bring the bottle.

"I apologize, Idol Yukita. I shall retrieve your champagne immediately!"

I move to collect the bottle, but Aleks stops me with a shout that's loud enough for the entire room to hear.

"Valet!"

"Yes, Idol Yukita."

"You expect me to stand here holding an empty glass?"

"No, of course not, Idol Yukita. Once again, I apologize."

"Don't apologize, just do your job!"

When I return with the bottle, I find Aleks has changed into a silver, leather A-line dress.

"Valet, prepare the Idol's vehicle for our departure," Mariposa orders.

"Idol Yukita, what about your breakfast?" I ask.

"My what?"

She's preoccupied with her reflection.

"Your breakfast, on the veranda, that came with this bottle of champagne."

"I'll have a NutriPop in the car. They come in fifteen different flavors and are packed with enough protein and vitamins to support even my active Idol lifestyle!"

"Aleks, you have to eat something! Something real!"

She whips around to glare at me.

"You're too familiar, Valet. I am the Idol, Aleksaria Yukita to you and everyone else here! If that is too long, you may address me as Idol Yukita! Do you understand? Does everybody understand?"

The room responds with over-enthusiastic agreement. Aleks waits for my answer with a cold stare.

"Yes, Idol Yukita," I say.

"Good. Now do as Mariposa asked and prepare my limousine."

I access the limousine's climate controls remotely, set the passenger cabin to 77 degrees, and tell it to meet us at the hotel entrance. Aleks and Mariposa move out of the room. I race after them like everyone else.

Kallista, with Crtr in tow, approaches us in the hallway. She wears a dark blue leather cat suit with thin, padded patches on the knees and elbows, and champagne gold zippers all over. The ensemble is finished with a long, champagne gold-lined leather cape.

"Kallista, darls!" Aleks shouts. "How are you?"

Kallista's initial shock turns into a broad smile.

"Fabulous, as always!" Kallista replies. "Aren't you just beyond about the LifeCast Dinner tonight? I can't wait to see what you're wearing!"

"I still haven't decided. Who are you wearing today?"

"Me! Do you like it?"

"Like it? I *love* it! It's decided, you're dressing me for the LifeCast Dinner tonight. Ride with me to Turner Leather, I want to hear all your ideas."

"Idol Yukita, I... I am honored!"

"The honor will be mine."

Aleks and Kallista link arms and walk together to the limousine. Crtr raises a confused eyebrow to me.

3 Beeps. Crtr.

"Aleks and Kallista are friends now? She just spent the last five hours complaining about how unfair it is that she's the Idol. This doesn't make sense."

"Nothing's made sense all morning."

"What do you mean?"

"I'll explain everything in the car."

"Can I drive?"

"No."

"Had to ask. Look, here comes Prianka."

Prianka sidles up to Kallista. She wants in on the newly-formed Idol clique. To my surprise, Kallista ignores Prianka. So much for childhood friendships.

I open the limousine door, and Kallista steps inside. Prianka waits by the door for an invitation.

"Sorry, Pria," Aleks says. "No more room. We'll meet you there."

Prianka gives a weak bow and walks back to her own car.

I close the door and move to the driver's seat. Crtr slides in beside me.

We wait in a long line as a motorcade of supply trucks and limousines enter the lowland port one at a time. When we reach the lowland, a dozen noble Guards fly above us in escort formation. Looks like Aleks' photo shoot sufficiently got her back in their good graces.

"So, what's going on with Aleks?" Crtr asks.

I fill him in on everything that happened between the Telladyne factory visit to now. Describing it all together reminds me of what Marena said about Vox. She became someone else, seemingly overnight, just like Aleks. Forget the escape plan. We can't leave until the real Aleks is back.

"The reels," Crtr says. "Maybe the rest of them can help us figure out what happened and how to reverse it."

"Loomi must have them all decoded by now..."

"Great, let's go!"

"It's not that simple. You're a full-time Noble Valet now, and I'm the Idol Valet. We can't disappear for hours on end like we used to. Remember, I already got fired for that once. I can't risk losing my post again."

"Then what are we supposed to do?"

"First, I need to get Aleks alone to see how far gone she is. We can talk about it more later. That's the tour stop up ahead."

The massive industrial complex of Turner Leather modular factories comes into view. We pull up to the main building which displays an ad starring Aleks.

In the ad, Aleks pours over clothing designs with a team of fashionable collaborators. The scene moves through the outfit's construction, from selecting the right leather, to final fittings. At the end, Aleks emerges from a limousine for some event. She wears an outrageous, haute couture dress with folded and draped silver leather. The words "Turner Leather" appear in white.

We stop at the main entrance and I escort Aleks along another blue walkway lined with workers and camera drones. She seems newly comfortable with the adoration. As we walk, Mariposa uploads information to Aleks.

"Our host, Canary Turner, took over leadership of Turner Leather after her mother's unexpected demise six years ago. Since then, profits have increased 147%."

"Can she be charmed?" Aleks asks.

"Canary Turner has been romantically linked to several high-profile Noble men and women, but there is no record of any particularly long-term relationships. With that in mind, yes, I believe seduction may be an option."

"Excellent. Thanks, Posey," Aleks says.

Posey? When did Aleks and Mariposa get so familiar?

Canary Turner waits for us at the factory entrance. She's easy to spot in a bright red dress. Turner pins up her ink black hair in two large curls. As we near, she takes a drag from a long ivory VaporLite holder.

"Idol Yukita," Turner coos in a velvety tone. "Thanks so much for swinging by. I trust you had a pleasant trip."

"It was fine, but so far this is the best part," Aleks says with a grin.

"Glad to hear it," Turner says. "Let's shake a leg, shall we?"

Turner's Valet appears. The NeuroNet tells me her name is Yele.

She's an older woman, probably the same age as Holt. Yele's shock white hair contrasts with her olive skin. Faint crow's feet and laugh lines reveal a full catalog of emotion beyond her stoic Valet facade.

We follow Turner into the factory atrium. Our footsteps click audibly on the polished concrete floor. Black, white, and brown cows wander around the room's perimeter behind glass walls. The cows gnaw on lush green grass at their feet. If my eyes were closed, I'd have no idea there were animals here at all. The glass must be sound and smell proof.

"Welcome to the slaughterhouse floor!" Turner shouts. "Most people have never seen a live cow in person, but we like to keep them around for inspiration. You see those hooks up there?"

We all look up to the ceiling where artfully-lit chains and hooks hang from the ceiling.

"Back in the old days we slaughtered these animals by hand. We'd hang their carcasses from hooks like those, move their bodies through the factory, and hack away whatever we needed."

"Sounds grueling," Aleks says. "Your family's inventiveness and ambition has clearly brought you far beyond such archaic methods."

"It certainly has. Let me show you just how far we've come."

Turner leads us toward a bank of dark archways. RXPen kiosks sit between the archways. The word "MaxDrive" rotates in light blue holographic letters above each one.

"Are these the new MaxDrive kiosks?" Aleks asks.

"They are," Turner responds. "Installed this morning."

"Wonderful! Your employees are so lucky to have MaxDrive available for free!"

Aleks skips over to one of the kiosks. A light blue pen dispenses. Aleks takes the pen, and spins around for a photo op.

I prep a pen from the MaxDrive pin in my sleeve and present it to Aleks.

"Idol Yukita, I've prepared a pen of MaxDrive if you like. Here."

"No, Valet, I need to be seen with a branded, pre-dosed pen."

"But Idol Yukita, the supply in my sleeve is likely more pure than that found in the kiosks."

"I said no! Now get back, you're ruining the shot!"

Aleks strikes different poses with the pen while she's painted by a flurry of white flashes. She ends the shoot by docking the pen and throwing it in the kiosk's disposal top.

So much for keeping Aleks away from MaxDrive.

Marena said MaxDrive eliminates the ability to critically think and basically makes people into mindless drones. No wonder Turner offers it for free. Telladyne isn't going to profit from MaxDrive as a recreational drug. They're going to make a fortune selling it to companies like Turner Leather. I'm sure Turner's happy to foot the bill if it makes her workers easier to manipulate.

We continue to an enormous room where hundreds of workers poke bubbling, sludge-filled baths. Dense gusts of chemical odors waft through the air.

Crtr nudges me with his elbow and sends me a NeuroText.

"Look over there."

A worker enters a booth at the room's edge. Glass doors close behind him, and white smoke fills the booth. After a little while, the smoke clears, and the worker exits into the room next door.

"It's a decontamination chamber," I say. *"They're common in factories like this."*

"I know. We're about to go through them."

"So?"

"So, it's small, only big enough for two people, max," Crtr replies. *"If you get in there with Aleks you'll have about 90 seconds alone with her. No one will be able to hear you, and once you trigger the decontamination they won't be able to see you either. Is that enough time to get some answers?"*

"Might be. Good thinking."

After Turner says a few words about the baths, she motions for the tour group to follow her.

"Idol Yukita, I hate to be a bother," Turner says. "But everyone who enters the tanning room must undergo a brief decontamination. I assure you that it is absolutely necessary in order to maintain the quality of our fine leather products."

"I completely understand, Lady Turner," Aleks says. "Care to join me?"

"After you," Turner replies.

Aleks moves into the booth. Turner follows close behind, but I leap ahead into the booth and snap the doors shut. White smoke surrounds us. Aleks turns around with a flirtatious smile that turns to rage when she sees me.

"Valet! What are you doing?"

"A Noble Valet never leaves his master unaccompanied in new and potentially dangerous environments," I reply. "Aleks, listen..."

Mariposa bangs on the booth door, but I ignore her.

"I asked you not to call me that."

"No one can hear us. Tell me what's going on with you. Is this all some kind of act to stay safe?"

"Act? This is no act, Valet. I'm simply free to be myself for the first time in my life."

"No, that's impossible. Aleks, this isn't you!"

"What do you know of the true me, Valet? You think because we shared a moment while you were sick that there's some kind of connection between us?"

"You know that isn't true. Aleks, are you in there? Please, I need to know you aren't gone!"

"Valet, what is true is that I am the most important person in The City, and you are merely a replaceable function of that."

Fans whir to life and clear away the white smoke. The doors open. A wave of dry, intense heat overtakes us. The sharp, unmistakable stench of formaldehyde fills the chamber.

"If I knew you were going to be this much trouble," Aleks says, "I would have let the Noble Guard take you. Oh well, Valets aren't known for having especially long life spans."

Aleks steps into the tanning room. I take a moment to collect myself and follow. Turner, Mariposa, and the rest of the tour party greet Aleks on the other side.

"Idol Yukita," Mariposa asks. "Are you all right?"

"I'm fine," Aleks says. "Why's it so hot in here?"

"The extreme heat expedites the curing process," Turner replies. "Let me show you around. And please, watch your step."

Toxic fumes fill my lungs, while the scent of rotted flesh saturates my sinuses. I never thought any aroma could be worse than the Vanderbilt Coliseum garbage chute, but I was wrong.

Steam rises through the metal floor grates. A worker to my right scrapes a large leather sheet with a razor sharp tool. Each scrape draws a thick build-up of pinkish-beige scum. The scum cascades down through the metal floor grates in putrid, viscous streams.

3 beeps. Crtr.

"How'd it go in there? You get any answers?"

"No, just more questions."

"We'll get her back. I know it."

Crtr puts a hand on my shoulder. It's a safe gesture because everyone else walks ahead with Aleks and Turner. Since we've fallen back, we can speak aloud.

"How can anyone think in this heat?" I ask. "It must be 100 degrees in here."

"117 degrees, actually," I hear from behind us.

"Noble Valet Yele," I say. "Why aren't you with Lady Turner?"

"I need to speak with you."

"How may I help you?"

"It's not me who needs help. After the Idol's public rebuke of the Noble Guard at the Telladyne factory, I thought she might be sympathetic to the plight of the workers here. Ever since Canary took over Turner Leather our monthly worker casualty rate has nearly tripled."

"What did she do?" Crtr asks.

"Canary's made operational changes everywhere. In this department, for example, she increased the heat by 20 degrees to dry the hides faster. You can't see it because of their V-Pros, but these workers are literally being baked to death."

"That is truly horrible," I say. "Unfortunately, the Idol may not be as sympathetic as you hoped."

All three of us look to Aleks, who clings to Turner's arm and flashes her a clench-lipped smile that poorly masks her disgust.

"She's very different than I expected," Yele says. "Please, promise me you'll talk to the Idol about the workers here. They're dying horrible deaths in droves, but all Canary cares about is profits. Like every new generation of Nobles, Canary is more ruthless than her parents ever were. Please, Bear, they need help."

Yele moves to re-join Turner. Crtr and I walk in silence for a bit, until Kallista spins around and shoots him an angry look. Crtr sprints ahead and leaves me alone.

Yele said the truth of the tanning room's horrific work conditions is hidden beneath the worker's V-Pros. She didn't understand the invitation she was extending. I take a deep breath and turn off my gem.

The V-Pros vanish. Every worker has the arms and legs of their boilersuits rolled up. Deep cracks cover their exposed flesh. Long trails of blood, from where their skin has dried and split, run across their limbs. But worse than any wound is who makes up the workforce.

Masked by elaborate hairstyles, flashy clothes, and ostentatious jewelry, the workers seemed so much older. I see now that they're among the youngest in The City. They're all around ten years old, fresh out of training. These kids barely had a chance to live before they were sentenced to this short life sentence of grueling labor.

I watch a young girl scrape a hide. Her yellow-tinged eyes bulge from her sunken-cheeked face. She's so thin I could wrap my thumb and pinky fingers around her forearm.

Between wheezy breaths, I hear the girl mutter to herself. She rattles off coordinate information, order numbers, and inventory data. She's split to work a second logistics job for Turner Leather. They've taken over her body and her mind.

An unsteady feeling rattles in my chest that moves into my throat. I feel compelled to scoop the girl into my arms and take her far away from this place. But even if I saved her, there would still be thousands of other suffering workers left behind.

Aleks screams. I flip my gem back on and run to her side. Once I get closer, I see that some sludge from a hide sloshed onto her dress. She stumbles back in disgust, and her heel sinks through the floor.

Aleks falls, seemingly in slow motion, toward the slop-covered ground. I catch her just moments before impact.

"This is unacceptable!" Aleks shouts. "Mariposa, how could you book me at such a squalid cesspool? I am *the Idol*, do you understand what that means? It means that if I twist my ankle on this slime-covered grate, I can't perform. If I can't perform, these stupid fours will lose interest in me! Then what? No wonder your nominee lost, Posey. Valet!"

"Yes, Idol Yukita."

"Make use of all those muscles and carry me out of here! I shouldn't even have to ask, aren't you supposed to think of these things on your own?"

"Of course, Idol Yukita. Right away," I lift Aleks off the ground.

"I agree!" Kallista adds. "Where have our Valets been this whole time? Valet! Do the same, I can't be expected to walk on these infernal grates!"

"Idol Yukita, I am truly sorry for any discomfort that you experienced during your tour," Turner pleads. "I simply wanted you to develop an appreciation for how the leather you wear is made. It goes without saying that I will replace your garment."

"Yes, it does go without saying! Get me out of here, Valet!"

"Idol Yukita, please wait!" Turner shouts after us. "I realize that your experience here wasn't ideal, but you must admit that our techniques are, from a technical standpoint, nothing short of spectacular!"

"Save it, Turner. You paid for my promotion and you'll have it. Meet me at the factory entrance."

"Thank you so much, Idol Yukita! Thank you!" Turner says with a series of bows.

Aleks lets me carry her all the way back to the factory atrium before she orders me to set her down. We're greeted at the factory entrance by the same mob of workers and camera drones from before. Cheers and applause fill the air.

Aleks and Turner stand side-by-side. They smile and wave to the crowd. There isn't a trace of the fit Aleks just threw on her face. She gestures for the crowd to settle, and they comply.

"Ladies and gentlemen of The City," Aleks begins. "Today I had the great pleasure of seeing first-hand how all of our fine leather goods are created here at Turner Leather. I must say that I was incredibly impressed by the technological processes within this factory and the overwhelming cheer of its workers. The positions here look so fun, in fact, that I demanded to get involved! As you can see from the stain on my dress, I wasn't a natural."

After the crowd's laughter subsides, Aleks continues her speech.

"Turner Leather is truly on the forefront of cruelty-free leather production, and I am proud to formally endorse their products. My only regret from today's tour stop is that I cannot stay longer. Lady Turner, you were an exemplary host. I would like to return the favor of today's tour by formally inviting to my Idol Estate whenever you like."

"Thank you, Idol Yukita. That would be lovely," Turner replies.

"Excellent! Now I must be off to the LifeCast Dinner. I hope that you, and the rest of The City, tune in to my very first LifeCast event!"

I look to Yele, who stands beside Turner, and send her a NeuroText.

"The Idol won't help you, but I will do everything I can for the workers here. No one should have to live and die like that."

"Thank you, Idol Valet Bear. That is a very kind offer, but I'm afraid there is nothing you can do. You and I are merely Valets, after all. I was foolish to put my hope in the Idol. At my age I should know better. Take care of yourself."

25

I yank the bodice strings of Aleks' dress so tight my fingertips turn red. This is normally something a stylist would do, but Aleks said they were too weak. With every tug, more light blue and silver wild flowers shed onto the floor.

"Pull harder!" she shouts. "I refuse to let this flower gown make me look chunky!"

"Idol Yukita, I'm afraid that I can't... get it any... tighter. I assure you that the fit is... exquisite."

"Put your foot on the window sill!"

I do as Aleks commands, and get another centimeter of string. Outside the window I see the dock float away as we depart aboard the Monarchs' airship, the Bonaventure III.

3 Beeps. Crtr.

"I know you're busy with the Idol, but I could use your help when you have a chance. It's Young Lady Telladyne."

"What's wrong with her?"

"She's in the ladies powder room on 6. She's throwing up everything she's eaten in the last year."

"I'll be right there."

"Idol Yukita, you look absolutely ravishing. May I please tie you in now?"

"Fin," Aleks says with a huff. "How long until I'm announced?"

"17 minutes," I say.

"Call back my makeup team for final touch-ups."

"Yes, Idol Yukita."

I do as Aleks orders and meet Crtr outside the powder room.

"She said all the flower smells were overwhelming."

"That's odd, Kallista's never been sensitive to floral aromas," I say.

I knock on the door as I open it and hear faint gagging sounds.

Kallista stands hunched over a sink with her dark blue flower gown slung around her hips. A black strapless bra provides her only coverage from the waist up.

"What do you want, Valet?" Kallista asks before she throws back a small single-use bottle of mouthwash.

Without a word, Crtr approaches Kallista and starts to redress her. She lets him.

"How long have you been ill?" I ask.

Kallista spits out the mouthwash.

"Couple of days, maybe."

"Do you have any other symptoms?"

"What do you care? You work for the Idol now."

"Despite your being an incredible brat most of the time, I can't help but care. If something happens to you, all my hard work protecting you from yourself will be in vain. Now tell me what's going on!"

"You think I'm a brat?"

"Of course I do! Forget it. If you won't answer my questions, I have other things to do. Good luck, Kallista."

My fingers touch the doorknob, and Kallista whimpers.

"Everything smells so strong. When I have an appetite, I can hardly keep anything down. All I want to eat is cucumbers and hummus."

"Cucumbers and hummus?" I ask.

"Yeah, everything else makes me wretch."

"Have you taken any new drugs lately, or mixed them in any new ways?"

"No new combo trips," She says. "The only new thing I've taken is ReBorn. But I've been taking that for weeks and I've only felt like this for a couple days."

I search the NeuroNet for Kallista's symptoms. Modern vaccines have eliminated every potential illness that appears. The only possibility, the one that isn't an illness at all, makes no sense. But I can't ignore it, absurdity aside.

"Young Lady Telladyne, I do not have an explanation at present," I say. "But Valet Crtr and I will keep you abreast of anything we discover. For now, it is best that you try and enjoy the LifeCast Dinner. If you notice any new symptoms, let your Valet know."

"Fin. I'll be in the parlor with the Idol," Kallista says on her way out of the powder room.

"Crtr, pull a wellness report on Kallista and tell me if her human chorionic gonadotropin levels are high."

"Human what?"

"hCG, check her hCG levels!"

"Done. She does have elevated hCG levels in her blood. What's that mean?"

"That the impossible has happened. Kallista is, somehow, pregnant."

A soft gasp emanates from a stall. I push against the door. It's locked. Someone heard everything. I knock on the stall door. No answer.

"Open this door or I'll bust it down!" I shout. "You have 3 seconds! 1... 2..."

The stall latch clicks, and the door swings open.

"Young Lady Patel," I say. "How much of that did you hear?"

"Enough," she says. "I knew something weird was going on with Kallista."

"Lady Patel, you can't tell anyone about this. The Highland hasn't seen a natural pregnancy in generations. There's no telling what effect this will have on The City."

"It's just one pregnancy. What's the big deal?"

"Are you joking? This news would send shockwaves through the entire Highland and beyond. But that's not going to happen because you aren't going to tell anyone."

"You don't tell me what to do, *Valet*! I am a Noble, an Idol Nominee no less! What's to stop me from giving an exclusive interview to Dahlia Delachort the second I leave this powder room?"

"You will do no such thing."

"Oh really? How are you going to stop me?"

"Do you really think Noble Valets don't talk to each other? We know all the Highland's secrets. My dear, you can't imagine the dirt I have on you... actually, you probably can."

"You wouldn't dare! You'd lose your job, *again*!"

"It'd be worth it to take down one of the Highland's most prominent Noble families. What I have to share won't just blemish your reputation. It would destroy the entire Patel Robotics empire. Surely you must know what I'm talking about?"

Prianka's face drops.

"No one would believe a Valet over a Noble..."

"They would in this case, Pria. You know it's true."

Prianka hikes up her purple gown and leaves the washroom. For all I know, she's pregnant, too, but I don't have access to her wellness report.

This must be ReBorn's true effect. A surge of natural births among Nobles would cause absolute chaos in the Highland.

"What were you talking about?" Crtr asks.

"What do you mean?"

"With Prianka. What's the big secret that scared her so bad?"

"No idea, but it must be pretty spectacular."

"Ladies and Gentleman," the ship's intercom announces. "The Monarch Family would like to once again thank you for attending tonight's event on the Bonaventure III. We should reach our destination, Nouveau Monaco, in just under three hours. In the meantime, enjoy your cruise, and please let our staff know if there is anything we can do to improve your time with us. Bon Voyage!"

3 Beeps.

"Valet, where are you? I'm about to be introduced!"

"I will be there at once, Idol Yukita."

Aleks and I stand behind a massive set of doors. Once the doors open, her first LifeCast will begin.

I check her hCG levels. She isn't pregnant. I need to make sure she doesn't touch ReBorn, or any Noble men for that matter.

An alarm sounds in my head. It's a reminder to give Aleks her daily supplement pen. I prep the pen and hand it to her.

"What mix did you use for this?"

"The same as usual, Idol Yukita, with slight modifications to equalize your stress levels, serotonin production, blood pressure, and heart rate. Allow me to send you the exact quantities."

I send Aleks the pen's drugs and dosages. She hands the pen back.

"Insufficient. Prepare this instead."

Aleks sends me a new order with unusually high doses of drugs that artificially produce dopamine, suppress appetite, lower inhibitions, and generally sacrifice health for momentary bliss.

"Idol Yukita, the pen you are suggesting simply is not safe. I cannot, in good conscience, prepare your request."

"Excuse me?"

"I apologize, Idol Yukita, but your order will have catastrophic long-term effects on your mind and body."

"This isn't a negotiation, Valet!" Aleks snaps. "No wonder you were kicked out of the Highland. You can't even follow orders when they come from the Idol herself!"

Aleks examines herself in a nearby mirror. She adjusts a few strands of hair and turns back to face the doors.

"Never mind," she says. "We'll find a way to rid ourselves of you soon enough. I'm sure your replacement will be more compliant."

If she could simply fire me, she would have by now. I became a part of the Idol narrative when Aleks named me at her Coronation. My sudden, unexplained departure would raise too many questions and detract valuable interest from her.

"Step aside, Valet," I hear Davis Vexhall bellow. "You're in my place."

Vexhall takes his position beside Aleks. A trumpet blares from within the ballroom, and the doors swing open.

"Ladies and Gentleman!" A deep-voiced man announces. "May I present to you, The City's 47th Idol, Aleksaria Yukita!"

The orchestra launches into a vibrant theme. Aleks descends a long staircase into the ballroom. Nobles huddled below stare and clap. I follow behind with the ends of her gown's long translucent wings in my hands.

Aleks' foot hits the green tile floor, and it ripples with the projected image of wind-blown blades of grass. Spring flowers climb the ballroom walls to an artificial, sun-filled sky. Swarms of bioluminescent butterflies float through the room like living fireworks explosions.

Various Nobles approach Aleks with outstretched hands like they've known her for years. They all say she looks gorgeous, that she was their choice for the Idol, and invite her to tour their factories. Aleks acknowledges each sycophant and moves on without missing a beat.

Through the gathered crowd, I see Aleks' former Idol competitors arrive at her LifeCast Dinner table.

Niko seats Prianka and fulfills her every request without a word. Marena sashays over and contorts into her seat without a single holographic waver. Dahlia Delachort's there, too. She's always at the Idol Table for LifeCast Dinners.

"Idol Valet Bear," Crtr says. "Would you please inspect the script on this new place card?"

I read "Mariposa Monarch," written in sharp calligraphy that shimmers with unusual life. My gem's product finder identifies the ink as a special, limited edition, Idol Blue #47. No lowlander could afford a drop of this ink, but for two points per day they can use the color in their NeuroText conversations.

The LifeCast Dinner is a festival of product placement that's meant to give The City a taste of what the Idol's full-time LifeCast will be like. Everything here is for sale, from the gingham tablecloths, to the drapes.

Crtr replaces Balliat's place card with Mariposa's on the table.

"Idol Yukita," Kallista says. "That piece looks increds on you! But you're acid rain in everything."

"I'm just the model, babes. Your design is the real star."

Davis peels away from Aleks to greet his sister. I almost forgot he and Marena were siblings. Marena yawns with obvious disinterest while Davis talks.

Mariposa appears at the table to little fanfare. She and Dahlia Delachort embrace like old friends. It's the warmest I've ever seen Mariposa act.

"Idol Yukita, I'd like to settle in with a drink before dinner begins," Davis says.

"An excellent idea! Drinks for everyone!"

I pull out Aleks' chair and feel an instinctual pang of excitement at the smell of her juniper shampoo. Even now, despite her abhorrent new personality, I can't forget Aleks' true self. I have to believe she'll return. There's no other option.

"Posey!" Aleks shouts over the floral centerpiece. "What are we drinking tonight?"

"That is Satine Debonay Pinot Grigio, Idol Yukita!"

"Excellent, thank you!" Aleks says and takes a sip.

A broad smile stretches across Aleks' face.

"Born of majestic plateaus with aromas of fresh-cut grass, Meyer lemon, and a touch of sunshine, Satine Debonay Pinot Grigio is the perfect wine to pair with any meal. Satine Debonay

Pinot Grigio, A Celebration with Every Sip! Valet, please make sure everyone has a full glass of this exquisite wine!"

"Idol Yukita," Marena says. "What do you mean by, 'a touch of sunshine?'"

"Excuse me?"

"You said that Satine Debonay has the aroma of 'a touch of sunshine.' What does sunshine smell like?"

"It just smells good, I don't know!"

As I fill Prianka's glass, I overhear her talk to Niko. She doesn't even NeuroText, which makes me think she wants someone like Dahlia Delachort to overhear her.

"They didn't even like each other before yesterday," Prianka says. "If the Idol ran into me in that hallway instead of Kallista I'd be sitting next to her right now."

"Most certainly, Lady Patel. How could the Idol resist your charms?"

"Right? Her outfit doesn't even make sense. What's with the winged cape? She looks like a giant bug. And a long-sleeved corset top with high-legs? The proportions are all wrong. No one would ever wear Kallista's designs without the Idol's endorsement. The Highland's going to become a laughing stock."

After everyone's glasses are filled, Aleks rises. She clinks her glass with a knife to capture the attention of all 14 surrounding tables. Two golden-robed publicists appear, and hold large gold-framed mirrors to the sides of Aleks' face.

"Dear friends," Aleks begins. "Nobles here and viewers at home, thank you so much for taking time out of your busy schedules to join me for my first ever LifeCast as the Idol!"

Aleks waits for the applause to peter out and continues.

"I would like to thank the Monarch family for hosting this wonderful event on their incredible airship, the Bonaventure III! If anyone knows what happened to the other two Bonaventures please let me know."

The crowd laughs as flashbulbs flicker.

"As we dine together, I hope that I may introduce you to a fine collection of products and services that will enrich your lives. But before we enjoy all of that, there is something I must address.

"It is no secret that my first tour stop at Telladyne Everglades Factory 168 was cut short by a group of unhinged radicals. My gracious hosts, the Telladyne family, were in no way responsible for the riots that broke out at their factory but were forced to endure them nonetheless. Unfortunately, these rioters struck at the end of my visit, which made my departure deathly dangerous.

"Yet, due to the strength, bravery, and heroism of one man, I stand here tonight. Had he not been there to rescue me, I fear my Idol tenure would have been cut tragically short.'

"Davis Vexhall, I wish to thank you publically, before the entire city, for your courage during the Telladyne Factory riots. I owe you my life. Please, stand and let us acknowledge you."

Vexhall rises to accept the room's unwarranted ovation. They have no idea he tried to leave us behind to save himself, and never will.

As the applause continues, Kallista throws back her wine and reaches for the bottle. Mid-pour, the bottle slips from her hand and crashes to the table.

I lunge to clear the area. Everyone in the dining room stares at Kallista. She slinks down in her seat with embarrassment.

Aleks breaks the tension with a hearty laugh.

"Get ahold of yourself, you drunken fool!" Aleks shouts in a joking tone as she shakes Kallista by the shoulders.

The dining room laughs along with Aleks.

I remove the broken dishes, WristVac the small shards, and re-set the table with dishes Crtr hands me. The tablecloth is designed to quick-absorb liquids, so there's no trace of the spill.

Kallista flashes an awkward smile and looks up just in time to see Prianka roll her eyes.

Oh no.

"Idol Yukita, have you ever heard the story of how Niko became the Patel family's Valet?" Kallista asks, loud enough for the entire table to hear.

"He used to work in one of their factories, right?" Aleks replies.

"Kalli, what are you doing?" Prianka asks, but Kallista ignores her.

"Oh, there's much more to the story than that," Kallista continues. "Prianka discovered Niko during a Southland factory tour. He had his boilersuit pulled down around his waist. The sight of his sweaty, glistening muscles ignited some kind of lewd lowlander fantasy within her.

"She checked Niko's NeuroFeed and saw he was obsessed with siloball. To get his attention, Prianka sponsored Niko in an exhibition siloball match near the factory. After Niko won the match, Prianka convinced her father to take him on as their Valet. In exchange for Niko's *full service*, the Patels agreed to sponsor him in siloball matches all over The City."

"By full service, do you mean..." Aleks asks.

"I do. Niko's been the Patel family's live sex toy for years. It's why their house is always such a mess. He isn't there to clean."

The entire city just heard Niko's origin story through Aleks' LifeCast. Prianka seems unfazed. Any reaction would lend credence to what is essentially a baseless rumor.

Kallista rises from her seat and raises her glass.

"I'd like to give a toast!" Kallista shouts. "To Prianka and Niko! May your days be filled with the kind of raw, untamed, animalistic coitus that only a lowlander can provide."

"That's enough, darls," Aleks says.

"No, no, I'm not finished!" Kallista continues, "I don't want either of you to feel one ounce of guilt about lying to all of us. Your countless erotic rendezvous required secrecy, I understand. But no more! I only hope that today's revelation doesn't spoil the novelty of surreptitiously screwing a lowlander."

"Kallista, that is enough!" Bertram Telladyne snaps from his table.

Master Telladyne stands with a hard stare that burns into Kallista. She responds with a fit of unrestrained laughter.

"Lady Kallista," Prianka begins. "I appreciate your kind words and am touched that you care so much about Niko and my well-being; especially in light of your own news."

"News?" Kallista asks. "What are you talking about?"

"Why your pregnancy, of course."

Confused chatter, along with a few gasps, fills the room. What Prianka said defies all logic, but the gossip-hungry Highland wants to believe it. They delight in being shocked.

"That's ridiculous," Kallista says with a laugh. "No one in the Highland's been pregnant for centuries!"

"It's true, check your hCG levels," Prianka responds.

"My what?"

"Your H-C-G levels. Check them and look up what they mean."

Kallista's laughter fades, and her face drops. The faces of Noble girls at every other table drop too. They all must have checked their own levels and gotten the same results.

Some of the girls break into tears and run out of the room, while others sit in stunned silence. So many different shouting matches erupt that it's impossible to hear any single one.

Every camera drone turns to Kallista and paints her with white flashes. Kallista's gaze darts around the room. Before she can respond, Master Telladyne pulls her away. Kallista squirms out of her father's grasp and returns to the table.

"What about you?" Kallista shouts at Prianka. "What about your H-C-G levels?"

"I'm sure they're normal! I don't sleep with every Noble boy in The City like you!"

"That doesn't matter, it only takes one!" Kallista says with her finger pointed at Niko. "Go ahead, check!"

Prianka stares down at the table for a moment.

"Come on, Niko. Let's go."

"What, Pria? Afraid to tell us about your half-breed baby? I'm sure it will be fine—probably just a little mental deficiency and facial asymmetry. At worst it might have flippers instead of hands, but any Highland surgeon can fix that!"

"I will love my child regardless of his appearance!" Niko shouts.

"So, it's a boy! Congratulations! I promise to tell my little girl to take it easy on him. It's rude to bully animals."

"We'll see whose child bullies who," Prianka says.

Prianka and Niko storm out of the room. A few guests stay planted in their seats, eager to see how the live drama plays out. Everyone else disperses in a frenzy. Aleks looks around like she's lost.

Suddenly, Dahlia Delachort shoots out of her seat. A single camera drone focuses on Aleks.

"Idol Yukita," Delachort asks. "What are your hCG levels? What is the status of your pregnancy? Is it a boy or a girl?"

"Lady Delachort, those are all valid questions," Balliat says, having appeared at Aleks' side. "I will alert you as soon as there is information to share on that front."

Just like that, Balliat is back. What was so important that he had to leave the new Idol?

Balliat leads Aleks away through throngs of camera drones.

"What's happening, Balliat?" Aleks asks.

"Due to tonight's unexpected revelations, we have terminated the LifeCast Dinner early and expedited our trip. We should arrive at port shortly."

"What about my sponsors? They'll be furious."

"A small price compared to the salvation of your brand."

This can't be. I was convinced Balliat was somehow controlling Aleks' mind remotely, which meant all I had to do was sever his connection. But he's here, and Aleks hasn't returned to normal. Things just got a lot more complicated.

I need to see the reels.

26

After we dock, Balliat, Aleks, and I enter our suite at the Hotel Notre Dame. Two masseuses snap to attention.

"Oh, right, the massage..." Balliat mutters to himself.

"Yes!" Aleks says. "That is *exactly* what I need!"

"Absolutely not! There's no telling who they work for!"

"Sir, we work for the hotel," one of the masseuses says. "The Hotel Notre Dame is known throughout the Highland for our deep relaxation treatments. It would be an honor to massage the Idol."

"You don't work for the hotel, you work for whoever gives you the most points! Collect your things and leave immediately!"

The masseuses scurry out of the room. Aleks tracks them with a pouty stare and flops onto a nearby sofa.

"How long do I have to stay here?"

"Until I return from my interview with Delachort, possibly longer."

"You just got back, why do you have to go?"

"Someone has to feed the wolves," Balliat says. "I still don't know if it's good or bad that you seem to be the only Noble girl who *isn't* pregnant. Until we determine a course of action, you are not to answer any questions about the status of your womb."

"Fin."

"Valet, that goes for you too. If you dare leak a single drop of inside information about the Idol's health you will never see the sun again. Understand?"

"Yes, sir."

Balliat leaves. Aleks lies on the sofa in a split stare.

"Valet, give me a pen of something to relax."

I'll need a fair amount of time if I'm going to see what's on the rest of the reels Loomi decoded. Aleks can't know I'm gone.

"Idol Yukita, a pen is merely a temporary solution. If you are feeling stressed, I recommend a pod treatment."

She shakes out of her split stare.

"A pod treatment? Are you joking? This moment will define me as the Idol! I have interviews to schedule, dirt to gather, deals to negotiate! If I play this right, my Idol reign will be legendary!"

"Idol Yukita, Balliat said not to speak to anyone..."

"And I won't! I'm simply preparing in advance for however we decide to proceed. Now give me the pen I requested."

"You don't need a pen right now, you need—"

"Need what, Valet? You don't know what I need! You don't know me at all!"

I stand speechless. No one knows Aleks better than I do, and she doesn't even realize it.

"I saw what you did for Kallista in the dining room," I say. "You saw her embarrassment and diffused the situation. That's something the Aleks I knew would have done."

"What? Oh, the drunken fool thing? Mariposa told me to say that. We have to protect our primary sponsor's reputation. Now give me that pen!"

Aleks lunges for my jacket, and I push her away. She stumbles backward onto the sofa.

My eyes shake with a mixture of remorse and rage. I can't let my emotions control me like this. For a moment, she was someone else entirely, even to me. If I, of all people, lose sight of Aleks' true self there's no hope for her.

"How dare you shove me like that!" Aleks shouts as she stomps back at me. "You're lucky Balliat insists on keeping you around."

"Fine, you want a pen, here!"

I prep a fresh pen with three doses of Diazapax. Aleks grabs for the pen, but I hold it out of reach. If I can ignite some spark of critical thinking in her, maybe she'll snap back, and I won't even need the reels.

"I'll give you this pen in exchange for an answer," I say. "Why are you the only Noble girl who isn't pregnant."

"I don't know! Now, give me that pen!"

"Not until you answer my question."

"I can't!"

"Yes, you can."

"No, I *can't*! Every memory of my old life was wiped when I became the Idol, so I would be unencumbered by my meaningless past."

"Your meaningless past?" I repeat. "Aleks, how could you—"

"I told you not to call me that!"

She charges toward me at full speed. When she reaches me to grab for the pen, I catch Aleks and hold her in a close embrace.

"Your life was not meaningless before you became the Idol," I say. "Look at this."

I step back, reach into my breast pocket, and remove the harmonica I've had since our last hunting trip. Aleks' eyes lock onto the instrument. Her furious features calm.

"Monarch," She reads aloud. "What is this?"

"It's an instrument called a harmonica. You blow into these holes and it makes different sounds. We discovered it together."

"Where?"

"The Monarch family archives."

"That's impossible. I've never seen this thing before, and I've certainly never been to the Monarch archives."

"Yes, you have. We used to be friends, best friends. You just don't remember."

"So when... *we* left, you took this with you?"

"They won't miss it."

"And the Monarchs had no idea you were there?"

"No."

"So you, Idol Valet Bear, trespassed in the archives of a Noble family and stole their property? This is amazing. Forget the pen, I can finally get rid of you!"

"Wait, Aleks—"

"I can't wait to tell Balliat when he returns. He'll probably fire you on the spot! No, this is too perfect. I have to tell him now!"

I spring forward and dock the pen into Aleks' wrist. She falls limp into my arms. I stand frozen for a few seconds to see if the Noble Guard crash into the room. If Aleks sent a panic message they'd already be here. I'm safe.

It was a stupid risk, but I thought I might be able to reach her. Our entire conversation is stored in her gem's visual record. If anyone sees that recording I'll be terminated, or worse, disappeared.

I move Aleks' limp body into her RejuviPod. She'll be safe there until I return from the True Born Collective. My only option now is to get Aleks back to normal before Balliat returns and she can report me.

The hotel hallways bustle with busy Valets and bellhops. Like Aleks, all the Noble children are confined to their rooms until someone tells them what to do.

I enter Kallista's suite to the sounds of coughing, gagging, spitting, and vomiting. I follow the sounds. Crtr turns a corner and nearly collides with me.

"Idol Valet Bear, what are you doing here?"

"I need your help. Do you remember that place where we met those strange people and you drove that fast thing through the dark?" I ask.

"How could I forget?"

"Good. I need to go back right now. You in?"

"I'd like nothing more, but I can't leave Young Lady Kallista in this state."

"What state?"

Crtr walks me to the bathroom. I peek inside to find Kallista hunched over the toilet bowl. In just her underwear, Kallista looks more frail than I've ever seen her.

A thick layer of sweat covers Kallista's body. There's an acrid, fermented smell in the air. Something's seriously wrong with her.

"She's been like this since we got back from dinner," Crtr says. "The nausea's come and gone for days, but this is new. Nothing in my sleeve seems to help."

"It's not just Kallista," we hear a familiar voice say.

Crtr and I look back to find Marena Vexhall. She wears a plush white hotel robe, comfortable slippers, and has her hair piled atop her head.

"Young Lady Vexhall," Crtr says. "How may I help you?"

"I'm actually here for Bear, but let me give you some advice. Don't give her anymore pens."

"Why not?"

"Once everyone's pregnancies were confirmed, their Neurogems activated a long dormant purge protocol to protect their unborn children. Kallista's body is trying to expunge any chemicals, toxins, or poisons that could harm the fetus."

"Everyone's pregnancies?"

"That's right, every Noble girl in this hotel has her face in the toilet, same as Kallista. The best thing for her right now is a pod treatment. It will purify her system, rehydrate her, and relieve her of this unpleasantness."

"I'll give you a hand," I say. "Marena, you may want to disappear for this part. Kallista won't react well if she sees you here."

Marena nods and fades out of sight.

Crtr and I enter the bathroom. Kallista does a double take when she sees me. Her pale white face turns beet red.

"Valet, what is he—" Kallista gags into the toilet. "Doing here?"

"Idol Valet Bear is here to help, Young Lady Telladyne."

"Don't you have an Idol to tend to?"

"Never mind that. We need to get you into a RejuviPod. It will make you—"

"You're not stuffing me in there! Get out, both of you!" Kallista shouts, which triggers another round of vomiting.

As she spits into the bowl, I crouch down beside Kallista. She looks up with tired, wet eyes. Black tear streaks run down her cheeks that connect with thick smudges of bright red lipstick. The memory of applying her makeup for the first time rushes to mind.

Kallista was so excited to try every color of eye shadow and lipstick. That first make-up session took hours, but it was full of smiles and laughter. She was so innocent then.

"Kallista," I say. "Your body is trying to evacuate all of the drugs and alcohol in your system for the health of your unborn child. Please trust me."

Kallista sniffles and gags into the toilet again but nothing comes. I extend my hand to help her up. She refuses, and pushes herself up on shaky legs. Crtr drapes her in a bathrobe.

After Kallista's pod fills with pink vapor, Crtr slumps onto a nearby sofa. He undoes his messy bun of thin braids and runs his hand back through them. Marena reappears.

"Bear," Marena says. "What can you tell me about Aleks' personality shift? When did it start?"

"I don't know, it was so sud... the jalapeno popper."

"Excuse me?"

"She loves jalapeno poppers, but she spit one out in disgust... at the Splendido Hotel, before her last pod treatment."

"Why didn't you tell me that night?"

"I thought she was just delirious with exhaustion. When she came out of the pod, she was a different person."

"There must be something else!" Marena says. "With more data I might be able to find a safe way to restore her mind."

"Do you know an un-safe way?" Crtr asks.

Marena's eyes drop. She looks at the ground with a distant, frozen stare.

"Vox," I say. "Before she jumped. How'd you do it?"

"That isn't an option, you saw what happened."

"Aleks isn't Vox! She could react differently."

"It didn't work! Vox is dead because of my impatience! That's why I'm trying to get as much information as possible!"

"I may have something useful. Crtr, you coming?"

"How are we supposed to get out of here without drawing attention? There's an army of NeuroCasters and camera drones camped outside the hotel."

"The premium escape port," Marena says.

"What premium escape port? Isn't that something the Idol Valet would know about?"

"If the Idol had to make an emergency escape, DiMelino would surely tell you about it, in exchange for a usage fee. Lucky for you, I already found it. Go to the parking garage, drive between a pillar labeled D5, and an unmarked green door."

Crtr and I drive the Idol limousine where Marena explained. We pass straight through a V-Pro wall into a small lowland port that drops us onto a closed highway off-ramp.

I enter traffic and weave through LaborLiners like the road is empty. We don't know when Balliat will return, and the last thing I need is to be attacked by radicals.

"Where we meeting Locke and Loomi?" Crtr asks.

"They don't actually know we're coming."

"Are you serious? What are we supposed to do, waive our arms and shout 'It's all right everyone, we're just here to see The True Born Collective! Never mind the limo and the Noble Valet uniforms!"

"Of course not."

"Then what's the plan?"

"I don't know... I didn't really think this part through."

"There's no other way to reach Locke or Loomi?"

"No, they must use a private, encrypted NeuroNet signal. Let me try Pach."

I send Pach a NeuroChat request, but there's no answer. Maybe Zola can put me in contact with him.

"Bear, how are you?"

"Fine. Is Pach around?"

"Oh no, afraid not. They took him for testing."

"What, when?"

"The night of the Idol Coronation."

"What kind of testing, I thought they were finished with him?"

"Me too, but the white coats came in and took him. Didn't say why."

"When's he coming back?"

"Don't know."

"OK, I have to go. Tell him to contact me when he gets back. Thanks, Zola."

"Every time you call asking for Pach you're either in trouble or about to get into trouble. Be careful, Bear."

"I will. Thanks."

We reach the exit and sink into the clave. It's eerily calm like last time. That is, until the gunfire starts.

A trail of bullets travels across the limo's side. I punch the throttle and tear down the crumbled road. More shooters fire upon us as we speed deeper into the clave. Our prismatic panel blur must stand out against the still landscape.

They expected us last time, but tonight we just look like Noble fools who wandered off the highway. The limo's taillights burst. We need to find cover. I pull into a dark alleyway, but the bullets follow. As I reverse out of the useless hiding spot, a rocket-propelled grenade explodes where we were parked.

I skid around a corner toward the palace. Webs of thin cracks spread across the limo's windows from the barrage of bullets.

No time to drive on the circular path to the palace entrance. We pop onto the lawn. The limo's tires spin on the wet grass before we gain traction and launch forward.

The back window bursts into glass shards. More rear windows shatter into a crystalline storm. The wet grass makes evasive maneuvers impossible. The slightest miscalculation could spin us out.

We close in on the two abandoned powercycles from our first visit. I swerve to evade the powercycles and trigger the booby trap I expected.

A heavy mortar detonates beneath us that shoots the limousine's back-end high into the air. Every remaining window shatters and drowns us in sprayed glass. I think we might flip over until we crash back down with angry force. The car's steel-reinforced undercarriage saved us from being evaporated.

The limo crawls forward on its front two wheels. I drive straight up the palace stairs and crash through the main entrance. Bullets continue to pelt the car, but we're somewhat obscured by the crash debris dust cloud.

Crtr and I climb through the front windshield. We cough and stumble behind an old desk for cover.

"You remember how to get back to that kitchen where we docked those ReBorn pens?" I ask.

"I think so, come on!"

Crtr bolts down a nearby corridor. I wait for a break in the gunfire and follow. A few strides into my run, another rocket-propelled grenade hits the limousine. Flames spew from the windows of the dead car's carcass.

Crtr sprints down a circuitous path. More shots ring out. We're being hunted, possibly even corralled. Crtr seems lost in the palace's maze-like halls.

The gunfire stops. Unsettling silence. They're trying to sneak up on us.

3 Beeps.

"Over here!"

Crtr motions to a pair of familiar double doors. He found it! We bound inside, shut the doors, and barricade them with a heavy table.

Crtr activates his WristVac flashlight and shines it around the room. I do the same.

"What now?" Crtr asks. "There aren't any other exits, we're trapped!"

We hear a faint crackle of static followed by a high-pitched screech. The screech stops. We aim our flashlights at the sound's origin. A tiny speaker hangs in the room's darkest corner.

"Bear...car!" the speaker shouts in a broken voice. "I th... you..."

We run to the speaker. Another burst of gunfire explodes in the hall. They're still in pursuit and getting closer.

"Loomi? Locke? We need to see you!" I shout.

"Le... me... There, is that better?" Loomi asks.

"Yes, better! Loomi, they're almost here! Help us!"

"All right, stand clear."

"Stand clear of what?"

Nearby counter cabinets shift to reveal a small square hatch in the floor. A long cart on tracks sits inside the hatch.

"Get in the cart and lie flat!"

We do as Loomi instructs. The floor seals back up over our faces, and the cart lurches forward, then plummets.

My stomach climbs into my chest as we careen in a chaotic descent. Flickers of neon green light our journey. Crtr's maniacal laughter rises above the squeal of metal wheels against the track.

The green lights go out, and the cart's brakes squeal.

We wobble to a stop. Crtr continues to laugh as we climb out of the cart. He looks back at the tracks and shakes his head. I'm glad we were unconscious for the first trip.

After a few minutes, Locke and Loomi arrive.

"Follow us," Locke says.

She and Loomi lead us to a narrow pathway. The winding, almost service tunnel-like route is a far cry from our first, very public, visit.

"Is this how we get to the powercycles?" Crtr asks.

"No powercycles this time," Locke says. "Too conspicuous. If Rork's followers knew you were here, they'd execute you on-sight."

"Why?" I ask.

"Two men got lost in the tunnels during your escape," Loomi says. "They're presumed dead, and Rork blames you."

"They were trying to kill us!" Crtr shouts.

"Shh!" Loomi says. "We know. That's why we didn't leave you back there. You'll be safe once you're in our lab."

"You mean like last time?" I ask.

"We've improved our security since then," Locke replies.

We travel through more dark, damp tunnels until Loomi stops. She pushes on a wall that lowers at her touch, and we step inside the lab.

"Let's get started," Loomi says. "We don't have much time, and from the looks of it, neither does the Idol."

27

The words "87th Annual Noble Leadership Summit" scrawl across a black title screen. An auditorium of clapping Nobles fades into view. When Dr. Monarch walks on stage, the applause explodes into a standing ovation.

Dr. Monarch wears his familiar black lab coat and orange tie. Now that I see him again, he looks like a more intense version of Balliat. Instead of long, straight silver hair, Dr. Monarch's falls in soft waves. His skin tone is also slightly richer in color, and his teeth are even more electric white than Balliat's.

The applause peters out.

"I have come today to share an astonishing breakthrough in behavioral science, one that will benefit every single person in this room. Maya Sandivall has become our city's first Idol. Understandably, many of you questioned a capricious Noble girl's ability to genuinely and consistently promote your products. After all, tastes change.

"People develop tastes for certain flavors over time and can experience overwhelmingly positive associations with new scents based on where they were first smelled. This human pliability is both the inspiration for my research and the key to my success.

"Ladies and gentlemen, the Idol has more potential than we ever anticipated. Today, before your very eyes, you will see Maya Sandivall transform from a stubborn, opinionated girl into a powerful tool for commerce. So, without further ado, let's jump right into the first step of our process, which we call, "Removal of Self."

The words "Part 1: Removal of Self" fade to reveal a stark white room, saturated by blinding white light. There's a shiny metal table at the room's center and two metal chairs. Maya Sandivall strides into the room.

She sits down at the table with casual indifference. Dr. Monarch joins her. He wears a pair of dark sunglasses and the same black lab coat. I know this scene, we saw it before in the other reel. Maya drinks the Pomm Fizz, spits it out, and lunges for Dr. Monarch. The black clad men catch her mid-leap, and sit her back down. In response, Dr. Monarch simply rises from his seat and walks out.

Maya gives chase, but the door snaps shut. While she shouts at the closed door, the white lights dim to near total darkness.

The metal table lowers into the tile floor. Small droplets of water drip from the ceiling. There's nowhere for Maya to take cover from the rain. The drips turn to streams, and the streams build to a torrential downpour.

The reel cuts back to Dr. Monarch onstage.

"Obviously, she didn't care for the Pomm Fizz," Dr. Monarch says, to a pop of laughter.

As Dr. Monarch continues to speak, a time-lapse video plays behind him. At several points, the water stops, and the bright cell lights flick back on. Dr. Monarch enters the room with two black-clad men in masks. The men force Maya back into her chair. After a brief conversation, Dr. Monarch leaves, and the cycle resumes.

"To reach optimal pliability, the subject must experience intense disorientation," Dr. Monarch says. "She cannot know how long she's been held captive, cannot receive any nourishment, or be given any sense of routine. The water makes it difficult for the subject to control her own body temperature, and the darkness makes it impossible for her to know the time of day. The number and duration of my visits are random as well. Let's take a look at one of these visits in closer detail."

The reel cuts back to Maya's cell, now in real-time. She sits crouched in the corner with her knees to her chin. Her makeup isn't streaked because it's long washed off. I can practically feel her ferocious shivers through the video. How could anyone do this to another person?

The cell door opens. Maya shoots to her feet and sprints for the door, but the black-clad men plant her back in her chair.

"Let me go!" She shouts. "What do you want? Points? Endorsements? Tell me, and I'll give it to you!"

The metal table rises. Dr. Monarch brings in his own dry chair and sits down.

"Hello, Idol," Dr. Monarch says. "Do you know why you're here?"

"No! And I don't care! As the city-elected Idol I demand you release me!"

"You are here because of the choices you make. Your inability to think of others around you hurts everyone in our society."

"What are you talking about?"

"The way you dress, the things you buy, the food and drink you consume. Your motivations are purely selfish. You don't care about The City. You only care about yourself."

"Is this about that drink you gave me? I'll say I like it, I'll say I like whatever you want! Just let me out of here!"

"There's a difference between *saying* you like something and *actually* enjoying it, Idol. I didn't expect you to understand. Your ignorance endangers our society's advancement."

Dr. Monarch exits the room.

"What does that mean?" Maya calls after Dr. Monarch. "Come back! Please!"

Maya bolts for the door, and one of the men in black whips around to shock her with some kind of baton. She shakes, stumbles backward, and trips on the lowering metal table.

"The subject's disorientation opens her mind to truly believing that she is hopelessly flawed," Dr. Monarch says. "Eventually, the subject will grow so desperate for answers that she will accept any truth presented to her. That truth being that she is inherently bad and must change for her sake and the sake of society at-large. In the next phase of our process, the subject will enthusiastically betray herself in the pursuit of betterment."

Applause fills the auditorium as Dr. Monarch leaves the stage. Another black screen appears with the words, "Part 2: Betrayal of Self." Dr. Monarch returns.

"I hope everyone had a nice break, enjoyed some refreshments, and gave some thought to Part 1. Last we saw the Idol, Maya Sandivall, she was still defiant, and refused to accept responsibility for her selfishness. After several days of rain, starvation, and negative reinforcement we finally achieved our first breakthrough! Let's return to Maya in the examination room."

"Examination room?" Crtr says. "Torture chamber's more like—"

"Shh!"

It's difficult to watch, but I can't miss anything. There's no telling what bit of information may help Aleks.

Maya lies facedown on the cell floor. The lights flick on again, and she climbs into her chair, where she draws her knees up to her chest. Enormous black circles hang beneath her squinted eyes. There's hardly any life left in her and certainly no fight.

Dr. Monarch strides into the room, along with his two black-clad guards and sits down.

"Idol, do you deserve to be here?"

"Yes... I do," Maya responds.

"I'm sorry, Idol, you'll have to speak up."

"Yes! I deserve to be here!" She shouts in a quick burst.

"I'm glad to hear that."

Dr. Monarch reaches into his lab coat and removes a bright silver gun.

"This will sting, but only for a moment."

"What is it?"

"Idol, do you deserve to be here?"

"Yes."

"Then you will have to trust me. Now tilt your head."

Dr. Monarch moves around the table. He presses the gun behind Maya's ear and fires. She winces. A thin trail of blood travels down her wet neck, and soaks into her dress collar.

"Very good, Idol. Now we can begin our work."

The reel cuts back to Dr. Monarch onstage.

"At this point in the process, subjects will say whatever they believe is necessary to secure their release. Vigilance is crucial to ensure that the subject is being truthful. As an expert in behavioral psychology and masterful observer of interpersonal mannerisms, I was confident that the subject was ready to begin the next stage, Betrayal of Self. In this stage, the subject will actively attack herself in order to destroy the perceived corruption inside of her.

"As you saw, we also introduced the latest Neurogem technology! This technology allows us to monitor the subject's biometrics to ensure our treatments are working.

"At this point we will begin to introduce small kindnesses to the subject. These kindnesses will build trust between the subject and, in this case, yours truly. Through this trust-bond, I will draw out confessions to further support the subject's betrayal of her self. Let's watch."

The film resumes. Dr. Monarch sits back down and waves away the black-clad men.

Maya recoils in terror as Dr. Monarch reaches back into his lab coat.

"It's all right, Idol. Here."

He sets a candy bar on the table and motions for Maya to pick it up. She approaches the bar hesitantly at first then tears open the wrapper.

"That's better," Dr. Monarch says. "They finally let me give you something to eat. I kept telling the higher-ups, 'she needs to eat something, she's starving!' Eventually they listened. It kills me to see you like this, Idol. I want to help. Tell me, why are you here?"

"Because..." Maya says between bites. "I'm selfish."

"In what ways are you selfish, Idol?"

"I only think about myself, like, literally only myself..." Maya says. "I watch clips of myself constantly. I practice facial expressions in the mirror for hours... While my friends are high, I sneak into their closets and throw away all their best clothes so they never look better than me... I have sex with workers at my family's factories, and afterwards I have them unassigned so I don't run into them again."

Maya's eyes go wide. She freezes and breaks into deep sobs. Her fragile mental state made it impossible to censor herself. Dr. Monarch watches Maya weep without the faintest sympathetic gesture.

"Idol, if you want my help, you're going to have to be *completely* honest with me. I'm sorry, but what you have told me isn't enough."

He gets up from the table and exits the room.

"The process has begun!" Dr. Monarch announces onstage. With a single candy bar, the subject opened up a trove of her darkest secrets. This purging of darkness will expose Maya's truest, worst self, which we can hold up as a mirror to further, deconstruct her identity. Let's fast-forward a bit to see how this eventually plays out."

The video cuts back to Maya's cell. The blinding white lights are already on. She lies on the ground with her arms over her face. Her water-soaked silk dress clings to her starved, emaciated body. She's probably too weak to sit up on her own.

The two black-clad men move Maya to her chair. She doesn't even look up as it happens. Dr. Monarch enters and sits down across from her.

"Idol, do you like having the lights on?"

"Yes."

"These are awfully bright. Wouldn't you prefer something a bit more subtle?"

"That would be nice."

"I thought so. I can give that to you, but first you need to tell me, Idol, why are you here?"

"I'm here because I am selfish and I make poor decisions. As the Idol, my selfishness hurts The City. Because of this I do not deserve love, or friendship... or... or sympathy."

"Is there anything else you would like to tell me about? Anything in particular that's been on your mind?"

"Yes."

"Go on."

"My sisters and I... we wanted more from our parents. They gave us everything, but that wasn't enough... We wanted the empire... to take control of the business. We made a plan to kill them, make it look like a factory accident. Everything was in place. When the day came, my little sister backed out. I..."

"You what, Idol?"

"I told her she was weak and that she would never survive as a Noble because she couldn't make hard decisions. My sisters and I called her ugly and stupid—too ugly to find a lover to support her once her points were whittled away by her stupidity. We said she'd never be like us, and we wouldn't help her when she falls; that she wasn't worth our time. When we were done, I left her in her room with enough pens to..."

"To what?"

"To... overdose."

"And?"

"She docked everything in sight. Our Valet found her hours later. Raeka's body was stone stiff... purple. She was only 12... She didn't deserve that. I did. I should have been the one to die."

"I see," Dr. Monarch says. "So, do you agree that you cannot be trusted to make decisions for yourself?"

"Yes."

"Do you want to be a better person?"

"Yes."

"I can help you, Idol, but you must trust me *completely*. Doing so will transform you into a great leader for our city. Can you do that?"

"Yes, please help me!"

"Excellent. We will get started right away, but first, a promise is a promise."

Dr. Monarch snaps his fingers, and the cell's blinding white lights dim to a soft, warm orange hue. He removes his sunglasses.

"Now, isn't that better?"

"Yes."

The auditorium sits in stunned silence. Dr. Monarch lets the gravity of Maya's confession sink in for a moment.

"There you have it, the subject's darkest secret, laid bare. She now accepts that she cannot be trusted to make decisions for herself. The subject understands that change is possible but only through the guidance of a trusted confidant, a handler. When we return you will see how we rebuilt the Idol from the ground up."

The screen fades to black and the words "Part 3: Rebuilding of Self" appear. This is the part we already saw on our first visit here.

I feel like I'm going to vomit. It's all too much. They stripped Maya down to nothing by assaulting her physically, mentally, and emotionally. Meanwhile, Dr. Monarch seems unfazed, even delighted by the process.

"Aleks didn't go through any of this," I say. "How'd they change her personality so quickly?"

"This video was made a long time ago, back when Neurogems were first invented," Loomi replies. "Gem science has advanced a lot since then."

The auditorium explodes into a standing ovation when the footage of Maya ends, and Dr. Monarch returns to the stage.

"The Idol's never been in control of her endorsements," I say. "The Monarchs can make her promote anything with absolute conviction. She's just another tool of the Highland, another way they control the lowland... no, she isn't a tool... she's a trusted confidant!"

"What do you mean?" Crtr asks.

"The Idol! She's the ultimate handler, just like Dr. Monarch was to Maya! The rain, the darkness, the way everyone in the lowland has a four letter name... you, me, everyone below the mist was born into that wet cell! Our basic humanity was stripped from us at birth, which left us open to suggestion! This experiment didn't end with the first Idol. It expanded to consume us all!"

"No, the Idol can't be in my head like that." Crtr says. "I see lots of ads for stuff I don't buy!"

"But sometimes you do. When you're hungry, there's an ad for BurgerNite. Tired? Have a Hot Shot. Thirsty? Pomm Fizz! The Idol's always there with a solution to meet your needs. We're all her captive audience, and if the need is strong enough, we'll buy whatever she tells us to. Loomi, how much is left?"

"Just one more part."

"Play it!"

The words "Part 4: Re-Birth" appear on screen. We see another time-lapse video where Maya sits bored in her cell but dry and somewhat comfortable. Things are better for her now, though she's still imprisoned. Dr. Monarch comes in intermittently with something else for Maya to taste, or wear, or dock. The black-clad men aren't around anymore.

Maya and Dr. Monarch rise from the table again and the time-lapse video freezes. Dr. Monarch appears back onstage to address the audience.

"The subject has come a long way. Surely you remember the beginning of this experiment, when she was assertive and head-strong. Given the chance she would have stabbed me in the neck with my own pen and left me for dead! But now look at her, sub-missive, pliable; the perfect Idol. At the start of this talk, would you have believed the subject would ever be inclined to do this?"

The video behind Dr. Monarch un-freezes. Maya and Dr. Monarch embrace each other in a warm hug. When they release, Dr. Monarch rests his palms on Maya's shoulders and looks into her eyes.

"Idol, you've done so well, but your journey isn't over yet. Do you trust me?"

"Yes."

"Very good."

The cell walls shake and lift into the air. Sunlight saturates the platform where Maya and Dr. Monarch stand. In the distance, highways of delivery drones weave through stratoscrapers that aren't separated by mist.

Maya squints as she takes in her bright, surprising surroundings. This is the birth of the Idol, as we all know her and the re-birth of The City. Nothing would ever be the same.

Before she can ask a single question, a team of stylists wheel over a makeup chair. Dr. Monarch motions for Maya to sit, and she does. The stylists get to work.

"Idol, these stylists are using Jezebel Cosmetics to rejuvenate your appearance. Going forward you will only use Jezebel Cosmetics. They are the finest cosmetics in The City and you are lucky to have unlimited access to them! Jezebel Cosmetics: Free Your True Beauty. Here, this should make you feel a bit more lively."

Dr. Monarch removes a pen from his lab coat and docks it into Maya's wrist. She sinks into the chair.

"Soothicane," Dr. Monarch says. "It is the absolute best anti-anxiety medication on the market today and is available in all convenient Telladyne mobile pharmacies. Feel Smooth and Sane, with Soothicane. Isn't it lovely?"

"Yes, it's smooth... and makes me feel... sane."

"Excellent! Be sure to say it, just like that, whenever anyone asks what you think of it. 'Smooth and sane with Soothicane!'"

The stylists complete their work with Maya and she rises from the chair. She doesn't look at all like she just endured a horrific gauntlet of sadistic, mind-bending abuse.

"The City is yours, Idol Sandivall," Dr. Monarch says. "You are different now, better than you once were. We still have plenty of work to do, but if you trust me and follow my instructions, you will do great things for our society. From this point on, I will be your handler, which means I will assist you in all decisions from here on out. Does that sounds good?"

"Yes!"

"Excellent."

Dr. Monarch appears back onstage where an exuberant standing ovation fills the room. He revels in the applause for several minutes.

"As you can see, the subject is now entirely under my control. After many hours of training and reinforcement, I am pleased to say that the Idol has become an entirely new person. But why tell you about her, when I can show you? Idol Sandivall, please join us!"

Maya walks out to another standing ovation. She looks magnificent in a shimmering gold jumpsuit with a jewel-encrusted belt.

Maya hugs Dr. Monarch and kisses him on both cheeks.

"Idol Sandivall, thank you so much for being here today."

"How could I refuse the opportunity to address all these fine Nobles?" Maya asks.

"Indeed. Now, Idol Sandivall, please tell us, how has it been being The City's greatest role model?"

"It's been fabulous! Honestly, I feel so lucky to promote so many fantastic products! It's why I was so excited to come today. I wanted to tell everyone here how much I appreciate what you do for The City and that I would be ecstatic to star in campaigns for any of you!"

"For a price, of course..." Dr. Monarch adds, to another pop of laughter.

Maya shrugs and laughs along.

"Now, Idol Sandivall," Dr. Monarch says. "I know this is a difficult subject, but I want to talk about the time right after you became the Idol, your time in the cell. Do you remember that?"

"I do, yes," Maya says with sudden severity.

"What do you remember?"

"I remember that I was a broken person, a terrible, vile human who only thought of herself. And I remember you, Dr. Monarch..."

"Me?"

"Yes, of course! I remember how you saved me. Without you I would have destroyed myself and The City in the process. I owe everything to you, Dr. Monarch. Thank you."

"Idol Sandivall, I am truly touched. Thank you for letting me be your handler. Ladies and gentlemen, please, another round of applause for *your* Idol, Maya Sandivall!"

The audience stands to applaud, whistle, and cheer. Maya and Dr. Monarch wave as the screen fades to black.

"Wait, that's it?" I ask.

"I said there was only one more part."

"But we didn't learn anything! Aleks changed in a matter of seconds, not days!

"What did you expect?" Locke asks.

"I don't know, some kind of answer. Maybe a secret phrase, or a program code to release her mind! I wish we never found those damn reels. They were nothing but a waste of time!"

"Hold on," Loomi says. "Like I said before, Neurogem technology has evolved exponentially since then. If Aleks' entire transformation happened in just a few seconds, that means it had to be done entirely through her gem."

"What are you getting at?" I ask.

"A person's personality is comprised of memories, reflexive responses, emotional development, and so much more. All that information is stored *throughout* the brain. You can't simply pluck out someone's personality and slot in a new one. It's not that simple."

"But they did, Aleks is a totally different person now!"

"No, they couldn't remove her personality without risking fatal brain damage, but they could suppress it! With Aleks' alpha personality suppressed, the Monarchs could overlay a new beta personality without conflict..."

"Conflict?"

"Well, yeah. Two simultaneously active personalities, no matter how similar, would contradict each other on a fundamental level. The host would experience extreme emotional imbalance."

"So, you're saying Aleks is still in there?" I ask. "Can you remove the new personality and restore her original one?"

"Theoretically, but this is all speculation. I'd have to perform a local Neurogem diagnostic to see what's really going on in her mind."

"I can get you to Aleks, but we have to go, now! Balliat could be back any second—"

"Why should Loomi help you?" Locke interrupts.

"What?"

"You heard me. Why should Loomi, a member of the True Born Collective, help save the Idol? The Highland, and every Noble in it, is our enemy."

"This is bigger than the Idol," I say. "Tell me, Locke, why make every Noble girl pregnant? What's the end game?"

"I don't see what bearing that has on this conversation."

"Please, humor me."

"The pregnant Nobles will cover every aspect of their pregnancies on their NeuroFeeds. They'll buy baby clothes, decorate their nurseries, wear designer maternity fashions, and unwittingly promote natural pregnancy to the entire city."

"All the Nobles I saw looked terrified," Crtr says. "What's to stop them from terminating the pregnancies?"

"They may have been initially shocked, but a Noble would never willingly give up another way to flaunt their wealth. Naturally-born babies will become essential status symbols. Like all Highland trends, natural birth will permeate lowland culture. Lowlanders will demand the ability to become pregnant. The Highland will see myriad new opportunities for profit, and an entirely new industry will develop, practically overnight."

"And UteroCube's stock will plummet," I add.

"One of many happy side effects," Locke replies.

"I see... Wouldn't your plan be more effective if the Idol was pregnant?"

"The Idol's pregnancy is essential. Her endorsement is required for natural pregnancy to gain city-wide popularity... are you saying she isn't pregnant?"

"Doesn't bode well for your plan, does it?"

"How is that possible?" Locke asks. "All Noble girls ever do is take drugs and have sex!"

"Aleks isn't like other Noble girls. It's why I'm trying to save her. Help me free Aleks' mind, and escape The City. Once we're gone, a new Idol will take her place. I know for a fact that the Idol runner-up is with child."

Locke calls Loomi over. Their whispered argument almost reaches audible levels before they turn back to us.

"All right," Locke says. "You can get Loomi into the Highland undetected?"

"I can."

"How are we supposed to get back?" Crtr asks. "Our car was destroyed."

"Follow me," Loomi says.

Loomi throws a couple of hooded coats to us. We put up our hoods and follow Loomi to a large, open mechanics shop. A disorienting clamor of welding sparks, rivets, metal cuts, and hammering fills the air.

We arrive at a stall where a dingy tarp covers something large. Loomi pulls away the tarp to reveal the BT-27. It's completely restored to its original factory polish.

"I'm surprised you didn't dismantle it for parts," I say.

"We've actually taken it apart and put it back together hundreds of times. It's value as an educational tool is far greater than any of its individual components. You're lucky it happens to be re-assembled today."

"Yes, I'm a very lucky person," I say. "Let's go."

I slide into the driver's seat. There's something comforting about sitting in the BT-27 again. For a moment it's as if everything is back to normal. Back when the chaos in my life was somewhat predictable and Aleks was still Aleks.

My gem doesn't work down here, so I activate the manual control override. The dashboard gauges surge to life.

From her crouched position on Crtr's lap, Loomi directs me out of the shop and back out onto the highway.

28

En route back to the Hotel Notre Dame, I split to check on Balliat's interview with Dahlia Delachort. Hopefully it'll give me some sense of when he'll return to the hotel.

"So tell me, Balliat, you're closer to the Idol than anyone," Delachort says, and my hands instinctively strangle the steering wheel. *"Is she pregnant like all the other Noble girls?"*

"This is certainly a complicated time for everyone in the Highland as we find so many of our sisters, daughters, and even mothers inexplicably with child. The Idol's pregnancy status will be revealed soon enough, but for now, I ask that the media respect the Idol's privacy during this difficult period."

"Really, that's all you're going to give me?"

"I'm afraid that's the best I can do for now, Dahlia."

They saved that question until the end to keep viewers hooked. If Balliat leaves right after the interview he could be back at the hotel any minute.

The premium escape port returns us to the hotel garage. It's perfectly normal for Crtr and me to walk through the hotel, but Loomi would instantly draw attention. We'll need to sneak her into Aleks' suite. She's small, so we have that going for us.

Crtr retrieves a room service cart. Loomi rolls her eyes but climbs into the cart without protest. As we wheel the cart through the halls several bellhops stop to ask if they can take it for us. More and more of them appear as we proceed. This isn't a coincidence.

We turn down the last hallway toward the Idol Suite and see the hotel's owner waiting for us. Our cart's atypical journey, and our refusal to release it back into circulation, caught his attention.

"Idol Valet Bear, may I ask what you are doing with that service cart?"

"Oh, this. It's for the Idol, a special request. I'll send for someone to fetch it when we're finished," I say, and attempt to advance through the door, but he doesn't budge.

"Idol Valet Bear, this is highly unusual. As you know, security is of the upmost importance to us at the Hotel Notre Dame. That security requires the maintenance of strict order within these halls. For the safety of the Idol, and all of our guests, I must insist that you relinquish custody of this cart to me at once."

"Sir..." I lean in to whisper. "Between the mass pregnancies and the strain of her dizzying Idol Tour schedule, the Idol has been under a lot of... pressure. I'm afraid she went a bit too hard with the pens, and now she's... passed out on the mist lounge floor. I need this cart to move her..."

"A strapping Valet such as yourself should have no problem moving a small girl!"

"That is true, but the task becomes much more difficult when that small girl is hand-cuffed to a Noble fellow who is even bigger than me... Surely you can appreciate the delicacy of the situation. It is why I chose a service cart instead of, say, a medical gurney, and why Noble Valet Crtr is with me."

The hotel owner thinks for a moment. He's deciding whether to leak the information for a quick publicity boost, or stay quiet and secure continued Idol support. The choice should be obvious.

"Very well, you may use the cart. Naturally, the Idol is entitled to whatever she needs. Next time, please alert me of such situations in advance. It is not my intention to collect gossip, I simply must know what is happening within my hotel."

"Of course. I apologize for not informing you sooner. Now, if you will excuse me..."

"Yes, yes, go ahead. And tell the Idol that her secrets are safe with me."

Once we're inside the suite, Loomi rolls out from the cart. Her chronic annoyed expression turns to wonder as she takes in the room.

"It's amazing, isn't it?" Crtr asks.

"Amazing?" Loomi replies. "It's repulsive. The cost of one of these tiles could feed a hundred people for a week."

"Bear, who is this?" Marena asks before she fully appears.

"This is Loomi. She's here to help Aleks. You can trust her."

"Loomi, this is—"

"Marena Vexhall," Loomi says. "I've always wondered how you get your projection so crisp."

"You can do pretty much anything with enough points and practice," Marena replies.

"I see. Where's the Idol?"

I lead Loomi, Marena, and Crtr to Aleks' pod chamber. As expected, she's still unconscious when I open the pod. After I lay Aleks on a large, square ottoman, Loomi unpacks her bag of aged instruments.

The clunky metal devices are covered in wires and antenna. Every dial and switch looks worn away from decades of excessive use. She also has several crude 3D holographic projectors that flicker in and out of focus.

"How are those ancient machines supposed to help Aleks?" Crtr asks. "They look older than Neurogems themselves."

"If you have better gem diagnostic equipment on-hand I'd be happy to use that."

"No, sorry."

"Don't worry, there's enough processing power here to see what's happening inside her head."

Loomi hooks the machines up to Aleks' head with electrodes and wires. Once everything's in place, a 3D hologram of Aleks' brain with highlighted lines and sections appears above her body. Loomi's fingers dance across a small keyboard.

"This gem program is remarkable," Loomi says. "I assumed the Monarchs uploaded a new personality through Aleks' gem, but that's not what they did at all... They essentially hacked her perception of the world."

"I don't understand..."

"The gem program suppressed Aleks' natural responses to stimulus and constructed alternative ones in line with what her controller wanted."

"Her controller?"

"Yeah, someone was inside Aleks' mind, controlling her like a puppet. It's probably the easiest way to hard-code desired responses. All they had to do was act how they wanted Aleks to act and she became the person they wanted. The good news is that Aleks is still in there, she's just buried beneath a tangle of neural detours."

We all hear someone enter the suite. Loomi, Crtr, Marena, and I stare at each other while we wait for another noise to confirm our suspicion. The suite's front door clicks closed.

We scramble. Loomi packs up her instruments. I pick up Aleks and stuff her back into the pod. Marena flies out of sight while Crtr and Loomi hide in a nearby closet. The pod fills with pink vapor as the chamber doorknob turns.

Balliat strides into the room. He's all smiles on the heels of his Delachort interview, but his smile fades when he sees me.

"Valet, how's my girl?"

"She's fine, but I am afraid she passed out from a volatile pen cocktail after you left. The pod treatment I just started should promote her quick recovery. How was the interview?"

"You didn't watch? I heard the ratings were phenomenal. No matter, you can purchase the entire interview, plus bonus material and exclusive behind-the-scenes content on the NApp Store right now. I highly recommend it."

He never stops.

"I will do that, sir. May I help you with anything in particular?"

"No, Valet. My team and I will return when the Idol's treatment ends. Make sure your clothes are changed by then, you look... rumpled."

"Of course, Master Monarch."

I listen for the suite door to close. Once Balliat's gone, everyone returns. Loomi spreads her instruments back over the ottoman while I retrieve Aleks.

She looks serene. I rest Aleks' arms at her sides, touch her cool cheek, and stare into her gentle face. The thought of someone manipulating her mind like she's some kind of hollow machine cuts like ice in my blood.

"It was Balliat, wasn't it?" I ask. "Her controller."

"Yeah," Loomi replies.

"How long will it take to remove the overlaid personality?"

"Not sure, but we have another problem."

"What?"

"All Neurogems have intense security protocols that prevent external tampering, even the oldest models."

"But you just diagnosed her. Didn't that require access?"

"That's different, gem diagnosis doesn't require the alteration of operational code."

"So how long will it take to gain access to her gem?"

"Honestly, I could be working for years without cracking it. The gem's security protocol algorithms regenerate constantly."

"Could you simulate an access request to her Neurogem from Balliat?" Marena asks.

"No, that would require forging a NeuroSig, which is impossible."

"If gaining access is so difficult, how did the Monarchs do it?" Crtr asks.

"You saw the reels," Loomi replies. "The Monarchs have been reprogramming Idols from the beginning. They probably have some kind of exclusive deal with Neurogem that gives them access to every new Idol's gem."

"Loomi, think!" I shout. "There must be another way!"

"There might be, but you aren't going to like it."

"Try me."

"The external gems we harvest for the Collective are easy to re-program because their security protocols are already dropped. This happens automatically after death to make gem autopsies easy to perform. Gem autopsies are still done all the time, which means modern gems likely have the same trigger."

"What are you saying?" I ask, afraid to answer the question myself.

"If we can cause a very brief—"

"No."

"Just a brief instance of brain death—"

"No! That's not an option, end of discussion!"

"It would be minutes before significant brain damage set in—"

"What if we flooded her mind with memories of her life before the change?" Marena asks. "Could that restore her original personality?"

"Yes, but she wouldn't like it," Loomi replies. "The suppressed personality would conflict with the overlaid one, impulse conflicts would occur throughout her mind, and she'd go mad."

"So it was my fault..." Marena says, and her hologram freezes.

"What was your fault?" I ask.

"I sent Vox a wedding gift before the ceremony, a slate box tied with turquoise ribbon.

"I remember that box," Crtr says. "It was the one Vox opened before all that light blew up in her face."

"Right, yes," Marena confirms. "It contained a concentrated data stream of light. When she opened it, Vox was bombarded with photo, video, and audio clip play requests. I forced her to acknowledge our history in the hope of getting her back."

Marena's hologram freezes again.

"Marena," I say, and she snaps back. "What kinds of memories were in the data stream?"

"The specific memories don't really matt—" Loomi starts.

"Quiet! Marena, please."

"All sorts of little moments," Marena says. "There was a recording of the first time we met. Vox poured a cup of coffee into my mug, and it spilled straight through to the floor. Then there was the time we raced the dragon suits for our Idol Nominee introductions. Our handlers were furious.

"My Neurogem visual archives contained a wealth of material. There was a kinetic longing for each other in every moment I found. More than anything we merely wanted to touch, if only for a second... I thought a concentration of powerful, authentic emotion might restore Vox to her old self... why do you ask? Do you have an idea?"

"No," I say. "I'm sorry she's gone."

"Marena's plan isn't an option for Aleks. You have to know that," Loomi says. "Her entire life would be an endless fight against re-wired impulses."

"It would be worse than death," Marena adds. "Aleks would never be sure if her words or actions were truly hers or the remnants of Balliat's reprogramming."

"The Monarchs won't ignore Aleks' sudden change either," Crtr says. "If Balliat got in her head once, he can do it again. We need to restore Aleks' mind, then you and her need to get as far away from The City as possible. It's the only way either of you will ever be safe."

Crtr demands that I understand his words with a deep stare. He's right, of course. They all are. We stand in silence so quiet I can hear every heartbeat in the room before I look to Aleks, and will my mouth to speak.

"How long will it take?"

"Won't know until I'm in. All I can say for certain is that it takes about 180 seconds for lasting brain damage to occur."

"Then you have 179 seconds," I say. "Aleks would want us to try. I know she'd rather die as herself than live as someone else. Loomi, tell us what you need."

"First, I need you to mix a precise drug combination that quickly cuts off oxygen to Aleks' brain. Also prep something to bring her back fast. Probably Adrenalex and... I don't know, you're the Valet. Crtr, get a bucket of ice water and a towel."

"Got it!" Crtr says, and takes off.

"Crtr!" I shout after him. "Get a box of Schollner du Sant chocolates, too. There should be some in the pantry."

He nods, and dashes away.

"Marena," Loomi continues. "I need you to post as many micro-drones as you can around the suite. If anyone drops in, I need to know immediately."

"On their way. Anything else?"

"Yes. Give me big red numbers on a black background. Start at 179 and decrease by 1 every second. I won't always be able to look up, so make the countdown clicks louder as they approach zero."

"Done."

Marena turns into the exact clock Loomi described. Crtr runs back into the room. He doesn't look twice at Marena-as-a-clock. He's super focused. We all are.

"Loomi, what else?" I ask.

"That's it. I'll start when you dock the pen and the security protocols drop. Ready when you are."

I stare down at Aleks' expressionless face. No passing onlooker would detect the poisonous program tucked deep inside her mind. Am I being selfish? Am I about to risk Aleks' life because I can't stand the thought of losing her?

Yes, I am being completely selfish. But this is the only way.

I kneel beside Aleks with the pen that will suffocate her brain. For nearly 3 minutes Aleks will be technically dead, and I'll be the one who killed her.

Loomi cracks her knuckles and twiddles her fingers. Crtr's left without a job during the procedure, but I can tell he's ready to help with anything at a moment's notice. The red numbers of Marena's clock are so bright they feel warm against my face. It's time... it's time.

"Loomi," I say. "On the count of 3... 1... 2... 3!"

I dock the pen into Aleks' wrist. Her face and body somehow fall more still.

Loomi pounces on her keyboard.

"Protocols are down. I'm in."

I hold Aleks' revival pen in one hand and her cold wrist in the other. The chill in her skin runs up into my body. All I can do now is wait for Loomi's signal.

The clock hits 156 seconds... 155... 154...

"They didn't just overlay," Loomi says. "They interwove! I have to write a subroutine to..."

Loomi trails off.

142... 141...

My lungs gulp in air; I stopped breathing when Aleks did. My thumb slides back and forth over her wrist. Loomi's face moves between devices in a blur.

114... 113... 112...

"Shit!" Loomi whispers.

"What's wrong?"

Loomi ignores my question and adjusts her equipment. Her hair clings to her sweat-covered brow. I didn't think Loomi's large, bright eyes could get any bigger.

She slows down for a moment. Her delicate hands tremble. Loomi's used to working with machines and gems, but not under these circumstances. What was I thinking? How could I risk Aleks' life like this?

65... 64... 63 seconds left...

"There's so much to go through," Loomi mutters. "So much code."

"You got this, Loomi!" Crtr calls out.

I realize my fingers are clamped around Aleks' wrist like a vice and release my grip. An anxious shiver runs through every part of me except the arm that holds Alek's revival pen. I won't let nerves sabotage my role.

41...40...39...

Loomi types faster. She pushes her face up against the projection of Aleks' brain as different areas light up, expand, and rotate.

"What, how is this possible?" Loomi mutters. "Why?"

I want to ask what she sees, but every second counts. Loomi turns the dial on one of her instruments with quick jerks. She's fighting against something.

I watch closely for any sign that it's time to dock the revival pen. If I wake Aleks before Loomi's finished, her mind could be torn apart.

22...21...20...

At 20 seconds Marena's beeps get shrill. Loomi makes more lightning-fast adjustments. The projection splits to display multiple parts of Aleks' brain simultaneously.

10...9...8...

Every beep passes my ears like a bullet. The metal objects in Loomi's hair whip back and forth as her eyes dart between projections. Come on, Loomi, it's almost time!

5... 4... 3...

"Bear, now!"

I drop the revival pen straight into Aleks' dock. The projection of her brain explodes back to life with a kaleidoscope of bright synapses, but she doesn't move.

"Aleks? Aleks, are you there?"

I shake her arm, and slap her cheeks, but she's unresponsive.

Aleks mutters something inaudible.

"Bear..." she whispers.

"Aleks, I'm here!"

"Bear!"

Her eyes jolt open and she looks right at me. Without hesitation, Aleks rises into my waiting arms. She clenches my body so tight I fear her arms might shatter.

"It's all right, Aleks," I say. "You're safe now."

She pushes away with an urgent, almost crazed look in her eyes.

"I'm not safe," She says. "None of us are! If Balliat realizes he's lost control of me, he'll cut his losses and destroy you, me, and everyone we know!"

"Don't worry, we'll figure all that out. How do you feel?"

"I feel like a LaborLiner crashed through my skull... are those Schollner du Sants?"

I hand Aleks the box. She tears off the lid, grabs one of the chocolates, and shoves it into her mouth.

"Here," she says through a mouth full of chocolate. "Take this one, before I eat them all."

She hands me the chocolate dome with liquified cinnamon, topped with cherry powder on a honeycomb wafer—my favorite. There's no way an imposter would know my favorite chocolate, we only ate them when our gems were off. It's really her, Aleks is back.

"He hardly let me eat," she says between chews. "I was living on booze, a few bites of sponsor foods here and there, and these horrible nutrient crackers."

"Aleks, if it's not too difficult, can you tell us what happened?" I ask.

"Sure... At first it was like watching the worst LifeCast imaginable. I couldn't control my body or my actions. After a little while I started to regain control, but things were... different. It's hard to explain. Waves of rage overtook me at the slightest disappointment, and everything disappointed me. My only relief came from making Balliat happy."

"How do you mean?"

"Whenever I did something Balliat approved of, like perfectly delivering a sponsor's slogan, snuggling up to Davis Vexhall, or being cruel to you, a wave of euphoria washed over me. It's as if, for a moment, everything made sense. Oh Bear, I was so terrible to you."

"Aleks, look at me. That was *not* you, how could it be? Balliat rewired your brain. His family's been manipulating Idols since Maya Sandivall. They made you into a vehicle for promoting anything they want, and Balliat was in the driver's seat. That's what was on those reels we found. I know it may be too soon, but are you feeling like yourself again?"

"It's hard to say. Normal seems so distant lately. But I know one thing for sure."

"What?"

"I need a change of clothes. This outfit is ridiculous."

We both laugh. With everything going on I forgot all about her absurd, Kallista-designed dress.

"Come on, let's find you something more comfortable. Balliat thinks you're unconscious in your pod, so we have time, but not nearly as much as we need."

"Need for what?"

"Our escape plan. We're getting out of here, away from The City."

"Good, I have some ideas."

"Already?"

"When my own body became a prison, all I could think about was escape."

Aleks changes into casual clothes, and we meet Loomi, Crtr, and Marena in the suite's mist lounge. Everyone sits on a large wrap-around sofa surrounded by floor-to-ceiling windows that provide a scenic view of the churning mist.

They've already started brainstorming. Together, we bring a formidable amount of insight to the table, but we can use all the help we can get. I send a quick NeuroText, and a few minutes later there's a knock at the door.

"Idol Valet Bear, it is glorious to see you again," Niko says with a bow.

"Likewise, Niko. Thank you for coming, please follow me."

I close the door and walk Niko to the mist lounge.

"Idol Yukita!" Niko shouts and drops into another bow. "I am honored to stand in your presence once again! Idol Valet Bear, I see you have assembled an intimate party. Is this why you summoned me, to entertain your guests?"

"No, but I do mean to cash in your favor."

"Ah, yes my sworn oath of fealty! How may I be of service?"

I look straight into Niko's eyes. Even if I don't yet understand how it will happen, I already know Niko's role in our plan.

"I need you to kill the Idol."

Niko's face drops out of the permanent smile he wears.

"Idol Valet Bear, you wish for me to kill this Idol? The Idol Yukita?"

"I do."

"Oh, Idol Valet Bear. I thought you a better man than that. I am truly saddened that this is how you wish to redeem my loyalty," Niko says, and turns to Aleks. "I apologize, Idol Yukita; you seem like an innocent, but I must keep my vow."

Niko moves toward Aleks in a fighting stance. Before he strikes, I command him to stop. He turns to me with a confused look.

"Your commitment is admirable, but that's not what I meant. Take a seat."

Each of us lays out our own unique resources and skills. We need to use everything at our disposal for our plan to succeed. Escaping The City is a feat by itself, but escaping with the Idol adds multiple layers of complexity. If Aleks so much as sneezes, it's considered breaking news that's broadcast to millions of people city-wide.

Hours pass like minutes until the sun rises over the mist. Slumped in our seats, we review the final plan one last time. Everything needs to happen like clockwork. Every piece of choreography and timing must be flawless.

"Aleks' pod treatment is over soon," I say. "It's showtime."

We rise to say our goodbyes. Crtr and Loomi leave for the True Born Collective. Niko returns to his room with a tired half-bow. Marena fades away with a wave.

Aleks changes back into her LifeCast Dinner outfit and steps inside her pod. I take her hands in mine. As our fingers intertwine. An anxious tremor starts in my stomach and vibrates through my body. If all goes to plan, the next time Aleks and I are alone together we'll be running for our lives.

I step into the pod and kiss Aleks with a mixture of passion and longing. She hooks her fingers into my beltloops and pulls my hips closer. Her legs weaken as she succumbs to the pure pleasure of the moment, but I hold her up against the pod cushions. We've craved each other since she was trapped. I should be enjoying this long overdue moment, but something gnaws at me.

"I should have found a way to free you sooner," I say.

"No. You risked your life to save me. Anyone else would have given up."

"I could never give up on you. Aleks, I love you."

A melodic chime tells me Aleks' treatment ends in three minutes. She must see the disappointment on my face.

"It's time, isn't it?"

"Yeah."

I gently kiss her cheek, her temple, her forehead, her nose, and end with her lips.

"Ready?" I ask.

"Ready," she says with a sigh.

I close the pod over Aleks and refill it with pink vapor. When the pod timer hits 0, Balliat flings open the pod chamber door and strides through. I stand at attention beside the pod.

The pod face slides back open. Aleks' mouth forms into an ecstatic smile. She leaps from the pod and runs straight to Balliat. After they greet each other with cheek kisses, Aleks jumps up into his arms.

"Spin me, Balliat!" Aleks shouts.

He does as asked, and they both laugh.

"Idol Yukita, I see your treatment was restorative!"

"Oh Balliat, I had the most fabulous idea for how to end my Idol Tour! It will boost my interest points *and* give us the chance to rid ourselves of that insipid Valet! I'll tell you all about it while I get dressed!"

Aleks and Balliat leave the room arm-in-arm.

She plays the part of a spoiled Idol perfectly, and the morning proceeds as expected. On our way to the day's first tour stop, I receive a city-wide visual message from Monarch Media.

The video begins with Aleks in a dark room. She looks contemplative as the screams of Siloball fans and announcers build. Clips from the Idol Nominee Ceremony Siloball Match play across her pensive face.

The ad cuts to similar scenes of Niko, Jita, Pinz, and me. I don't even question how they got the footage of me looking like that, I'm sure there's plenty of examples of me looking sullen on the NeuroNet. We all raise our heads with determined looks straight into the camera.

A darkened Siloball pool appears, followed by the words "The Rematch," and a date. It's only a few days from now.

29

Aleks stands at the center of the Vanderbilt Coliseum green room, surrounded by excited Nobles. They compete for her attention with their best anecdotes and sickening flattery.

With a flick of her wrist, she commands me to fetch a mini lobster roll with wasabi vinaigrette. Aleks has me working before the match to keep up appearances.

I slip through the crowd like a shadow. Even though I'm one of tonight's five competitors, no one here looks twice at me. I'm still the help after all. But outside the green room walls, I'm one of the most recognizable people alive.

Tonight's match has been promoted non-stop since it was announced. The promotion wasn't limited to highway barriers and building facades—it penetrated every aspect of culture. Exclusive, rematch-themed Hot Shot pens were released; animated rematch murals appeared in NeuroNet in-game worlds; and exclusive fragrances were designed to represent all five competitors.

As if the rampant product placement wasn't enough, every factory has played our first match, peppered with rematch ads, on a constant loop. Everyone in The City will be watching tonight.

A dull force collides with my shoulder.

"Watch where you're going, LEF," Pinz says.

"You ran into me. I hope you'll be more careful during tonight's match."

"The Idol's point transfer went through, I won't harm a single hair on your lumpy lowland head. I always knew you were a coward."

"I'm not a coward, Pinz. I'm the Idol Valet. Why risk my life over a stupid game?"

"Tell yourself whatever you need. Just stay out of my way. I can't be held responsible for any accidents that occur."

"Don't worry, I'll have no problem staying away from you."

Pinz walks away. He's despicable, but he's also a professional. He'll leave Aleks, Niko, and me alone for the match. Pinz doesn't know it, but Aleks paid Jita the same amount to focus solely on him.

I make my way into the kitchen where I prepare Aleks' lobster roll. As I grate wasabi root, Crtr enters.

"Have the necessary preparations been made?" I ask.

"They have."

"You're certain?"

"Yes. I have confirmed the locations and inventory. Everything is in place."

While we talked, Crtr assembled the lobster roll. All that's left is the wasabi vinaigrette in my hands.

Crtr's come so far since we met. His ability to improvise and anticipate needs makes him a good Valet, and an invaluable ally. I wish we could take him with us, but our plan wouldn't allow it.

"Crtr," I say. "Thank you, for everything. I am truly lucky to have known you."

"It's been an honor..." Crtr's face contorts. "Good luck, Bear... The City won't be the same without you."

Crtr springs forward and hugs me tight with his thick arms. At first, I'm afraid someone will walk in and see us, but so what if they do? I raise my arms and return the hug.

Crtr and I never had the chance to simply sit and talk like people, and there's so much to talk about. Ideally, we could relax in a couple of comfortable chairs and reminisce about the adventures we had over a few drinks. But as always, there's no time for that.

The green room lights dim and brighten.

3 Beeps. It's an automated NeuroChat from Dahlia Delachort.

"Attention, all players! Report to your assigned Siloball pool entrance positions. We are live in 45 seconds. Repeat, we are live in 45 seconds! Report to your places at once."

I return to Aleks.

"Your miniature lobster roll with wasabi vinaigrette, Idol Yukita."

"Where's the champagne?"

"I apologize, Idol Yukita, you did not request champagne."

"I shouldn't have to request it! How am I supposed to eat a lobster roll without champagne?"

"Once again, I apologize. I shall go retrieve a glass right away."

"Forget it!" Aleks snaps and swats my tray aside. "I'm needed elsewhere, so are you. I hereby release you from my service until the match is over."

Instead of getting in line with the rest of us, Aleks leaves the green room.

The glass wall rises, and the room fills with screams and cheers. Even though Idol Nominees aren't escorting us to the pool tonight, our entrances will reference those from the first match.

Niko walks out to energetic Indian music as purple flames explode. The Coliseum lights turn green, and Jita descends the ramp through a haze of emerald glitter. I'm up.

Champagne gold leaves fall from the sky. I walk with focused determination while the details of our escape plan flood my mind. In my contemplation I almost forget to turn on the announcers.

"Haystacks and honeycombs, here he is! Winner of the last Idol Nominee Siloball Match, Idol Valet Bear! Look at that stare, Bulloxy! The Idol Valet's here to show everyone that his first victory wasn't a fluke!"

"Do you think he'll be brave, or stupid, enough to attack his master, the Idol tonight?"

"How could Bear possibly betray the Idol after saving her in the last match! If not for him, we would have lost the Idol Yukita before she was elected!"

"Let's hope Bear doesn't spend the entire match defending her. That would be such a waste of his talents."

I take my position and Pinz descends the ramp. He stares me down while he walks, but I'm certain Pinz won't turn against me. If word got out that he betrayed a client for personal reasons, he'd never work again.

The instant Pinz steps onto his mark, everything goes black. Gentle music, reminiscent of Aleks' original entrance begins. Soft blue light glows into existence throughout the Coliseum, and a biting chill sweeps through the air.

Countless snowballs fire from the silos. The balls explode mid-flight into blankets of snow that fall upon the Coliseum. As the snow falls, it reveals a previously invisible track that swirls down from the Coliseum roofline, over the spectators' heads, and ends at the center silo.

A spotlight shines on Aleks at the roofline. She wears another bright gold replica of Vox's wedding dress.

While everyone beams up at Aleks, I look down at the siloball pool. Snow settles upon its frozen surface. The snow, laced with a solution Loomi calls "Ice X," froze the water solid. So far everything's going to plan.

Aleks waves to the crowd and casually skates down the track. Every time her skate blades hit the track, thick layers of ice spread beneath her and more ice crawls down the Coliseum walls. She looks like the serene, but powerful spirit of cold, come to compete against us mere mortals.

When Aleks reaches the center silo, she whips into a dizzying spin. As she spins, long fissures form across every ice-covered surface in the Coliseum. Seconds later, all the ice explodes into trillions upon trillions of tiny shards.

Aleks' V-Pro dress vanishes to reveal an iridescent, ice blue siloball suit. Like all of us, her suit is covered in sponsor logos, the largest of which is MaxDrive. The Coliseum explodes with cheers and applause.

"Can you believe it, Chip? What an incredible, spectacular, unforgettable entrance by the Idol Aleksaria Yukita! Isn't she something?"

"Igloos and isotopes, I don't even care that those ice capades broke our underwater cameras! It was worth it!"

Perfect. Good work, Loomi.

Aleks takes her position facing the blue outer silo. The crowd continues to cheer and scream as giant silver numbers surround the Coliseum.

10.

I want to check in with Aleks one last time but don't want to risk someone intercepting our NeuroText.

9.

Part of the arrangement with Pinz is that he'll always go for the opposite outer silo as Aleks.

8.

He and I will pass each other at the match's start. If Pinz intends to betray us, that would be the perfect opportunity.

7.

I look at Jita to my right. Her eyes are dead-set on the orange silo.

6.

Niko flashes me a quick glance that tells me he's ready.

5.

We've only rehearsed our part of the plan a few times, but we have to be perfect.

4.

If we fail, I'll be disappeared, but Aleks...

3.

Balliat will realize he lost control of her and replace Aleks with someone who's easier to manipulate.

2.

Like every previous Idol, she'll die a theatrical death to make room for someone new.

1.

No! I won't let that happen. I need to focus. Focus!

0.

I turn and bolt toward the blue silo. Pinz races past me. I leap onto a corner silo cable after Aleks.

"Limericks and ligaments, Pinz is avoiding the Idol! Speaking of the Idol, she's off to the blue silo with Bear close behind! Is he trying to take her out early?"

Aleks gets to the blue outer silo first, grabs the ball, and flees. I'm close on her tail as she zips to the center silo.

"Cobras and candelabras, here comes Niko! He abandoned the orange silo and is coming for the Idol!"

Aleks hits the center silo in a full sprint. Niko touches down and makes a B-line for Aleks, but he's too far away to catch her. I leap forward to hook my grappler onto Aleks' leg.

She stumbles enough for Niko to catch up. With pure bloodlust in his eyes, Niko smacks together his grapplers. He takes a powerful swing at Aleks, but she deflects the attack with her own illuminated grappler. I join the fight, and we launch into a furious three-way grappler battle.

Neon purple, ice blue, and dark blue streaks slice through the air as we lunge, parry, slash, and dodge. Aleks still has possession, but we've pushed her far from the point tube.

Niko swipes at my legs. I leap into the air and counter with a slash at Aleks' head. She ducks and stabs her grappler toward Niko's bare chest.

Niko twists the strong base of his grappler against the weaker tip of Aleks'. She tries to pull away, but Niko's in control of her blade's direction. He uses his control to push all three of us to the silo edge.

"Niko's locked in his famous bind! The Idol's trying to break it, but... yes! There it is, the double bind! Niko has both the Idol's blades tied up! What's she going to do? Will Bear come to her aid?"

Aleks looks panicked. I ignore Niko and grab for Aleks' ball but can't dislodge it.

I send a flurry of distraction slashes toward Niko. He releases one of his binds to deflect my grapplers. Aleks pulls back, but her and Niko's grapplers hook together at the ends.

Niko grabs my suit and throws me at Aleks. He follows up with a merciless kick to my chest that hammers me into Aleks and knocks us both off the platform. I feel the back of my head collide with her face.

We plummet toward the water. Aleks appears unconscious.

"Niko, what have you done? Hacksaws and haymakers, this can't be happening! The Idol's grapplers are still electrified and she's headed for the drink!"

I power down my own grapplers, but Aleks' continue to glow. In the nanosecond before impact, I hold Aleks tight and let myself hit first.

30

Furious pain explodes across my back. The air gets pushed from my lungs. All I hear is the slosh of water. My body went limp upon impact, and I let go of Aleks.

Darkness surrounds me. Pressure crushes my eardrums. My lungs choke for air. If I don't take a breath soon, I'll drown.

Someone grabs my suit. A pair of familiar lips lock onto mine and breath life into me. Tendrils of silken, weightless hair envelop my face. The lips pull away, and a re-breather gets shoved into my mouth.

I want to suck in deep, but resist the urge and manage a controlled inhale. My breathing steadies, and I open my eyes. It's dark down here. We must be near the pool bottom.

A high-pitched beep carries through the water. Crtr rigged up the sound to help us find the base of the silo.

Aleks and I reach the beep's origin and find two face masks. With my mask cleared, I locate a heavy latched door in the silo. I nod to Aleks, she nods back, and I open the door.

Two lifeless decoy bodies emerge, and float past our faces to the surface. I can't help but fixate on my own. That's what I'd look like dead—limp, expressionless, empty. To say I'm creeped out would be an understatement.

Aleks and I turned off our gems when we hit the water, so we can't see the Coliseum's reaction. Maybe that's for the best.

We swim to a loosened drainage gate at the pool's edge. An underwater tunnel takes us to the Coliseum pump room. I pop my head above water to confirm no one's around, and we climb out of an enormous water tank.

A nondescript bag sits on the floor nearby. Our first supply drop. I grab the bag and reach inside. When I pull out a small mirror, an anxious shiver runs through me, and I drop it. The mirror shatters, and we crouch down.

"We can't let our nerves get the best of us," Aleks whispers. "Slow down. Be deliberate."

I pull two uniforms from the bag. The uniforms consist of an ivory jacket with a high purple collar, purple epaulettes, purple cuffs, and a tight line of brass buttons down the front. Dark purple pants and a purple pillbox hat complete the look. The uniforms are exact replicas of the V-Pro ones Vanderbilt Coliseum workers project over their boilersuits during service.

We dry our hair and strip off our siloball uniforms. Aleks stands completely naked just inches from me. Her bare skin radiates a warmth that I feel through my entire body. As much as I want to, there's no time to steel even the briefest glance let alone let my hand grace any part of her smooth curves.

I pull on a wig of long, ice blue hair with a side braid just like Aleks'. Aleks doesn't need a wig to blend in, but I brush and re-braid her hair so it looks tidy. Next, we use archaic makeup tools to apply facial prosthetics to each other.

I apply a wider nose over Aleks' real one. She also gets bushier eyebrows and rounder cheeks. Last, Aleks gets a pair of dark brown contact lenses. All these effects could be easily accomplished with V-Pros, but we have to keep our gems off.

"How do I look?" Aleks asks.

"Nothing like yourself."

"Perfect. Your turn."

Aleks affixes the fleshy shell of a prosthetic around my nose. She applies more pieces to my jaw and neck that make me look heavier in the face. After some new eyebrows and a pair of cartoonishly green contact lenses, my transformation is complete. Aleks looks at me in awe.

"What's wrong? Is it convincing?"

"You look so different."

"Different enough to throw off a facial recognition scan?"

"Definitely. How you feeling?"

"Better. The adrenaline from that fall is starting to wear off. You?"

"Getting there. Those clones really got to me. I never thought I'd shake hands with my own corpse."

My job was merely to release the flash clones, but Aleks had to put her Idol ring on her clone's finger. That must have been chilling.

I stuff our siloball suits, grapplers, boots, and re-breathers into the bag and tuck it out of sight. Crtr will come retrieve the bag later so there's no trace of our escape.

We stop at the exit. Through a small window, we watch busy workers speed-walk through the Vanderbilt Coliseum tunnels to fulfill Noble requests. They push carts that overflow with exotic fruits, carry wooden crates of rare champagne, and lead swarms of drone fans for overheated guests. The workers' mouths flutter in a constant stream of verbal order confirmations.

"Ready?" I ask.

"I am. You'll be behind me, right?"

"I will. Remember, stare down at a 45-degree angle, don't make eye contact with anyone and never stop talking."

Aleks nods. She lets out a long, shaky breath, and rests her hand on the door.

"No one will recognize you," I say. "We'll be outside soon."

Aleks pushes open the door and steps into a passing lane of foot traffic. I watch her through the window until she's out of sight. My turn.

I step into the hallway and slide between two focused workers who don't notice me enter. A flood of random commands pours from my mouth.

"West in tunnel 4C to the Telladyne luxury box, picking up two cases of Satine Debonay to replace older vintages within 4 minutes. Current status 1 minute 32 seconds. Possible delays include congestion in the tunnels, alternate orders, order changes. Stock is full, should be no issue retrieving bottles..."

It's all nonsense, but I need to appear suitably overworked. My commands are convincing because I've lived a life of service. But Noble Valet service is nothing compared to what Coliseum workers face. All their splits are constantly used to process inbound orders, responses, stock checks, and team coordination.

Because their splits are occupied, and workers need to know what's happening in the Coliseum to anticipate needs, a live stream of Coliseum events plays across the tunnel walls. There's no audio, but whenever I turn a corner, I catch another glimpse of the siloball pool.

Niko, Pinz, and Jita continue to play. Siloball matches continue if a player dies, but no one cares what happens now. Everyone in the Coliseum, except the siloball competitors, wears a V-Pro of Aleks' ice blue hair with her signature braid. Their faces glisten with fresh tears as they weep and wail.

I turn another corner and see Dahlia Delachort walk toward me. As we pass, Delachort looks into my face. I drop my eyes, but feel her gaze linger on me. Nonetheless, she strides past.

I reach a dark storage room at Southwest Exit 457B. Aleks should be here already. I check Crtr's supply drop. Everything's here.

Did Delachort somehow recognize me and alert the Noble Guard?

No. If Aleks was caught the whole Coliseum would be on lockdown. Without a gem-based map, there's no sense going looking for her. All I can do is wait.

The second supply drop is simple, just a pair of long, hooded, silver raincoats and two archaic wrist watches. Kallista designed the coats, which are available to everyone in the lowland as a V-Pro. There are hundreds of pointless zippers, buttons, and belts that all need to be fastened for the coat to look right.

I finish putting on the coat and secure my watch. Where is she?

Footsteps! Aleks appears in a full sprint. No time for questions. She hurriedly motions toward the door. I throw her a coat. She slips it on mid-stride, and we burst outside into the lowland downpour.

Lowlanders in grey boilersuits and shaved heads fill the quiet streets. We're so conspicuous among them, yet no one looks twice at us. Our outfits and hairstyles are similar to the V-Pros they wear, the ones we can't see with our gems deactivated.

We walk North to a LaborLiner stop. LaborLiners to and from the Coliseum are free during Idol events. A free ride means we won't be tracked by our payment. We're exactly where we need to be, with only a slight delay.

"53 minutes until delivery," I say and hand Aleks a watch that's synchronized to mine. "What happened back there?"

"Every Coliseum worker matching my height was ordered up to the luxury boxes."

"Why?"

"Don't know, but I couldn't get three steps without someone else reminding me where I was supposed to be."

"Why were you running?"

"Trying to make up for lost time. Don't worry. No one saw me."

We board the LaborLiner and squeeze between throngs of sullen-faced lowlanders. Some openly sob, while others stare downward with the sheen of dried tears beneath their eyes. I stand and Aleks holds onto me as the LaborLiner eases into traffic.

We both see a small girl nearby with a doll clutched in her hands. The doll has Aleks' ice blue hair and wears the same silver wolf pelt outfit from her Idol Nomination performance.

A real doll with such incredible detail must have cost the girl a fortune. She compulsively strokes the doll's hair with absent intensity. There isn't a tear on her face. She's in shock.

Aleks clenches the lapels of my raincoat and buries her face in my chest. Warm tears penetrate the fabric of my Coliseum worker uniform. I rub her back with my free hand. It's terrible to admit, but Aleks' sadness helps us blend in.

"What have we done?" She asks in a whisper.

"This is the only way we can be free," I say. "The City will recover, they always do."

"That doesn't change the fact that we caused all this pain."

"The Monarchs won't go through the whole nominee process again so soon after the last. Kallista will become the next Idol, and The City will have someone else to follow."

"They deserve better. Even though I never wanted to be the Idol, I thought I might be able to do some actual good with that kind of power. But Balliat would never allow that. There's no hope for them—any of them."

What she says is true. We're leaving to save ourselves, but then what? The City and everyone in it will continue in their endless cycle of production, consumption, and death.

That girl with the doll will forget all about Aleks once Kallista becomes the Idol. She'll be bombarded with a new series of ads until her whole life becomes a compulsive pursuit of Idol-approved products. Her whole life—however long that is.

We pass the private road to a parabolic jumper launch bay. Multiple tiers of black overhangs rise around the private road entrance. To passersby the tiers are just garish design, but I know better.

Noble Guards in prismatic stealth armor stand beneath each tier so the rainfall doesn't give away their positions. It would be suicide to try and sneak through that gate, which is why we're approaching from a different location.

The LaborLiner closes in on our stop. Aleks' face is still nestled into me. I brush back her hair and whisper in her ear.

"We're here."

She pulls away.

"You're still in this, right?" I ask.

Aleks nods.

We leave the LaborLiner and walk down the crowded sidewalk. With the whole city in a melancholic stupor, foot traffic is even slower than usual. No one notices or cares as we duck into a forgotten alleyway.

The narrow alley stretches between two tall, ancient buildings. Garbage rains over the passage onto enormous piles of trash that obscure our view of the alley's end. No map of The City displays this cramped passage because it's filled solid with generations of apartment and factory refuse. The Nobles, in their typical arrogance, have their nicely paved entrance well-fortified but have left this route to the jumper launch unguarded.

"42 minutes," I say.

Aleks sprints ahead. She leaps off a broken RejuviPod to a length of rusted pipe. Her bounds look effortless, as if she's following an obvious, clearly defined path. By contrast, my first step onto a sturdy-looking steel girder sinks my leg knee-deep into sludge.

I pull myself from the decades-old muck and scramble upward. My hands move like excavators through the wet heap of food wrappers, discarded rubber conveyor belts, and antiquated machine parts. Noxious stenches fill my sinuses with each swath of trash I displace.

I reach the top. From here the terrain evens out a bit, but there's still an endless landscape of discarded debris to traverse.

I leap over chunks of porcelain toilets, stomp through particle board furniture that's turned to pulpy mash, and wade through tangled nests of corroded plumbing. Aleks waits for me where the terrain drops backs down.

Once she's confirmed I'm still with her, she leaps over a shopping cart, onto a dumpster, and kicks into a lateral spin over an industrial crate. I start after her, immediately trip, and stumble to my knees.

Aleks closes in on a huge pile of enormous wooden crates, the kind used to transport heavy machinery. The pile of crates is even higher than the mountain of trash. These kinds of crates are built for strength, which is why even after being dropped several stories they're still intact.

Aleks climbs the crates without a second thought. She's about 15 feet up when something above catches my eye.

"Aleks! Jump!"

She leaps straight back off the crates. Seconds after her feet leave the wood, a massive metal object crashes through four levels of crates and falls behind them. Aleks lands on the soft, garbage-padded ground like a cat.

We're running out of time, and I can't climb as fast as Aleks. The crates have reinforced corners and frames, but their sides are only a few inches thick. I dig my heels into the ground and charge ahead.

I let out a guttural roar as I bust through the back of a crate. The ground drops, and I fall into a disgusting, dreck-filled slurry.

I push my hands into the salmon-colored soup and rise to my feet. The alley slopes toward the back here, which means every ounce of trash liquid collects in this sinkhole. Kallista's raincoat is treated with a liquid repellent, so the slop slides down my body in slow sheets.

"Thanks for the head's up," Aleks says from behind. "You look good in pink."

"I've always been a 'Spring.'"

Aleks eyes something up ahead. I turn to see the jumper launch. The dizzyingly tall, black, tubular structure extends straight up into the mist.

"26 minutes," Aleks says. "Let's go."

We peel off our facial prosthetics and wigs, turn our silver raincoats inside-out, and put them back on. Unlike Kallista's original design, our coats are lined with long strands of wild grass that match the huge lawn around the launch.

I unfold flaps at the coat's hem and sleeves that cover my legs and hands and flip up the hood. Once we're changed, we lie on our stomachs and crawl toward the imposing black spire.

The sharp, prickly tangle of grass scratches our faces. At least the lowland rain makes the ground slippery with mud and easy to slide over.

A spotlight shines across our bodies. We freeze. My limbs vibrate from a sudden surge of adrenaline. The light passes, but we stay frozen for a few more seconds.

There must be NeuroSig detectors all over this lawn, but they obviously aren't a threat. Along with the grassy liner modifications to our coats, they also include a layer that hides us from thermal imaging. The Noble Guard relies so heavily on their technology that our analog approach makes us practically invisible.

All advantages aside, we aren't moving fast enough. I check my watch. We're barely halfway there with only have 19 minutes left. If we miss our window, we'll be trapped in The City forever.

I swing my hips in a wider crawl that speeds my progress. Aleks matches my new pace. It's a risk to move so aggressively, but there's no other option. Our increased speed makes the bramble scratches deeper and more painful, but I ignore them. The pain fades when I realize our risk paid off.

We snap to our feet and flatten against the launch tower in a narrow crevice that leads all the way up to the mist. I look up at the towering spire, let out a deep sight, and nod to Aleks. She nods back.

We put our backs together and interlock arms. I plant my foot against the wall while Aleks does the same. After three arm flexes, we jump up and push against each other. The even pressure suspends us over the ground.

We take small, coordinated steps up the vertical wall. Our steady climb feels natural. Unlike other phases of our plan, we were able to practice this maneuver in every suite hallway we encountered. After we learned to compensate for our size difference, our bodies synchronized in a way I never thought possible.

We knew this would be different. Our practice sessions took place in short, narrow hallways. This climb is 10 times higher than we ever attempted, and we're doing it after everything else tonight.

High overhead, a drone flies toward the tower and disappears through a delivery hatch. That's our destination, only about 20 feet left.

I feel Aleks shake.

She squeezes her arms once to tell me she needs a break. As we press our backs hard against each other, I observe Aleks' breathing. Labored inhales and stuttered exhales have replaced her rhythmic breathes.

Aleks' lithe, agile body has been through too much raw exertion. I'm a blunt object that's suited for punishment like this, but she's a precision tool intended for more nuanced tasks. I wish I had the right words to motivate her, to make Aleks somehow forget about the pain in her spent muscles. Even if I did, we can't speak aloud here.

I close my eyes and hum one long, low note. The hum's vibration carries from my chest, through to my back, and into Aleks. It's all I can think of.

Aleks returns the hum. Our combined vibration flows through us like a gentle, restorative tide. After we taper into silence, she squeezes her arms twice, and we continue our ascent.

I've never been more aware of my body than I am now. Every one of my abdominal muscles feels like a bubble that's ready to pop. The sinewy tissue that connects my lower back and leg muscles is frayed like the over-played strings of a jazz guitar.

The grated catch beneath the delivery hatch must be eight feet up, maybe seven. Aleks lets out an unconscious meep. We stop. I squeeze my arms twice to see if she's OK. Aleks squeezes twice in return, and we continue.

Every step brings us closer to the catch. Only a few feet now before Aleks can jump for it. I feel three quick flexes against my arms. Oh no, she's panicked. I tilt my head as far back as possible without arching into Aleks.

A huge drone flies for the tower. The drone carries a large white crate. It's Marena's delivery, the one that will open the hatch enough for us to climb through. We aren't close enough.

Aleks takes a larger-than-usual step that I try to match. My step is too big, and we wind up lopsided. She takes another step while I hold my body still. Once we're realigned, we try another larger step that works better.

"Mm! Mm! Mm!" Aleks hums in high, quick bursts.

We still have a way to go before Aleks' jump to the catch is safe.

"Mm Mm," I respond in low tones that convey my disapproval.

"Mm Mm *MM*!" Aleks returns.

She's certain. If Aleks thinks she can make the jump, I have to trust her. I give three quick arm squeezes and Aleks returns them.

"Mm," we hum unison.

"Mm."

"Mm."

"Mm!"

Aleks kicks off the wall with both feet. While she's airborne, I shoot my arms and legs straight out and wedge my palms and the soles of my boots against both walls to create a platform. I take several deep breaths and visualize solid objects—concrete bridges, steel beams, graphene pylons.

Aleks climbs to her feet near my shoulders. My entire body shakes from strain. Beads of sweat fall from my brow in a chain. I watch them fall until they mix with the rain. 50 feet up looks a lot higher from here.

Aleks' feet press into my shoulder blades as she prepares to jump. She dips low once, twice, three, four, five... Come on, Aleks, jump! I can't stay like this much—

She leaps upward. The world goes silent while Aleks is in mid-air. I can't tell what's happening while we're disconnected.

If Aleks missed the grate she would have crashed back onto me by now. She made it! The small victory fills me with a shot of untapped strength, but it only lasts a moment. No amount of visualization can compete with the exhaustion of my muscles.

My vision blurs and explodes with hazy waves. Sharp tingles burn across my arms. On the other end, my locked legs are numb, but I feel their weight like two heavy anchors.

My foot slides down the wall. The slide sends shivers through my arms, and they shake out of my control.

Something heavy hits my back, something limp and thick. A rope! I twist around and grab the rope. Luckily, I still have some grip strength left.

Compared to holding Aleks and my weight across a six-foot wide chasm, the rope climb should feel like a vacation, but I can hardly put hand-over-hand. Aleks opens the delivery hatch doors when I finally arrive.

I tumble inside, scramble behind some large objects and lie flat on my back. We have to keep moving, but my destroyed muscles need a second to recuperate. Aleks sits beside me, but she seems like a mirage.

She whispers something, but my ears popped from the climb. Her face looks blurry. I feel like I'm back underwater. Finally, I hear something.

"Water!" she shouts. "Bear, drink!"

I sit up against the wall and gag as water passes my lips and re-hydrates my desertous mouth.

"Bear!" Aleks shouts. "Bear!"

I must have blacked out for second.

"I'm back, I'm back!"

"We're almost there. Can you keep going?"

"Yeah... yes. Let's go."

Aleks helps me up onto my rubber legs. I take a few more swigs from the water bottle. My vision's returned, but everything has an ephemeral glow.

Aleks leads us out of the delivery bay. Under cover of darkness, we descend back to ground level. Marena demanded that no maintenance staff be present when she reserved the jumper, but the journey still feels perilous.

The sleek, ivory jumper sits in wait. We do a cursory sweep, determine the area is clear, and scurry forward. Even Aleks looks clumsy given all we've been through. Our tattered bodies can barely run, but we use each other for support.

Something rises in my chest, a feeling of excitement. I can't believe we made it, after all that. We're here! A smile creeps onto my face, but it gets spiked back into my heart when I see movement.

The jumper hatch opens. Aleks and I freeze in position. There's nowhere to hide. We've already been seen. Maybe they can be reasoned with. Aleks is the Idol after all.

I see a bright white jacket sleeve. It can't be.

It is.

Davis Vexhall descends the jumper staircase with a glass of champagne in one hand, and a custom, yellow gold RXSleeve attached to his arm. The smug grin on his face sends furious pulses through my body.

"Idol Yukita," Vexhall says. "So nice of you to join me."

31

Vexhall saunters forward. I remain frozen. The slightest sign of aggression could trigger a call to the Noble Guard. Aleks takes a different approach.

"Davis, lovey! What are you doing here?"

"My sister never books jumpers," Vexhall replies. "When I heard she reserved one during tonight's highly-anticipated Siloball match, I simply had to investigate. Imagine my surprise when instead of finding Marena, I stumbled upon the newly-dead Idol and her faithful servant."

"You caught us, and I'm so glad you did!"

Aleks leaves my side and sashays over to Vexhall.

"Life as the Idol is so exhausting. I just had to get away for a spell. Surely you can understand."

I follow, but not close enough to seem threatening.

"What about your sponsors? Without the Idol, they'll lose fortunes."

"All of which will be regained, many times over, upon my miraculous return! *Our* miraculous return. Yours, and mine."

"What?"

"Come with us, Davy! My Valet's only here to fly the jumper, but I don't want to spend my holiday with him! No one understands me like you. We were made for each other. You know it's true. This is the trip we need, our chance to get away from The City and finally be together!"

"Where would we go?"

Aleks presses her body against Vexhall's and rests her head on his chest.

"I've always wanted to make love on the dirt ground like a wild animal. Wind over my skin, rocks against my back, leaves in my hair... deep in the Baron Hills, I could scream at the top of my lungs and no one could hear me. And who knows what will happen when we return? The City does love an Idol wedding..."

Aleks closes her eyes and cranes her neck upward. Vexhall leans into her waiting lips. The sound of their kiss pierces my ears. I'm forced to watch Vexhall's thick tongue lunge into Aleks' mouth with serpentine thrusts.

Vexhall opens his eyes to stare straight at me. He runs his hand over Aleks' waist, caresses her backside, and moves up her spine. With his fingers at Aleks' scalp, he grabs a fistful of her hair, and yanks her away from his face. Aleks screams from the sudden jolt of pain.

"Did you actually think I would fall for your pathetic seduction? You've spent too much time with this LEF, Idol. It's made you simple!"

"Let her go, Vexhall!"

"Let her go? Then she'd run away. I can't spend all night chasing her around this tower. No-no-no, our Idol stays right here while you and I have a little chat."

Vexhall sucker punches Aleks in the face. She collapses into his arms. He shoves Aleks' limp body at me, but I'm too far to catch her, and she falls to the ground between us.

I check her vitals. Breathing and pulse are steady. She's still alive.

"It's a good thing I ran into you when I did," Vexhall says. "You've obviously been terribly rough with the Idol. You're a monster, Valet. A monster that must be stopped."

Vexhall removes an empty pen from his jacket, preps an array of drugs with shocking efficiency, and docks them.

He drops his custom RXSleeve and jacket, pulls off his cuff links, and folds up his sleeves. A bright red rash crawls down his arms.

The red rash continues up Vexhall's neck to cover his face. His body expands and contracts with violent breathes. He stares at me with wild, beastly eyes.

"Strike me, Valet!" Vexhall shouts. "Tear me asunder with your mighty lowland fists! I dare you!"

This can't be a coincidence. Vexhall knew we'd be here. From what I can tell, he doesn't have a weapon, which means he also expected us to be exhausted.

"What are you waiting for?" He shouts. "Do it! Or shall I summon the Noble Guard? When they see the vicious assault you've perpetrated against the Idol and hear about your plan to kidnap her, I'm sure they'll waste no time disappearing you."

"If you were going to call the Noble Guard you would have done it already. What do you want, Vexhall?"

"I want you to suffer. Suffer and die with the knowledge that the Idol belongs to me now."

I look down at Aleks. She's alive, which means there's still hope for our plan. At full strength I might be a match for Vexhall, but my body's seen too much abuse. The only way to dispatch him is to fight smart. Holt always said strength is no match for wit.

Rather than rush him, I amble toward Vexhall until we're face-to-face.

"You want me to hit you?" I ask.

"I want you to try."

I throw a fake left punch to his ribs and connect a right hook. Vexhall stumbles backward. A stream of blood bursts from his nose, but he barely reacts.

"Not bad, Valet. This should be fun."

He runs his knuckles through the fresh blood and charges at me.

Vexhall moves with surprising speed. His assault comes so hard and fast that my worn body can't keep up. He lands countless punches and knees me in the face.

My eyes open. I must have blacked out.

Vexhall drags me across the floor by my collar. He thinks I'm still unconscious.

I wedge my hands beneath Vexhall's grip and snap his middle and index fingers. While he clutches the newly broken fingers, I pop to my feet and kick him hard in the face. Without strength enough for a follow-up attack, I retreat to collect myself.

"You ridiculous four, why can't you learn your place!"

Vexhall runs at me again. So many blows connect with my body that I can't tell them apart. If he let up for a second, I'd fall to the ground, but the force of his strikes keeps me upright.

His slack, broken fingers slap me with every other punch. All I hear is the compression of my flesh, peppered by Vexhall's bloodthirsty growls.

I manage to dodge a punch, but Vexhall turns the failed strike into a lift. He hoists me high into the air and slams me back down to the polished concrete floor. My organs feel burst open upon impact. I try to crawl away but don't get far. He grabs me by the ankle and drags me toward the jumper.

I flail to escape his grasp, but Vexhall's too strong. Aleks still lies motionless several feet away. There's no one around to intervene and nothing within reach to use as a weapon.

Vexhall grabs a long chain. As he moves to wrap the chain around my neck, I land a desperate head butt to his nose. He doesn't even flinch.

Vexhall closes the chain around my neck, drops me, and sits on my chest. He pulls the chain tight. I kick with my whole body, but Vexhall doesn't budge.

The chain links sink deep into my neck. I can feel the life being squeezed out of me.

Vexhall's eyes bulge with sick excitement as he stares down into my panicked face. His lips are clenched into a tight, expressionless line. He's tapped into a murderous, inhuman part of his psyche.

I can taste the metal chain in my throat. My gasps for air come out as faint squeaks. I stop struggling to conserve energy. A ravenous headache overtakes me. My vision blurs and skips.

"Beg," Vexhall says. "Beg me to stop."

Vexhall loosens the chain enough for me to speak. I use the break to take a gulp of air. He pulls the chain tight again, even tighter than before. My lungs start to spasm. I cough spittle into the air. The room gets dark, darker, so dark all I can see are the bright white teeth of Vexhall's sadistic smile.

He drops the chain and leaps off me.

Someone's on his back! Vexhall thrashes to shake off the thin limbs wrapped around his body.

Aleks!

There's something in her clenched fist, but I can't tell what. She jams it into Vexhall's wrist. With Aleks' grip weakened, Vexhall whips her to the ground. She smacks hard onto the concrete but recovers with a roll.

"You think a little Diazapax can stop me?" Vexhall shouts. "There isn't enough Diazapax in that sleeve to slow me down, you vile LEF lover."

Vexhall closes in on Aleks. She stares up at him with unwavering focus. Run, Aleks! I crawl to my feet, but before I'm fully up, Vexhall stops.

A tremor starts in his hand that travels up his arm and through Vexhall's entire body. His bright red skin returns to normal but fades even further to an ashen, pale hue. A fine sheen appears on his skin as his pores erupt with sweat.

He scratches his arms, his neck, and everywhere else in a frenzy. Golden buttons burst into the air Vexhall tears open his shirt.

The sheen on his skin turns pink. Blood. He's sweating blood.

Vexhall mutters a string of inaudible words. His tremors turn to full body quakes, and he collapses onto his back.

I limp over to Aleks. Together, we watch Vexhall scratch and writhe in agony.

"What'd you put in that pen?" I ask.

"Don't know. I just prepped all the pins Holt taught me to avoid. Come on!"

Aleks puts my arm around her shoulders, helps me inside the jumper, and lowers me into the pilot's seat. The seat's cushions cradle my broken body. No one part of me hurts because the same pain radiates through every organ, muscle, and bone.

Aleks begins the pre-launch sequence while I collect myself. As she works, I notice a decorative wooden box to my left. It looks familiar. There's a little white note on the top.

"Nothing is more unpredictable than the unknown.

These might come in handy.

Good luck.

-M"

I lift the box top to find the pistols Holt gave me. Marena somehow recovered them from my loft. I never even considered taking them. Guns have always been tools of destruction that I avoided at all costs, but in Marena's infinite pragmatism, she sees them simply as tools. They could be useful in the wilderness.

"Pre-launch complete," Aleks says. "Sure you can fly?"

"Yeah, but I'll need your help."

I back the jumper into the launch mechanism, and it rises into position.

"The gold button," I say. "Activate the launch sequence."

Aleks presses the button. The launch tower whirs to life. Rings of blue illuminate our path up and out of the tower. The countdown begins.

10.

Countdowns are a Highland luxury.

9.

There aren't any countdowns in the lowland. Things are just terrible until they suddenly get worse.

8.

I hope Crtr's all right.

7.

I guess I'll never know.

6.

I won't know if anyone we're leaving behind is OK for that matter.

5.

In just a few seconds, Aleks and I will be gone forever. But life will push on for Crtr, Marena, Holt, Zola, Loomi, Locke, even Pinz.

4.

Life will push on. Time will march forward. The City never stops, not for anything.

3.

It's a massive gear that churns eternal. Sometimes things catch in the spokes, but they quickly shatter and fall away.

2.

That won't happen to Aleks, not now.

1.

Maybe someday we can return... No, that's impossible. The City moves on fast, but it never truly forgets.

0.

The jumper snaps upward. We flatten against our seats from the momentum and fire into the sky with a thunderous clap.

I flip the thruster throttle in my seat arm. We bound higher. Aleks' face contorts into joyful tears and a broad smile. Her reaction brings the same relieved tears to my face.

We're in the air. We escaped.

Shoonk!

What was that? Maybe we hit some satellite debris.

Shoonk! Shoonk-Shoonk!

Three more objects. We aren't hitting something, something's hitting us, and sticking!

Shoonk! Shoonk-Shoonk! Shoonk! Shoonk-Shoonk-Shoonk!

More and more objects attach every second—too many to count. An emergency siren sounds throughout the cabin.

"What's happening?"

"I don't know, but we're being weighed down! If we dip below 7 miles per second we won't break through the atmosphere!"

I push the thrusters to maximum power, but nothing happens.

Shoonk-Shoonk! Shoonk-Shoonk-Shoonk! Shoonk-Shoonk-Shoonk-Shoonk-Shoonk-Shoonk!

More mysterious objects come hard and fast. The jumper feels like it's about to shake apart. Something bright red flattens against the windshield.

A Noble Guard? The objects are Noble Guards! They're trying to pull us back down to The City.

Our speed drops faster than the gauges can display. Eventually we come to a complete stop, and level off with the horizon. I can practically feel the hundreds of armored hands that hold us in mid-air.

"Are there any weapons we can use to break free?" Aleks asks.

"No, parabolic jumpers don't have onboard defenses. Nothing like this has ever—"

An explosion rings out from the cabin. I rise and turn toward the cockpit door as a Noble Guard flings it open.

The guard advances with emotionless authority. There's nowhere to run, nowhere to hide. Even if I could stop this one, there are infinite others outside.

I flip open the wooden box, pull out a pistol, undo Aleks' harness, and grab her. My face forms into a crazed expression, and I press the pistol to Aleks' temple.

"Bear, what are you doing?"

"Shut up! Don't come any closer, guard, or I'll paint the inside of this cockpit with the Idol's blood!"

The Noble Guard halts his advance.

"Aleks, listen to me," I whisper through grit teeth. "This is the only way you'll be safe. You have to tell them I took you. You have to tell them you were scared, that you had no choice."

"No! You'll be disappeared!"

"As long as you're alive I'll never disappear. I wish there was another way, but there isn't. I love you, Aleks. I love you. Stay back, guard! I'll do it! Everyone wants the Idol, but they don't understand! She's mine! We're meant to be together!"

"Lower your firearm," the Noble Guard says. "There is no escape."

"Why don't you leave us alone? Can't you see? The Idol loves me! She wants to be with me! This is all for her!"

I shove Aleks back into her seat and fire at the guard. My bullets ricochet off his armor like dry grains of rice against a steel door.

The guard advances on me, unfazed by my shots. One of the bullets deflects off the guard's armor and grazes my leg. I stumble but catch myself on the pilot's seat.

By the time I recover and re-aim my pistol, the guard is so close that the barrel touches his chest plate. I pull the trigger.

Before the shot fires, I feel a sharp sting in my neck.

PART IV

32

I inhale through my nose. Air flows deep into my lungs, and reanimates my body. The hard, smooth ground feels cold against my face. I open my eyes to total darkness.

Wasn't I shot?

I reach down to feel the bullet wound on my leg. My fingers slide across the fabric of fresh Noble Valet trousers. There isn't even a scar.

The walls are such a dark black that I can't tell how big or far away they are. I turn around and discover a massive transparent wall that overlooks Neurogem Square.

Countless ads featuring Aleks scrawl across every building. One ad plays larger than the rest.

Aleks lies poolside. She's draped in a sheer, ice blue robe.

"After a long day of being the Idol, I need a... release," Aleks says. *"Something to... relax my mind and de-stress my wary... body. That's when I reach for Arctic Freezers. With seven exotic flavors, my indulgence is never ordinary. Don't forget to pair your freezer with MaxDrive, for a truly scintillating experience."*

Aleks!

I run to the nearest black wall and feel my way around the room. Opposite the transparent wall, I feel the thin seam of a door. I pound on the door and shout.

No one comes. I press my ear to the door, but hear nothing. Even though my cell looks out over Neurogem Square, I don't know precisely where I am. Once I know that, I can figure out who has me captive.

I request location coordinates from my gem. Instead of coordinates, I hear Aleks' voice.

"Error. Due to ongoing judiciary proceedings some Neurogem functions are temporarily suspended. Pending the outcome of your trial, these Neurogem functions may be restored."

My trial? I look back at the transparent wall in time to see a ramble of orange butterflies fly across every ad. They're accompanied by a dramatic score. The butterflies clear and leave behind a black screen with gold text that reads, "Special Presentation."

Special Presentation? Doesn't matter, nothing's more important than Aleks. I turn back to the door and continue banging. The music stops. I can only hear the audio if I can see its source. For some reason, my captors decided to keep that Neurogem function active but suspended the others.

It's no use. I'll have to wait until someone comes for me. I turn back around and am shocked to see myself.

There's a close-up of my snarled face as I shattered Pinz's knee with my grappler, footage of me pushing someone over a security gate, and a visual slice of me screaming and holding a gun to Aleks' head.

The montage cuts to me following Aleks. My stoic face scans for threats until my eyes fix on the camera. The shot freezes with my blank expression and fades to black.

A single spotlight shines on Dahlia Delachort. She stands posed in a lacy orange gown, with a scarf wrapped around her head that obscures one eye. Her microphone is embedded in the handle of a solid gold sword.

"Seven days ago, The City thought our cherished Idol, Aleksaria Yukita, was killed in her prime."

Seven days ago! I've been out for seven days?

"While we mourned the Idol's sudden, untimely death, the Idol's captor stole her away in secret. Never before has our City seen such a brazen act of treachery.

"I, like you, have so many unanswered questions. Who could perpetrate such a crime? Why wasn't he stopped sooner? What were his plans for the Idol? And how is the Idol recovering? All these questions and more will be answered, along with a special appearance from the Idol herself, tonight on: Sinister Service: The Trial of Idol Valet Bear!"

Lights and pyrotechnics explode around Delachort, who stands center stage in an extravagant Highland amphitheater.

Thunderous applause erupts from the live audience of thousands. Delachort leaves the stage to make room for a troupe of dancers in revealing Noble Valet-inspired outfits.

This is why my audio/visual access remains, so I can watch The City turn against me. I'd look away, but then I couldn't hear anything and Delachort said Aleks will be there. Like everyone else watching, I need to know how she's doing.

The dancers finish, and Delachort returns.

"The MaxDrive Dancers, ladies and gentlemen! Aren't they spectacular? To think, had the Idol Valet Bear's plan succeeded, we never would have seen the Idol dance again... Now before I introduce our first guest, let me explain the little meter to my left."

Delachort motions to a long white line at the side of the screen. On the line, my scowling face appears inside a tiny cartoon rocket ship.

"This is my own, patented, guilt-o-meter! During tonight's trial, we want to hear from you! Download our Sinister Service NApp for just 5 points, and your opinion will appear in real-time for all The City to see! It's obvious that the disgraced Idol Valet is guilty, but you have the power to decide if he is simply detained by the Noble Guard indefinitely, or if he is launched from The City and banished for good!'

"If that little jumper-looking thing climbs all the way above 99%, Bear gets shot deep into the wilderness! I hear that we've already had 84 million downloads. Let's see the guilt-o-meter in action!"

The little rocket with my face on it climbs as a percentage beside it increases. It stops at 65%. The show's just begun and more than half the population already wants me exiled. I'm the most hated person in The City.

"Dah-lings, dah-lings, settle down! We have so much evidence to cover! Our first guest is a distinguished one. He was the last person to face the Idol Valet Bear before he nearly absconded with our beloved Idol. Ladies and gentlemen, please welcome, Davis Vexhall!"

An exceptionally flattering hologram of Davis Vexhall walks onstage. Even though he's Marena's brother, Vexhall's low quality projection barely touches realism. The live crowd explodes with applause.

Vexhall's hologram sits beside Delachort.

"Young Master Vexhall, may I call you Davis?"

"Of course, call me whatever you like, dah-ling."

The theater fills with laughter, as if Vexhall just said the funniest quip imaginable.

"I wish I could be there in person with all of you beautiful people, but unfortunately, I am still recovering from the former Idol Valet's surprise attack."

"Indeed," Delachort says. *"Thank you for making the effort to join us at all. It must be so difficult to recount the events of that evening. You must be so... angry."*

"Angry? No, no. More than anything I feel remorse—remorse that I couldn't save the Idol from the hands of that lunatic. If I'm angry at all, it's because the fight between that sadistic ex-Valet and myself wasn't fair."

"If it isn't too painful, would you please tell us what happened?"

"I'm happy to, Dahlia. It all started after the Siloball match. I, like everyone else, thought the Idol was dead. My dear sister knew I would be devastated. To preserve my sanity and protect me from the press's attention, she booked a jumper to our home in the Southland. It was a difficult decision, but the Idol was gone and I was powerless to change her fate.

"You can imagine my surprise when I entered the jumper launch and found Aleks... I mean, Idol Yukita unconscious. I ran to her side and right into Bear's trap. He viciously assaulted me before I could escape to safety with the Idol, or even defend myself!"

"That must have been terrifying," Delachort says. *"I understand you've decided to share a visual slice from that evening. Is that correct?"*

"It is."

"Thank you, Young Master Vexhall. You are so brave. Ladies and gentlemen, what you are about to see is never-before-seen, uncut footage from the night of the Idol's kidnapping. It contains graphic material that may not be suitable for younger viewers."

Scenes from Vexhall's perspective flash onscreen. They lied. The slice is heavily edited. My weak blows barely affected Vexhall when we fought for real, but whoever doctored the footage added screams of agony whenever I punch or kick. Aleks' motionless body lies in the background.

Vexhall blinks, and when his eyes reopen, a pinkish hue clouds his vision. I stand over his writhing body with a cold stare. This time, Vexhall's agony is authentic. Even though Aleks stood right beside me when this happened, she's been removed from the footage. Eventually Vexhall's vision blurs out of focus.

The screen cuts back to the amphitheater, which sits in stunned silence.

"We love you, Davis!" Someone shouts.

The audience launches into a standing ovation.

Before he was folded into Aleks' Idol storyline, no one in The City cared about Davis Vexhall. He was just another privileged Noble who spent his days doing drugs and practicing extravagant hobbies. Now he's seen as a righteous defender of the Idol, a hero.

The interview continues. Vexhall shares past encounters with me and says my unhealthy obsession with Aleks started long before she was the Idol. Their conversation is so riddled with lies that I can hardly stand to listen, but I need to stay glued. Aleks could make her appearance any moment.

Delachort thanks Vexhall for joining her, and he exits to another standing ovation.

The guilt-o-meter rises to 76%.

After a brief intermission, Delachort introduces Niko as her next guest. He recounts a series of memories about me that never happened and paints me as a depraved narcissist with delusions of grandeur and a psychopathic fixation on the Idol. By the end of his segment, the guilt-o-meter rises another 7 points to 83%.

Niko kept his word. I made him promise to assassinate my character if we were caught. That way the focus would be on me and Aleks would look like a victim instead of a co-conspirator.

More guests and witnesses are called over the course of several hours. They all describe me as a loner, a schemer, the kind of person who should never have been allowed above the mist.

I never could have imagined an entire Special Presentation, projected live to the entire city, about what a horrible person I am. The lies pierce my skin and burn through my bones, but I keep watching.

The guilt-o-meter's at 94%. At this point, I can't believe there are still holdouts for my banishment.

A cast of dozens clears the stage. They just performed a song from an upcoming musical about Aleks' Idol reign.

Delachort returns. The theater lights lower.

"By now you must understand the kind of wanton insanity that drove the Idol Valet Bear to his actions. We've heard the testimonies of those who have interacted with Bear, but none of our guests could ever truly convey his madness.

"On behalf of all our city's citizens, I demand answers. Ladies and gentlemen, I thought long and hard about the decision to do this, and ultimately decided that we cannot banish this criminal without understanding his mind first-hand. Former Idol Valet Bear, how do you plead?"

Delachort looks straight into the camera. What's happening?

I hear a faint buzz behind me. A small camera drone floats into my face. I stare down the drone lens. Delachort's probably asking a litany of follow-up questions, but I can't hear any of them. The drone zooms in and floats closer.

"The Idol loves me!" I shout. "I'm the only one who can take care of her! The only one who can love her how she needs to be loved! I see her! I see beyond her title and wealth! We belong together!"

I grab the drone in my hands and hold it inches from my face. Something's taken hold of me. The injustice, the sheer, unadulterated lunacy of my position hits me with full force.

"I did this for her! It's all for her! The letters, the NeuroTexts, the gifts, none of them were ever enough! Her father never understood! The Telladynes never understood! We belonged together, always! I couldn't wait any longer! I couldn't let her be destroyed by all of you! It's me you want, Aleks! Can't you see? It's always been me!"

I slam the camera drone to the ground, and it shatters to pieces.

The only way to sell my absolute guilt was to contort my true feelings for Aleks into something shallow and demented. I stand in the dark silence. How did this happen? How did we get here?

I turn back around. Delachort stares in shock.

The guilt-o-meter rises to 98%. I'd like to think that last 2% thinks I need help and feels sorry for me, but more likely, they relate to my obsessive lunacy.

"Wow, that was..." Delachort begins. *"I've seen crazy, I mean, I'm crazy, but that was... I apologize ladies and gentlemen. I had no idea how deep Bear's delusions ran. With that, there's only one person left to hear from. The person you've waited all evening to see. Ladies and gentlemen of The City, it is my pleasure to present, for the first time since her harrowing ordeal, the Idol, Aleksaria Yukita!"*

Music blares, ice blue fireworks ignite, and the audience stands to raucous attention as Aleks walks onstage. She wears a short, silver sequined dress with long sleeves, and a plunging neckline. Fresh tear streaks run down her cheeks. She hugs Delachort and stands beside her.

The hysteria around Aleks' entrance continues for an exhausting amount of time. Eventually, the theater quiets.

"Idol Yukita, it is so wonderful to see you here with us tonight, safe and sound."

"Thank you, Dahlia. It is truly an honor to be here."

"I see you've been crying. It must have been difficult hearing from your captor."

"It was, yes. To be honest I've never really heard him talk like that. It was... so—"

Aleks bursts into tears and covers her face with a sleeve. The audience reacts with an, "Aww." Delachort rubs Aleks' back with compassion that almost seems genuine.

"He's never said anything like that to you before?" Delachort asks.

"No. We've barely spoken, actually. I saw him at a few parties here and there, but he never approached me. I don't remember anything from the k-kidnapping. I must have been drugged."

"What about the letters he sent you? The gifts? Did they seem strange at all?"

"I couldn't tell you. As a performer in the Highland Dance Company, I received so many letters and gifts from people all over The City. His never stood out especially."

"But your LifeCast, during your Idol Nomination, you said such sweet things to him! We were all convinced you actually loved this Valet!"

"I wasn't speaking to him, Dahlia," Aleks says through sniffles. *"I was speaking to you. To the entire city! That moment was a chance for me to proclaim my love for all of The City's people. I wanted to be your guide, your savior! I wanted you to see that my feelings for you were true. Those feelings are still true, more so than ever! I love this city, and everyone in it!"*

It's a ridiculous explanation, but they'll believe it coming from the Idol.

"Then why did you ask for the Convict Bear during your Coronation?"

"I heard he was in Noble Guard custody, but didn't know why. He did so much to help me become the Idol that I couldn't let him be arrested. It wasn't until after I saved him that I found out why he was apprehended. He tried to sneak into the luxury boxes to find me. Who knows what would have happened if he did?"

Aleks is doing the same thing as me; twisting our relationship into a narrative that makes sense to The City. Standing up for me would only implicate her. She'd be killed so another Idol could take her place, and I'd still be disappeared or banished.

"I shutter to even think about that!" Delachort replies. *"Idol Yukita, thank you for your candor in this extremely vulnerable time. Please accept my*

sincerest condolences on behalf of everyone in our city for the events that transpired that fateful evening. We all love you, just as you love us."

The audience applauds. Aleks wipes away her tears, cracks a smile, and chuckles to herself.

"What's that smile?" Delachort asks.

"I'm not sure, disbelief, maybe, and relief," Aleks says. *"When I regained consciousness inside the jumper, next to that psychopath, I never thought I'd see anyone else ever again. The thought of being without all of you was devastating."*

"Indeed. Now, before we sign off, I understand that you have prepared a statement. Please, Idol Yukita, the stage is yours."

"Thank you, Dahlia. Friends, both above and below the mist, and at every stretch of The City, thank you for your outpouring of support during this difficult time. Without you, I would not be standing here right now. My love for you has never waned, and I know that this one unspeakably horrific act does not represent The City's people as a whole.

"This act was perpetrated by one incurably sick individual. By attempting to kidnap me, Bear selfishly attempted to steal a piece of all of you. This man hurts without mercy, and destroys without sympathy. That is why he must be banished, so that he may never harm another member of our city again."

The guilt-o-meter hits 100%.

33

I expected the banishment to happen immediately, but no one came for me. It's been a little over two days now.

My captors haven't fed me a single bite of food or given me a drop of water. I haven't had any human contact since the jumper. All I know of the outside world comes from the NeuroCast that accompanies Aleks' LifeCast.

I don't have LifeCast access, but I devour every moment of Aleks' NeuroCast from the largest projection in Neurogem Square. If I'm to be cast out of The City, never to lay eyes on her again, I want to burn as many memories of Aleks into my brain as possible.

I watch her practice choreography, give interviews, model the latest Highland fashions, act in ads and shows, and eat indulgent meals with new Noble friends.

Aleks seems like a stranger in her NeuroCast. Perhaps this is the real Aleks, and my memory of her is the fabrication. Could all our adventures together merely be elaborate fantasies I concocted? Why would a Noble girl like her spend so much time with a servant like me?

No, that's impossible. My memories are too vivid. I can still feel my fingers on her boilersuit zipper, smell the scent of her juniper shampoo, and hear her soft exhale as my breath hit her neck. We've been inseparable since we were children. That can't all be in my mind... can it?

Hunger pains radiate from my stomach with loud grumbles. Every projection in view that isn't Aleks' NeuroCast is a food ad. Even though most of my gem functions remain restricted, Monarch Media still gets updates about my hunger.

I'm forced to find satisfaction from the food Aleks eats.

She sits before a little spearmint-colored cube laid within a copper doily. It's decorated with a thin zigzag of dark purple. Aleks takes a small bite from the corner and sets it down.

"That was delicious, Ovash!" Aleks says. *"What is it?"*

"I'm so glad you like it, Idol Yukita!" Says a squat, round man with bushy green hair who sits across from Aleks. *"That is our latest creation at VegeTime, The Green Cube! That one small salad-flavored truffle contains all of the nutrients of an entire chef's salad, in a single, portable, one-inch cube! The explosion of flavor you experienced came from our famous Balsamic Island dressing, but the Green Cube comes in a variety of mouth-watering flavors. Would you like to try another?"*

"I would love to, but my guests are waiting. Please send me a case of each variety, and I will be sure to try them all. I highly recommend that everyone in The City pick up a box of Green Cubes to add a dash of freshness to any meal!"

"Yes, Idol Yukita, most certainly! Thank you so much! It has been a pleasure meeting with you."

"The pleasure was mine. Good day, Ovash."

Aleks rises from her seat and proceeds through the wide, sunlit hallways of her newly constructed Idol Palace. She stops at a full-length mirror to show her outfit off to her LifeCast viewers.

A sheer, light blue cover up hangs from her shoulders down to a pair of polished wood sandals. Peaks of a silver laser latex bikini peak out from the open cover-up. Aleks puts on a large pair of sunglasses.

The air fills with cheers and applause as Aleks steps outside. She works her way through the crowd with personalized greetings to everyone she passes.

Vigorous laughter and the pop of champagne corks punctuate the pool party's bop-woo-pop soundtrack. It's a sensory overload nightmare filled with people I know she can't stand. Aleks is imprisoned like me. Her cell's just a lot brighter.

"Aleks, darls!" a familiar voice calls out.

Aleks turns and walks over to Kallista, who stands inside a poolside cabana. Kallista's laser latex suit is the skimpiest I've ever seen. Balliat's there, too, in shimmery orange shorts covered with gold butterflies.

Kallista greets Aleks with a glass of champagne and kisses to both cheeks.

"Idol, this party is major-domo! Where'd you find all these fit new boys?"

"They're my brother's siloball friends. You probably haven't seen them around because they hardly ever leave the training pools. It's no wonder they act like children."

"They're just having a good time," Kallista says. *"Everyone in The City should be celebrating the banishment of that horrid Valet we shared."*

"Indeed," Balliat adds. *"It is a relief to know that in a few short hours The City's collective nightmare will be over."*

"A few hours?" Aleks asks. *"The launch isn't scheduled until tomorrow!"*

"The Convict Bear's launch has been moved up to this afternoon. We're using it as a lead-in to your reunion with Young Master Vexhall."

Aleks pauses for a moment.

"Where's the meeting I asked you to arrange?"

"Idol Yukita, why do you insist on facing your captor? No good can come of it."

"I agree, let it go," Kallista adds. *"What could he possibly say that makes any difference?"*

"I don't expect him to say anything, I expect him to listen. I want to look that coward in the eyes and make him understand the gravity of his crimes. He needs to know that if we were allowed to execute him, I'd offer to do it myself on behalf of the entire city."

"Very well. If that is how you feel, I shall arrange a meeting between you and the convict prior to launch."

"No, it needs to happen now. And remember, no LifeCast. I refuse to give that monster an audience. Summon my car!"

Aleks stomps back into the palace.

She's coming here, right now! A wave of excitement breaks within me.

The screen outside switches to highlights from the previous two hours of Idol LifeCast coverage. Dahlia Delachort appears on screen.

"What a revelation!" Delachort says. *"The Idol Aleksaria Yukita has decided to face her captor before he's shot off into the wilderness! More on that in a moment, but before we continue, let me introduce our guest host..."*

No need to watch the recap. It never has new information.

I pace around the dark room. We won't have much time, and I have so much to tell her. What will I say?

Should I continue my stark raving lunacy, in case there are hidden cameras? Should I be callous and push her away to save her heart? Will I even have a chance to speak or will the Noble Guard throw a muzzle over my mouth before the meeting begins?

There's one other scenario I don't want to consider but creeps in nonetheless. Maybe I *am* an obsessed psychopath. Maybe our entire story, Aleks and mine, was an elaborate fiction I composed to cope with my station as a Noble Valet.

Several loud bolts release. The cell door opens, and two Noble Guards march toward me.

One of the guards positions me at the room's center, while the other guard shackles my ankles to the ground. A bright white circle illuminates around me. Chains descend from the ceiling. The guards move to shackle my wrists.

"That won't be necessary," Aleks says.

"Idol Yukita, the restraints are for your safety," a guard responds.

"He can't move past the white line, correct?"

"Correct, Idol Yukita."

"Then I'll stay behind the white line. Leave us."

The guards exit. We stand in silence while each door bolt falls back into place.

I can tell she came here in a rush. She only had time to throw an ice blue raincoat over her silver bikini.

The cell's final bolt falls into place, and Aleks rushes forward. She leaps over the white line and wraps her arms tight around me. I let myself melt into her embrace, but my senses soon return.

"Aleks, cameras," I whisper.

"There aren't any cameras in here, I'm certain."

Warm tears run down my neck. I don't know if they're mine or hers. Aleks' body feels freshly baked by sunlight.

"I'm so sorry, Bear. I don't know what to do. I've been trying to think of ways to get you out of here, but security's too tight and I can't reach any of our friends for help."

"It's OK. There's nothing we can do now."

"I can't believe I let them convict you!"

"You had to; it was the only choice. Otherwise, we'd both be disappeared. Create an Idol persona and do everything you can to curry favor with The City. As long as your interest points remain strong no one can touch you, not even Balliat."

"That's the thing, I can't keep this up! They want so much, and the more they take, the less of me is left.

"Aleks, look at me. You are the smartest, strongest, most resourceful person I know. If your points start to fall, make adjustments and be diligent, but don't trust anyone. Promise me that."

"I will, but on one condition."

"What?"

"You'll survive... survive and come back to me."

"From the wilderness? I can't promis—"

"No! You put all this faith in my ability to survive here, I need to have the same for you out there! We *will* see each other again, but that's only possible if we *both* live. Do you promise?"

"I do."

"Good. Me too."

We dive into each other like it's the last time. I reach into her jacket, lay my hand across her warm skin, and pull her closer. Aleks' breath hits my neck. She kisses upward and bites my earlobe, which sends a shiver up my back. I plunge my fingers into her hair and savor the taste of her lips.

I want to somehow take a part of her with me, collect a shard of her heart, a splinter of her mind, a mere whisper of her spirit to give me strength on my journey. And I want to give myself to her—anything and everything that might help.

One of the cell door bolts clicks. No, we've barely had any time at all!

"I don't want to go, not yet!"

"Remember our promise. We will be together again."

"I love you, Bear."

"I love you too, Aleks, more than I can say..."

Another bolt clicks.

She needs something to show for our secret meeting—proof that it was contentious and even violent. I know what I have to do.

I drive my fingers around the sides of my RXDock and pry the edges away from my skin.

"What are you doing? Stop!"

I ignore Aleks' plea, there's no time to respond. The flesh around my dock sears with burning pain as it separates. Blood pours from the dock's edges, flows down my wrist, and cascades onto the floor.

"Bear, stop! Stop!"

With one last strong pull, I tear the dock from my wrist. The sudden, incredible blood loss makes me lightheaded. Before I crumble to the ground, I shove the dock into Aleks' hand and close her fingers around it.

"Take it!" I demand. "You have to commit. Make them believe you hate me, that I'm nothing to you."

The last bolt clicks and the cell door swings open. Two Noble Guards enter to escort Aleks out. The second she steps foot outside my cell, Aleks' NeuroCast resumes.

Aleks opens her fist to reveal my bloody dock to her viewers. After a moment, she tosses the dock aside like a worthless trinket.

"Have a medic treat the convict's wound," Aleks says to a nearby guard *"We can't have him bleeding to death before the launch."*

I fall into a calm trance. All I feel is the blood pour from my wrist. Time stands still while my eyes wander around the dark cell.

A medic, flanked by Noble Guards, enters. After a cursory examination, the medic cleans the wound and applies a synthetic flesh patch.

"You aren't replacing it?" I ask.

"I'm not wasting a new dock on you. Besides, it won't do you any good out there."

When the medic is finished, my wrist looks like it never had a dock implanted at all.

I hardly get a chance to observe my newly smooth wrist before a Noble Guard picks me up. He shackles my wrists once more at the center of the illuminated white ring.

A custodian trades places with the medic. As he cleans up my blood, I expect to see a thin braid fall from his cap or for him to flash me a conspiratorial grin. Neither happens. The custodian leaves, and I hang alone in the dark cell.

Faced away from the NeuroCast, the dark silence crushes me. I feel trapped at the edge of reality, weak and exhausted—just short of death.

34

A bright orange butterfly appears. The butterfly flutters along the wall and is soon joined by dozens, then hundreds, then thousands more. The ramble of projected butterflies overtakes every inch of the black cell walls and paints them in undulating, iridescent orange.

The cell door opens to reveal the backlit silhouette of a tall, thin man. His broad, sharp shoulders taper to a narrow waist. Long strands of straight silver hair sparkle around his face. He poses in a casual lean against the doorway.

Is this being broadcast? All this pageantry can't be for me alone. I look around for camera drones, but don't see any.

"Orphan Bear, Valet Apprentice Bear, Noble Valet Bear, Idol Valet Bear, Convict Bear," Balliat says in a sing-songy voice as he strolls into sight. "You've had quite a journey."

Every cell in my body ignites with hatred. Balliat violated and manipulated Aleks' mind for his own selfish gain. If these shackles suddenly released, I would break every bone in his body with my bare hands.

But I need to stay cool. One emotional slip of the tongue could put Aleks in even more danger.

"I like to stay busy," I say.

"Indeed, that's something we have in common. You must, then, understand my frustration at having to take time from my packed schedule to come speak with you."

"Don't stay on my account. I promise not to be offended if you leave."

"I would love to, but unfortunately, I have a question that only you can answer."

I stare at Balliat with a blank expression.

"Let's see, where did I put tha... a there it is!" Balliat reaches into his breast pocket and produces a gold harmonica. It's the same one I took from his family's archives.

He steps closer.

"Now, how did you come to possess this object?"

"I don't even know what that is."

"No? It's called a harmonica. Before there was a Monarch Media, our family made our fortune through the manufacture of instruments such as this. Such humble beginnings. Who would have thought back then that we would someday control all of The City's media?"

"You should have stuck with instruments."

"Oh really, why's that?" Balliat asks.

"You don't need a Neurogem to see a harmonica, or feel it, or play it. All your ads, V-Pros, NeuroCasts, LifeCasts, they're all useless without Neurogem technology. You used to manufacture and sell goods, now you just peddle noise."

"Quite an astute observation for a lowland-born. You're absolutely right, Convict Bear, my business demands a delivery system. That's why Monarch Media acquired the Neurogem Corporation ages ago."

"What? How is that possible?"

"It is a common misconception that the Neurogem Corporation is this ominous, endlessly profitable mega company that controls The City, but that's actually quite far from the truth.

"You practically said it yourself, 'what is Monarch Media without the Neurogem?' But the real question is, what is the Neurogem without Monarch Media? Think about it. Everyone in The City receives a Neurogem at birth for free. They have no inherent value. A Neurogem is a vessel, a conduit for Monarch Media's catalog of revolutionary media offerings."

"So, you lose money on each Neurogem?" I ask. "Doesn't seem like a very lucrative business model."

The longer Balliat monologues, the closer my launch time comes, and the quicker I'll be rid of him.

"Each Neurogem pays for itself almost instan... Oh, I see what you did there. You tried to change the subject, make me lose my train of thought. You're clever, Bear; I'll give you that. But like I said, I'm here to find out one simple thing. The Noble Guard found this harmonica among your personal effects. Where did you get it?"

"I found it."

"Where?"

"I don't remember."

"Convict Bear, this is a first press, limited edition Monarch Harmonica. This instrument is literally centuries old but has somehow remained in pristine condition. By now the engraved flourishes should be rubbed away, the metal casing should be tarnished, and the chambers should be clogged, but they aren't. This artifact was stored away someplace safe for a very long time... You found this in my family's archives, didn't you?"

His face is so close to mine that our noses nearly touch. I can practically taste his hot, espresso-scented breath. There's no reason to answer, so I don't.

Balliat backs up, twirls the instrument between his fingers and examines my face.

"I'm not actually upset in the least that you stole this from me. In fact, here, think of it as a parting gift."

He slips the harmonica into my handkerchief pocket.

"What I really want to know is how you evaded my security system, entered my home, and made your way into the Monarch family archives undetected. That's all."

"I have no idea what you're talking about."

"Oh Bear, yes you do. You snuck into my home undetected the same way you snuck out of Vanderbilt Coliseum. Come on, you're about to be launched into the wilderness—never to be seen or heard from again. You can tell me..."

Balliat walks closer, close enough to whisper in my ear.

"How do you turn off your gem?"

"What?" I ask with a laugh. "That's ridiculous! No one can turn off their Neurogem!"

Balliat steps back with an exacerbated exhale and runs his fingers through his hair.

"That, right there, *that* is why Nobles find lowlanders so infuriating. All you ever do is whine and cry about what you deserve; less work, more living space, the ability to split five times instead of four. It never ends! And yet, rather than respecting us, the ones who actually have the power to change your lives for the better, you lie right to our faces.

"Even worse, you lie to yourselves and blame us! My family has spent generations studying the human mind, and the one absolute truth we've found is that people, more than anything, want to be entertained. It's why splitting was invented, so people didn't have to miss their favorite programming while they worked. But that wasn't enough. You started using splits to take on more work, so we gave you more splits, and more, and more!

"Don't you think I'd love to kick back, dock something to relax my nerves, and split four ways to consume the Idol's LifeCast and all the NeuroCasts I hear so much about? Of course I would, but I don't have that luxury. My family has given up our own freedom so fours like you can live how you truly want. No responsibility, constant pleasure, endless entertainment.

"You're like our children. Our job is to foster your development. But when you lie to us, you make our job impossible. When you lie to me, it's like you take all of my sacrifice and effort, and set it ablaze. Do you have any idea how that feels?"

I don't even know how to respond to Balliat's skewed worldview. Since birth, Balliat's been told his family is The City's savior. He has no concept of what life is like below the mist, but thinks he knows what's best for everyone who lives there.

"You honestly think I don't know how that feels?" I say. "To have everything that matters to me stripped away in an instant? You know nothing of true loss, Balliat. You're just another spoiled Noble child with an immeasurable ego and utter lack of empathy."

"If empathy means understanding the perspective of others, I have more empathy than you know. Now tell me how you turn off your gem."

"I'm telling you, I have no idea! It's impossible!"

"I was afraid you'd be difficult."

The cell door opens again. A gaunt, shirtless man with an empty rice bag over his head falls through the door. Pinz Baylor enters next. He pulls the faceless man to his feet, handcuffs him to the wall, and pulls off the bag.

"Pach!"

Pach squints to look at me.

"B-bear! Say n-n-nothing!"

"What are you doing? He has nothing to do with any of this!"

"Doesn't he? It was Pach who forged the maintenance documents that let you access the garbage chute at Vanderbilt Coliseum. Given your unique participation in the Idol Coronation, I thought Pach here would be a good investment. He's been my honored guest since then, and now he's finally going to prove his value to me. That's where Mr. Baylor comes in. Thank you for joining us, by the way."

"It is my pleasure, Master Monarch."

"Please, have at it," Balliat says with a flick of his wrist.

A sinister snarl crosses Pinz's face. Grapplers emerge from Pinz's sleeves. He knocks the grapplers together and they glow bright red.

Pinz delivers three vicious slashes to Pach's back. Pach screams with pure agony.

"Balliat, stop!" I shout. "He's an old man, he can't take this kind of abuse!"

"Then tell me how you turn off your gem!"

Pinz kicks Pach in the ribs. Pach's pained howls turn to hacking coughs.

"Bear, no!" Pach shouts, clear and true for the first time I've ever heard.

"Keep! Your! Filthy! LEF! Mouth! Shut!" Pinz shouts and punctuates each word with another slash.

Pach falls broken against the wall.

"Pinz, stop! You'll kill him!"

"He won't stop until I give the order," Balliat says.

Pinz continues to beat Pach without mercy. Pach is in so much pain he can't even whimper. The only sign he's still alive are the sharp, spasmodic jolts his body makes with each new blow. Cauterized black lines cover Pach's skin like a ghastly spider web.

"Tell me how you turn off your gem!"

Pach doesn't want me to tell Balliat anything, but I can't let him get beaten to death.

"What difference does it make?" I ask. "Even if I could turn off my gem, who cares?"

"It makes all the difference!" Balliat replies and signals Pinz to stand down with a subtle wave. "Convict Bear, you may not believe this, but my one true goal is to make the citizens of our city happy."

"You're right, I don't believe it."

"It's true! Happy citizens are more productive. If our people aren't productive, then the very foundation of our city crumbles. Neurogems ensure a constant supply of happiness, on demand, that enriches the lives of everyone in The City and keeps our economy strong."

"You don't care about anyone's happiness but your own! All you've done is dope everyone with mindless distractions. You even fooled us into buying into the ludicrous concept of the Idol, as if one person can tell millions of people how to live their best lives! It's absurd!

"And if they don't follow your prescribed road to happiness, they lose their jobs, starve, and die in the street! If you really cared about their happiness, you wouldn't let that happen!"

"I do care! But those who refuse to contribute to our society as both producers and consumers do not deserve to benefit from The City's luxuries!"

"Luxuries? Are you joking? Even the lowlanders who live exactly as you want struggle to survive. You've stolen everything from the lowland, even their basic humanity! We're born in cubes to corporate parents and forced to work impossible hours from the moment we can walk! We eat your food, play your games, watch your NeuroCasts, and spend our hard-earned points on products you relentlessly push on us at every turn!

"We're addicted to the small dopamine rush that comes from every little purchase, and you dangle that rush before us like a carrot until we die. That's no way to live; I wouldn't even call that living.

"But that means the ads are working, which means you get paid. That's it, isn't it? Why you're so eager to know how I turn off my gem. You're terrified that if The City can turn off their gems they'll finally see past your veil of distractions! They'll see the truth!"

Balliat chuckles to himself, which quickly turns into a hearty laugh. Pinz joins in with a gravely, forced chortle.

"The truth?" Balliat says. "I gave you too much credit before. Your understanding of the world is as simple as any lowlander. You want to know the truth? The truth is that without people like me we'd all be living in caves, hunting for every meal, dying from easily treatable diseases, and rubbing sticks together so we didn't freeze to death. Humanity's very survival is thanks to me. Now tell me how you turn off your gem."

"Why do you insist I can turn it off?"

Balliat locks eyes with me. The muscles in his jaw protrude as he clenches his teeth.

"Enough! No more games!" Balliat shouts. "I know for a fact that you can turn off your gem because you told me, right to my face. Your whole idiotic escape plan hinged on it! How else could you get out of the Coliseum and climb up the jumper launch without being detected?"

"How did you—"

"It doesn't matter! What matters is that you *can* turn off your gem, and if you don't tell me how, I know someone else who will. Aleks is *my* Idol; she belongs to me! I can make her reign easy and simple, or I can magnify her suffering every day until her last, horrific breath. Tell me how you turn it off, or I'll make sure Aleks does."

"So it's t-true," Pach says and gets another slash from Pinz.

"What's true?" I ask.

"He can t-t-tap into any gem at w-w..." Another strike silences Pach before he can finish.

"At will," I whisper to myself. "You knew our entire plan before Aleks even proposed the siloball rematch. Why didn't you stop us?"

"I needed to know if you could actually turn off your gem and keep it off for a sustained period of time. Vexhall was supposed to prevent your escape, but obviously he wasn't up to the task."

"So, you can just spy on anyone with a Neurogem whenever you want?"

"If the need arises. The Idol isn't the only one with a LifeCast, hers is just the only one that's broadcast. There are so many LifeCasts at my disposal that I have to be selective about the ones I monitor. Trust me, it's mostly pretty boring. You, however, with your existing relationship to the Idol and natural inclination toward rebellion, peaked my interest early on."

"I always sus-suspected," Pach says, and winces in anticipation of another slash, but none comes.

Pinz's grapplers remain at his sides as he stares at Balliat. Even to a Noble, this news is shocking. They live their entire lives thinking they're untouchable, at the top of the food chain, and that their privacy is absolute.

"What?" Balliat asks. "As long as you follow the laws of The City and don't do anything suspicious, we leave your LifeCasts alone. Is that so difficult?"

Pach and I join Pinz with our own stares of disbelief. Balliat's arrogance has blinded him to the true evil of his admission. That's the real reason why he cares so much about gems that can be turned off; any deactivated gem is a blind spot in his omniscience.

Pinz deactivates and retracts his grapplers. Without a word, he turns and walks toward the cell door.

"Mr. Baylor, wait!" Balliat calls out.

Pinz turns around.

Balliat pulls a polished gold revolver from his jacket. He clenches his eyes shut, and fires round after round. His arm flails from the gun's recoil. Somehow the awkward shots hit their target. I watch the life leave Pinz's eyes before his body drops to the floor.

"Balliat, he was walking away!"

"Mr. Baylor apparently had little respect for confidentiality agreements. I've never actually fired a gun before. Gem-assisted aim makes it so easy! Now listen, convict, my patience is spent. Tell me how you turn off your gem or Pach won't leave this room alive, and your dear friend Aleks will live a life of pure suffering! You have 5 seconds. 5!"

Another countdown.

Balliat wouldn't believe me if I told him there's no single line of code, or magic word. You have to start with a true desire to turn it off and can't be afraid that it won't reactivate. From there, it's a matter of teaching yourself with practice, and dogged discipline.

"4!"

He already killed Pinz in cold blood and will surely do the same to Pach, regardless of what I say. After I'm gone there won't be anyone around to hold Balliat to his promise about Aleks. He'll exploit her to death, like his family has done to every other Idol.

"3! Tell me, convict!"

Balliat holds all the cards. I have no actual control over anyone's fate, which makes his threats meaningless.

"2!"

"All right, all right! I'll tell you. But please, let me see the Idol one last time."

Balliat glares at me with his arms crossed. He walks behind me. My shackles shake, and the platform within the white circle rotates. Balliat stands beside the translucent wall, through which I have a clear view of Aleks' NeuroCast.

Aleks walks through a parlor high above the mist. Wherever she is, it's swarming with Nobles. Everyone wears immaculate, hand-tailored formal wear. This isn't just another cocktail party. It's an event. The Launch. They've all gathered to witness my expulsion together.

"There!" Balliat snaps. "Now tell me how you turn it off!"

"How I turn off my gem..." I start. "Well, it all started in the orphanage..."

"Cut the backstory!"

"Do you think figuring out how to turn off my gem was easy? It took years of practice. I have to start from the beginning or my technique won't make any sense."

Balliat's already scheduled the launch. Now that I can see Aleks' NeuroCast I'll know exactly how long I need to ramble. Before I start into a meandering anecdote about being inspired by a training module, Aleks calls everyone at the party to attention.

Camera drones from all over the parlor move to surround her. A live feed of Aleks' face takes over every projection in Neurogem Square. Balliat notices my preoccupation and spins around to watch. Aleks clears her throat.

'Ladies and gentlemen of The City. As you know, this afternoon I met face-to-face with the Convict Bear in a private meeting. The purpose of this meeting was to understand his motives, and *his methods.'*

"After a short, but grueling interrogation, I learned that while his motives were simple obsession, his methods were far more sinister. As I stated during

the Convict Bear's trial, I awoke on the jumper with no memory of the events that brought me there. The Convict revealed that he was able to control my mind and actions with an extremely high dose... of MaxDrive."

Camera flashes paint the NeuroCast white. A slew of questions overtakes the audio. Balliat grips the handle of his gun so tight his arm shakes. Aleks ignores the questions and continues.

"Above all else, I must be true to myself and to The City. With the knowledge of MaxDrive's potential dangers, I can no longer endorse it. As the Idol, my charge is to present you with The City's greatest innovations. On the other hand, I must protect all our citizens from dangerous products, such as MaxDrive, that have the potential to destroy us. Following this statement, you shall never again hear me utter the word MaxDrive. That product is a scourge on The City, and is best forgotten by time."

Coverage of Aleks flips to shots of a parking garage elevator. The elevator doors open to reveal Kassian Telladyne. A caption on screen reads, "Kassian Telladyne: Acting CEO of Telladyne Industries." Kassian must have ousted his father after MaxDrive was released.

He tries to cover his face with his jacket, but camera drones catch him from every angle. Kassian's Valet, who isn't Crtr, swats at the cameras. Before he ducks into his car, Kassian addresses the cameras.

"Our extensive research has not indicated that any of the Idol's claims are true or even possible. I have already assembled an in-house team to investigate this allegation. In the meantime, Telladyne Industries has suspended the production and distribution of MaxDrive, effective immediately."

Balliat turns to me with wild eyes. He's typically so composed, even after he shot Pinz, but this is different. The Idol just renounced her flagship sponsor to the entire City.

"Aleks can't be controlled like all the other Idols," I say. "She's different. You know it's true. Your tactics will only make her stronger. She'll turn your power and greed against you, embarrass you at every turn, and make you wish your name wasn't Monarch. By the time you realize she's beaten you at your own pathetic game, it'll be too late."

I hear Pach laugh behind me.

"Your time is over, Monarch," Pach says with more surprising clarity. "Good-bye, Bear."

The next thing I hear is Pach's body slump to the floor.

"What is this?" Balliat asks. "What happened?"

"He died on his own terms," I say. "A luxury most lowlanders don't get."

Pangs of sorrow surge through me. Pach gave Aleks and me the tools to explore both sides of the mist and imparted the wisdom to appreciate both. I release a long, hot breath from my nose, clench my teeth, and suppress my tears. Balliat won't see any weakness from me; not today. Not ever.

One of the cell door bolts clicks, followed by the rest. Balliat rushes forward and pushes the tip of his revolver to my temple.

"Tell me, convict!" he shouts. "Tell me how you do it or I will destroy everyone and everything that you have ever known. Zola, Holt, the Breaker Ward, that Clave you were always going to, I'll burn it all to carbon dust! Now tell me!"

The cell door opens. Two Nobles Guards march into the room.

"Get out! We aren't done here!"

"The Convict must be prepared for launch," one of the guards says.

"I said we aren't done! Wait outside, that's an order!"

The guards ignore Balliat's commands. Not even he can delay the scheduled event.

One guard undoes my ankle shackles, while the other releases my wrists. I collapse to the ground, lame from exhaustion and hunger. Each guard takes an arm, and they drag me out of the cell.

Balliat's gone silent with impotent rage. Even though he failed to extract any real information from me, I feel far from victorious. Pach, my mentor and friend, is dead. Aleks is still the Idol. And in a few minutes, I'll be shot deep into the wilderness with nothing but the clothes on my back.

Pach was so confident when he told Balliat his time is over, but I know the truth. There's no fight left in me. I lost. *We* lost.

35

The Noble Guards throw me into a dark elevator, and I crumple into the corner.

My mind turns over the promise Aleks and I made to each other. We have to survive—both of us. Once I'm gone, Balliat will focus fully on Aleks. I should be more worried about her, but I'm not.

Aleks' press conference about MaxDrive confirmed everything I've always known about her. She won't wait for Balliat's first move; she'll bring the fight to him. Now I need to keep my end of our bargain and stay alive.

This elevator ride is taking forever. The launch bay must be far above the Highland. Neurogem Tower. It's the tallest building in The City. I suspected that's where I was being held, but wasn't sure until now. The guards lift me to my feet.

The elevator doors open to a raucous Noble cocktail party, the same one from Aleks' NeuroCast. The party's curio-jazz background music suddenly switches to a down-tempo, funeral dirge.

One guard stays behind, while the other leads me forward. Countless camera drones lock onto my position and blind me with white light. I stumble in a disoriented zigzag while Noble onlookers shove me back and forth.

"You belong outside, LEF dog!"

"Traitor!"

"You won't last 30 seconds in the wild!"

The heckles soon merge into a single, indecipherable clamor. Someone pushes me hard, and I fall to my hands and knees. The insults turn to riotous laughter. Canapés topped with beluga caviar and other extravagant hors d'oeurves pelt me from all sides. I'll need my strength to survive outside The City, and this may be my last chance to eat for a while.

I lift my face and open my mouth. The predictable Nobles see my pose as a challenge and lob fistfuls of bite-size food into my face. Disparate flavors mash into a revolting paste on my tongue, but at least I got some calories.

The guard lifts me back to my feet.

"Convict Bear, how are you feeling right now?" I hear Dahlia Delachort ask. "What's going through your mind? Do you have any remorse for what you've done?"

Delachort pushes a microphone into my face. I don't respond.

The flood of white light recedes as the camera drones clear a path. There's a large glass enclosure up ahead. Inside the enclosure, the tool of my banishment awaits.

It's a sleek rocket covered in glossy sponsor logos. Two paltry wings stick out from the rocket's sides, and a powerful cluster of afterburners juts from the back. A large sliding door rests open at the rocket's side. Even the lone seat has "Turner Leather" emblazoned across it.

That's all this is, another sponsorship opportunity. Advertising space on my rocket must have cost a fortune. Balliat will be rid of me and turn a nice profit at the same time.

The guard walks me inside the launch bay. A glass wall closes behind us that seals with a vacuum. The rabid vitriol directed at me quiets.

"Convict Bear," I hear Balliat say from the edge of the room. "I'm so glad you were able to catch a meal. Unfortunately, there won't be any food or beverage service during today's flight."

The Noble Guard sits me inside the rocket and straps me down with a collection of thick restraints and buckles. All I can do is turn my head.

While the guard cinches the final straps tight, I look at everyone gathered at the glass. Practically every Noble I've ever encountered is here.

Kassian fled the party in disgrace before I arrived, but Kallista stayed behind. She makes faces at me to illicit a reaction. Even now, after everything we've been through together, she's trying to make this moment about her.

What will she do with a baby? What will any of them do? I've spent so much time thinking about Aleks' fate that I never considered the True Born Collective's victory. Even without the Idol, there's bound to be fallout from such a huge cultural shift.

Nobles at the glass separate to let Aleks through. They all try to engage her as she passes, but she ignores them. Aleks stares at me with a calm, neutral expression.

Her fingers faintly grace the glass wall between us. It's the closest we'll ever be to touching again.

No, I can't think like that.

We *will* see each other again. It may not be tomorrow, or the next day, but if we both stay alive no force on earth can keep us apart. I'd give anything to hold her in my arms—to hear her whisper just one more word in my ear before I go.

Balliat crouches in front of me and blocks my view of Aleks. He's recollected himself since our conversation in the cell. His face is twisted into a faux-sympathetic expression.

"You know, Bear," Balliat says. "I can save her life, I have that power. It's too late for you, but she doesn't have to... expire like all the other Idols."

"What are you talking about? You couldn't even reschedule this launch."

"Launch times are complex, but saving Aleks would actually be quite simple for someone in my position. She doesn't have to die. I know that she can also turn off her gem. It wouldn't take much effort to extract the information I need from her, but I'd rather not tarnish our relationship with such... unpleasantness. You can save her. All you have to do is tell me how you turn off your gem."

I stare at Balliat but say nothing. The rich flavors of Highland food linger rancid in my mouth. I can actually taste the same grotesque privilege that turned Balliat into the delusional monster before me.

Balliat removes a pocket watch from his jacket. I recognize the watch; it's the same one Holt wears. The gesture isn't lost on me. He has Holt, just like he had Pach.

"Would you look at that," Balliat says. "It's almost time for my address! You have until I'm finished speaking to consider my offer."

Balliat rises, but crouches again.

"Oh, one more thing. After I traveled to my family's archives to confirm that our harmonica was missing, I noticed something else. It appears that whoever stole our harmonica also happened upon some old family films.

"I'm confident that anyone with the technological savvy to evade my home's security *and* reverse the Idol Yukita's re-training could surely decode the true content of those spools. Wouldn't you agree?"

Balliat waits for my response with a smirk. He's giving me a chance to remember what I saw on the reels. My hands unconsciously clench into tight fists.

"Unfortunately, because the Idol proved resistant to our modern re-training efforts," Balliat continues. "I will be forced to revisit some of the more... archaic methods from those early experiments."

I explode toward Balliat, but the restraints hold me down. The straps and buckles bruise my flesh as I fight against them. Balliat's threat unearthed buried stores of fury I didn't know existed.

"Balliat, you can't do that! Listen to me, she's a person!"

He turns to walk away.

"Balliat, look at me!"

If I could just get a single buckle loose, I could undo the rest. Nothing gives; not even a little. I have to warn Aleks!

Tears stream down her face, but she remains composed. I know she can't hear me, but I have to try.

"Aleks! Don't trust him! He's evil! Balliat will destroy you! Find Crtr! Find help and escape! There are worse things than death!"

Two Noble Guards pull Aleks away from the glass. Before she's out of sight, Aleks wriggles out of the guards' grasp and returns to the window.

Her eyes lock back onto mine. She's mouthing something. It's a word, the same word over and over again...

Sir. Vive. Sir-vive. Survive. Survive. Survive.

Aleks gets pulled back out of sight.

"Oh, that reminds me!" Balliat says. "Noble Guard 3182018 dash 3, please remove your helmet."

The Noble Guard obeys Balliat's order. Several thin braids fall from beneath the helmet. My stomach drops.

Crtr stands at attention in the same bright red Noble Guard uniform that plagues the lowland. Dark circles hang below his vacant eyes, bulging veins travel up his swollen neck, and his jaw clenches with intense severity.

"No! Crtr! Crtr can you hear me? It's me, Bear! Crtr, wake up!"

This is my fault. All Crtr ever wanted was to help us live free. Now he's become a slave to The City's greatest destructive force.

Balliat flashes a sly grin. I gave him exactly what he wanted—one final unhinged outburst to prove my insanity. The best way to generate interest in my launch is for The City to see that I'm a crazed lunatic, even to the last.

I stopped caring how The City sees me long ago. They have no idea that they voted to shoot an innocent man into the wilderness. But it's not their fault. As usual, Balliat manipulated everyone with the illusion of choice.

My credibility's gone, but they still deserve to know the truth.

"We all have LifeCasts!" I shout. "They never stop! The Monarchs can watch you all! They're always watching!"

Balliat steps onto a podium inside the glass launch bay. He raises his arms to accept a rousing applause from the assembled Noble crowd. I can't hear what he says over my own screams. Only a few Nobles care to look at me, and their looks are filled with disgust.

My dry throat burns as I shout long and loud. Balliat must be broadcasting his words through a NApp that filters out excess noise, like me. I keep shouting in the hope that I'm visible in the background.

"Your secrets aren't safe!" I shout. "The Monarchs see everything! You're never alone! Turn off your gem! Turn off your gem!"

Balliat says something that throws the crowd into hysterics. As they laugh, I catch sight of Davis Vexhall's hologram at the glass. Even through a projection, something about Vexhall's stare confirms that he's gone completely insane.

Davis Vexhall, Kassian Telladyne, Balliat Monarch; they've all come untethered from reality. I'm suddenly reminded of what Yele, Canary Turner's Valet, told me.

Each Noble generation is more ruthless than the last.

At the time I took her words in stride, but now I understand what she meant.

They're all so desperate to grow their family's businesses that they've resorted to ever more brutal tactics. Their singular focus on points makes it easy to relocate factories and displace thousands of workers on a whim, or invasively tap into people's heads without their knowledge. They'll do whatever it takes to win, regardless of the pain it causes. No wonder I'm sitting in this rocket.

A single camera drone turns away from Balliat to focus on me. I take the opportunity to drive my message home.

"Turn off your gem! Think for yourselves! Turn off your gem! Live your *true* life! Turn off your gem! Turn! Off! Your! Gem!"

Crtr, with his Noble Guard helmet back in place, turns to me with mechanical precision. He marches forward. Hydraulic actuators in his suit hiss as he crouches down.

"Crtr!" I shout. "Listen! You're not a Noble Guard. You're my friend. Don't you remember? All the things we did together, everything we saw. It's not too late; you can still save yourself. Just remember! This isn't you! Remember!"

Crtr remains frozen. I don't know which, if any, of my words are getting through to him. In a flash, Crtr's fist reels back and punches me straight in the nose.

The blow dazes me. I'm too disoriented to shout or focus on anything. A warm, salty trail of blood runs over my lips and down my chin.

Ambient noises fade in and out. Crtr wasn't listening to me. He was analyzing my face. Noble Guards are experts at immobilizing their targets. He applied exactly enough force to silence my cries but keep me conscious.

The blurry mass of Nobles beyond the glass applauds. Powerful engines behind me whir to life. The scent of hot grease and dust envelops me.

Someone approaches. Once he's closer, I see it's Balliat.

"Convict... Convict Bear! Can you hear me?" Balliat asks. "Time's up. I need an answer."

"An... answer?" I reply.

"I told him to shut you up, not scramble your brain. It's so hard to find competent help among lowlanders. Tell me how you turn off your gem. If you do, you have my word that Aleks will live well beyond her Idol reign."

"Your word?" I ask. "The word of an... echo is... meaningless."

"An echo?"

"Yes, an echo..." I collect myself and refocus on Balliat. "You're an echo, the mere... repetition of your ancestors. With every generation your obsession with points and power has... grown at the cost of your humanity.

"You're a tool for progress, just like a common lowlander. Long dead Monarchs have engineered you from the grave to ensure that their business lives forever. You think how they would think and act how they would act. Balliat Monarch doesn't exist. It's just a name. Your word is meaningless, Balliat, because it isn't yours to give."

Balliat looks deep into my eyes like he's trying to read my mind.

"Your naivety is truly remarkable," he says. "You may think me the villain, but it's your stubbornness that has sealed the fates of all of your misguided allies."

"You already have me. Leave them alone."

"Let me put this in terms you'll understand. You can't expect to free a garden of weeds by plucking the stem. You have to remove them completely—from the flower to the roots. Good bye, Convict Bear."

The rocket door slides shut. I hear two quick pats on the outside, one last send-off from Balliat.

I look down at my clenched, sweat-filled fists in the dark red cabin light. My hands blur as the rocket starts to shake.

I have no clue what's out there. The wilderness has always been this abstract idea; a fanciful wasteland made real by rumors alone. I've heard stories of wild beasts perfectly evolved to kill, torrential storms that make the lowland's rainfall look like a trickle, and arid plains hot enough to totally dehydrate a human in seconds.

The cabin temperature rises fast. My eyes burn from sweat drips I can't wipe away. The warm metallic flavor of blood puckers my mouth. I growl and struggle against the restraints. There's no escape, nothing I can do to stop this one-way trip out of The City.

The red cabin lights go out. I sit in total darkness. My heart races as pure terror fills my chest. They aren't banishing me; this is an elaborate form of execution.

The smells of sulfur and molten metal fill the air. A deafening explosion erupts behind me, and the rocket fires forward with ferocious speed. The dark red cabin light flicks back on as I'm driven deep into my seat. My chest feels hit by a battering ram.

Massive G-forces pin me down. Every breath is a battle.

The cabin goes fuzzy. Black shadows creep in from the borders of my vision. My eyeballs fill with tiny flashes that tingle and sting.

Am I right side up, upside-down? My panicked breaths refuse any kind of stable rhythm. I want to vomit, but the battering ram at my chest holds everything in. The shadows around my eyes grow as I fight to stay conscious.

All I see is a tiny pinhole of dark red light. The rocket shakes into a violent blur.

Waves of blood drain from and back into my head.

I let out one more hoarse, desperate scream to summon any remaining strength.

The pinholes go black.

36

"... Self-destruct in 60 seconds."

Aleks?

"Please evacuate the aircraft. Self-destruct in 55 seconds."

My eyes flutter open. The cabin's dark red light strobes in time with a siren. Red, black, red, black... The rocket is still. It feels lodged into the ground at an awkward pitch.

"Please evacuate the aircraft. Self-destruct in 50 seconds."

Painful lines burn across my body beneath the restraints. A buckle at my wrist is free. It must have released upon impact.

"Please evacuate the aircraft. Self-destruct in 45 seconds."

45 seconds? 45 seconds!

I fumble to free myself from my restraints and lunge for the door handle. The handle glides in a wide arc, then jams.

"Please evacuate the aircraft. Self-destruct in 40 seconds."

I press my foot against the doorframe and pull again with both hands. It doesn't open. The resistance is soft, with a bit of bounce, as if the door's using my own strength against me.

A vacuum!

I pull the handle again and pry my hand into the narrow door gap. With the very tip of my finger, I feel an air-filled rubber seal.

"Please evacuate the aircraft. Self-destruct in 35 seconds."

I pull the handle again. The narrow crevice feels like a gruesome machine designed to separate flesh from bone. I ignore the pain and press forward.

If I lose grip of the handle, the door will slam shut and lop off my fingers like carrots in a guillotine.

"Please evacuate the aircraft. Self-destruct in 30 seconds."

I feel the rubber seal again, but can't get around it. If I can't break the seal and get out, I'll explode inside this miserable tub. Worse, I'll break my promise to Aleks.

My fingers won't work. I need something thin—thin and relatively strong. My eyes dart around the cabin. Every other second casts total darkness, which makes my search even harder.

"Please evacuate the aircraft. Self-destruct in 25 seconds."

Something thin. Something flat. The strap buckle? No, too short. A piece of the seat? It's all bolted down. No time to wrestle with that. A thin piece of metal... is there anything in my pock... the harmonica!

I reach into my handkerchief pocket and remove the first press, limited edition Monarch harmonica. With the handle pulled, the harmonica slides easily into the door gap. I fish around to try and hook the rubber seal.

"Please evacuate the aircraft. Self-destruct in 20 seconds."

The harmonica wedges into something soft. That's it! I pull hard on the harmonica while my other hand holds the door gap open. The harmonica's polished metal finish slips in my gloved hand.

"Please evacuate the aircraft. Self-destruct in 15 seconds."

I'm thrown backward as the door slams shut with a loud pop. Something happened. The pressure released! I move back to the handle and see the harmonica. It's lodged in the shut doorframe, irreparably bent into a right angle. Sorry, Balliat.

"Self destruct in 10, 9, 8..."

I wrench the heavy door open.

The harsh sound of scraping metal fills my ears. A whip of fresh air hits me. I stumble through the opening and fall to the ground.

I run to put as much distance between me and the rocket as possible. A single shard of shrapnel from the self-destruct explosion could kill me.

Trees. Trees everywhere. The countdown will end soon. I duck behind a massive trunk, hunker down, and wait.

A second passes, and another, and another. What's happening back there? Where's the concussive, earth-shattering blast? The torrent of blinding flame? The cloud of sharp metal bits that fly like bullets through the air?

I listen close and hear a light gurgling sound. Against my better judgment, I peek around the trunk. I'm shocked to find the rocket engulfed in lathered shampoo-like suds.

I step out from behind the tree. Dry leaves and twigs crinkle with each step.

Purple bubbles cover the rocket. Whenever a bubble bursts, it briefly reveals a newly corroded bit of the rocket's hull.

A new sizzling sound joins the foamy chorus. Small tendrils of smoke rise from the chemical mess. Caustic fumes burn my eyes and sinuses, so I step back. The bubbles increase in volume and size. Over the course of a few minutes, I watch the entire rickety rocket reduce to a sheeny pool of toxic goo.

With the rocket dissolved, and my feet firmly set on solid ground, I finally have a moment to collect myself.

I look up. A cover of long branches extends far above my head. Dappled sunlight travels through the forest canopy and paints the dirt orange gold. Sunset. It'll be dark soon.

I try to access my gem for a topographical map of the area, but it doesn't work. Of course it doesn't work, I should have known. Inside The City, accessing the NeuroNet is automatic like breathing. For some reason it didn't occur to me that my gem would be useless outside The City.

I found sanctuary in turning off my gem at will, but I still relied on it often. Skillful navigation of the NeuroNet gave me limitless information to handle any situation. I became dependent on it.

How can I survive a single night out here with so little knowledge of my surroundings?

Aleks' advice during our escape comes to mind. Slow down. Be deliberate.

I'll have to start with what I know.

I'm in a dense forest filled with trees and bushes. I close my eyes to listen. There are bugs out here—bugs and small animals. Their subtle buzzes and croaks surround me. I'll need a better vantage point to collect more information. If I can't access a topographical map, I'll have to build one from sight.

I follow the sloped ground upward. The hors d'oeurves filled my stomach for a moment, but I burned so many calories getting out of the rocket. I'm starving, and it's not like there's a BurgerNite around.

Something rustles in the brush nearby.

I stop to look back. Nothing.

I need to get as high as possible. Holt taught me that the key to success in any new situation is understanding the terrain. From there, he said, you can determine your tactical advantages, and address any potential pitfalls.

The brush rustles again. Something's following me. I stop, but again find nothing. My fear of the unknown has me paranoid.

This hill seems endless. I can't even see the top. After the sun sets, I won't be able to see anything. And if some creature is stalking me, it's probably best to get off the ground.

I open my arms wide at the nearest tree trunk and hug tight. The deep, rough bark feels strong enough to hold. With a small jump, I press my shoes into the trunk's grooves and inch my way up.

There aren't any branches this low on the trunk. My ascent requires brute strength combined with delicate foot placement. Eventually I reach a branch and scramble up through the tree.

I emerge through tangles of pine-scented nettles at the treetop. The orange setting sun makes silhouettes of trees that extend far beyond my vision in all directions. Wisps of pulled cotton clouds add texture to the brilliant, fire-colored sky.

A cool breeze rustles the branches around me and carries a familiar scent—juniper.

I close my eyes again. This is how it felt to turn my gem off in The City. The noise faded, and everything became simple. All Aleks and I ever wanted was to feel this way, to live like this together. We dared to dream, and that dream was stolen from us by Kassian Telladyne, Davis Vexhall, and Balliat Monarch.

If Balliat hasn't already started attacking Aleks' mind, he will soon. I have no doubt she'll survive, but in what state? With control over all The City's media, the ability to tap into any LifeCast at will, and a warped moral compass, Balliat is practically unstoppable.

The truth is that everyone I love is in danger, and I have to save them. But before I can do that, I need to keep my promise to Aleks.

I scan the horizon again for fruit trees, streams, caves; anything to make my survival easier. No luck. Even if I could see something from here, it'll be dark soon. The forest is probably crawling with nocturnal predators; one of which might be waiting for me below.

Horrific danger aside, I can't deny the beauty that surrounds me. The natural world lays bare before my eyes, like a scene from one of the landscapes hung in Telladyne Manor. The concepts of stratoscrapers, modular factories, and freezing mist seem impossibly foreign to this view. I wish Aleks could see it.

I'll have to sleep rough in these branches tonight. Everyone knows natural sleep can cause cognitive delay, muscle atrophy, and emotional imbalance, but I have no choice. RejuviPods don't grow in the wild.

I close my eyes again. The day's last light warms my face.

Survive.

ACKNOWLEDGMENTS

First and foremost, this book was made possible by the incomparable support of Meryl Opsal. Not only is she a keen and honest editor, but a source of constant inspiration.

To my son, Jasper, whose birth allowed me see the world in an entirely new way.

Kudos to the first-round readers who read versions of LIFECAST that were far longer than it needed to be: Anne and Russell Ephraim, David Kennedy, Emily Himmelright, Matt M. Smith, Miki Stein, and Tracie Rajasankar.

Much appreciation goes to Michele La Belle whose fine-toothed comb brought a level of polish to this text that I didn't know was possible.

And a great thank you to Adriann Ranta Zurhellen, whose patience with my myriad questions was nothing short of saint-like.

Goldshif Publishing is a small, independent publishing house established in 2020. While we publish books that inspire big ideas, our marketing and promotion budgets are not so big—especially compared to larger publishing houses. If you enjoyed this book, and would like to see more like it, please review it on Amazon and/or Goodreads. Thanks!